Willing

ALSO BY SCOTT SPENCER

Fiction

A Ship Made of Paper

The Rich Man's Table

Men in Black

Secret Anniversaries

Waking the Dead

Endless Love

Preservation Hall

Last Night at the Brain Thieves' Hall

Scott Spencer

Willing

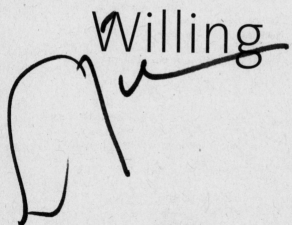

AN ECCO BOOK

HARPER ● PERENNIAL

NEW YORK ● LONDON ● TORONTO ● SYDNEY ● NEW DELHI ● AUCKLAND

HARPER ● PERENNIAL

A hardcover edition of this book was published in 2008 by Ecco, an imprint of HarperCollins Publishers.

P.S.™ is a trademark of HarperCollins Publishers.

HarperCollins books may be purchased for educational, business, or sales promotional use. For information please write: Special Markets Department, HarperCollins Publishers, 10 East 53rd Street, New York, NY 10022.

FIRST HARPER PERENNIAL EDITION PUBLISHED 2009.

Designed by Kate Nichols

The Library of Congress has catalogued the hardcover edition as follows:
Spencer, Scott.
Willing / Scott Spencer. — 1st ed.
    p.   cm.
ISBN 978-0-06-076015-1
I. Title.
PS3569.P455W56   2008
813'.54—dc22
2007028230

ISBN 978-0-06-076016-8 (pbk.)

09 10 11 12 13   ID/RRD   10 9 8 7 6 5 4 3 2 1

to my mother

What did we care?

MARK TWAIN, *THE INNOCENTS ABROAD*

1

SO THERE I WAS, Avery Jankowsky, New York City, early twenty-first century, not terribly well educated in light of all there was to know, but adequately taught in light of what I had to do. I wasn't someone you could push around, but I was not a leader, not a standout. I was a face in the crowd, a penitent on the edge of a Renaissance painting, a particularly graceful skater in a Breughel, the guy in the stands at the World Series, right behind the crepe bunting, his hand on his heart and his eyes bright with belief during the singing of the national anthem. Why would you even give him a second look? But you do. Physically, I was of the type no longer commonly minted, a large serious face, a little heavier than necessary, broad shoulders, sturdy legs, hair and eyes the color of a lunch bag. I had a kind of 1940s manliness—perhaps the doomed manliness of the father I had never known—and, unfortunately, I had a kind of 1940s income, too. Thirty-seven years old, and I had studied a chart that had run in one of the monthlies I sometimes wrote for, and in terms of income I simply wasn't where I should be. The thing is, if I'd had more money, it could be that none of this would have happened. Heracleitus taught us that Character is Fate. I don't want to argue, but money is, too.

Did I *need* more than I had? To that, I would have to say Yes. Did I *want* more than I had? Here, the Yes is unequivocal. Not that I was one of the Gimme Gimme people. I was not hatching schemes to make millions. I was not one to shove my way to the front of the line. I was not plotting the downfall of my competitors. Here's the way it was with me: I was staring at my half-empty plate with the absurd hope that my sad, hungry eyes might one day inspire someone to heap some of the world's bounty on me.

Be careful what you wish for,

But before that, before I got what I wished for, and more, which is, as most people know, another way of saying Before I got what I wished for, and less, I was, to be perfectly blunt about it, still absorbed with the Sisyphean task of getting over my childhood, which was not at all how I wanted to be spending my brief flicker of existence, but was, to my perpetual chagrin, what I seemed to be stuck with.

When I asked myself *Why am I me?* I usually didn't look much further than the fact that I was a man who had had four fathers.

Each time my mother remarried she took her new husband's name, and I did, too. If we were to meet when I was fifteen and I said, as I would have, because I was rather formal as a teenager, How do you do, my name is Avery Jankowsky, I would be giving you relatively new information. Jankowsky was my fourth and final name. First there was Kaplan, after my first father. I don't like to call him my *real father* because he was around for such a short time, certainly not long enough to corner the market in realness. I wasn't yet walking or talking at the time of his death, and I have no independent memories of him; all I have are my mother's handful of repeated stories about him, memories I have more or less incorporated as my own, something in the way ethnic minorities in the former Yugoslavia have heard the stories of the crimes committed against them by the Moors in the time of Suleyman and somehow take these experiences as their own. I don't like to call him my birth father, either, since he didn't give birth to me, and Ejaculation Father is just nutty and rude, so for the most part I have simply called him Ted, though sometimes I have referred to him as Mr. Kaplan.

After I was Avery Kaplan I became Avery Kearney, out of my second father, Andrew, who was Ted's partner in a flag and banner business, and who was himself a stern Irish miser, with large ears and icy hands. The marriage lasted eight years, until my mother was caught in an affair with the man who would become the third and by far the worst of her husbands, a sadistic, sarcastic bully named Norman Blake. And so I became Avery Blake, wearing his name like a crown of thorns. In Einsteinian-emotional time, that seemed like the most protracted of her marriages, though, in fact, it lasted three years, which I would say was an embarrassingly short time for a marriage, except my one marriage was even briefer than that. After Blake was swept into the dustbin of conjugal history, I had my mother to myself, relatively speaking, for eighteen months, and then, just when the gears of our shrunken family began to mesh, she met and fell in love with my fourth and final father—Gene Jankowsky. Gene was a painter, a maker of large busy canvases, full of reds and oranges and darting little arrows indicating the flow of energy, that is, God's presence. He was tall and thick, with a Russian mystic's beard and hair down to his shoulders. His clothes and hands smelled of turpentine and his breath carried the yeasty tang of B vitamins. He loved van Gogh, St. Francis, Gandhi, and Martin Luther King, and, to my great relief and surprise, he loved me, too. He saw me as a helpless boy tied to the zigs and zags of a childish woman's life, like a water-skier hitched to the stern of an out-of-control speedboat.

My mother was born to Jews, and her first husband, Ted Kaplan, was Jewish, too. Kearney and Blake were both Catholics, though Kearney seemed only to believe in pleasure, his own pleasure, and Blake believed in science, without, quite frankly, having much of a grasp of it. Gene, however, was a devout Christian, though his religion was largely homemade. He was not what is called a cafeteria Christian, someone who helps himself to the easy and attractive parts and ignores those parts that are inconvenient or call for self-sacrifice. But his devotion didn't fit into any particular dogma; it was a homemade goulash of do-unto-others, prophecy, and joy. Gene's last work of art was a piece of silversmithery, a crucifix two and a half inches high, an inch and a half wide, the silver stripped and scored to look like petrified wood. He made a few of them to sell at local crafts fairs, and then a Humpty Dumpty of a man in a powder blue suit and aviator glasses came into possession of one of them and bought the rights to the Jankowsky Cross for a small Tennessee company called Calvary Products, and in the last year of his life Gene was making quite a bit of money.

Dear Gene died of congestive heart failure when I was a freshman in college. He had left his financial affairs in surprisingly good order. Relatives he hadn't seen in thirty years were considerately remembered, soup kitchens, community art programs, a fellow whose animal rescue operation Gene had learned about on the local news, the War Resisters League, all were given small sums of money. More remarkably, he bequeathed a thousand dollars each to fifty-three people who had made generous gestures in Gene's direction over the course of his lifetime, some of these charitable acts going as far back as Gene's semester at the San Francisco Art Institute. I had my hands full trying to locate these far-flung earth angels, finding them all was a tedious process, but I owed it to Gene. He had always treated me with such kindness, a kindness that extended itself beyond the grave. I was bequeathed 8 percent of the annual income from the Jankowsky Cross, a sum that was enough to cushion me from the full force of financial disaster, though—and this may have been Gene's intention—it never gave me enough to live particularly well, not even in the year preceding the millennium, when national jitters ran high. I was a freelance writer, and I was always grateful for the income, though there were times when I was convinced it actually held me back. The trust was like being tied to a balloon that was too small to lift me to great heights but just big enough to create a few inches of space between my feet and the pavement, making it difficult for me to walk like a normal human being.

I've already mentioned my brief early marriage. When it ended I was not even twenty-four years old, and I had to wonder if I was embarking on an emotional journey similar to my mother's, fated to lunge from one matrimonial catastrophe to the next. I had beginner's luck in my relationships and already had in my little neural notebook of romantic memories a dozen gorgeous commencements. Now as the only divorced twenty-four-year-old I knew, I was worried if courtship and a ferocious few months were all I was made for. Beginner's luck is fine if you get the hell out of there before it runs out; if you don't, it's worse than having no luck at all. I became careful to keep my entanglements solely with women who were manifestly unsuited to long-term engagements: women who were already married, or who seemed only mildly interested in me, or who lived a time zone or two away, or, as I aged, who were too young for me, which brings me to my relationship with Deirdre Feigenbaum, the end of which began the adventures I am about to impart.

Deirdre and I never spoke of marriage. I thought there was an unspoken agreement between us that our relationship had an expiration date on it, one that took a bit of squinting and close examination to read, but which was indelibly there nonetheless. I also thought this expiration date was there for Deirdre's benefit; it was her ticket home when, say, she was nearing thirty and I had rounded the bend at forty and was in full gallop toward fifty. Now she was twenty-seven and I was thirty-seven. Deirdre was gracious about the decade I had on her. Thirty-seven, she told me, is the new thirty-five, so we're almost exactly the same age. Nevertheless, I dwelled on the age difference, privately and out loud, obscuring the fact that I had fallen in love with Deirdre. I was so convinced that it was temporary that I was in effect fondly remembering her even when we were in medias res. She was a graduate student in Russian history at Columbia, and her spoken intention was to move to Moscow or St. Petersburg once she had her PhD, which wouldn't take terribly long. Nothing did with Deirdre. She was tall and fleshy, with extravagant waves of red hair, freckles, auburn eyes, a sharp nose that pointed at you like a finger. She was quick and efficient, in her reading, her cooking and eating, her showering and dressing, her walking, her decision making; she was even sexually quick and efficient. Bringing her to climax was like pulling a cork out of a bottle of champagne; if you knew what you were doing, there was nothing to it.

We had met at a book party, a desultory affair in a bar on University Place—the waiters were eating canapés off each other's platters; the author was huddled in the back talking furiously into his cell phone. After a decade of relationships that all seemed to last twenty-six weeks, I hadn't had the company of a woman in months and I felt awkward, constrained. I carried my desire within me like a tray filled with too many little cups of ceremonial wine: one false step and the whole thing comes crashing down. Deirdre started it, and sensing she was somewhat drawn to me was like hearing the little bass and drum riff that begins your favorite song. We left the party, took a long walk that ended up in my small apartment. Afterward, she draped her hefty leg over me, propped herself up on her elbow, and said, "You're perfect." I was taking a drink from my water glass at the time, and her praise touched something antic in me. I opened my mouth and let the water drool out, as if I were, as my third father used to say, *subnormal*. Deirdre's laugh was loud, masculine, like a locker room punch on the arm. "And you're funny, too!" she said.

Two weeks later she moved out of the apartment she was sharing with three other students and moved into my place, and then three weeks after that Deirdre, who could find virtually anything on the Internet, found an apartment we could afford, and I gladly allowed myself to be carried along in the wake of her enthusiasm. We moved to an apartment on Seventh Avenue, near Fifty-fourth Street, a gloomy place, the walls soft from a century's paint jobs, the sound of traffic like a steel river seven floors below.

My mother wants me to ask you a question, Deirdre said during a meal somewhere near the end of our first month at the new apartment. This sounds fatal, I said. She took my hands in hers. Our hands were the same size. My mother wants to know why you never married. But I *was* married. Didn't you tell her that? Avery, come on, you were married for two months, that's not really going to settle the issue. Issue? So now there's an issue? Come on, Avery, don't play word games with me. There's no need, you're perfectly safe here. I stopped myself from saying, Safe? Is my safety an issue? Instead, I asked So what did you tell her? Deirdre smiled and said I told her I would ask you. I disengaged my hand from hers. We were eating a roast chicken Deirdre had prepared according to the instructions of Marcella Hazan—a couple of pierced lemons inside, salt and pepper. No fox or weasel had ever enjoyed a chicken more than I enjoyed those roasters Deirdre now and again brought to our table. I was trying to come up with a smart retort. But as the silence lengthened, and deepened, it took on weight like a punctured hull takes on water, and I found myself sinking into despair. I'm pretty good at the early stages of love affairs, I said. That's very true, said Deirdre, smiling her encouragement. I'm good in the beginning, it's true, I said. I'm good at zeroing in on someone and getting her to care about me. I'm good at trying to know everything about her. I like telling the story of my stupid little life, the four fathers and all that. But after that, I said, something goes awry. I don't see myself as one of those eternal boys in the magazines. I don't fear commitment. I'm not a *commitment-a-phobe*, I added, trying to italicize the word, to let Deirdre know I was deliberately saying something tacky and absurd. However, nothing of the irony registered in Deirdre's face or in the steady, piercing sanity of her gaze. Despite having presented this as a question her mother had posed, Deirdre was surely waiting for an answer, and as I slowly realized this I also realized that what I said next might be something I would have to live with. I don't get tired of people, and I don't screw around, I said. She frowned. Do people get tired of you, and then they screw around? Sometimes, I said. But mostly the energy runs out, like an old wooden top that spins slower and slower, until it's just sort of wobbling and you can see every nick in the paint, and then, boom, it stops, and it's just this weird little piece of wood with a big belly lying on the table. Okay, then, I'll tell my mother. I'm sure she'll be fond of the top analogy. More chicken?

I may have been older, but I always wondered if I was in Deirdre's league. She was ambitious, optimistic, full of plans, schedules, energy. She had a pure, open heart. Her innate happiness, her optimistic turn of mind, were as alluring and exciting to me as her soft skin, her warm scalp, the smell of her, like a crushed orange and fresh bread. We never quarreled, though sometimes I was irked by what I imagined she was thinking—like why didn't I write a best seller or get a job at ABC News, as if these things were available if you wanted them. She seemed to think you could just register for them like putting your name on the sign-up sheet for the Chess Club. I was sure she wondered why I, the oldest man she had ever been with, had the income of a boy. Deirdre's father, Ronald Feigenbaum, was an intellectual property lawyer who dropped names like Vonnegut, Coppola, Grisham, and Sontag; her mother, Lena Rosen, was a classics professor who dropped names like Ovid and Aristophanes; and her brother, Adam, a pediatrician in Vermont, was also a rising star in the Democratic Party and dropped names like Clinton and Dean. Deirdre herself was surely headed for a life of achievement and material comfort. Without even having begun her dissertation, she had been offered a job in Citicorp's Moscow office, and four think tanks were in touch with her. I felt a little threadbare compared to Deirdre. Yet her choosing to be with me was a source of encouragement to me. She had so much of what I lacked, which awakened in me not a sense of covetousness but a sense of relief, and validation. I had, against considerable odds, been chosen by a woman whose life was rich and secure—which must mean she saw something at least potentially rich and secure in me. Yet this sense of accomplishment her affection bestowed upon me cast its own shadow, a darkly opposite sense of foreboding that, through the animating magic of neurosis, took on a life of its own.

Before long, the misgivings and historical pessimism that I had harbored from the beginning of the relationship were all but eclipsed by my growing suspicion that Deirdre was unfaithful. I could not stop thinking about the time she'd asked me if women had ever screwed around on me. I was also struck by the flimsy but pesky fact that since that night she had never cooked lemon chicken again and, in fact, had all but stopped doing her share in the kitchen. As a freelance writer I had plenty of free time in which to perfect my jealousy, spinning out scenarios, sharpening vague suspicions into a fine deadly point, like a prisoner patiently whittling a Popsicle stick into a murder weapon. I sneaked uptown in order to lurk around Columbia, dreading and hoping to catch sight of her kissing some brilliant, irresistible professor, or walking arm in arm with some policy wonk of the future. If she seemed to lack sexual interest in me even for one night, I could not help but believe it was proof that her erotic energies were being spent elsewhere.

And then it happened. Like so many of life's disasters, it came at a quiet moment. We were shopping for food at a nearby market. I was pushing the cart—half size and in surprisingly poor repair for a store selling cherries at fourteen dollars a pound—and Deirdre was picking out the items we were going to have for that night's dinner. We were going to make a pasta to go along with some fresh halibut; she pulled a can of tomatoes off the shelf and seemed to be studying the label. Her back was to me, and I assumed she was reading the ingredients, as she was generally careful to avoid products that were laced with preservatives or corn fructose. I found myself distracted by a display of carving knives on the other side of the aisle, lethal-looking things encased in heavy plastic. They looked as if they could be used not only for slicing steak but butchering cows. I remember thinking *We should get some really good knives and get serious about living together,* and when I turned around again Deirdre was still studying that tomato can. I wondered how long it could take her to read a can of crushed tomatoes, she who could zip through two hundred pages on the Sino-Soviet split in an hour. Are you okay? I asked her. At first she didn't answer, but then she shook her head. Her shoulders moved up and then down. Her voluminous red curls swung back and forth, and when she finally turned toward me her face was luminescent with fright. She was breathing through her mouth. You're going to hate me, she said, and you should, you should; I am such an idiot. I felt like a child watching helplessly while everything falls apart. For all of my stupid tedious jealousy, I had never really believed Deirdre would deceive me. I had been playing a terrible emotional game, and now all my worst case scenarios were coming true. I've been seeing someone, his name is Osip, and I don't know what I want to happen at this point. I turned away from her, stared at the little display of knives. *His name is Osip? How dare she say his name! It would have been all right to tell me if I asked, but I hadn't asked.* You dope, I said, you're never supposed to say the name.

That night, we made dinner anyhow, set the table, and sat across from each other—we thought if we acted normally it would make things easier. But as soon as we were seated, Deirdre burst into tears. And through tears that seemed genuine to me, she said she was glad she was finally telling the truth, and that she cared too much about me to lie any longer, and I said Whatever happened to carrying the terrible secret? You just keep it to yourself, let it rot you out. You carry the weight even if it drags you right down into hell! I didn't really want to give her a hard time but it was clear to me that even as she wept and apologized, she was maintaining her power—the power of being the one who knew everything, the power of knowing what it felt like when she and Osip went at it, the power of knowing what took place last Thursday afternoon, last Saturday morning, the power of Time, which is the power of God.

I tried to grasp hold of what tiny fizzling little mitigating remarks she threw in as she sobbed out her confession. She said that while she was attracted to Osip, she didn't really *like* him very much, but the more I thought about that the worse it made things. It made the connection seem compellingly dark, compulsive, and sexual. Then she said Osip had a mean streak a mile wide and could barely speak English, and he was actually sort of married, to a woman he had left in a mental hospital in Moscow, and he, finally, was not even going to stay in New York much longer. The general tenor of the remarks she threw my way was that I was a known commodity, tested, and branded, while Osip was something available only on the black market. I was Tylenol and he was heroin, to which I thought *Thank you very much for the underwhelming praise. Don't you fucking know me well enough to realize I would rather be heroin?*

What I ought to have done was marshal what dignity I had left and walk slowly into the bedroom, pack my bags, and leave. Or maybe I ought to have looked at my watch and said You have an hour to get your stuff together and get out of here. Leave your keys in the blue bowl next to the door. But I didn't. What I did instead was try to get her into bed. Sorrow carried within it a backlash of desire, sheer savage lust, as if with a few violent thrusts I could cleanse myself of the loss, and cleanse Deirdre of the memory of all she had done, to inhabit her totally and force out every other thing.

And so, with our stinking halibut still on our plates, I reached across the table for Deirdre, as if I could just fuck our troubles away, bump and grind my way back into contention, back into the great game of life. We went to bed; we made love; she cried some more; I stared stoically ahead. Nothing was solved; nothing was salvaged.

And then the real hell began. We continued to live together, and I was plunged into a wretched state. We became roommates, and I became more wretched still. It was as if everything that had once been mine had been picked up and carried away by a tornado, and I was simply glad to be alive, and wholly unable to move. I was just going to sit there pretending the storm had never hit. Wretcheder and wretcheder. We were condemned to cross paths in the apartment while trying to make ourselves smaller and quieter. Our shame was razor wire; one false step and we'd be bleeding. We both wished the other were someplace else, a thousand or so miles away. It was madness of the grimmest, most degrading sort to continue living together on Fifty-fourth Street but neither of us had anyplace else to go. We were both looking for an affordable place to move to, but I thought she should be the one who moved, and she probably thought it should be me.

In the weeks following Deirdre's supermarket confession, I worked feverishly. I believed what Freud said about the two things you need for happiness: Love and Work. Now that the former had let me down, I doubly committed myself to the latter. I told myself and others that the plan was to make enough money to move out of my befouled Fifty-fourth Street nest, though ever making that kind of money in my chosen field seemed unlikely.

About half of my modest annual income as a freelancer came from writing company reports for a few corporations where I had old college friends. The rest came from articles, profiles, a travel piece when I lucked into one, more celebrity journalism than I would have liked, but for which I was generally grateful. Despite the compromised nature of my particular craft, I held on to a secret ambition to one day create something extraordinary.

Sometimes I wrote pieces that called for my putting myself through some arduous or strange experience. I lived for two weeks in a retirement community in Florida. I got a job in a puppy mill in New Hampshire. I took a menial position in a firm called Swept Away, which did the night maintenance in several downtown banks and brokerage houses—this turned out to be my most affecting piece. I found myself oddly and unexpectedly touched by the little signs of humanity left behind by the bond salesmen and computer programmers; the family snapshots, the little Buddhas, the list of nearby AA meetings, even the candy wrappers and rosary beads seemed steeped in pathos in the stark fluorescent light of those empty glass boxes.

Shortly after Deirdre dropped the Scarlet A Bomb on me, *Esquire* finally ran a piece I had submitted eight months earlier, about having four fathers.

FOUR KINGS

Chances are I haven't broken any more laws than you. Neverthe-less, I have had four surnames. I have been Avery Kaplan, Avery Kearney, Avery Blake, and the byline you see on this piece: Avery Jankowsky.

Which brings me to my mother. My mother is what used to be called the Marrying Kind—though I think that tag was meant for men who adapted easily to the married state. Her first marriage, to Theodore Kaplan, took place three days after her eighteenth birthday. She came from a nonreligious but fiercely Jewish family. Both her parents believed that every Jewish child born postwar was spit in Hitler's eye, and even though they were poor and lived in five warrenlike rooms, more of a dovecote than an apartment, in a part of Brooklyn called Ditmas Park, my grandparents had nine children, concluding with so-called Irish twins, of which my mother was the distaff side. My mother's fa-ther, Grandpa Sam, delivered for Dr. Brown's soda; his back was always sore; his hands were a catastrophe of bruises and breaks. Grandmama Doris did piecework at home for a mean-spirited cousin who sold aprons with funny sayings on them.

Which is to say that love my mother as they surely did, Sam and Doris Cohen were exhausted, their finances were stretched thin, and they were not sorry to see her go. Each of those chil-dren might have been spit in Hitler's eye, but, let's face it, spit-ting at Adolf was easy compared to what's involved in raising a family that size. The shoes, the pants, the fevers, the meals, the mess, the drama, the worry, the tedium, the feuds, the tears. Not all of the children married; not all of them moved. So when little Naomi was being courted by my father—an Upper West Side boy, a stranger, not terribly polite, with no great prospects, a couple years of college, a vague desire to travel—he escaped all scrutiny. And when, after a few weeks of courtship that in-cluded who knew how much sex, because this was the Golden Age of Sex, she announced she was going to marry Ted Kaplan, no objections were raised. Good luck, good-bye, don't let the door hit your *tuchis* on the way out! Was this hasty sendoff, this mumbled mazel tov, wounding to my mother? Did it set her on her path as a serial matrimonialist?

In fairness to her—and, believe me, I want nothing more than to be fair to her—her first and fourth marriages did not result in divorce. My first father killed himself—gently, I might add, asphyxiating himself in our garage. (I still wonder why a Jew, just thirty years past the Shoah, would choose to gas himself.) My fourth father, whose name I now bear, died of congestive heart failure.

This was my final father. If my mother remarries again, I am now well past the age when I can be either forced or persuaded to give up my name. My second name, Kearney, was slapped over Kaplan like hastily hung wallpaper in a room in which a crime has been committed. Not only did my father gas himself, but he did this terrible thing to himself in direct response to having been caught with his hand deep in his company's till, a flag and banner manufacturing company he co-owned with none other than Andrew Kearney, my second father . . .

Etcetera. I hadn't spent much time agonizing about cannibalizing my personal life for a few inches of copy and enough of a payday to make rent for four months. I didn't feel I was prostituting myself; I was only using the materials at hand. But my mother, who, in the past, when she happened to see something I had written, could usually be counted on for a polite little note or a phone call, was furious with me and experienced the article not only as a breach of good taste but as a thoughtless betrayal of her. Some things are personal, Avery, she'd said to me over the telephone, I never thought you would compromise the privacy and dignity of your family just to make money. So how are things in Costa Rica? I asked her. She was down there for the duration, living comfortably on her share of the Jankowsky Cross. It's none of your goddamned business, you little brat. Mom, come on, there's no need for that. Don't you tell me what there's a need for. You better watch out, Avery, and I mean it. I'm going to come up there and really let you have it. You've gone too far this time, you really have. I've already spoken to my attorney, and he tells me that suing is going to be too hard, but there's more to life than lawsuits and you better believe it—I'm going to make you sorry you ever did such a thing to me. Me! Who gave up half her life to take care of you. How could you do this to me? Your one and only mother? Haven't you ever noticed that everyone in your life has found a way to get rid of you, and I'm the only one still here?

2

IN THE DAYS following Deirdre's confession, I had little luck standing up to the hurricane of grief and shame—let's say the levees of the ego did not hold. I was stuck on the shaky idea that something—*something*—had to be done to make what had happened between Deirdre and Osip not to have happened. I wanted her to be unfucked. In this insanity I found kinship with certain species of dragonfly, whose genitalia are veritable Rube Goldberg inventions, a penile balloon with sticky hooks and a scouring brush added on for good measure—all designed to remove the sperm of rival dragonflies, in a tireless competition for the prime real estate of one female's reproductive organ. But of course the nice thing, for the dragonflies, is that there are others, billions of other dragonflies, they all look good, and you can try your luck elsewhere. The only thing you can't do is mope around; evolution makes short shrift of the mopers. You only have so much time and then: your DNA dies with you. The body is not here to write celebrity profiles or try new restaurants; the body is here to reproduce.

Forget the flies. We've got closer relatives designed for unfucking. The bush babies, our little pocket-sized cousins, scurrying up and down the dark green trees, their eyes large and glassy, with a kind of imbecilic shine. The bush babies have elaborate genitalia, crooked, twisting Roto-Rooter penises a riot of spikes and knobs, so the males might compensate for the waywardness of female desire by literally going after the ejaculate left behind by other males, piercing it, hooking it, scrubbing it out, and thereby increasing the chances that I, King of the bush babies, I, the Inimitable bush baby, my seed will be the one to germinate.

Yet there are not even any *myths* about human women who have had sex suddenly having that act erased. When you are fucked you are fucked is the one thing we have always been able to agree upon—not when you're dead you're dead, not if dreams can or cannot foretell the future, not if we are or are not ruled by the stars, not if we are or are not destined to be reborn and have, in fact, already been popping up here and there throughout history, once, say, as a baker, then a banker, then a biker, then as a water moccasin. All of these possibilities have been put forward, sometimes strenuously proposed, sometimes just as strenuously denounced. But whether or not once you've been fucked you do or do not remain fucked has never been subject to debate.

I could not make it unhappen. All I could do was build a wall between what she had done and the pain it was causing me. As to what that wall would be made of—I already had the first component, Work. The second, which I had initially thought was Love, might have to be Sex, a bit of last-minute substitution with which all builders are familiar, because you have to know how to use the materials at hand. Yet these two ingredients—only one of which was actually at hand—were not in themselves sufficient for the wall. The wall needed something to hold it together; it needed cement; it needed insulation: it needed money.

Money, money. I had never needed it more. My yearly take from the Jankowsky Cross was but a mockery of my needs. When it arrived I thought about taking the whole thing—less than five grand, unfortunately—and going over to Atlantic City or maybe out to that Indian casino over in Connecticut and putting it all on red at the roulette table, and doubling it with one spin of the wheel. (Some people in difficult straits ask themselves *What would Jesus do?* I, however, was wondering *What would Dostoyevsky do?*) But even if I won, my money woes would still be on me like that proverbial stink on a monkey. All you got with a red/black bet for five thousand was even money, another five thousand, and even if I took the whole ten thousand and let it ride, and won again, I'd only have twenty, and if I let that ride and won again, I'd be up to forty thousand, a nice piece of change, to be sure, but mere pocket lint when it came to buying an apartment in New York, setting down roots, living a life of some dignity and stability. For that I would have to win twenty times in a row—and there was no chance of that, none whatsoever.

I sat at my silver and peach Piedmont computer, trying to generate ideas for work. I sent my poor agent, Andrew Post, a flurry of pitches, or pitches for pitches, most of them, I see now, insane and unsellable. Nearly all my ideas for articles—as well as a couple of TV pilots that struck me as sure things, even though I knew nothing about writing a TV pilot and almost nothing about television itself—involved putting myself into some kind of jeopardy or predicament. A couple were attempts to get some editor to assign me a task I was otherwise trying mightily to resist. For instance, I proposed writing a piece called "Stalking," in which I would "assume the identity" of someone obsessively following someone, say, a woman, say, just for the sake of illustration, a woman with whom the writer either is or has been involved , and what it is like to trail after her, making deductions as to her activities based on her movements around the city, how close you can get to the person you're stalking, what taxi drivers actually say and do when you tell them urgently to Follow that cab, how to cope with the inevitable human dilemmas you encounter along the way, such as where to get out of the rain, where to take a leak, what to say and do if you happen to run into someone you know and they are curious about what you're doing walking around with your jacket collar up and your Mets cap pulled down over your eyes. I also proposed a piece about interviewing and then hiring a private detective to follow and photograph someone; the pitch included an estimate of what I would need by way of expenses, since it wasn't likely I could put various New York investigators through their paces free of charge.

Not all of my ideas were so transparently wounded. I thought it might be interesting if I went out to Colorado and hung out with the guys who were building a see-through walkway over the Grand Canyon. I wanted to cover one of the Enron trials. I proposed profiles of Mark Knopfler, Judy Pfaff, Francine Prose, Paula Abdul, Randy Newman,

Gillian Welch—at one point I just started writing down the names of musicians whose work was in my iPod and then doing an Internet search to see if anything had recently been published about them. And not all of my ideas were sane. I spent hours working up a pitch for some enterprising, imaginative editor to send me to Costa Rica, where I would confront my mother and somehow fathom the mystery of her multiple marriages—but was there really such a mystery to untangle? Anyhow, these were coals I had already thoroughly raked in "Four Kings." Now they were cold.

I sent my ideas to my agent via e-mail. When I wasn't trolling the Internet for still more ideas—I needed more than just one or two to sell if I was ever going to escape the minute-by-minute humiliation of staying put—I was checking my e-mail to see if anyone had bitten. But there were no takers—I got a Maybe on the Knopfler idea, but *Rolling Stone* only wanted five hundred words at $2.25 per word. (Do the math, as the sadists say.) Not only that, but my agent was barely responding to my ideas. I was becoming a pest, and I knew it. But somehow knowing it was not quite enough to force me to stop.

I could not just sit there and do nothing without filling up with jealousy and sadness, and a feeling of such overwhelming shame I was almost ready to believe that everything in my life that had ever gone wrong was entirely my own fault, every wound self-inflicted, every slap in the face accompanied by the stinging of my own palm. Inundating myself with images and information from my computer was like running a white noise machine in your apartment to drown out the sounds of traffic. I was drowning out wondering where Deirdre was, and what she was doing, and with whom, and I was drowning out the coyote yowl of my own loneliness.

It was hard for me to leave the apartment during business hours; I thought my agent might call at any time, with some rescuing good news, news too vital to my survival to trust to my cheap cell phone. If I were to be plucked from the pit of my own personal hell, I wanted it to happen on a land line; I wanted to hear every word, every number, and I wanted the privacy to fall to my knees with relief, I ran a few simple errands—milk for my thousand cups of coffees, rum for my Diet Cokes, pints of prefab tuna salad—but for the most part I might as well have been under house arrest, with an electronic sensor around my ankle. The evenings were, of course, more difficult; they always are. The introduction of electric light and our gradual evolution into a twenty-four-hour-society have done little to cut down on the intrinsic peril of the hours between eight and eight. I wasn't worried about the things my night-fearing distant relations had once feared: saber-toothed tigers, rampaging Cossacks. What unnerved me were my thoughts of Deirdre—what a thing to fear! I feared the woman upon whose breast I had slept, the woman whose body I had so casually enjoyed, the woman whose youth I had always assumed made her an unsuitable match; I feared creamy soft red-haired freckle-shouldered Deirdre. I dreaded her coming into our penitential apartment and sensing the internal rot of me, I feared what I might say to her, I feared what I might do, and I feared, above all, what I would—and did—feel when she failed to come home at all.

The streets, restaurants, clubs, theaters, and shops of New York are filled with people who would rather not be in their apartments at night. Whereas once I had experienced this constant activity as a kind of ceaseless frantic unbounded commercialism, a nonstop effort to soak up as many dollars from as many people as possible, I now saw the we-never-close side of Manhattan as a great humanitarian effort on behalf of those of us who not only would rather not be at home but could not be at home. What would I have done if I had been in my predicament in Joliet or Eugene? But in New York there were always movie theaters I could slip into, where I could watch depictions of other people's troubles. There were a million bars. Within walking distance of my apartment, there were places to listen to jazz, blues, bluegrass, Persian classical music, klezmer, suburban hip-hop, samba, Afro-Cuban, Turkish, Greek, and Russian music, and where you could ride out the evening on a carpet of song. No one looked at you twice for being alone. I saw plays by Shakespeare, Mike Leigh, Brecht. These were awfully tough on the purse, but they filled the time and they provided people for me to sit with and share an emotional experience. I wasn't the only one alone in these places, nor was I the only one who walked the streets by myself. Yet I felt loneliness filling me up. A man without a woman is a wretched thing, prone to disease, mental illness, crime; and a man alone whose woman is on the frolic with someone else is exponentially more wretched still. Women rushed by like white water, and they moved past me as if I were a rock. More than once, I thought about just bumping into one of them, just to have the feel of human flesh. Between the theaters and my apartment there were dozens of pornography shops and before long it was more than I could do to resist their sneaky rancid allure. Every once in a while I ducked into one of these Lysol-scented storefronts with their purplish lighting and recently paroled clerks and there I would stand as if in a fugue state and look at pictures of naked women, like a castaway looking for a little dot of hope on the horizon. For a minute or two the sight of these unknown women made me stop thinking of Deirdre (and Osip), and then, when I put the magazine down, I couldn't even say I was back where I'd started from, because, in fact, everything was a little bit worse.

ONE EVENING, I got back to Fifty-fourth Street, and Deirdre was not yet home. Her perforated gray Swedish slip-on shoes were there, her maroon backpack, the yellow grin of a half-eaten toasted cheese sandwich. The emptiness of the apartment was squeezing me like a vise. It was terrible to be skulking around those rooms when Deirdre was home, but it was no better when she was away. She had at one point told me that she had stopped seeing Osip, but I did not believe her. I did not believe her for one simple reason: it was a lie.

I knew it was a lie because I had proof. Two days after the confession, feeling so humiliated I avoided mirrors, I found Deirdre's diary, stowed in a defiantly obvious place, between the mattress and the box spring. What was I doing waving my hand around in this cramped space? Looking for the diary. I knew she kept one. I had seen her write in it, and there it was, in the very first place I looked. I stood in the bedroom, my heart hiccuping. I held the tall, narrow notebook, with its decorative, marbleized cover and mock Victorian leather corners. I knew the rules governing privacy, boundaries, et cetera, but I was unable to resist. I opened to the first page: there was a list of the classes she was taking, the professors, the times. I opened to the middle and found a log of phone numbers: embassies, doctors, computer repair shops. On the next page there was one sentence, written in Deirdre's neat, conventional script: *I'm so so tired of my hair.* Fuck you, I'd said, so loudly that I startled myself, and then on the next page: at last, *Poor Avery, I have bruised his ego. I guess my dream of him and me staying friends is never going to be.* Him and me? What an ignorant, ungrammatical tramp.

He's such a sweet guy. The gentlest. Maybe too gentle for me? I can't believe the way I've screwed everything up. And for what? Vanity and curiosity? Come on, Deirdre, when are you going to get a clue? I'm still in that head space from when I was fourteen. Poor Avery. I don't even know why I keep thinking of him like that. I have to keep reminding myself how many times he told me that our love was just a shipboard romance, and that we would never end up together. He probably thought he was being honorable telling me that over and over, but each time was like a slap in my face. I was never fucking mean to him! Like about how sometimes he smells weird. I could have said so, but I didn't. I never wanted him to feel that bad.

I had never read anything quite so shocking in my whole life. I rolled up my shirtsleeve, sniffed my forearm. It smelled faintly of soap. Surely she could not have meant that. I smelled my hands, my shoulders, my underarms. What was the problem? I tried to put it out of my mind . . .

Then, on the next page: *Osip tonight. Yippee!* It wasn't so horrifying as reading about my so-called smell, but it was close. Of course, it's what you risk when you snoop. It's what the cuckolds must feel when the detectives they hire come back with evidence confirming their worst fears. Photographs, theater programs, telephone bills, hotel registrations, tickets to Jamaica. Yet this wound, this wound of proof, I could not stop inflicting it on myself. It was like some vicious erotica created just for me. Day after day, while Deirdre was away at school, or at night, when she was supposedly out with friends or studying late at the library, I walked (whistling an insanely jaunty little tune) back to the bedroom, fished out the diary, and read the latest installments. There were days that went by in which nothing was recorded, days I would experience the blank page with a mixture of frustration and relief. And there were days in which the entries had nothing to do with Osip or anything else of a sexual nature, entries devoted to daydreams of her postgraduate life, or accounts of her conversations with family members, or lists of books she needed to read. But there were also a shocking number of entries devoted to Osip and their ecstatic couplings, all recounted in great detail, with a kind of pornographic concentration, as if she planned one day in her lonely old age to relive these memories and recall herself at the peak of her vitality. In the mouth, on the table, on the floor, in a rocking chair; they could not, it seemed, be with each other for more than an hour without exchanging fluids. Even her occasional criticisms of Osip were daggers to my heart.

O says I have been wasting myself with American boyfriends. LOL, he thinks that sex is a Russian specialty. I don't think he even understands that for women it's about emotions. Not ALL about emotions, of course.

And, a page later:

O was really in a rush, like we had to finish before the secret police knocked on the door. I clamped my legs closed to try and keep him inside me. Stay stay, I feel like crying when he pulls out. But he won't. Grrrrr. He takes himself elsewhere, leaving nothing behind but the faint odor of bread.

I really had had no idea she was so olfactorily inclined. And that bit about the bread? I had said that to Deirdre. About *her*. She was using *my* tune while she danced with him.

Throughout the day, I had white-knuckled it through my hours alone in the apartment and forced myself not to look at her diary; the grim restless sexual energy was spent, instead, surfing the Internet. But coming back one night after sitting comatose through a supposedly rousing and artful Chinese martial arts epic, all I could think of was now it was time to check in on Deirdre's journal. I really didn't want to. I sat on the sofa for a few moments, gently rocking back and forth, wondering if I ought to go back into the bedroom, take the diary out, destroy it, or perhaps read it all carefully, page by page, banality by banality, let the full force of the thing go into me like nails hammered in by a furious drunken carpenter, maybe even have the filthy thing out on my lap when Deirdre returned from whatever sexual calisthenics she was engaged in.

I've got to pull myself together, I thought, and the first step would be to stop reading her fucking diary, since that's what it literally *was.* I drank some gin, took a Tylenol PM. I pulled out the sofa bed, slapped away some dust and popcorn kernels that had slipped through the cushions and onto the sheet, took the down comforter out of the cabinet, and spread it across what was now my bed. Buying a new goose down comforter had taken some of the grimness out of sleeping on the convertible sofa, though I sometimes wondered what had become of the goose itself. Did they simply pluck every last feather from it, or had it been butchered? I looked at the bed, tried to think well of it. *Nice, nice,* I said to myself. *Very nice.*

Somehow I fell asleep, and when I awoke it was still dark—but it was always dark in that apartment. I looked at my watch. Three thirty in the morning. Deirdre was home, in the bedroom, with the door closed. I heard music playing, Bach unaccompanied cello sonatas. She had lately been lulling herself to sleep with music—following the line of the melody got her off the hamster wheel of her own thinking. I lay there, listening through the door to the sadness and tenderness of the music, this spire of sound that reached all the way to heaven. I couldn't help myself, the music made me think about getting into bed with her. The body's great joke at the soul's expense was that since that terrible evening our three separate nights of sex were the most passionate and uninhibited of our lives together. Let's do unmentionable things, she had whispered to me. She had always been free with her body, eager for pleasure. I spontaneously combust, she said, and I, unable to relinquish my position as elder in our village of two, the purveyor of maturity and wisdom, said that spontaneous combustion was no way to heat a home; you needed something regular, controlled; you needed to know you could twist the dial on the thermostat and the furnace would ignite. And Deirdre said Then do it, just shut up and twist my dial, and before I could argue it any further, she rolled onto her side, took my hand

and guided it toward where she wanted it. But she said other things, too. She said Oh, not now, and she said I don't think we'd better, and she said Let's not do things that make us sad. I could not bear to be turned away by her; it was too much, on top of everything else. Do you love me or do you not? I finally blurted out, and her wide placid face darkened—for a moment I thought she was going to slap me, and finally she said, Why didn't you care when it still mattered?

The bedroom door opened, and Deirdre emerged. She stood motionless for a moment and then, before I could say anything, she rushed toward the bathroom and closed the door behind her. I heard the light click on in the bathroom, saw its diffuse glow leaking out from beneath the door. Then: the rodenty squeak of the sink's faucets twisting open. The rush of water. The clatter of the toilet's lid, hastily lifted, hitting against the tank. Through the white noise of the rushing water, I heard her voice, a small cracked suffering groan. I wondered if there were something I ought to do. And then—of course, I should have guessed—the sound of retching. I thought I heard her say "Osip," but it could have been "Oh shit." The toilet flushed thunderously, more retching, more flushing—and then she turned on the shower.

She must have had a great deal to drink, I thought. I could see her, with him, downing shots, losing inhibitions . . . And then, suddenly, without knowing what train of thought had brought me to this point, I was standing, moving toward the bedroom. I listened to make sure the shower was still running, and then I crouched down, reached under what had once been my mattress, groped around, felt something hard and rectangular, and pulled out her diary. I stood up quickly, dizzily. The digital readout window of her boom box cast a dark blue light in the little bedroom; every other moment the word *Good-bye* flashed. I loathed that I was acting so dishonorably, but there it was. I'd always wondered how low I could sink. Yet even now I felt more anxiety than guilt. Shame and conscience prove to be rather small next to the looming fear of being found out, discovered, seen through. I turned on the bedside lamp; the bulb was still warm. I opened the journal, turned to see if she had written anything new since last I looked. She had! *Tonight was grim. First an hour of him holding forth on global warming. Then the moment of truth! He's been lobbying for me to try "it," and I finally gave in. I told him a little lie and said I had never done it like that before. Well, it was sort of true. I never did it with A or with G. G was so big it would have killed me anyhow. So it's been 2 yrs, the way I see it I am a virgin there again. O was so excited I don't think he knew where he was or who I was. I tried to experience his excitement. Forget it. All I could feel was Ow. And it's like pooping in reverse.*

I gasped, shut the book, tried to prevent what I had just read from sinking in. Suddenly I was aware that I was no longer hearing the shower, and I shoved the book back under the mattress, turned off the lamp, and hurried back to my sofa bed, feeling sick with jealousy and shame, plus murderous rage.

A few moments later, I lifted myself up on my elbows in what I thought was a fine mimicry of a man just coming awake as Deirdre emerged from the bathroom.

Are you okay? I asked, to which she replied Ichhh, and hurried past.

I lay flat again. The mattress felt like a few sheets of newspaper spread out over scaffolding. I wondered if Deirdre's growl of disgust was meant to refer to her stomach or to me. I thought about this, and then a kind of soft nothingness filled my mind, like dim, diffuse light from a hidden source. I felt something akin to peace. Life for a moment was a little less mysterious. Deirdre was heartless; I was worthless; it was all pretty simple. . .

In the morning, I opened my eyes to the timeless gloom of the living room. I smelled coffee, the burned edges of a fried egg. I assumed Deirdre was in the kitchen, and I hurried to the bathroom, washed my face, teeth, tongue. I would have liked the physical gravitas of a hangover; it might have counteracted the anxiety I felt upon waking, that nerved-out high hum pulsating through my brain.

The kitchen was messy, and Deirdre was gone. I sat at the half table we were able to squeeze into the tiny space, finished the dregs of her sweet coffee, and ate the couple bites of toast she had left behind. There was something abject and canine about eating her scraps that held some sort of appeal, the dank pleasure of slipping down another notch.

I filled the teakettle, set it atop the blue chrysanthemum of the gas flame, and, seemingly without thinking about it, walked into the bedroom, dropped to my knees, and plunged my hand into the space between the mattress and the box spring. My fingers groped, felt nothing but darkness. I slid my palm back and forth. I felt . . . something. Not the journal, however. I pulled it out. An envelope. With my name on it, written in pen. My heart was beginning to race. I opened the envelope carefully, as if I might have to reseal it, put it back. There was a single piece of pale green notebook paper in it, its edge ragged from having been ripped out of its spiral binder. I unfolded it. A single sentence, written in Deirdre's plump cursive. *Shame on you, Avery, shame shame shame on you.*

I trudged back to the front of the apartment and walked to the windows overlooking Seventh Avenue, looked out through the grime that was so thick it was like gauze. Seven stories below, traffic was stopped; in the middle of a congestion of yellow cabs, a red and white ambulance from St. Clare's Hospital sat, its lights frantically flashing. Every so often the ambulance let out a siren whoop, a cry of anguish, but no one budged; it was like the blow of an ax against a frozen sea, completely hopeless.

3

DEIRDRE MOVED OUT, temporarily, saying that in her view the apartment was hers but I could stay there while I looked for someplace else, and I tried to comfort myself with nihilistic thoughts about the eventual extinction of life on Earth, the catastrophe of which dwarfed my own little purse of nickel miseries. Francis Crick, who worked with James Watson in decoding DNA, believed that the first DNA came to Earth from deep space, from a star, and that eventually, we, that is humanity, this vast aggregate of soft machine whose main purpose is to house, protect, and spew DNA, eventually will return to our origins, to that distant star from which we çame. That is why we are able to play so fast and loose with our planet, unable to stop fouling our little round nest—threatening it with extinction through atomic fusion, shredding the protective skin of our atmosphere, polluting our water supply, melting our ice caps, turning the once frozen tundra into a tepid trampoline.

I, too, was going elsewhere, not to another planet, but surely I was not meant to spend much more time wallowing in my own mess. Not to equate finding another apartment with emigrating to a distant galaxy, but I couldn't even accomplish that. Not to equate finding some other arms to hold me while I endured the slow-motion evisceration of living with Deirdre with actually facing and understanding why I had gotten myself into this fix to begin with, but I couldn't accomplish that either.

Failing to escape into deep space or into a new bed, I found a degree of relief and diversion on the Internet. Some of my travel from site to site was entirely wholesome. I read British magazines, took a virtual tour of the Hermitage, listened to archived interviews on the National Public Radio page, checked out hotels in Lisbon, browsed through New York real estate listings. Wherever I went, ads popped up on my screen. It was as if someone knew how desperately I wanted to make some money; nearly all of them were trying to lure me into the supposedly limitless profit opportunities of precious metals, touting gold or silver mining stocks selling for a dollar, tin mining stocks selling for fifty cents, wildcat oil drillers working the seas from Baja to the Bering Strait. *This was who the world is for*, I thought, *the men who split the world wide open and suck it dry.*

And then I typed the words *So Fucking Lonely* into my search engine, and it was as if a bridge appeared, upon which I was welcome to walk across the moat that had previously separated me from the countless portals in the skin trade. One little click and there it was.

No one forced me to walk across it. But I did. I'm not sure I have ever been able to turn away from the sight of a naked woman. The picture might be anthropological, medical, or forensic, it might fill me with horror, or compassion, or anger, but no matter what, there is always a limbic hiccup, one little rivulet of reaction that goes like this: she's naked. And now here they were, the images, millions of them. And not only were they naked, but they all claimed to want to know me.

It was madness and a kind of crime against humanity, this nonstop proliferation of images of women living in Click World, pretending they wanted to have something to do with you, except there was no You, save to the extent that you existed as a credit card number. I was going around and around and around. I had no idea who I was looking at, or where they lived—was I seeing them in Russia, China, Argentina, Las Vegas, perhaps somewhere within my own apartment house? My brain was sick, engorged, and reeling from the feeding frenzy as screen after screen of visual information flickered before me. I began to see that the human male's sexual response had been originally forged for creatures who saw perhaps one hundred—or, say, one thousand—people in a whole lifetime. Then, when we lived in roving bands, in tribes, in towns with the population of my apartment building, the trigger-happy promiscuity of desire may have been necessary to animate the great human project of populating the earth. You saw something beautiful—you went for it. But this susceptibility to beauty could not get out of hand because how many staggeringly beautiful women did we see in a lifetime? We had very narrow choices. Now our hardwired susceptibility to beautiful women has remained essentially unaltered, unevolved, while our ability to *see* beautiful women has grown by leaps and bounds. In paintings, then in photographs, then in movies, and now, as we sit smoking and unshaved in front of our home computers. So now, with our hardwired susceptibility to the sight of a desirable woman, millions of men are inundated with visions of women, women who strike to the core of our need for prestige, our instinctual mission to improve the species. These images drive us mad, and without any undue effort we can view a thousand of them every day. Our ability to summon them forth and dismiss them with a keystroke makes the life of a sultan seem ascetic indeed. What happens to our wiring when we see not one or two attractive women, but dozens of them? And then dozens become hundreds and hundreds become thousands? In Click World there are hundreds of thousands of naked women, and they are pointing at their sex organ and saying Come on and fill me up; that's just how things are done in Click World.

Somewhere along the way, like a traveler lost in a dark wood, I began putting one virtual foot in front of the other, clicking from site to site, link to link, less and less sure of where I had just been, more and more surprised by what came up next. Soon, I was no longer following paths that led me to pictures of naked women. Now I was flitting about sites that were offering for sale the women themselves.

I had passed hookers on the street many, many times before. In fact, my apartment was near several hotels around which streetwalkers orbited, in their vertiginous heels and short skirts. But whenever I was near a street prostitute I was careful not to look at her too closely. I didn't want to give her the impression that I was cruising her, evaluating her wares, squeezing the fruit, as it were, and then tossing it back into the bin. I avoided eye contact out of good manners. I did not want to intrude on their consciousness. I was also, quite frankly, a little afraid of them. It seemed to me that that line of work would attract more than its share of psychopaths. Was it really so unlikely that, say, 1 percent of the women trying to make a living selling sex on Seventh Avenue were in a murderous rage? Throw in another 2 percent for women in the grip of drug psychosis, which brings us up to 3 percent, and we can stop there. If, say, a thousand women are prowling the streets looking for someone who will pay to have sex with them, that means *thirty* of them are extremely dangerous. So I cut them all a wide berth, for fear that one of them would cut *me*.

In the gloomy, hypnotic safety of the Internet, with its ceaseless presentation of a world that was full of spectacle and danger, I was completely safe because it was fundamentally not real. It was a world where I could see them but they, as far as I could tell, could not see me, and I was free to examine hundreds of women doing business within a two-mile radius of my apartment, without the slightest risk—except, of course, the risk that the women in those pictures were not real, and the images were put forward with the same cunning with which a trout fisherman baits his hook with little pieces of plastic and sparkle to fool the hungry fish into thinking the lure is an actual meal.

There followed days of dithering, in which I could barely do my work but instead went around and around such local call girl sites as New York Pink, Desirez, Do Me, Empire State Tens, Manhattan Courtesans, and literally hundreds of others, looking at the pictures, reading their mission statements: I love what I do and U will 2; I am an international runway model; I am here from Brazil for just a little while and love meeting new people; I have a sweet, bright, unforgettable smile that will leave you speechless when we meet; my all-natural measurements are 36C–24–34, and I stand 5'7" and weigh 115 lbs. of pure elegance; I exclusively cater to mature, upscale, distinguished gentlemen who appreciate the finer things in life; I am here to pamper you with my seductive charm and grace and make you feel as comfortable as possible; I am well educated and can adapt to any situation; I am finally legal. None of these were necessarily true, but, then again, the offering statements of several recent IPOs also turned out to be fairly fictitious. Then I made a new discovery. Just as investors in stocks have the Securities and Exchange Commission to look after their interests and protect them from fraud, the men cruising the Internet in search of flesh had a site to consult, which rated the various women advertising their services and told you whether the actual woman you would end up seeing looked like her picture, and rated on a ten-point scale the quality of the services she provided. Of course, one couldn't tell to what extent this consumer protection site had been penetrated by the providers themselves, but the same misgivings were appropriate when it came to the SEC, as well.

I knew it was just a matter of time before I went from voyeuristically clicking on ad after ad, looking at the women, to actually making a call and arranging to see one. The first woman I chose was named Stephanie, a standard-issue male fantasy: her photograph, showing a long-legged blonde in a turquoise bikini bottom, thrusting her breasts up toward the sun, looked as if it had been taken in Florida or Southern California, and probably wasn't even Stephanie. Further investigation revealed that she charged $1,400 per hour, putting her well out of my pay grade. I couldn't even afford to be defrauded by her.

The majority of the women advertising offered outcall, which meant they would come to you, which, in my case, was out of the question—however grimly entertaining it might be to have Deirdre walk in on us. Limiting my pursuit to the women who offered in-call services—and ruling out the majority of these, because they were Korean or Thai, and I had recently read that many of the Asian sex workers were in fact slaves, and while I was willing to sink a bit, there was a limit to how low I was prepared to go—I eventually narrowed my search to one particular provider, whose listing I returned to over and over. If this had been taking place in the physical world rather than on my Piedmont computer, she would have been standing on a street corner or sitting in a club chair in the lobby of a hotel, and I would be the hapless john who continually circled her, who got within a few feet of her and then got a faraway look in his eyes, as if he had just seen something that needed his immediate attention, or snapped his fingers as if some important detail that had slipped his mind was suddenly back on the mental radar, and then scurried away, only to return in a few minutes, at which point the pathetic, ambivalent charade would begin again. But because this was all taking place in the toxic privacy of the Internet, I was free to click on her name, visit her Web site, look at her picture, take note of her schedule and fees, over and over and over and over again, until I was beginning to fear that there was some aspect to the Internet with which I was not familiar, some little tracking capability, some way of registering visits, and she not only was aware of me but was getting irritated with me, just as she would be if this all-day approach and retreat were taking place on Seventh Avenue.

Her name was Chelsea, almost certainly not her real name, but, I thought, an interesting choice, a vaguely hippie, Clinton-era name, friendly, not aggressively erotic. She had dark hair, parted in the middle, cut just above her shoulders. Her eyes were soft and melancholy, beneath dark brows. She looked like a girl who had had to defy a strong unreasonable father. She had a stubborn jaw but a wide, open smile—she seemed fond of whoever had taken her picture. She was posed shirtless in jeans, with her arms folded demurely over her breasts. *Hi, I'm pretty new to this. I hope you like what you see. I promise this is me—some people say I look even better in person. I'm a down-to-earth girl, I like to laugh, and I like making people feel good about themselves. I offer an unrushed, full girlfriend experience (GFE). If you are a clean, respectful upscale gentleman and have three hundred roses, then make an appointment with me. You won't be disappointed.*

It was four in the afternoon when I called her; she had a dry, sleepy, scratchy hello, startlingly intimate. I saw your ad, I said. Oh, she said, drawing it out, as if she was just remembering it, as if she had posted it in a moment of madness and now she was forced to deal with the consequences. I heard the faint rasp of a match being struck, then a sharp little intake of breath, an exhalation. Would you like to make an appointment? she said in her flirtatious crackle. Yes I would. To whom am I speaking? she asked. I hesitated for a moment. I didn't want to give my real name, but I wasn't prepared with a false one. Osip, I said. Osip? It was as if she had never heard anything so ridiculous. Yeah, it's Russian. Are you Russian, Osip? How far could I go with this? I wasn't going to suddenly come up with a credible Russian accent. Not really, I said. My grandfather was. Okay, she said, again drawing it out, letting the long *a* cast a shadow of doubt over the whole thing. So, I said, where are you located? (It's what you say when you can't say Where are you? or Where do you live?) I'm in the Upper Midtown area, she said, on the West Side. Really? I said, momentarily forgetting to be false. So am I. What time did you have in mind, Osip? I was thinking maybe now, if you have an opening. She was silent and I realized I had just made a smutty little pun. All right, she said. Go to the corner of Fifty-fourth and Seventh, and call me, and I'll tell you where to go. Now it was my turn to be silent. Fifty fourth and Seventh was *my* corner. Could this so-called Chelsea be operating from an apartment in this very building? Okay, I said, I'll call you in . . . what? Ten minutes. Make it half an hour, she said. Okay, that's fine, half an hour. I was about to hang up, but I heard her say, Osip? You're not a cop, are you? Absolutely not, I said. Sorry, she said, I have to ask, a girl has to feel safe. I don't mind, I said. And, Osip, she said, one more thing. I tell this to all my new friends. It'll be so much nicer if you take a shower. If that's a problem, there's a nice shower here you're welcome to use. Okay, I said, no problem. My voice sounded husky and deferential.

I showered, shaved, flossed, and gargled, with all the nervousness of someone getting ready for a date. I put on a pair of jeans and the most expensive shirt I had ever purchased, a Savile Row blue oxford I bought at Saks, when American Airlines made a three-article deal with me for their in-flight magazine. I closed down my computer, cutting the power source of all the thousands of real and imaginary women swimming around its inner workings, and then I went to a nearby ATM and took out three hundred dollars for Chelsea's fee, an extra hundred for myself, or for a possible tip, if it should come to pass that she would bring me to the brink of a pleasure that would cost extra. I put the three hundred in my front pocket—the one bit of folk wisdom I retained from Father Number 3 was a manly man does not put money in a wallet; he carries it neatly folded in his right front pocket—and five fresh twenties in a back pocket. It was a warm, still afternoon; the sky was the color of cod. I stood on the southeast corner of Fifty-fourth and Seventh, near a diner, one of those Greek-owned places that never close, and where the waiters always seem to be coming down from forty-eight hours on Dexedrine. I had had countless breakfasts there, especially since the Crushed Tomato Confession, and, as I dialed Chelsea's number on my cell phone, I was also smiling and waving at Theo, who earlier that day had served me a cheese omelet and coffee. We had a special bond; he was the first person I'd met who wore an actual, bona fide Jankowsky Cross. He was forty: he lived with his sister and her husband in Queens. Theo seemed to spend his tips on lottery tickets. Even this morning, he had a couple of them in his shirt pocket, clearly visible through the thin white fabric. He had a lucky spot at the counter where he sat when he scratched off the numbers—at least he called it a lucky spot, though as far as I knew all Theo won were a few bucks every so often, money he used to increase his weekly investment in lottery tickets. Now, he stood at the window, his dark hair combed back, his eyes full of resignation, holding two of the diner's heavy menus, one cradled in each arm, like Moses holding the Ten Commandments.

Chelsea picked up her phone, and I slowly turned my back on Theo, in case he could read my lips and would figure out what I was up to. Are you on Fifty-fourth and Seventh? Chelsea asked, and when I said I was she said Good, now I'd like you to go to Fifty-sixth Street, between Broadway and Eighth. She gave me an exact address and told me to call her once I was standing in front of it. In ninety or so seconds I was standing in front of the address Chelsea had given me. It was an old commercial building, which, in my short time in the neighborhood, I had seen go from a shoe store, to a Broadway ticket broker, to its most recent incarnation as a doomed little enterprise called the Healthy Donut. Now the storefront window was covered by plywood, the door was chained and padlocked, and all the windows in the three upper stories were also covered in plywood, except for one on the very top floor. Was the building condemned, or had it simply changed hands and was awaiting renovation? Was Chelsea hunkered down behind that one extant window? I didn't see how I could venture into that building. A person would have to be half insane even to walk in there, let alone trudge up to the top floor and take off his clothes. *Just get out of here,* I said to myself. *Go home, behave, stop acting like this.* But all those hours wallowing on the Internet, all those pictures, descriptions, consumer reviews . . . They had taken me farther than I had realized. Which is to say that even though I was quite sure entering that building was a stupid, reckless thing to do, so much so that no one would have the slightest sympathy for me were I to be found dead on the fourth floor, I was still not able to abandon the idea of spending an hour with Chelsea. I had worked myself up into a state of desperate longing. I was not in my right mind. I was, in other words, exactly where she wanted me.

Doing as I had been told, I dialed her number. It rang several times, and when she answered it she said Call back in three minutes, without even asking who it was. I waited and looked up at the one glass window, trying to catch signs of life, but there were none. A cop drove by, slowly. He looked at me standing there, probably wondering what business I could have in front of an abandoned building. I dialed on my cell phone, in an attempt to look busy, and, having no one else to call, I dialed my home number and listened for any messages that had come in, though I hadn't been out of the apartment more than eight minutes. To my surprise, there were *two* messages. One was from Andrew Post, saying that an editor from *Gig*, a not-yet-published magazine for men, wanted to know if I was interested in doing a Major Piece about men and elective plastic surgery. That Andrew sounded so enthusiastic about this idea—an idea that struck me as ten years past its expiration date—was more proof of how desperate my situation was, if more proof were needed. And then the second call: Deirdre. Are you there, Avery? If you are, pick up, please. I don't know where Deirdre got the idea that I didn't answer the phone if I was home. Oh, all right, she said, with an audible sigh. I just wanted to let you know that I'm . . . Her voice trailed off. *You're what?* I wondered. *Sorry? Wishing we could put it all back together again?* I'm going to have to come over and get some of my summer clothes, it's getting so warm. I'll call again and find out a convenient time. She cleared her throat, and her voice brightened. She was relieved she was through with an uncomfortable call. All right, Ave, take care. Hope work's going well, and . . . well, see you. And then, before she pressed the off button on her phone, she turned to someone, probably Osip, and said Okay, let's go.

I was Osip, too, for now. I hurried to call Chelsea, not wanting to give Deirdre's last words a chance to work their way through me. Are you standing in front of the building now? she asked me. I'm right here, I said. What are you wearing? she wanted to know, and though none of it seemed right to me, I just went along with it—getting robbed

and beaten or even arrested seemed, for the moment, a better alternative than walking back to my apartment. I stepped back, looked up at
the building's uncovered window, thinking I could catch a glimpse of
her, or at least see something that would tell me in no uncertain terms
that it was time to flee, and I told her what I was wearing. A man in the
largest Yankees shirt I had ever seen, a morbidly obese guy in his forties,
with dark circles under his eyes, and mournful, downward sloping eyes,
stopped for breath right next to me, eclipsing me. I don't see you, Osip,
Chelsea said, and I said Just wait a second. Oh, okay, Osip, I see you,
she said. Now turn around—see that building right across the street,
between the deli and the parking garage? That's my building, and I'm
in apartment 402. Okay, I said, be right over. It was a homey little high-
rise, narrow, about fifteen stories high, porcelain-colored bricks, and a
jaunty little green awning over the front door, like a card dealer's visor.
The only discomforting note: standing in front was a guy in a leather
jacket, shaved head, a Roman nose, with a red-and-yellow scarf hung
loosely around his neck.

I crossed in the middle of the block, as we do in New York. I squeezed
between the rear bumper of a shiny white Jeep and the front bumper
of a beat-up Toyota with several parking tickets fluttering beneath its
windshield wiper. My heart was with the scofflaw, the perpetrator of the
victimless crime. Apartment 402, I reasoned, must be facing front. How
else could she have seen me?

A high percentage of people driving cars around New York City
drive professionally—cab and limousine drivers—or, in the case of
couriers and delivery people, as an integral part of their profession.
Compared with traffic in other cites, where custom and design allow
and even encourage the casual driver, the traffic in Midtown Manhattan
is largely made up of cars whose drivers know the streets very well and
know how to keep their wits about them, and who view stoplights and
double-parked trucks and unpredictable pedestrians as part of the
workplace, as a factory worker would see the furnaces, the lathes, the
eyes-in-back-of-his-head foreman.

Which is to say that what happened next was almost certainly my
fault. I darted out from between two parked cars and then found
myself directly in the path of a Lincoln Town Car. Judging from the

lichenlike rust on the chrome around the headlights, and the slightly off-the-grid quality of its midnight blue paint job, the car was about ten years old, probably picked up second- or third-hand by the driver, who had scraped together enough money to go into the livery business himself.

The misery was divided into three parts. First—and perhaps foremost—was the psychological, all the fearful images that flashed through my mind as I saw what was about to happen to me. I saw death, I saw paralysis, I saw myself lying in a pool of my own blood, I felt tires running over my torso, and all of it occurred in the space of a heart thump, one wretched squeeze. I was sick, frozen, deluged with fright. If fear were snow, it was as if a winter's worth of it had fallen in one second. And then my troubles really began. I stuck out my arm, my hand, Superman stopping a speeding car. I skidded backward as I pressed my palm against the Lincoln's sun-baked hood. Distantly, I heard my voice saying Whoa, whoa.

I experienced this first contact with the car as a surge of sudden heat, a wild leap of my internal temperature beginning with the heel of my hand. It's amazing how much you can see in less than a second. I saw the driver, a man in his forties, with rich brown skin, with blueblack hair wet-combed straight back, small, decisive eyes, abrupt brows, a broad flared nose. He wore a blazer, a white shirt, a red and yellow tie. A guide to the city streets was fixed to the top of the dashboard by a chain and a suction cup. A couple of dowdy old pigeons were hopping and shaking around a puddle on the side of the street, taking a sad afternoon bath. A skinny white girl was practically bent over while pulling a huge amplifier down the street on its unreliable wheels; she was following a tall black man in a black gaucho hat with a pink silk band, who took long magisterial strides, with his chin thrust forward, and who carried two guitars crossed over his chest. An elderly woman in a Chinese silk jacket was spitting something out into a wire trash basket.

The front bumper knocked into my shin. Any pain in my shin is electric, unbearable—feeling it makes it possible for me to imagine myself being mauled by a lion. Being hit in the shin—blamelessly, by the corner of a table; punitively, by my third father, Norman Blake, and his five iron—makes me frantic, as if I were being suffocated. I would rather be punched in the nose or kneed in the balls than have my shin hit with any force. The edge of the bumper sliced right through my Dockers, and the next thing I knew I was tipped up into the air, and falling forward, which was the setup for part three of my small catastrophe. I landed on the hood, slid along the hot metal sticky with sap and soot until the side of my head collided with the windshield, not with enough force to spiderweb the glass, nor even with enough force to render me unconscious—at least not for more than a moment or two—but with a dull cracking noise, a kind of muffled crunch. Like stepping on a glass wrapped in a towel. Beneath the heavy-hanging grayish sky, which sagged above me, come to think of it, like a chuppah.

4

THERE WAS an antiwar demonstration in Central Park, and a small contingent of protesters, frustrated by the orderliness of the march— why should the protests be so peaceful, while the war, anything but peaceful and orderly, went on and on?—stirred up some trouble around Columbus Circle. Nothing of any great impact, considering the stakes. Disrupting traffic, spray-painting NO BLOOD FOR OIL on the side of a building. But the police were having none of it—maybe they were as frustrated as this activist faction of young protesters over the essentially pro forma nature of the Central Park march, and they were looking for a chance to show their collective muscle, and their patriotic scorn for the antiwar kids. Several hundred officers, nightsticks drawn, surrounded the fifty or seventy-five protesters. All of them were arrested, most of them were roughed up, and quite a few of them were hurt badly enough to end up at the nearest hospital, which was Roosevelt.

They began arriving minutes after me, and though the hospital was not unlike a police station, the sudden influx of cracked skulls, broken hands, and missing teeth created enough chaos to make me suddenly a low priority. I sat alone on an examining table, dangling my feet, and making calls on my cell phone, ignoring the sign on the wall directing patients and visitors to keep their cell phones off. I called Deirdre, though I wasn't sure what I would say to her. I did think she ought to know that I had been hit by a car and that I was in the ER. However, she didn't answer my call, and the next thing I knew I was calling my mother, though I had no idea what a call to Costa Rica would run me. She, too, failed to answer, but this time I didn't just hang up. Hey, Mom, I said, not to worry but I wanted to tell you I got hit by a car this afternoon and now I'm sitting here in the hospital, waiting for someone to take a look at me. That's about it, except Deirdre and I broke up. Well, Deirdre broke up with me, and I was on my way to doing something a little stupid when I got hit, so maybe it's all for the best. Anyhow, it's not too bad, just a bump on the head. In fact, just forget I made this call. Sort of a mistake. Bye.

Shortly after, a doctor came into my little curtained cubicle, looked at me with palpable impatience, as if I were some crazy person who was constantly showing up in the emergency room and he had had enough of me. The bleeding on the side of my head had already stopped, and the doctor said stitches might be in order, but it was up to me. If it's up to me, then I'd rather not, I said. What was mostly bothering me was I couldn't really remember how I'd gotten here, but I didn't dare say that for fear of being further detained. He shrugged and said It's your call, but I have to tell you I think you're making a mistake. But he didn't really give me a chance to change my mind. He simply left, and I sat there for a few minutes, feeling a bit dizzy, with a kind of underwater fullness in my ears, and a little neck soreness, until I remembered that I was supposed to meet my uncle Ezra for drinks at the Oyster Bar, and I simply put my shoes back on, checked over my shirt, gazed at myself in the looking glass over my cubicle's little sink, was satisfied that I didn't look all that much worse for wear, and walked out of the emergency room, through the corridor and the waiting room, where some of the protesters were making calls to families, friends, and lawyers while they waited for medical attention. I walked out of the hospital, where, as luck would have it, an air-conditioned taxi was waiting.

I was going to see Uncle Ezra, which was also a lucky thing. Ezra had always cast a kind eye upon me. As my father's older brother, he may have carried some guilt over my father's suicide. Ezra was the type who liked to fix things for people, and he may have wondered if an emergency loan of a few thousand dollars might have saved Ted Kaplan's young life.

Ezra had gotten rich off buying insurance settlements from poor people at about forty cents on the dollar. If, for example, a poor woman had the wrong teeth yanked out by a hasty dentist and managed to win a settlement for, say, $50,000, that money in many cases would be paid out in installments, say, over the course of five years. The plaintiff, especially if she or he were poor, often could not wait for the entire payout. Enter Ezra, who would pay a lump sum $20,000 for the value of the suit. Instant, though diminished, gratification! The theory behind the business was Ezra could afford to ride out a five-year, or even ten-year, payout, collecting a drip here, a drab there, while a poor person generally needed a lump sum ASAP, the day before yesterday if possible, to make a car payment, get a beagle neutered, rent a motorized wheelchair. Ezra's clients were the people who could not wait, and even as he picked up the rights to their insurance settlements for a song, he imagined himself as a benefactor. When he was younger, he had enjoyed delivering the larger checks himself. His office displayed several color photographs of Ezra being embraced by grateful recipients of his largesse.

Ezra was an operator, and now, near sixty, he looked it, too. He was stout and sleek. On either side of his smooth polished skull, he had two well-tended swaths of hair, black as the fenders on an old Buick. He was a bit of a dandy, especially for a man who spent the best part of the day on the telephone. He wore jewelry, nail polish, and his clothes were all high quality, custom tailored, with notched collars, working buttons on the sleeves, and cut in a way that streamlined him. (When Ezra brought me to the Russian steam bath on East Tenth Street, I was surprised to discover that beneath all that cleverly cut cashmere Uncle Ezra had more or less gone to pot: his skin hung off of him like melted candle wax, and he was covered in brown spots.) Unless Ezra and his wife, Sheila, were on Long Island or otherwise traveling, or I was away on a writing assignment, Ezra and I met on the first Wednesday of every month, at the Oyster Bar, in Grand Central Station. American Transfer Rights was just a few steps away, on the tenth floor of a nearby office building—and what a dive that place was: nicotine-tinged air, dusty Venetian blinds, rows of metal file cabinets, and a staff of three stooped, clay-complexioned clerks Ezra seemed to have spirited from the nineteenth century.

Ezra's preferred spot at the Oyster Bar was at the counter—he thought it looked a bit fruity for two men to sit together at a table, with a flower in a vase between them. Side by side at the counter, like sitting at a bar, with plenty to look at. Ezra was usually fifteen minutes late, his way of letting me know he had many irons in the fire, and today was no exception. I took a seat at the counter and resolved not to tell Ezra that I had just sneaked out of the emergency room. He would have little patience for someone careless enough to walk in front of a car, and he would worry, too. All those years on the outskirts of the insurance game had filled his head with stories of unlikely disasters, and the delayed catastrophe was one of his specialties, people being in worse shape than they imagined: the food poisoning that hits twenty-four hours after the meal, the whiplash that appears a week after the fender-bender, the belated discovery of a surgical sponge lodged in your abdomen. If I told Ezra what had happened, he would more likely than not insist on taking me back to Roosevelt Hospital or, failing that, to his own personal physician.

Look at you, Ezra said, sliding onto the stool next to me, you not sleeping or something? You look like something the cat dragged in. And what's that on your head? Ezra reached for the little clot of blood above my ear, but stopped before touching it.

I just bumped my head, I said, smiling. I'm fine.

You bumped your head? Why would you bump your head?

Well, it's not as if I meant to. It's like you said. I'm not sleeping all that well. Ezra narrowed his eyes, pursed his lips. He was simply a man to whom you told things. You couldn't just say Hey, I'd rather not talk about it. So I said, Things are a little shaky, and he nodded sympathetically. It's a very competitive field you've chosen. I don't know how you stand it sometimes. I hated to tell Ezra about Deirdre's infidelity—Ezra barely knew Deirdre, referred to her mostly as Your young friend, treated the whole thing as a dalliance, a by-product of the footloose life. But I didn't want my uncle to think that I was suffering over career problems. Somehow, right now, that seemed the greater humiliation. It's not that, Uncle Ezra. It's Deirdre. She's been—I stopped myself, suddenly feeling choosy about what words to use. She's been somewhat less than loyal. Ezra's little round eyes opened to their fullest aperture. She's fucking around? She's doing that to you?

I made a helpless gesture. Handing over to Ezra the raw materials of Deirdre's behavior and letting him shape them according to his own understanding of the world was like asking a gangster to help you collect a debt—things were going to be a little rougher than you might prefer. I felt I must come to her defense. She feels as bad about this as I do, just about. Oh, I'm sure, I'm sure, Ezra said, his voice shimmering with contempt. I'm sure she's all racked up. A waiter was approaching to take our order, but Uncle Ezra waved him away. Then he laid his hand over mine. I'm sorry, Ave, I know it's rough. But I'll tell you what. You want to know what I think? To me, Ezra pointed to himself, Deirdre was a perfectly nice—Is, Uncle Ezra, not was; she's not dead. Ezra put up his hands in a pantomime of surrender. I never said I wanted her dead. It's just that the moment I met her, do you want to know what my first impression was? I thought this is a very nice girl, big, sexy, looks like a lot of fun, and certainly bright, with her history classes and all those family connections. He held up a finger, perhaps to say that was point number one, perhaps to keep my interruptions at bay. Too young for you? Sure, but what the hell? It's her choice, right? And let's face it, the girl's never too young for the guy, the guy's too old for the girl. Anyhow, it's not like she's in it for the money or the security. I winced, but it didn't seem as if Ezra were trying to insult me; he was just stating the case. There was no second finger, though the first one remained aloft, and then, as if keeling over from its own weight, it slowly began to point directly at me. Main problem? He went silent, and remained so until I gave him a so-say-it-already look. Sure you can take it? Ezra reached into the little bowl of oyster crackers, picked up a few, rubbed them between his well-manicured fingers, let them drop. She put me in mind of your mother. My mother? I exclaimed far too loudly. The walls of the place were black and white tiles like the inside of the subway and sound bounced around. I'm surprised you didn't see it, Ave, to me there was a lot of similarities. Similar bodies, that sort of sexy bottom-heavy situation. And they both are not set up to look after anyone but themselves: they're not caregivers, you know? Not the maternal type. Me? I like the maternal type. Which Sheila is, by the way, even though we were not blessed with children of our own. This Deirdre's shrewd, like your mother.

I shook my head, No, no, my mother's not shrewd. If anything she's a little spacey. Ezra winced as if tasting something sour. It's an act. I'm sorry, Ave, but that's how it is. When your father died it took two seconds for your mother to find someone else, and when that didn't work out . . . Well you know the story, it was your life. One man in, another one out, a revolving door, and meanwhile there you are, her one and only child, who she should have been putting first, there you are, the most confused kid on earth, not even allowed to keep your name, afraid of your own shadow, never knowing which way was up.

I was fine, I said, my life wasn't so bad. I tried to summon up the will to defend my mother from Uncle Ezra's attack, but, in fact, since Gene Jankowsky's death, and her move down to Costa Rica, I hardly ever saw her, and we spoke on the phone only occasionally, and those conversations were generally taken up with whatever had happened to her that particular day, matters mainly pertaining to the social life of the little tropical expatriate enclave where she lived, a Pacific coast town called Nosara where enterprising Costa Ricans lived with hundreds of tourists who had come to meditate, study yoga, and take digital photos of the howler monkeys.

Ezra was hungry and he called the waiter back over. No matter how many times we ate there, I could never really draw a distinction between the wide variety of oysters on the menu; as usual, Uncle Ezra ordered for me, and when the waiter slowly walked away Ezra took a handful of oyster crackers and put them into his mouth, as if to stop himself from speaking further. He chewed patiently, and, when the crackers had formed a kind of paste in his mouth, he took a drink of ice water to wash them down.

The waiter placed a bowl of crab bisque in front of both of us. Why thank you, thank you very much, Ezra said, as if the soup had come compliments of the house.

We ate our soup in silence for a minute or so, until, suddenly, Ezra put his spoon down, turned in his seat so he was directly facing me, his bright button eyes full of life and promise. I'm going to tell you something that I want to keep strictly between you and me.

This guy I know, off and on for many years. An old buddy named Lincoln Castle. Fifty years ago, he turned his father in to the FBI for being a commie spy. Or maybe not a spy, but a commie all the way. Again, that smile. Since getting his dental implants, Ezra showed his convincing teeth at every opportunity. But stories of betrayal did truly amuse him. Can you imagine? They wanted to put the father on trial, put him on the hot seat, but he sneaked out of the country. I think he actually went to Moscow. Anyhow, Linc's been into everything. He studied premed in college, where I met him, but he never got licensed, not that it stopped him from practicing, until it looked like he was going to get busted. Basically, at heart, he's a hustler. He's a whiz at coming up with ideas—he promoted a bunch of concerts for Ozzy Osbourne, he sold algae that's supposed to pep up your prostate—but there was always a problem. And I loaned him a few bucks along the way, figuring I'd never see the money again.

Then one day I get a postal money order—Linc's never had a checking account, he likes to minimize the paper trail—for something like twelve grand, with a little Post-it showing how he computed the interest. And also a business card. LINCOLN CASTLE, PRESIDENT, FLEMING TOURS. Written on the back, Call me, which I do, and that's where you come in, Avery. He tells me something, and as soon as I hear it, I think of you. And now that I hear you're single again . . .

That's nice of you, Uncle Ezra. But what made you think of me? I was distracted for a moment—a couple of waiters on the other side of the cavernous room were sharing a long, merry laugh. The sound of it somehow touched a reservoir of worry over Deirdre—where was she, and with whom? What a mistake, putting my ego in someone else's hands. Never again. Never.

Fleming runs sex tours. Ezra's voice was suddenly confidential. As he lowered his voice, he raised his eyebrows, pursed his lips, nodded, exactly as he had when I was young and he would cut me in on some insider information about the unseemly behavior of adults: bought judges, cops on the take, women who married for money.

Our waiter arrived with the oysters, set in a diorama of rock salt and lemon wedges.

I was quiet for a moment. You don't mean going around having sex with kids, do you? Ezra looked at his me as if the idea were preposterous. Of course not. Women, beautiful women. Grown-up women for grown-up men. I was aware of a certain quickening of my attentions. I felt so strange, hearing this. Like I was falling down the stairs, but painlessly. Or falling through the Internet, clicking away. So where do they go? I asked. Thailand? Ezra shook his head vehemently. No, no. That's old stuff. Too raunchy. Lincoln takes his tours to places like, I don't know, Scotland, Sweden, Liechtenstein for crying out loud, and he charges a hell of a price—a hundred and thirty-five thousand dollars. Everything first class, all inclusive. Totally. If you know what I mean. He explained it to me, broad strokes. He doesn't even hire the women directly. He has contacts all over the place—mostly women, by the way—and they're in charge of finding eight, ten, twelve, however many women, depending on how many subscribe for the trip, and what they seem to be looking for. There's a questionnaire, you're supposed to fill it out. Lincoln pays each of his contact people some huge wad of cash so they can hire really great-looking women, and what the contact people pay is up to them. They supposedly know what's what. Lincoln's not worried the contact people will cheap out on him because with the kind of clientele he deals with, believe me if there's anything wrong he's going to hear complaints, and if he hears complaints the contact people are out of a job. He gives them enough so the women make maybe four, five thousand dollars a night, with enough left over for the contact people to make a nice profit—that's his whole philosophy right there: everyone has a nice little payday.

You'd think men who have that kind of money could have all the sex they want, I said. Ezra gave me pat on the face, not particularly gentle. You think you're the unhappiest man in the world, Avery? Well, you're not. Do you have any idea how many men in this city alone are walking around in a state of lust-induced psychosis? And anyhow, if guys want to screw around a little—who are they going to do it with? Women who work for them? The nanny? Thank you very much for the sexual harassment suit. Their friends' wives? Ladies in the neighborhood? What a shortcut to disaster. It's not so easy. People are isolated. Did you hear that thing on the news? Very few people even go on picnics anymore.

But come on, Ezra, aren't there plenty of hookers right here in the USA? Sure, there are, Ezra said, but have you ever been with one? I'd come close, but, technically speaking, I hadn't, and I told him so. You want to know why you haven't? Because you are not insane. Ezra slurped an oyster out of its shell; the sound was like two pieces of Velcro separating. Don't get me wrong, America has some great hookers, but mostly no. Mostly, even the pretty ones are drug addicted, diseased, all kinds of underworld connections. It's dangerous business. Ezra tapped his finger on the side of his head. I wondered if it was a symbolic tap on *my* head; I wondered if he was somehow perfectly aware of what I'd been up to this afternoon.

So here's Lincoln's concept, Ezra said. He figures why not go some-place beautiful, somewhere safe, a lovely little destination where no one knows you, and you just have your fun, get the hell out, and no one's the wiser. Everyone's prescreened for health, police record, cleanliness, education, so the women Linc gets are fantastic.

The women better be fantastic, I said, for that kind of money. Christ! A hundred and thirty-five thousand? Ezra smiled. That's all-inclusive, he said. Private jet, hotels. How about meals? Meals? What the hell's wrong with you, Avery? I'm talking about jetting to Europe and making love with women you'd be lucky to even *dream* about, and you're won-dering if meals are included?

I felt like a child. Of course the world was made by—and for!—men who took what they wanted. If they could loot pension funds and pol-lute rivers, what was a little commercial nooky compared to that? They blasted holes in the earth and sent lesser men down and down and down and down, risking their lives to bring out the diamonds and the gold. They herded thousands of animals through stockyards, stunned them, killed them, chopped them up into little pieces, and if a few of the animals were diseased they sold them anyhow. They smuggled, they slashed and burned, they tossed their enemies into the river, they deep-sixed reports that might reflect unfavorably on their product, they burned down businesses that failed to show a profit, they celebrated their daring and their bounty, while men like me walked around knock-kneed going tsk-tsk, that's not very nice.

Do you think you'd like to go on a trip like that? Me? I asked. If I had a hundred thirty-five thousand dollars, I'd spend it on an apartment and get out of that place on Fifty-fourth Street before I hang myself. Forget the cost, think of it without the cost. Do you think you could enjoy something like that? I shrugged. I'm not sure. Wouldn't I basically be paying women to have sex with me?

All right, Ezra said, suddenly at the end of his patience. I think you need to give a little thought about what it means to be a man. To be a man you have to understand the importance of having something that not everybody else has; you have to have a leg up. You understand? You can't be a drop of water going over a waterfall. You can't be the same as everyone else because no one else is playing the game like that, and if you're the only one being like everyone else, that means you're not really with everyone else, you're all alone, and not all alone on top, either; it just makes you into a sucker. You've got to have a rock in your hand. You just can't walk around empty-handed like a little shmucky boy who's going skip to my lou with daddy on one side and mommy on the other. You've got to be carrying a rock, or a gun, by which I mean money. I don't need to tell you, Avery. You're a bright young man. You know the things money can buy: shelter, food, safety, respect, and you may as well include the most beautiful women in the world.

Well, money is one of the main things I don't have, I said. Let me put it like this, Uncle Ezra said. It's yours, if you want it. Lincoln comped me for the next trip, for favors granted. He comped you for a hundred-thirty-five-thousand-dollar trip? Yes, he did, very generously. Welcome to the world of men. There's probably another fifty thousand in extras, I said. Ezra shook his head, No extras. They even supply a car and driver to take you to the airport.

I picked up an oyster, felt its rough shell, looked at its slippery shiny grayness, then let it fall back into the mound of rock salt. It's so embarrassing to be cheated on, I said.

Forget embarrassment. And forget cheating, forget the word even. It doesn't have any meaning because everyone does it, and if everyone's doing it it's not cheating, it's just how things are. You think Aunt Sheila cheats on you? I asked. But Uncle Ezra paid the question no mind. What you need to do right now is forget all that hand-wringing bullshit, he said. This is life! Life is like a wind: it keeps coming, carrying things inside it, you breathe it in, you can't control it, no one can. So? Are you interested? Lincoln's holding a spot open for me, but I have to let him know.

Today?

What you don't know today, you won't know tomorrow. What are you? Thirty-seven? In twenty-three years you'll be sixty, and let me tell you something about sixty. It's not great. And I'll tell you something else—those twenty-three years? They go like this. To demonstrate, he slurped an oyster out of its shell.

I need to move, I said, quietly. I need a place to live.

You're still living with her?

I nodded. The thing is. I'm not really used to wanting something, aching for it. But now . . . that's all I do. I want to get out of that terrible place on Fifty-fourth Street. I'd do it, I'd go on your friend's trip, if I could write about it, Uncle Ezra. I can't do it just to do it. But to write about? That could be something. I could make some money. Would your friend object to that?

Ezra tossed the oyster shell onto the mound of rock salt and smiled. As far as Lincoln and the Fleming Tours people are concerned, you're my nephew, your life is in the shitter, and I'm giving it to you as a little pick-me-up. That's your story, and like all good stories it's more than half true. But, sure, you could write about it. It's what I figured. He flicked the end of my nose. From someone else it would be a contemptuous gesture. I'm way ahead of you, kiddo, he said. But you got to step on it. They leave the day after tomorrow.

5

I WENT STRAIGHT TO WORK, or what passes for work in my profession. That is to say, I telephoned my agent. I was never sure Andrew Post would take my call. I was not a valuable client; I had never earned more than $25,000 in a year, netting his agency $3,750 at the high-water mark. But the assistant didn't treat me as if I were worthless; she put me right through and I told Andrew about the sex tour idea. Post was in his seventies. There was something deeply embarrassing to be talking to him about going from country to country having commercial sex, though I did suspect that, in his prime, he had had sexual adventures the number, intensity, and theatricality of which I could scarcely imagine. Nevertheless, I found myself emphasizing the tour's deluxe trappings, the high price of the ticket, the promise of posh hotels, the private jet. Mention of the jet launched Post into a rambling story about a trip he and his recently deceased partner had taken a year ago to Los Angeles for the Oscars on a plane chartered by another venerable old agent who didn't forget his friends. Remembering your friends, it's a noble thing, don't you agree? Post said, but I had to jump in. I think I've got something worth something here, Andy. I hated to interrupt, but right now time was of the essence—maybe it always had been, and always would be, and I was just learning that crucial fact. I wanted some sort of publishing deal in place before I got on that plane. Do you think you could sell something like this fairly quickly. Oh, I don't know, Avery. All the publishers are running scared. I've never seen anything like it. Why not put something in writing, just to give the flavor? Post's voice was frail, wavering; I wondered if he had much hope for the whole thing. All right, I said, I can do that; I can do it right away. I can have it on your desk tomorrow morning. Well, he said, you don't want to rush it. These things take time. And I won't be in tomorrow morning. Then I'll be there in the afternoon, I said. My, you're really charged up! Well, okay then, tomorrow afternoon. But remember, Avery, less is more, so keep it short. Everyone's so terribly busy these days. Let's make it easy on them.

I wasn't vain about my writing. To the people in charge of assignments, what I mainly had going for me was a reputation for *never* being late with my copy, and *always* remaining good-natured about being edited, no matter how severely. Even when radically altered pieces ran without the editor showing me the courtesy of checking the changed copy beforehand, I maintained an affable, professional air. The idea had always been: We're all professionals, let's get the job done and what's the use of pretending we're talking about high art here. I was perfectly aware that I was not writing *The Odyssey* or the Bill of Rights, and, above all, I did not forget that everything you write for a newspaper or a magazine ends up at the bottom of some poor canary's cage. I knew where the caged bird craps.

Nevertheless, composing the pitch for the sex tour book was slow going. I set up shop in a nearby Starbucks and went over and over the page and a half from five in the afternoon to midnight, and then I crept back into my apartment and continued work until nearly three in the morning. I didn't feel the slightest fatigue. Fantasies of riches coursed through me like waste water from a methamphetamine lab. When the time I had allotted myself to put something on paper was at its end, this is what I'd come up with.

THE SEX TOUR

OR

IF THIS IS TUESDAY, YOU MUST BE BELGIAN

Many people, upon first hearing the words *organized sex tours*, ask the following question: Do such things really exist? The answer, of course, is Yes. To many men, having access to beautiful, glamorous, desirable women—women at whom, under normal circumstances, they could only gaze with mute longing—would be the realization of their most fundamental fantasies. And so it is no wonder that while our government, along with many other governments and the United Nations, has curtailed the activities of sex tour agencies that promote child prostitution as well as trafficking, the sex tour industry as a whole is thriving, and it is today a large part of the multibillion-dollar-a-year sex industry.

For years, the most popular destination for sex tourists has been the Far East, most commonly Thailand. But as sex tourism has become more commonplace in Thailand, it has inevitably lost whatever cachet it once had, and, in the past few years, the preferred destination for the tens of thousands of men (and, in fact, sometimes women) who form this growing subculture has been the Dominican Republic, Cuba, Brazil, Russia, or Czechoslovakia. As with most commodities, there is a low end and a high end to sex tourism, and I have access to the highest end of the phenomenon—perhaps the most expensive and exclusive of all the sex tours. This is not the Cadillac of sex tours, it is not even the Mercedes-Benz—this is the Lamborghini of sex tours, where, for the clients, money is no object and no creature comforts are spared. The jet is private, the accommodations . . .

I MIGHT have been able to compose my pitch more efficiently had I not had visions of apartments dancing in my head. It seemed to me that people with their own address, their own closet in which to hang their shirts and sweaters, their own doors to lock were the luckiest people in the world. I viewed the lighted windows of the thousands of apartments I passed the way a brokenhearted lover views people walking through the park hand in hand.

After delivering my two-page pitch to Andrew Post, I went downtown to Perry Street to meet a real estate agent named Isabelle Rosenberg. Isabelle was Colombian and Israeli, with mink eyebrows, shiny shoulder-length hair, smartly dressed in a dark blue suit, like a senator.

It was drizzling by the time I reached Perry Street, but Isabelle was waiting outside the apartment house—a redbrick building, seven stories high, with new windows that reflected the street's flowering dogwoods. She carried a black leather purse, the size of a mail carrier's pouch.

I have always found it difficult to know how to act around someone who is trying to sell me something. In the end, the seller is always pushing to get a dollar more, and the buyer is, of course, hoping to pay a dollar less. All the smiles and the laughter, all the sentences that begin I'm only telling you this because, or To tell you the truth, all come down to the final dollar. I long ago conceded I would rarely if ever come out on top in any business deal—from buying a scarf off a street vendor, to getting a New York apartment—and since I was always having to defend myself against having salespeople take excessive advantage of me, I was generally a rather taciturn customer, brightening only at the very end, when nothing more could be extracted from me.

However, I did like Isabelle straightaway. Her eyes suggested a tragic sense of life, but she walked up the stairs to the apartment on the third floor with a kind of buoyancy, as if she was happiest when her body was in motion. She had an olive complexion, a wide romantic mouth. Twice, Isabelle touched my wrist, and, overall, she seemed friendly beyond the usual subterfuges of saleswomanship. What a special cozy place this is, she said, as if we were looking for a home for the two of us. Then she arched her luxuriant brows and asked Will you be living here alone?—to which I said Oh God, yes, letting her know my previous life was in shambles—to which she responded by walking quickly to the window and beckoning me to her side, so I could see the view of the street, with its dark dripping trees and somberly painted Federal houses, with their red wooden doors, all of it so melancholy, dignified, stable, and lush in the rain.

After she showed me the apartment, Isabelle suggested we have a coffee at a nearby café. She said I find the things you want to ask about a place always come to mind after you walk out, so this way I'll be right here to answer your questions and we can scoot back over if we need to. I'm not much for scooting these days, I said, going back to that idea of myself as a wounded man, which for some reason I thought she might find appealing, but then, from the look of her, I realized she thought I was turning the coffee idea down so I quickly added I could really use a cup of coffee. Isabelle put two sugars and a lot of milk in hers. She stirred it with the spoon in the cup's dead center and moved it in circles with great care, making sure there were no potentially nerve-racking clinks of metal against ceramic. Everything she did was modest, melancholy, and warm. I could feel my brain coming back to life, as I searched for clues to her character, as well as any indication of what she might be feeling toward me.

THE NEXT DAY, Andrew Post called and said he had so far gotten one call from a publisher. The initial offer was $375,000. I thanked Andrew, quickly hung up, and stood in front of the windows looking out onto Seventh Avenue and pumped my fists in the air and shouted. Then, that phase of my joy disappeared in a heartbeat and I burst into tears. I was simply overwhelmed by my good fortune. The sort of thing that had always happened to somebody else was now happening to me.

As I wept for joy, misfortune and confusion struck in the form of Deirdre walking in. Seeing me dissolved into tears, she quite naturally assumed I was grieving. She was wheeling in an empty suitcase, which she intended to fill up with her summer clothes, and she stood there for a moment, with her hand on the long handle, and our eyes met. Mine were no doubt small and scarlet, while hers were wide with apprehension. She said my name and moved slowly in my direction, pushing her valise in front of her like a vacuum cleaner. I put up my hand, which I had meant to signify that I was all right, despite appearances, but Deirdre thought I was asking her to leave me alone, and she said my name again, soothingly and imploringly, practically insisting that I accept the solace she was prepared to offer.

I see you've come to get more of your stuff. She shrugged, as if to leave open the possibility of somehow denying it. May I assume you are living with your Russian friend? She shook her head No, not trusting her voice to communicate the obvious lie. I dried my eyes with the heels of my hands, and heaved a deep, steadying sigh. It was starting to dawn on me that the chance to tell Deirdre I was about to strike it rich might be every bit as satisfying as the major score itself. Well, help yourself. I'm still sleeping on the sofa bed, so the old bedroom might be a bit musty, but you'll find everything as you left it, I trust. And then, with a desiccated little laugh, I added If trust has any meaning. I sounded arch to myself, a little nutty, but I couldn't help it. To adopt the persona of a British stage actor, some sadly wronged fellow in a quilted jacket, whose heart has been broken by someone not really worthy of him, was a comfort, for some reason. It just wasn't a moment I wanted to be exactly and unanimously myself. There were things going on in this room I didn't even want my self to know about. If you'd like, I'll give you a hand organizing your gear, I went on. After all, I do appreciate your taking the initiative and giving me a little time to sort things out. Are you all right? she asked. I'm fine. And you'll be glad to know that it looks like I'll be getting my own place to live. I'm buying an apartment. Deirdre nodded. I had expected her to say something like You are? and to be filled with amazement that I could manage such an amazing fiscal feat. But, of course, in Deirdre's world down payments were no more fantastic than subscriptions to *Vanity Fair*.

I think I'll buy this place down on Perry Street, I said. Deirdre nodded, looked sad. I love it down there, she said. Yes, I said. It's all very nice. So when? Deirdre asked. When does all this happen? Her eyes were slowly reddening. The wings of her nose were trembling, and it took some effort for her not to turn away. I couldn't have been more surprised if she had pulled a gun on me. I thought you'd be relieved. It means the apartment's all yours. Why would I be relieved? She was suddenly angry. Her voice, usually a serene alto, rose in volume and pitch. Did you ever stop to think why any of this was happening? Jesus Christ, Avery, do you think this is what I want?

Deirdre's flare-up had a strangely tranquilizing effect on me. Maybe not at this very moment, I said. But, yes, I do, I think this is what you wanted. Why else would you sleep with that idiot? It was a mistake! She almost screamed it, which only made me more composed. Really? Then why did you tell me about it? Jesus Christ, Avery, I told you about it because I'm an honest person and I didn't want there to be any lies between us. You can't use that against—she stopped suddenly, looked at me with a mixture of concern and dismay. Why are you smiling? Am I smiling? I asked. I'm sorry. You have every right to be annoyed. After all, what right do I have to smile? I leaned forward, cupped my chin in my hand. It's just that I notice you're saying *Jesus Christ* a lot, and you never did before, so I'm guessing that comes from Osip. Am I right? Is he one of those Russian true believers, with his little painted eggs and his corduroy jacket stinking of incense?

Deirdre looked crestfallen. Her broad shoulders heaved upward and then slumped down; she let out a little gasp and shook her head. What is wrong with you, Avery? You're making way too much of the whole thing. Don't say that, don't fuck somebody and then tell me I'm making too much of it. You don't get to set the parameters of my reaction. Okay? You broke my heart.

I admit I made a mistake, she said. I've already admitted it, and I'm admitting it again. If you must know . . . She stopped, walked around her suitcase, and sat across from me at the table, with its litter of newspapers yet to be taken out of their blue plastic pouches, toast plates, coffee cups, and various scraps of paper upon which I did fantasy sums, calculating how much I might receive for my book, and how much it would buy me, and how long it might last. Avery, she said. Deirdre, I answered. Listen to me, Avery, okay? He's a Russian. I never would have slept with him otherwise. Think of it like this: if I were your friend, a man, and I told you that, you'd understand. You'd say, that's a little weird, but I do understand. I was so curious, all the years studying Russia, and I had never really known a Russian. It really will never happen again. How do I know that? I said. What if you meet some other type of man you haven't had intimate knowledge of? What if you meet a Tibetan or some great Patagonian guy? But it's my *major*, she said, her voice rising plaintively, as if I were unreasonably withholding my compassion.

I'm going to pretend you didn't say that, I said. I only slept with him once, she said. Really? I said. You mean once today? She shook her head. Well, that's just a total lie, I said. Have you forgotten that I read your diary? As soon as I said that, I wondered if I had fallen into a cleverly laid trap. Had Deirdre just tricked me into reminding myself that I wasn't operating on a higher moral plane than she was? No, I haven't forgotten. But if you had read it more carefully you would have realized that we'd only been together once. I did read it carefully, Deirdre. I read it very, very carefully. And you slept with him many times, in many ways . . . I don't want to go into it; I can't even think about it. And, anyhow, it doesn't matter how many times. Nabokov said One is the only real number; all the rest are variations. Na-bow-kuff, she said, correcting my pronunciation. And then she lurched forward, grabbing her forehead and massaging it.

You always kept me at arm's length, she said, very softly. I loved you, I truly loved you. I loved your face, the sound of your voice. I loved how you never gave up on your dreams, no matter what. (I could have done without that, the portrait of me as the dogged little dreamer, the plucky little guy who no matter how many times he gets smacked down always dusts himself off and gets up again.) You never intended for things to work out between us, she said. She was composed again, confident in her despair. Just the way you always talk about our age difference.

How old is Osip? I asked. She waved away the importance of the question but could not help herself—a part of her would always be the chubby third grader with her hand up in the air because she knows the answer. Twenty-five. And it's not a long *O*, by the way, it's an *Ahh* sound. And I don't care how old people are, she said, with a little pause between each word. That's your thing.

The phone rang, and I stopped myself from answering it. After the third ring the answering machine picked up. Deirdre and I were quiet and attentive for this minor technological event. As I had anticipated, it was my agent. Post here, call soon, he said, and hung up.

Then a voice came out of my laptop's little speakers, announcing that I had just received an e-mail. I glanced at the bottom of my screen and saw it was from Andrew Post, and while it would have been rude to answer the phone, taking a look at the e-mail—I knew it must be urgent if he called and e-mailed within the same minute—seemed harmless. I clicked it open.

Avery, we're at four hundred but it's from _____ and it's pre-emptive. We have one hour to respond or he takes it off the table. Please advise.
Andrew

What's wrong? Deirdre said, with that slight hopefulness you can feel when someone with whom you are in conflict receives bad news, perhaps creating a little space into which you can insert yourself and offer comfort. Oh, nothing, I said, cat-and-mousing with the situation for a moment. Just a business thing. She nodded, either too disciplined to inquire further, or actually not that interested. I had to come out with it. It's why it looks like I can buy an apartment, I said. I came up with an idea, and my agent is selling it right now, as we speak. You know, Avery, just because something is in a journal doesn't mean it's necessarily true. Did you ever stop to think I was writing those things because I suspected you might be invading my privacy and I wanted to teach you a lesson? No, I never thought of that, mainly because it's not true. But guess what? This book that my agent is selling? My Piedmont chimed in again, announcing another e-mail. The electronic voice was strangely friendly, composed but enthusiastic, a noncompetitive male who wants the best for you, amiable but a little remote, like a neighbor's dog. I glanced down at the lower-right-hand corner of my screen. A little flag came up telling me that Post had sent another e-mail. I didn't dare open it—I was still digesting the last heaping portion of good news.

Yeah? Deirdre said. What about it?

It's about an around-the-world sex tour, which I am going on. I leave tomorrow, as a matter of fact.

Deirdre was silent, unblinking, I wasn't sure if she was even breathing. It was as if she were on the screen of a computer that had frozen. I waited. I wasn't at all sure what her reaction would be to my news. In the moments she spent just looking at me, I succumbed to the temptation to see what Post's last e-mail said and I clicked it open. My mind was going too quickly to tolerate any time without something new going into it, and if Deirdre was going to be quiet then I needed to hear from Andrew.

So?
A.

That wasn't very informative.

I feel like I've just been kicked in the stomach, Deirdre said. It seemed as if her natural pigmentation had drained from her face, her throat, her arms, and gathered into her hands, which were suddenly bright red. Why do you hate me, Avery?

I don't hate you. I said it with a sense not only of deep conviction but of discovery, as if I had just at that very moment come upon a map to my truest feelings. I loved being with you, I said, quavering. From the moment we met. There was nothing about it I didn't enjoy. Enjoy! Deirdre said, as if I couldn't have chosen a less substantial word. A paper cut of a word. Not only enjoy, I said. I loved watching movies with you, walking around, I loved going to bed with you. If you thought there was something wrong, something missing, then why didn't you say anything about it? I did! she cried. In a million different ways. I'm sorry, then, it didn't get through. I thought everything was okay.

When you told me you were with someone else—I'm not *with* him. I put up my hands, asking her to spare me the fine print. When you told me, I realized what a total fool I'd been. You could stay out late, you were here, you were there, I never asked a question. You think I didn't worry? You think I didn't picture it? But I never opened my mouth, out of respect, not once. Well, maybe you should have. Maybe I would have felt you cared. Please don't say that, I advised. That's just going to piss me off. You slept with someone else; I didn't. Everything I wanted sexually was right here. I pointed at her—perhaps a little too vigorously, because she backed away, as if I were going to poke her in the chest. And you want to know something else? I said. I had no idea what I was going to say. It was just happening, on its own. Do you want to know what it's been like, night after night and day after day, knowing you're with your new friend? I've gone through the hamper so I can smell your clothes, just for the intimacy of it. I've been scouring the porn shops, looking for pictures of women who look like you. Deirdre made a face, as if she'd just bitten down on something spoiled. Don't look at me like that, I said. I already feel grotesque.

You were so wonderful to me in the beginning, she said. Always glad to see me and interested in me. Then it started getting the way you said it would, the way you said it was with the other women. I was thinking that maybe our beginner's luck was over. She said this softly, almost interrogatively, as if she barely meant it, or was waiting for me to refute it with passionate force. But all that followed was a long, sad silence, until Deirdre asked Are there really women in porno mags who look like me? Not really, I said. You look more . . . comfortable. You mean fat? No, comfortable. Bourgeois. The women in the magazines are sort of tough. I just look for redheads.

And have you really been going through my laundry? I nodded Yes. Jesus Christ, Avery, is that supposed to be flattering? You're sniffing my private clothes? I'm not going to feel bad about that, I said. I like the smell of them. It pleases me. What you like, she said, are very specific parts of me, but not the whole thing. Isn't that the definition of pornography? I don't know about that, I said. But I could feel I was on shaky ground. And this round-the-world trip? Is that true, too? I don't need to be questioned, Deirdre. You don't exactly have the moral high ground here. I'd been so eager to tell her about what was in store for me a few moments ago, but now, with the stage completely set, I found myself hesitant. I didn't want to hurt her, nor did I want her to feel well rid of me. Is it true? Are you really going on one of those sex tours? What do you know about sex tours? I said. Everyone knows about them, she said. What are you going to do, go to Thailand and rape children? What is wrong with you, Avery? This isn't like you.

No Thailand, I said. No children. No rape. It's all very sedate and grown-up. All very first class. Private jet and all. We go to Nordic countries, for the most part. You know, the master race.

If this is supposed to make me jealous, it really doesn't. To me it's just sad. And kind of sketchy, too, morally speaking. Paying women to have sex with you? To which I said Thousands and thousands of dollars. I don't care if it's millions, Avery, it's still—she didn't finish the sentence, leaving it to me to fill in the blank. Well, if you must know, I'm going on the tour to write about it, not to have sex. I'm not going to have sex with any of them. I've never had sex under those circumstances, and I intend to keep my record unblemished.

There was no compelling reason to mention Chelsea or that my record owed its continued existence to a Town Car that happened to upend me on Fifty-sixth Street.

Just think of all the women you can tell your four fathers story to. That's not fair, Deirdre, and it's not very nice. Nice? Is nice a part of this? Is it nice to give some poor woman money so you can abuse her? What are you smiling about now? You look indecently happy. I'm sorry, I said, but more than one publisher wants to hear about the sex tour.

We're closing in on half a million dollars. Even saying this raced my heart; my blood zizzed through me like carbonated water.

I don't get it, Avery. You read my diary; you're messing with my dirty clothes; you're looking for women who resemble me in porn magazines. I can only imagine what these women are doing. And now this? Just fucking for fucking? With no feeling, no conscience?

I'm sure there will be feelings.

Not real feelings.

All feelings are real.

She shook her head, reached out for me, took my hand. You're a great guy, Avery. Thank you, I said. I just can't see you on this kind of trip, doing those things. With all those gross guys—did you ever think of that? Who you'll be with? Grist for the mill, I said. Avery. Really. Why are you doing this?

Because I can, I said. I was going to elaborate, maybe tell her about Uncle Ezra, his friendship with the guy who ran Fleming Tours; I was going to say there was something about having the power to do something that inevitably led to your actually doing it, like having a weapon, a bomb, you just can't keep it under lock and key forever; I was going to say there was a ratty little part of every man's brain that twitched and grinned at the thought of women easily available to him; I was going to say it was a rare man indeed who maintained his virtue if lack of virtue was easily accessible—but I left it at *Because I can.* There was something about it, a kind of no-frills truthfulness that made me leave it at that. As is.

Deirdre stood up and wheeled her suitcase into the bedroom and closed the door. I imagined what it would be like to go in after her, fall to my knees, and beg her to take me back. Or to let me take her back. Or to join me in pretending that none of the terrible things that had happened had ever occurred. But instead I picked up the phone and instructed Post, Take the four hundred thousand dollars. It's plenty.

6

THE NEXT AFTERNOON, I was picked up at my apartment by a Town Car and driven out to a small airport in Westchester. The air-conditioning made the air inside the car feel like the cold satin lining of a coffin. The driver took a route made up almost entirely of side streets. He zigzagged through the Bronx, and in Yonkers he took little residential streets, past culs-de-sac where beige brick bungalows stood shoulder to shoulder. There was a clicking sound coming from somewhere in the car. My second father used to talk about cars blowing a rod; I never quite understood what that meant, but I wondered if that's what was about to happen. I imagined it, the rod, shooting out into the cabin like a harpoon.

In the fading light, I opened my briefcase to make sure I had packed my notebooks, a box of pens, my micro tape recorder. All was in order. I had the pen-and-ink drawing of what I now thought of as my new apartment, which Isabelle had given me. I also had a sheet of her firm's stationery, upon which she had stapled the business cards from an interior decorator, a painter, and a carpenter. *Throw these away if you want to, but I couldn't help coming up with some ideas about your new place!* She signed off with her initials, which she had given an artistic flair, linking the *I* and the *R.*

I looked out of the side window at an elderly man with a watermelon-sized gut cradled in the mesh of his white, sleeveless T-shirt. The man stood on his little patch of lawn, his little share of the universe, frowning at the arc of water spewing from his salmon-colored hose. He sensed my attentions and looked up; the sinking sun detonated his wire-rimmed eyeglasses.

In the backseat of the hired car, I consulted the printed directions. Excuse me, but have you ever driven to this terminal?

This place? Sure. The driver had light brown hair, a meaty neck, an affable voice; he could easily have been one of a dozen guys with whom I had gone to high school on the North Side of Chicago—solid, realistic guys, somehow secure in their place in the pecking order, guys who knew they'd be taking orders from someone their whole life, but who also had the confidence that with hard work, and decent luck, they'd be able to push a few people around as well. Do you think you could turn the AC down a bit? But either he didn't hear me, or he wasn't interested in acceding to my request.

The cell phone rang in my pocket. Deirdre, once a great kidder, had months ago programmed the ring to play the first four notes of the Wedding March. She had always been deft with technology; it was all second nature to her. I looked at the caller-ID screen on my phone, which Deirdre had programmed so that her name appeared surrounded by throbbing hearts.

What's up? I struck the right casual, slightly distant note, and it felt good, the sweet spot of it. Have you left yet? Deirdre's voice sounded blurry. At first I thought it was just a bad connection, but then it seemed as if something else was wrong. Are you okay? I'm a little drunk, she said. You are? Aren't you at school? I am, but today was sad. Jeremy Fraser, my Soviet literature professor, announced he has lung cancer. Today was his last class—everyone went out afterward. It was so fucking sad.

I was seized by a desire to comfort her. What in the world was I doing? I should tell the driver to turn around and take me back home. Home! That gloomy nine-hundred-square-foot apartment on Fifty-fourth Street was where I belonged after all. It occurred to me that Deirdre had slept with Osip because what was best in her had been undermined by our relationship's corrosively casual nature. It was my own sorry fault, and somehow sharing the blame made it more tolerable; it gave me a place to stand, something to do; it was not exile, it was not being ridiculed, or passed over; it was a challenge to be a better man.

Avery? Why did you look at my journal? Why would you do a thing like that?

I don't know. I told you I was sorry. It was just jealousy, curiosity, masochism.

Try bad character.

Okay, bad character. There's nothing I can say. I just don't think you're in a position to start demanding apologies.

The driver's ears pinked. By now, we were in Westchester, driving past newly minted mansions. There seemed an inexhaustible supply of them, one after the other, and where there weren't huge houses there were earth-moving machines, there to bulldoze trees, level the terrain, and make room for more construction. *How can there be so many rich people?*

I'm not demanding an apology. There was a sudden instability in Deirdre's voice. It's just all so terrible, Avery. We've both behaved badly. And now you're going on a fucking sex tour? How is that supposed to make me feel? I cleared my throat. I didn't like hearing other people say what I was engaged in. I was taking a tour that dared not speak its own name. It's not supposed to make you feel anything, I said. It's not about you. And then, before she could jump back in, I said, I am painfully aware of my shortcomings, but let's face it, Deirdre, you're the one who started sleeping around. Sleeping around? How can you say that? I wasn't sleeping around. I made a mistake. A mistake, Avery, a mistake. Haven't you ever made a mistake? Yes, of course I have. According to you, I'm making one right now. I could see the driver's eyes in the rearview mirror. He was unabashedly looking back at me. Oh, baby, Deirdre was saying, are you sure this is what you want?

Why are you doing this now, Deirdre? Are you just trying to drive me crazy? Okay, sorry, sorry. She took a deep steadying breath. She was going to be good about this after all. Have a great trip, Ave. I'm going to miss you. And I'm so sorry, Avery, really I am. I never wanted things to go bad for us. Please don't blame yourself. I don't. A moment's silence. Well good, she said. You shouldn't. I fucked up. Big time.

Why are you saying this now, Deirdre? Because I'm actually going through with it? My hand began to tremble.

I cared about you a hell of a lot more than you cared about me, she said. You never said you loved me. Oh please, I said, what a load of steaming horseshit. Don't you fucking dare make this about something I did. But it was, Avery, it was. She was crying now. It was about what you did and what you didn't do. I never felt as if I were your destination; I was just a stop along the way. I seized on the cliché. A stop along the way? Where'd you get that one, Deirdre? Well, wasn't I? You said so yourself. I did? When did I ever say that? You . . . you . . . you said that it could never really work out for us because of the age difference. I didn't make the age difference between us, Deirdre. Am I supposed to take the blame for that? And here she was practically sobbing. I never cared about that, Avery. I cared about *you.* She was trying to appeal to my kinder nature, but it was as if I couldn't understand her language. You know what the biggest mistake I made was? That time in the store when you were so kind as to share your little secret with me? I should have fucking cracked your skull open.

For a moment it looked as if the driver was going to turn around in his seat and stare directly at me. The car went through an underpass, and a moment after that we were driving parallel to a ten-foot-high metal fence, behind which was a landing strip. My legs ached; my rage had carried within it a rancid residue and it had poisoned my muscle tissue. The runway was dark except for the cobalt blue lights and the occasional sweep of a searchlight. There were propeller planes and small jets parked here and there, in strikingly haphazard fashion—I would have guessed that such expensive equipment would be meticulously stowed, but each plane looked as if it had been hurriedly abandoned. Adding to the sense of dereliction and chaos, several planes were in various stages of repair, or perhaps decomposition—planes with their wings off, or missing propellers, or in the process of being repainted.

You want to know something about me, Avery? Something I never told you? *Not really,* I thought to myself, but I was good enough not to say it. We always talked about your four fathers, but I've got this family thing, too. She cleared her throat. Both my parents are really big. Big? I asked. Big how? Overweight, Deirdre said. Fat. Both of them. And

Adam is, too. And me, too, when I was young. And one day I'm going to be fat; I can feel it. It's what my body wants. My ass wants to be big, my belly, everything. Stop it, Deirdre, You're svelte, and you're always going to be beautiful. No matter what. But I would cut down on the desserts, if I were you. She laughed. Oh, Avery, she said, all I want now is for you to be safe, baby. To hear the old warmth and intimacy in her voice was completely unnerving; it was like having a loved one return from the grave.

A small blue and yellow sign reading FLEMING TOURS pointed toward a narrow, winding road that in a few moments led to a cyclone fence gate upon which hung an immense KEEP OUT sign. Two machine-tooled young men in blue and yellow Fleming Aviation jackets, one holding a clipboard, the other a flashlight. I'm at the airport, Deirdre. I have to hang up. Yeah, me too, she said, flatly. Poof. The ghost of love was gone.

The Fleming employee with the flashlight approached the driver's window and the guy with the clipboard rapped his knuckles against the smoked glass. Good evening, sir, the clipboard man said. He had blond hair, sun-sensitive skin, and one of those military voices: steely but with filigrees of politesse, like moonflower vines growing over a machine gun.

What's up? I was determined not to sound overly deferential. Nothing's up with me, sir. How about yourself? Just getting myself ready to go, I said. That's what we're here for, sir, the one with the knuckles said. He adjusted his eyeglasses. Name, please. Avery Jankowsky. That was never an easy thing to say.

My cell phone rang again. Now what? I said into it. I'd meant it to sound tough and aloof, but it came off like the growl of an overburdened civil servant. Avery? Through the whoosh and crackle, I heard my mother's voice. Avery? Is that you?

Mom, I said, as the gate closed behind us, and we rolled slowly toward the terminal. I pictured her, in her seaside village in Costa Rica. Feet in the pool, sunblock on the nose, a festive straw hat. She pursued happiness and relaxation like someone learning a new language—imitating the sounds, the hand movements, the tilt of the head. Avery, she said, I'm coming to New York. I've been thinking, thinking about a lot of things. I don't want to go into it right now, not on the phone. Mom? Listen. No, you listen, Avery. I'm coming to New York. I'm going to stay in that Sheraton near your apartment. I'm already at the airport in San Jose. Do you have a pen handy? I want to give you my flight number. Mom, I said, this isn't great timing. Whatever it is that you want to talk about—can it wait? No, it can't, Avery. I am on my way. And believe me, when I get there you'll be glad I did. Well, I'm not going to be there, Mom. Yes, you are; you make sure of it.

And with a rare display of maternal bossiness, she hung up before I could say another word.

THE ADRENALINE of my fight with Deirdre and my mother's call was still coursing through me as I walked through the departures lounge and then through double doors that led into a large room, with nothing about it that suggested air travel or anything else in particular. There were just blank walls painted pale blue, a black and white linoleum floor, and mismatched chairs, some leather, some vinyl, all of them well worn. There were skid marks on the linoleum floor. A sign on the wall read FLEMING TOURS, but it seemed to have been recently slapped up there. The smell of burned coffee was in the air and one of the fluorescent overheads was flickering, making the room twitch. All right. It was time to get to work. Time was money. I surreptitiously slipped my notebook out of my pocket and wrote: *This is the corporate presentation of a company that charges $135,000 for a holiday that lasts less than two weeks?*

I looked around at the men with whom I would be making my way. They were keeping to themselves, making calls, working on laptops, reading newspapers, no different from how men behave in the first-class lounge at any airport. Yet it did not take a great exertion of imagination for me to see these same industrious men conniving to undermine each other, shoving each other aside, outwitting, cheating, intimidating, threatening, shocking, awing, button-holing, high-hatting, or even bludgeoning each other.

I sat in a molded plastic seat, near a man in his late sixties. He had a booming voice, cue ball head, raptor eyes, and weirdly campy manner, a kind of forced, complicatedly coded foppishness. He wore a cologne that struck a deep, heretofore secret chord within me—whatever this man was wearing had also been worn by my second father. Then, blatantly disregarding the rule of time, dispelling thirty years with the suddenness of a sneeze, I was standing in the small beige and white bathroom in our eight-room house in Evanston smelling Kearney's cologne, and then, in less than a blink, it was a cold storming Sunday and seven-year-old me had found his lonely frightened way into the matrimonial bed where the sheets were redolent with the same signature aroma. Bright and citrus, with something fierce and discordant at its olfactory edge. What kind of man was this Andrew Kearney? What kind of man marries his ex-partner's widow, after it is revealed that the deceased had spent months siphoning company funds into his own pocket? What kind of man attends the funeral of his partner and then marries the widow? *Cold hands, warm heart,* my mother used to say, a little aphoristic alibi for her husband's freezing fingers.

Yet Andrew Kearney could not have been less like this man seated near me, and holding forth to a much younger man, who turned out to be his son, a fellow in his early twenties with half his face looking smooth and artificial as a doll's, and the other red and lumpy from catastrophic burns. The right sleeve of his white shirt and sport coat were both empty. I leaned back in my seat, hooded my eyes, and adjusted my hearing so I could eavesdrop on them. The father, in linen slacks, loafers, and tight hose that hugged his trim ankles, was telling his son a story about the boy's late mother. He spoke of her as if she had been a legendary diva, one of those imperious yet somehow broken women whose great performances and hopeless love affairs constituted the secret history of their times. The son listened politely. He had the sad, wrecked smile of someone who has endured great physical pain and the courtliness of someone who had to depend on the kindness of hired help.

Your mother and I loved to travel. We were always on the move, despite the demands of our careers, and despite the fact that your mother despised all forms of locomotion. Freud says that every journey reminds people of death, the son said, with a shrug.

It wasn't travel she hated, the father was saying, his voice rising. It was locomotion. Trains, planes, my God, she could barely stand elevators. A car was acceptable, but only if I was driving. He tilted his head, pursed his full, pinkish lips: his equivalent of a smile. There was a stiff cooling breeze of insincerity behind everything he said—he was the sort of man who gave irony a bad name.

Once, we were given two weeks in this perfectly awful old villa outside of Genoa, owned by one of my patients, Bernard Kellogg. Who, by the way, always insisted he had nothing to do with the great Corn Flakes fortune, but no one ever believed him about that—or anything else. But people liked him. Next to your mother's, he had the most beautiful legs I've ever seen on a human being. Bernard was also very generous with all that supposedly noncereal money he never seemed to run out of. It was simply inexhaustible. This was about three years before you were born. Reagan was just coming into office, and all your mother's friends were completely hysterical. She and Bernard Kellogg were part of this set of people in Evanston, I called them the Chicken Little Society. They were convinced Ronnie and Nancy were the harbingers of a new Dark Age.

At that moment, a side door to the room opened and Lincoln Castle came bounding in, like an old vaudevillian hitting the stage. He had everything but the theme music. He was an average-size man, average height, average weight, about sixty years old. All that was remarkable about his appearance was the size of his head. It was extraordinarily large, suggesting genius and/or imbecility. He had none of my Uncle Ezra's style; handmade suits and opening-night tickets wouldn't be a part of this man's life. He wore a Hawaiian shirt and baggy jeans, red sneakers. If the getup was meant to make him look young, it wasn't working. He seemed a little bit silly, yet as he got closer, I noticed his eyes. Beneath his pale, practically nonexistent eyebrows, they were dark blue, vulpine, cold and decisive, calibrated for quickly sorting the world into two categories: Want, Don't Want.

He walked directly over to the people next to me. Excuse me, gentlemen, he said. I want to welcome you to the tour. I'm Lincoln Castle.

The young man was quick to smile and offer his left hand. Oh hi. I'm Jordan Gordon. Hello, Jordan. And *you* must be Curtis.

Why must I? What if I'm tired of being that?

Jordan was quick to laugh, lest Castle fail to see the good humor in Dr. Gordon's remark.

Well, the nice thing about Fleming Tours is that you're welcome to be whoever you want, Castle said.

As he spoke. Castle slipped behind my chair and placed his hands on my shoulders. He rested them there, and then squeezed, and I thought *Get your hands off of me.* Followed by *He's on to me.* Are you Ezra's nephew, then? Is that who you are? Are you Avery?

I said I was, and he said Hello, Avery, you ready to roll? I twisted around in my chair so I could face Castle. His nostrils were filled with curiously bright silver hairs. They're just putting the finishing touches on our plane, Castle said. We've got some refreshments on the way. He jabbed his stubby wrinkled thumb toward a doorway at the end of the room. Meanwhile, why don't I introduce you around. He slapped me on the shoulder. Come on. We've got a great group. He stopped, looked me up and down, and added Wow, is it ever great to see you. Your uncle's been so important in my life.

I allowed myself to be trotted around the waiting room by Castle. The introductions began with the Gordons. Dr. Gordon gave me a baroquely strange look, a kind of silent double entendre, as if the two of us had once met under sordid circumstances and were going to keep quiet about it.

Chicago, Chicago, Castle said, pointing to Curtis and then to Jordan. Then, pointing at me, he said New York.

Actually, I'm originally from Chicago, I said. Nothing original happens in Chicago, Dr. Gordon said, and we're actually from Evanston, which is not quite the same thing.

Castle laughed and shook his finger at Gordon. I'm going to have to keep an eye on you.

A compact, exhausted-looking man stood before the room's sole window and looked out at the airfield. The sun was setting now; a long fiery orange crack separated the dark blue sky from the shadowy curve of the earth. The exhausted man, with dark brown skin and deep-set eyes, seemed to be checking the landing strip for some sign of our plane, but when he patted his thinning hair I realized he was using the window as a mirror.

Tony? The man turned toward Castle's voice, with an expectant look, as if he were about to be asked to perform a task. Tony was wearing a brown summer-weight suit and a pale yellow shirt, open at the neck. This is Avery, Tony. New York. Castle jabbed his finger in Tony's direction, as if pushing a series of buttons. Cleveland, right? Close, yes, but Akron. Tony's voice was heavy with the fatigue of sadness. He seemed like someone who recently endured a severe beating; he stood as if trying to minimize his clothes' contact with his skin. Castle shrugged. Well, I got the Ohio right. You know what, Tony? Maybe you can tell Avery the story of how you got the money to come on this trip. Tony looked worried, but he moved his head up and down in a show of willingness, not so much out of a desire to please but from a great anxiety to not *displease*. Maybe on the plane I can tell him, Tony said. As we shook hands, I noticed my own reflection in the darkening window, as well as a reflection of the back of Tony's dark hair, with comb lines furrowing down in eight perfect rows. I could not, however, see Castle in the window, and though I am not now nor have I ever been given to supernatural interpretations of everyday phenomena, I was startled by Castle's absence in the reflection. I moved my hand toward the tour leader, thinking that it was just the angle of vision that excluded him from the tableau, but, as I did so, Castle stepped away and beckoned me to follow. I glanced a last time at the window and moved on.

Next, I was introduced to a man with eyes of two different colors: one dark gray, the other light blue. I knew in that instinctual male way that this guy was going to be trouble. In fact, in one incarnation or another, he had been making things rough for me all my life. Like my third father, Norman Blake, my traveling companion was fit, wearing a form-fitting canary yellow T-shirt that showed off his sculpted muscles. Unlike Blake, this guy didn't seem as if he would be grousing at the back of the pack. He was most daunting of all things—a leader of men. You could imagine him shouting his war-weary troops up over the hill to their certain death. Castle introduced him as Webb, and Webb quickly supplied his last name—Doleack—in a tone that implied Reporting for duty. He looked me over. If Castle's eyes were programmed to make quick decisions about Want/Don't Want, Webb's main decision was Threat/No Threat. Castle continued self-testing his own memory by pointing at Webb and saying, Hillsboro, New Hampshire, to which Webb did not object.

Webb was chewing a wad of gum, which he moved from one side of his mouth to the other. His jaw muscles were as well developed as a bulldog's. Best private airport in the country? he asked. And then quickly answered, Would have to be Santa Monica. This place? He took our surroundings in with an impatient wave of the arm. Extremely substandard. My line of work, I travel all the time. These things come to matter.

What do you do? I asked, since the opening was there and it was, after all, my job.

I sell sporting equipment. Okay? We can leave it at that.

What he was saying had a peculiar sound to it, like the slightly hollow thud of a drawer with a false bottom. But I couldn't press the weight of my intelligence against it. I've never been able to discipline my mind; it goes where it wants to go. Monkey mind, as the Buddhists say. I had not been able to stop myself from needing to know what Deirdre had written in her diary, and now I could not stop trying to figure out a way to maneuver Castle so we could pass the reflecting window again. Most likely my eyes had been playing tricks on me, but I wanted to make sure. However, the window was to our right and Castle went left, to meet a small, soft man in his fifties named Sean. Castle was still trying to demonstrate his ability to remember where everyone lived. Los Angeles, he said, with great confidence, and then he added The verdant hills of Beverly. Sean, with a round, sun-kissed face, and an air of gentleness and agreeability, nodded, as if to say Close enough.

Standing near Sean was a man I would have bet money was a psychiatrist. He wore a jacket, vest, watch fob, and tie. Delicate hands, folded like the wings of a dove. His demeanor was so calm, it almost seemed as if he were in a trance. Like Freud in the standard pictures, he had closely barbered thinning gray hair and a well-tended beard, each bristle of which suggested wisdom and equanimity. He stood with one hand on his hip, and when Castle introduced us—Avery, this is Russell—he turned toward me and nodded formally in my direction.

Is that guy a shrink? I asked Castle as he steered me to another part of the room. Well, he said, I don't like to say, but I will say that's an amazingly good guess. He seems like a Park Avenue psychiatrist, I said. Ninety-third and Fifth, said Castle.

Then I was introduced to three athletically built men in their early thirties who seemed to be traveling together: one, called Hap, had an angular face, close-cropped hair, large teeth, a prominent Adam's apple; the next, named Olmo, had a reddened, weather-blasted face, which made his small squinting eyes look furtive, almost hunted; the third, called Hutton, had a little hipster's soul patch, broad shoulders, a trim waist, and was conventionally handsome enough to be a model, except he looked rather mean. They all had vigorous handshakes and used my name once or twice, probably something they had learned in an executive training weekend early in their careers.

These are our Metal Men, Castle said. Oh man, I fucking hate when you say that, Hutton said, but with a smile, as if he and Castle went way back and were used to teasing each other. But that's what you are, Castle said. What'd you do? Make a killing in gold, right? Or was it spot oil? It was actually tin, said Hutton, but don't call us Tin Men.

Hey, Lincoln, give me your take on this, said Olmo. He had a deep voice, like the bass in a country gospel quartet. He nodded his head continuously as he spoke. He combined an air of sincerity with a sense of wanting to grab whatever he could get his hands on. Hap here proposed to his girlfriend thirty-six hours ago. Well, I guess congratulations are in order, Castle said. Afraid not, Olmo said, with delight. She passed. Well, as a matter of fact she did, Hap said. She was very polite about it, which was how she was raised by two lesbians. He dried the corners of his mouth with his thumb and forefinger. Don't let me down easy is all I had to say, which is not a favor, since it's an insult. Plus I want you to think about it. If you really and truly think you can do better for yourself, then by all means pass on my offer. I'm keeping it on the table. But it's like any other offer, it doesn't stay there forever. And when I take it off the table, it's gone for good. Just watch. I'm not cowardly and I'm not lying.

My feeling about Candace is she goes for the artsy type, Olmo said. Hutton scratched his chin whiskers with his fingernails. She does have that tattoo, he said. That's the one real negative, Hap said. The paint? Olmo asked. No, no, the tattoo's fine. It's the artsy thing, that's a red flag. These girls who want someone quote unquote creative. It is so stupid. Some jackass who can do a little dance? Hap waved his hands around, with his eyes half closed. That's supposed to be manly or dignified? Oh, but they're so creative, they're so sensitive. He did a startlingly true approximation of a woman's tone of voice. Well, listen up, honey, he said, addressing that same imaginary woman, Mr. Arty Pants wouldn't even be able to make his fake-ass morning espresso if people like my friends weren't out there busting their asses getting the oil drilled, the coal mined, the tin, the copper—it's called the real world, it's called things that actually fucking exist, it's called reality. So do me a favor and do not even *mention* art, and singing and dancing and making little pictures because where I come from that is strictly child's play; it's just something to watch at night when you're completely exhausted and you're trying to relax, and there's nothing else on.

Just then, the door to the waiting room opened and an immensely large man in his early forties walked in, with the help of two canes. Despite the fact that simple locomotion was an event for him, he exuded an air of stunning self-confidence and enormous good cheer. He had silvery hair, dark brows, heavily lidded eyes spaced far apart, and a candy pink little mouth, through which he breathed, since the air he could take in through his nostrils was not sufficient. He had small square feet, like satyr's hooves. He was dressed in denim dungarees with an elastic waist and a voluminous red sweatshirt emblazoned with soccer balls, diving players, and the name of a Korean soccer team. Make way, make way, he said, and pretended to roll back and forth, as if he could barely control himself and might at any moment go careening into a wall or knock someone to one side like a bowling ball picking off a spare. This is the Jenny Craig tour, isn't it? he called out, and then laughed breathily at his own joke.

The potential value of my story had just increased—for this lumbering, panting man was surely Michael Piedmont, the computer software genius and billionaire, forced out of the company he founded by his once trusted lieutenants, victoriously reinstalled three years later, and then the object of an SEC investigation that he plea-bargained into a large fine and eighteen months in Allentown. Now he was a highly sought-after speaker, said to make $200,000 each time he addressed a trade group or a convention on the subject of Business Ethics in the Twenty-first Century. I was good at spotting notables, I had a radar for the boldfaced name. I had always been the first one to notice that Michael Douglas was sitting in a back booth in the coffee shop, or that Zubin Mehta was waiting on line to pay for an umbrella at Eddie Bauer; I could even spot less publicized people of accomplishment, the niche-celebrities whom few others noticed—Linda Lavin, Don DeLillo, Martha Reeves, Boris Spassky, Joshua Redman, bell hooks, and Bruce Jay Friedman.

Will you excuse me? Castle asked me, giving me a little See-you-later squeeze on the elbow and making his way toward Piedmont. I saw that Castle's path would take him past that reflecting window and I followed close behind, but Castle moved with surprising speed, his skimpy black loafers seemed to glide over the tiled floor, and before I could get myself into position, Castle had already passed the window and was greeting Piedmont with an upraised thumb, exclaiming You're just in time!

At that moment, I felt a gentle tap on my shoulder. I turned to see an expensively dressed woman in her late thirties, perhaps early forties. She had a round, old-fashioned looking face, soft and guileless, a comfortable, humorous, forgiving face. Her dark hair was luxuriously wavy, full of highlights. She looked like a youngish widow, pleasantly surprised by how far her late husband's pension could be stretched with a few small economies. You dropped this, she said to me, and to my horror she had my notebook in hand.

I overthanked her, masking my panic with gratitude. I'm Gabrielle Castle, Lincoln's wife, the woman said. I introduced myself, and Gabrielle went on to tell me that she was from Montreal and that she had met Castle on the inaugural Fleming Tour, and the two of them had married a few months later. Now she was making her livelihood working for Fleming.

Whenever we are in New York I take myself to a spectacular lunch, Gabrielle said. Montreal has very fine restaurants, and of course Paris. But to me New York is unique, not only for the variety but for the uniformly high quality of the cuisine. Yes, well, that is certainly true, I said. There's no question about that.

Gabrielle smiled radiantly, as if relieved to at last find someone who saw eye to eye with her about something. Right now, my passion is fusion, she said. I go alone. They say that the single women have difficulties in restaurants, getting a decent table, being served efficiently, but only in Zurich have I had this. In New York it's . . . how do you say? They smooth your silk. First thing, always, I ask them—Bring me a glass of champagne. This way they know that I plan to spend money; I'm not some little old lady with her fingers squeezing the top of her purse, afraid to let a penny escape. I always act as if I am pleasantly surprised by the prices. Oh! Thirty-one dollars for the seared goose liver and orange zest appetizer! I thought it would cost forty-one! I should have two, but I want to leave room for your wassail lobster ravioli, which you are practically giving away for sixty dollars. And I always bring a good book. There is something about excellent food that makes my brain hungry, too. She had strapped over her shoulder a gaily colored straw bag, such as you'd carry to the beach, and she reached into it and brought out a copy of *La Chute*, by Albert Camus, and she gave it a little shake. This is one of Lincoln's personal favorites, she said.

I was momentarily tempted to quote my favorite line from the Camus novel—the book's final sentence—but I refrained. I knew it only in translation—sort of knew it, anyhow, something about it being too late to save the drowning woman, too late, always too late, thank God—and for all I knew she wouldn't even recognize it in English. And there was the matter of exercising some caution. It was enough that Castle's wife had found my notebook on the floor; I didn't need to further advertise my literary bent.

Look at him over there, Gabrielle said, pointing toward Lincoln. So happy to be talking to the important man. Castle was speaking animatedly to Michael Piedmont, gesturing, shrugging, wagging his heavy head, like an old Russian innkeeper at whose humble establishment a nobleman has stopped. Gabrielle pursed her lips. Piedmont had plopped himself down onto a bench and was squeezing his hands together, reviving them after the difficult job of supporting his weight. Clever Lincoln, so anxious to please. How could she say such a thing? I was careful not to react. Once my mother had said something similar to Norman Blake. You're a brownnoser, that's what I think. She stood up, pushed her chair away from the table. It squeaked against the kitchen floor, and then she was gone, leaving just the two of us. I had been astonished by her gumption. It was like seeing a geisha suddenly spring into a jujitsu stance. What the hell are you smirking about? Blake said, and then, of course, it was time for me to suffer—no outright physical punishment on this occasion, but rather an assault of mimed pokes and slaps, so unnerving that I ended up in tears.

Are you looking forward to the trip? I asked Gabrielle. Oh yes, yes. It's very pleasurable. The men are always in a wonderful frame of mind. It's good to see them on their adventure. Often, at home, their lives are very sad. She gestured with her eyes toward the Gordons. Such a beautiful thing, she said. The boy was in the U.S. Army, he comes home so terribly injured, he thinks his life is over, he goes into the most terrible depression, and the father says No, this is not how it's going to be. We are going to enjoy life.

She sighed. As a girl, I always longed for travel. The museums, cathedrals, the most magnificent wonders of the world. The cafés. It's good to travel, no phones, no responsibilities. Sometimes I see old friends. I carry books, and I read at least one every day, without fail. When I was a girl I didn't have a chance at education. I was on my own from the time of eleven years old, my father—poof!—and my mother very sad, too sad to leave her room. So no one told me Gabrielle, go to school; Gabrielle, you don't want to be a backward, ignorant woman, do you? So now to read and see paintings and to have my own hours, it's very nice. A great privilege.

I don't think too many of the people on this trip will be looking at paintings.

I am here to show that you meet a woman, a girl on the tour and then you fall in love. I am proof it works. You can bring her home; you can marry. Or not. Just for enjoyment. You gentlemen have worked hard all your lives. You deserve these things. There is no judgment, no punishment, no harm. It is something that has always been. Napoleon, who I learned last week was unable to have sex for more than a minute, he would wait in his tent, and his lieutenants would bring him a woman. With one he even made a son. The film directors, you know, they are given big books from the modeling agencies with pictures of all the girls; they go through them like a mail-order catalog, and they point to the one they want. But of course. They are lonely, like all men.

I heard the squeak of wheels on the waiting-room floor. The two men who had been checking IDs at the gate outside were now rolling in refreshment carts. On the first were ruby and black grapes, squares of yellow and white cheese, each impaled by a ruffled toothpick, wicker baskets of dusty white crackers, tumblers filled with cashews, and a fish-bowl stuffed with miniature candy bars, such as you'd hand out to children dressed as serial killers and vampires on Halloween. The second cart carried drinks: wine, beer, Coke, bottled water, and carafes of fruit juice. Behind them was a woman in her late twenties or early thirties, with a slightly lopsided, friendly face, wavy brown hair. She looked like the unmarried sister upon whom the other siblings depend when their parents become aged and infirm. Judging from her clothes—a blue skirt and matching jacket, black shoes with two-inch heels—she was going to be our flight attendant.

Gabrielle noticed me looking at the attendant and said That's Stephanie, this is her sixth tour with us. Every time one of the men, drunk with success after so many beautiful women on our stops around the world, he makes a try for Stephanie. And it never happens. You understand? She is here only to do her job, nothing more. Message received.

Let me give you some good advice, Gabrielle said, tilting her head, smiling at me, as if there was something faintly bizarre in my personality. It's very simple. The ladies want to be treated like ladies. They like it if you speak politely, show some interest. They are no different from anyone else. A present, an offer of food or drink, all very good. But most of all they very much appreciate cleanliness.

Just then, Jordan began to cough. He bent over from the force of it, writhing, while the heel of his left foot beat against the floor, as if he were timing his convulsions. Dr. Gordon handed a handkerchief to him and poised his hand an inch or two above the boy's back, not touching him but creating some kind of paternal force field, his lips pursed, his chin high, his posture rigid, raking the room with his blue imperious eyes, daring anyone to come near.

7

A NOISY, none too smooth takeoff, though spirits on board were running high, and I may have been the only one to notice the turbulence, the precipitous dip of the wings, the thud of hydraulics, the high-pitched strain of the engines, as piercing as an ambulance siren. I scratched the side of my head and came away with a little blood on my fingernails. I wondered how I could still be bleeding. Being upended by that car seemed to be something that had happened a year ago.

And now I was here. Avery Jankowsky, all 192 pounds of me, borne aloft in this refurbished 737. The rows of seats had been torn out and replaced by big leather chairs, roomy enough even for Piedmont, and placed in such a way that most of us wouldn't have to have to sit near or even have visual contact with any of the other passengers. I was here to make my fortune, and I really ought to have been starting to accumulate pages right away, but the little bit of solitude afforded me by my seat's feng shui suited me just fine. Try as I might to connect with the other men and to begin filling my notebook with notes and observations, I was involuntarily shutting down, wanting only to be left alone, and hoping not to be noticed.

The seats could assume any number of positions: you could be as rigid as a defendant at Nuremberg, you could lounge like a starlet poolside at the Chateau Marmont, or lower yourself the full 180 degrees

and transform your seat into a coffin-sized bed. We each had a private
TV, a DVD player, and access to a quirky collection of movies. They
seemed as if they'd been picked up at a flea market, starring lesser-
known actors like Tom Sizemore and Lolita Davidovich. Along with the
obscure little films was a full complement of pornography—with titles
ranging from smirking *Hole-y Ghost* to the punishing *Ass Torture*, but,
for the most part, so-called erotica from mainstream sources such as
Playboy and *Penthouse*, featuring nurses, cheerleaders, and naked skiers.
We were also given a travel kit, containing moisturizer, mouthwash, slip-
pers, sleep mask, inflatable neck brace, and, the only discordant note,
in my opinion, a so-called Power Pak, a little cellophane pouch filled
with B vitamins and extract of ginseng, reminding me of those supple-
ments they display near the cash register at truck stops along the inter-
state. We were each given a little globe made of semi-transparent blue
glass, upon which was etched our route and destinations—Reykjavik,
Oslo, Riga—each one signified by a charming little red heart.

Stephanie, the flight attendant, was crouched in the aisle toward
the back of the plane, fussing over Jordan. She had served him a fruit
and cheese plate, and now she was pointing out things on the platter:
the grapes, the brie, the figs, the Stilton. The Metal Men were playing
cards. The table between them was already a chaos of candy wrappers,
Coke cans, and money. Sean was dozing, a script in a bright red CAA
binder tepeed on his chest.

I heard a clicking noise. My first thought was that something was
going wrong with the plane. How fitting it would be, a planeload of
men off on a sex tour going down in the Atlantic. How little we would
be mourned. None of the other men seemed to notice it, or else they
weren't bothered by it. I looked at Stephanie, but she was teaching
Jordan about Spanish goat cheese.

I played *Hole-y Ghost* on my video screen, in the unlikely case someone checked out what I was watching. (The Ghost was a formidable
brunette with a muscular, angry-looking body, dressed in a red night-
gown, who hovered over a sleeping man, one of those skinny guys
with plenty of tats and a billy club dick, and whispered Fuck Me into
his ear.) While this flickered on the plasma screen in front of me, I
concentrated on eavesdropping on the man closest to me: an African

American at least six and a half feet tall, wearing a caramel-colored suit and a dark green shirt. His long legs were stretched out, his ankles crossed; his voice was deep, with something amused and generous in it, a lubricating willingness to think well of people. His name was Len Cobb, and, it turned out, he was a professional basketball player whom I had actually seen play a few years back at Madison Square Garden, when he was a reserve forward for the visiting Phoenix Suns in a game against the Knicks. Len was talking with the short, brown skinned man I'd met in the waiting room, Tony, fretful Tony, with his small hands, delicate wrists, and nascent belly. Len was asking Tony where he was from, and Tony said Akron, but added that his mother was from Syria and his father from Naples. Which reminded Len of his days playing in the Italian League, where he got back into shape after missing a season due to knee surgery. Len still knew some Italian, which he tried out on Tony, who only smiled, showing his small melancholy teeth, and shook his head, explaining that the little Italian he knew he had forgotten many years ago.

By now, Stephanie had left Jordan. She was standing next to Webb; it took me a moment to realize Webb had her by the wrist and was holding her there.

Len was sketching the outlines of his life for Tony. Cobb was friendly, but it was an empty friendliness, the patter of a man used to life on planes, used to talking to strangers. He knew how to boil it down: child-hood in Oakland, scholarship to the University of Nevada, Las Vegas, drafted by the Seventy Sixers, knee surgery, Italy, Turkey, a foolish marriage to a Dutch model, the less said about her the better, the return to the NBA, and now retirement at the age of thirty-seven, with plenty of money and half a century to spend it. Now I do business, he said. It's what I studied in college. I've opened up a Lenny's Car Wash in fourteen markets, and I've got other things, too. I've got a share in a ski resort in Utah, and I'm negotiating an interest in this place in Mas-sachusetts called Jiminy Peak. Ever hear of it? Me? asked Tony. No, no, I don't ski. Hey, me neither, said Cobb, and put out his fist, inviting Tony to bump knuckles in solidarity.

A crescent moon swayed above the rushing clouds. Castle had taken a seat across the aisle from Michael Piedmont. He was having him sign some papers; my guess was that Piedmont had booked the tour at the last minute and the paperwork the rest of us had completed before boarding was being completed now. The multitier system of expectation and privilege was in effect, even here.

Mr. Castle said I should ask you how you made your money, Len was saying to Tony. He said I would find it interesting.

I won the lottery in my home state of Ohio, Tony said. You did? Len said—he sounded alarmed. The whole thing? Yes, the whole thing. Jesus, Len said, but Tony interrupted him. Please, don't say that, only in prayer. All right, said Len, so tell me, how much did you win? One hundred million dollars, said Tony, with the kind of sadness with which a doctor delivers a fatal diagnosis.

My microrecorder was in my pocket, a Sony the size and shape of a pack of smokes. I pressed the red RECORD button without taking it out of my pocket.

Before I won I had nothing material. I was borrowing money from my brother, my sister, my cousins. There was no end in sight.

So, uh, how many tickets did you buy?

Only one, and there was an outcry against me because the money I used, the two dollars, people said it was stolen.

You stole two dollars?

More like a dollar and forty cents. I already had sixty cents.

How do you steal a dollar and forty cents? What did you do? Rob a five-year-old?

Pennies. I took pennies. Starting at seven in the morning. I was visiting a friend who worked in a Cumberland Farms store. On the counter, near the cash register, there was a bowl, like a cereal bowl, and when people had an extra penny they'd throw it in, and when someone needed a penny, they could take one out. It was an honor system.

You took the pennies from the extra pennies bowl?

Yes, I took the pennies. Not all of them. Some I got other places. There was an Exxon station, there they had the pennies in a paper cup. The 7-Eleven keeps them in an ashtray.

So you went around stealing pennies so you could buy a lottery ticket?

No, I needed money to buy ointment for athlete's foot. I had terrible fungus between the toes on my right foot. I was constantly taking off my shoes and socks and sitting on a chair, or a stool, or the ground and scratching the itch on and on until I was bleeding. Now, you might ask me: Tony, why didn't you simply borrow the money for a tube of Lotrimin, or some other over-the-counter medication? And to that I would have to say Pride, my friend, pride. There was not a person I knew who I didn't owe money. I could not ask another person for another thing. Was I a criminal? No, that's not Tony Dinato. I took pennies. The government is thinking of doing away with the penny; the mint and the people who work there have better things to do with their time, so no more new ones, and they're going to phase out the old ones, that's how worthless they are. I know that what I did was not something I can be proud of, but technically speaking, those pennies I helped myself to belonged to no one. They were left by customers, for other customers. A lawyer said to me that the pennies in question were in a gray area between transactions. They did not belong to the store, and they no longer belonged to the people who dropped them into the cup. People had gotten rid of them; they had washed their hands of them. It was rude to take them but not illegal.

What happened to the athlete's foot cream?

I had no idea it was so expensive. For the smallest tube, eight dollars. I stood there in the pharmacy, with my two hundred pennies in my pocket, so heavy they were pulling my pants down, and I realized that I would have to continue on the great American penny hunt for the rest of the day, the rest of the week maybe, in order to afford my medicine. And so I walked out, a dejected man. I walked back to where my good friend was working, Cumberland Farms, with the idea that at least I could buy a coffee and a buttered Kaiser roll. But they had no more rolls. They had bagels, but I didn't want a bagel. They had coffee, but I didn't want a coffee without a Kaiser roll. I was not looking to get an acid stomach, you understand. So I bought a lottery ticket. I dumped all my pennies on the counter, and my friend and I counted them, and put them in little stacks of ten each, and counted all the little stacks to make sure there were twenty of them, and he gave me the ticket. Three days later I was a rich man.

Even from a distance I could sense the toll this story was taking on Cobb, how it churned at the pit of his stomach, as if he had eaten something soft but alive, something that seethed in its own sour persistence, and which must be vanquished and digested, using pints, quarts, even gallons of bile to get the dirty job done. He had been continually shaking his head in disbelief when Tony was telling his story, and now he was silent, gazing at the crescent moon and meditatively rubbing his stomach. Well that seals it, he finally said. I am never going to buy another lottery ticket. Why not? Tony asked. Because there is no way I am going to meet a winner and be a winner—you either get one or the other, never both.

Suddenly, I heard a woman's voice in my ear. We're opening a beautiful bottle of wine. Startled, I looked up at Stephanie. She wore an apron over her blue skirt and jacket—a little gesture of costumery to indicate that now she was a waitress—and she held a wineglass by the stem, offering it to me. It's a '99 Beychevelle, chosen especially for this flight by Gabrielle. Sure, I said, love some. My ears were congested, and my voice sounded buried in the middle of my head. May I bring you some pâté and olives to enjoy with your wine? *How had they known?* I wondered. *Had that been on the questionnaire?* That would be nice, I said. Then I'll be right back. I'm Stephanie, by the way.

When Stephanie retreated to the galley, I heard someone shouting behind me, his voice raw and deprived. I felt an instinctual cringing at the sound of that male rage, as well as a degree of morbid curiosity. Men gravitate toward violence, but fearfully; violence spills out of a barroom, and the cowards race out into the street, to watch, thankful it's not them trading blows. It was Webb. I could have guessed. He was standing in front of a soft, middle-aged guy in a blazer and gray slacks, with high wavy hair, like a country singer, who I would later learn was named Romulus Linwood, from Pennsylvania, the owner of a hugely successful company called CutMax that sold kitchen utensils, primarily knives, door to door. This was Linwood's third foray into sex tourism, and it may have given him an extra measure of detachment; he listened to Webb and kept his own face devoid of expression. He ought to have been sitting with the Metal Men playing poker; you'd never have any idea what he was holding. You want to be careful around me, Webb was saying. I am not someone you want to fuck with. Linwood rubbed his hands together, as if to warm them, and then shrugged and turned away. Webb caught him by the shoulder—he was certainly not going to let Linwood simply walk away from him. As soon as Webb touched him, Linwood whirled around and shoved Webb, pushed his hands hard against his chest, and sent him stumbling backward. Webb, of course, could not let this stand. Once he righted himself, he launched himself at Linwood. However, the Metal Men were on the case, and they intercepted Webb before his hands could find their way to Linwood's throat. Linwood tried to look defiant and amused, but even from a distance I could see his face had drained of color.

I looked up and down the aisle to see what Russell was making of all this. In fact, I had already picked him out as the tour member with whom I would probably having the most conversations. He would certainly give my book an added dimension. However, I could not find him. I slowed my gaze, thinking I must somehow be skipping over him as I looked up and down the length of the plane. Sean, from California, was watching something on his video monitor. He gripped his left shoulder with his right hand and wept at whatever was on the screen. His small, sensitive mouth was turned so radically downward it almost seemed like a pantomime of sorrow; the tears, however, were unquestionably real.

Stephanie returned with my wine, pâté, and olives, presented them to me on a tray, along with a neatly folded napkin and a small vase holding a single white orchid on a long curving stem. Here you go, Avery. Thanks, I said. You know that guy Russell? The psychiatrist? she said, opening my armrest, pulling out the table, and placing the tray before me. Yes, I said, I was looking forward to talking to him. Getting a little free psychiatric help while I was at it, I added with a laugh. Oh, he had to suddenly change his plans, Stephanie said, glancing over her shoulder. Really? I said. He never even got on the plane? I felt stricken, as if Russell had abandoned me personally, deliberately.

I picked up the wineglass, swirled the contents, sniffed it—the smell of wine often reminded me that life can be good. I gathered myself in. May I ask you a question, Stephanie? She straightened up, looked faintly surprised. Of course you can. I made a couple of self-deprecating gestures. Well, I guess you get this all the time, but . . . isn't this sort of weird for you? She knit her brows, choosing to pretend she had no idea what I was talking about. And I, suddenly concerned that I might be insulting her, waved my hand, taking in the lot of the Fleming travelers. I mean, look at us, we're a pretty motley crew. I'm very happy with my job, she said, clearly offended. I love flying, going new places, and meeting people. I work two weeks, and then I have twenty days off, and I make what I was getting at Delta, but with a lot of free time. She showed her teeth, registering a willingness to smile, if not a smile itself.

As Stephanie made her way down the aisle, Castle emerged from the cockpit. Gentlemen! he cried out. His voice was full of holes. May I have your attention? If Tony's every word was steeped in sadness and held within it the heavy breath of a sigh, there was a kind of joshing merriness in Castle's tone; winks fluttered within it like butterflies.

I want to welcome you to Fleming Tours. As I'm sure you noticed, we were a little late getting up in the air . . . He paused, did the old jack-o-lantern. Let's just hope that's the last trouble any of us has getting anything up.

The laughter was vague. Castle clapped his hands together, made a clownish grimace—he knew how to work not getting a laugh into the general routine. Sean switched off his movie, stowed the screen, and dried his face with the heels of his hands.

Stephanie had set up a bar at the front of the cabin, just to the left of the curtain leading to the cockpit. Castle walked over to it, poured himself a club soda, and yanked loose a bunch of ruby red grapes. He dropped a couple of them into his soda and popped one into his mouth. He chewed carefully, like someone who just came from the dentist. What I am about to say is not a rule, it's a suggestion, something I've learned from experience. He paused, shrugged, did his best to undercut the air of authority he had assumed. I'm not here trying to tell anyone what to do, but I can promise you something, I've been on a number of these trips, and I've come to see what works best. And it all boils down to this: leave your troubles behind. Don't e-mail the office, don't. One of the Metal Men raised his hand, though he spoke without being called on. We're spot traders in oil and other commodities, he said. Our business moves as fast as computers allow. And every six months it gets more difficult than the six months before. You understand what I'm saying? Hundreds of millions of dollars are at stake, and—Castle stopped him with a raised hand. These are only suggestions. I wouldn't presume to tell you how to run your business any more than you'd tell me how to run mine. One of the other Metal Men called out Oh he might tell you how to run your business, if you give him a chance. All three of the Metal Men laughed at this, though the one who had spoken first threw a macadamia nut at the one who had made a joke at his expense.

All right, Castle said, pulling off another couple of grapes and shaking them like dice in his half-closed fist. Some of you may need to keep in touch with wives or whatever, fine, but if I were you, I'd keep it to a minimum. A weak current of laughter moved through the plane, like a rivulet of warmth—highly questionable warmth—through a pond. And in terms of each other, let's really do what we can to keep it on an even keel. My best advice on that score? No politics. Our country's in a war right now. Piedmont called out, A poorly planned and poorly executed war, in which we are getting our asses handed to us! The less said about that kind of thing, the better, Castle said. We're certainly not going to solve it on this plane or on this trip. And, come on, guys, we've got a returning soldier on the plane.

We all did our best not to turn in our seats to glance at Jordan. We might not all see eye to eye on politics, Castle said, but I think we all agree that the men and women doing the fighting deserve our gratitude. There was a smattering of applause. Castle put his hand up, as if to quell an outpouring of support, though the two or three people clapping had already stopped. Honestly speaking? I wouldn't even read the news. Go on a ten-day news fast. We'll closely monitor the world situation ourselves so we don't accidentally go somewhere we'd all rather skip. Cell phone, e-mail, all that kind of thing—forget about it. You want to know what I always say? Turn in your cell phones! Hand them over to me, or Gabrielle, or Stephanie, and we'll hold on to them for safekeeping until we're back in New York, and I promise you you'll have an even better time. Men have always traveled, always explored the world, and they did it without holding little pieces of plastic up to their face, telling someone a million miles away every little thing that takes place. My personal opinion? All this electronic checking-in is bad for you; it isn't even manly, if you really want to know what I think.

All right. Now you've heard the Lincoln Castle cell phone rant. Now I want to say a couple of things about the girls we'll be meeting. We're very proud of the talent we've gathered for you fellas. Make no mistake; you'll remember this trip for the rest of your lives. Notice our itinerary—no typical stops made by a bunch of guys looking for female companionship. If what you want is to go to a bar or a massage parlor in Thailand, then you don't need Fleming Tours. These are the kind of girls—women—you see at the movies, or sometimes even *in* the movies and you ask yourself: How come there's no one like that in my life? Why do I work day in and day out and never enjoy this kind of beauty? These are the kind of girls you see when you're driving past an American college campus and you see one walking with her friends, with a sweet little oval face and dark brown hair down to her shoulders, wearing a sweater and jeans and carrying a book bag, and the next thing you know, you've almost crashed your car into a tree because you've been staring at her. These are girls you see on expensive beaches or coming out of expensive stores. Are you getting the idea these ladies are expensive? Well, they are. They are not whores, let's get that settled once and for all. They all have lives that are far outside what we'll be sharing with them. They're students, teachers, nurses, dancers; all they have in common is their uncommon beauty and their willingness to tiptoe out of the straight and narrow now and again and earn themselves a hefty fee. And if they have one little weakness in common, it's this: they *love* American men.

These are girls you actually *yearn* for, not *just* because they've got dynamite bodies but because they're just simply beautiful, in and out. These are God's grand-slam home runs. Think unattainable girl next door. Think of your best friend's daughter or your daughter's best friend. Grown up, of course. We're not doing anything that UNICEF or anyone else is going to be coming at us for. We're grown-up men meeting some very special grown-up women. And now I can tell you something I couldn't, according to Legal, tell you when we were on terra firma. There is very, very little that is out-of-bounds with these very special ladies. They are all committed to the proposition that you men are going to roar like lions, and if there's something a little special you want—guess what? They want it, too.

By now, Castle had worked up most of the group into a kind of low-key call-and-response. They were all into it, except for Webb Doleack. Holding a small leather toiletries bag, he walked directly in front of Castle and went into the lavatory.

Let me tell you guys how I got into this. To make money! one of the Metal Men called out. True enough, Castle said. But also to . . . He stopped himself, looked, breathed a long sigh, and a pained look crossed his face. So many men go to Paris, he said, or St. Petersburg, on business, flying first class, staying at deluxe hotels, enough per diem to choke a horse, and they just assume if they want a little female companionship it's there for the asking. Well, maybe it is, and maybe it isn't—but most guys either come up empty or end up in some fantastically unpleasant situation. These places are supposedly crawling with beautiful women, but where do you find them? The ancient myth of the bellboy or the elevator operator or the doorman? Forget it, if those guys know any women, trust me, they're not women you'd want to take to bed. Unless you want to try your luck with some forty-year-old hooker weighing in at a cool one hundred seventy-five pounds, or some sweaty little freak with a rose tattooed on her tailbone, trying to scrape together enough money for her next fix. Criminal connections, the worst of intentions, a penchant for petty thievery, maybe even violence. How do you get from that beautiful hotel room with the satin-covered headboard and the chocolate-covered mint on your pillow into *that*? And that's if you get lucky. Most guys never can figure out where the hell these so-called available women are. I've known guys reduced to looking in the phone book under escort or massage and just crossing their fingers that whoever shows up, if anyone shows up, won't be too terrible. Or those free weekly papers with all the sex ads in them? I mean,

what kind of hooker is putting ads in giveaway newspapers? What kind
of experience are you going to have?

All right, road warriors. Enough talk. You've all worked hard; you're
all successful. Only the best will do. That holds for cars, suits, houses,
and, at least as long as you're with me, it holds for women, too. Fleming customers are often some of the hardest working people in the
world. Why shouldn't you have whatever it is you want—as long as no
laws are broken and no one gets hurt? Right? Right. Everyone should
just relax, get to know one another. We're going to be in truly magical
Iceland in a few hours; you're not going to believe this place, or the
women. I trust you'll find the ride a pleasant one—we're very proud of
our fleet. This bird's going to be our second home, and I must say we've
outdone ourselves in making this cabin as spacious and comfortable as
we know how. Our safety and maintenance standards are the highest in
the industry, but, knowing you guys, you're probably well aware of that.
We find that our clients do a lot of research before embarking with
us—which is fine by us. In fact, we welcome it. The closer you look at
us, the better we look.

8

I HAD EXPECTED the North Atlantic to be an icy tumult, fierce and treacherous, but it looked calm as the plane prepared to land in Iceland. Occasional whitecaps ruffled the sea's smooth surface; from two thousand feet they looked like handkerchiefs someone had dropped. My stomach was contracting and expanding like a sour heart.

Up and down the aisle, the men were stirring, displacing the stale air with extravagant stretches, yawns, great, shameless belches, a flying fraternity of happy animals. The only one out of his seat was Webb, who was tilted forward with his hands pressed against the bathroom door and his feet as far back as possible. He seemed to be stretching out his Achilles tendons. I wondered if he thought we were going to have to chase the women down.

Gabrielle, her feet tucked beneath her, wrapped in a blanket so that only her neck, head, and one arm were visible, read her small biography of Napoleon. Stephanie was in the galley, the curtain drawn. I could see her feet, her sensible shoes. Perhaps she was busy at work, but her feet were not moving, and I wondered if she were just standing there, helping herself to a few minutes in which she didn't have to smile or ask if anyone needed anything. A little hiccup of desire—for reality, plain talk, for love—went through me, leaving a faint peppery taste of itself behind. I readjusted myself, looked out the window again. The gray-blue ocean was turning into land with no noticeable transition, no cliffs, no breakers, no seaside community, just a lone coastal lighthouse throwing out its long tangerine-colored beacon of light. The landscape was lunar—while dozing, I had half-heard Castle telling someone that NASA once used Iceland to train the crew for the moon shot.

AT THE REYKJAVIK AIRPORT, we were shepherded onto a mini-bus, which would take us into town. It was five in the morning Iceland time, about midnight New York time, not terribly late, but I was fried. I felt a kind of isometric exhaustion from pushing back a thought that had been trying to enter my mind since the ride to the airport: that not only was I making a mistake, but I was going to be a party to harming others. My blood felt like sand. I wanted to sleep. I wanted to be stretched out flat on cool sheets. To the other men on the bus, however, the night was young. This was what they had paid for; this was why they were here. Knees were jiggling, jokes cracking.

I tried to imagine what the women who were awaiting us were think-ing. Were they sitting with their arms folded, rocking back and forth, their faces blank, their private parts anesthetized with dread? Were they smoking crack, or bent over ceramic dishes snorting up long lines of coke? Were they napping, applying makeup, perfuming and anointing themselves? The enormity of the wrong we were about to do presented itself to me, and then it was gone, and when it reappeared a moment later it seemed smaller, just a matter of how things were and always had been. I watched out the window as the bus drove through the heavy gray dawn. The damp steely road wound through the rubble of volcanic rock, covered in lichen, dark green, and moist as creamed spinach.

As we closed in on the women, I thought about all of the services I had paid for in my life. It didn't really improve matters, but I thought about these things nevertheless. I had paid to have the wax flushed out of my ears and felt a morbid satisfaction upon seeing the dark amber stalac-tites emerge from the cave of my auditory canal. I had just a few months ago paid Dr. Tarnovsky to insert an educated finger up my rectum to make sure everything was copacetic, prostate-wise. I had treated myself to a manicure administered by a silent, manifestly homesick Korean woman who worked in a nail salon near my apartment. I had sat there, feeling a mixture of passivity and abashment, as she soaked my fingernails and dislodged their freight of bacteria into a little bowl of soapy water, and I studied her pensive, sad face and searched for some flicker of revulsion as she snipped away at my cuticles. At the end of the process she made a brusque little bow, and I tipped her a fiver. I had the plaque scraped and chipped off my teeth, and believe me I did not fail to note the twinge of disapproval on the hygienist's masked face—it was just a little pucker of the brows, but I saw it. I'd had a boil lanced. Deirdre sometimes splurged on a housekeeper and when she came to the apartment I took some reading material to the nearby diner while a stranger sterilized our toilet, scrubbed the grime off the stove, swept up swirls of dust, soot, skin, and hair. In hotels, I was capable of leaving a heap of wet towels on the bathroom floor, newspapers strewn about, and, on at least one memorable occasion, semen-stained sheets on the bed; in Portland, Oregon, I allowed a man who was seventy years old if he was a day carry my two suitcases *and* my laptop from the lobby to my room on the fifth floor, after the desk clerk informed me that the elevator was out of order. True, I had just taken a long flight, but *come on.* There is something fundamentally wrong with the world when a seventy-year-old man is straining his muscles and breathing mightily through clenched teeth with the hope that someone half his seniority will give him a nice tip. I had tried to take one of my bags away from him, but he jerked it away and shook his head emphatically—he might have been too winded to protest verbally. At any rate, I might not have tried hard enough to wrest control of my luggage. I walked a few steps behind him, my eyes cast down.

That was bad, but my guess was that I was heading toward something worse. As willing as I had been to pay others to *do* for me, I still had never paid for sexual pleasure. It had not taken any exercise of self-control. Before the breakup with Deirdre, I never thought that hiring a sex partner would be enjoyable. In fact, I always thought it would be depressing, possibly humiliating, and even dangerous. Clap, herpes, AIDS, mockery, robbery, stabbery. I had had periods of loneliness when I would have been thrilled to touch a woman and have her touch me, and times alone in cities other than my own when I saw the available women along the downtown streets or in the hotel bar—in some cities there even were escort ads on cable TV. But the loneliness I felt was never so very corrosive, or maybe it just didn't last long enough. Maybe loneliness had to drip and drip and seep and sink and waste you away like acid over a period of months, or even years, until it ate a hole right through everything you once believed about yourself. But on the other hand—and here the Other Hand was a fierce hairy claw—what power does the idea we hold of ourselves, the pious wish, the urgent, magical lie, have against the brute reality of our animal nature?

I glanced around the bus. I hadn't had any success getting near Michael Piedmont on the flight, and now Piedmont was seated in the van's last row, with Len Cobb on one side of him and Lincoln Castle on the other. Piedmont's lips were parted; his hands were folded in his lap; his heavy chin rested on his chest. Castle was saying something to Cobb and Cobb shook his head vigorously, but then Castle wagged his finger at him and both the men laughed; Castle put out his palm, and Cobb obligingly slapped him five. *How very merry*, I thought, with that familiar revulsion I so often felt around male strangers.

I was seated next to Sean, who Castle had said was from Beverly Hills but who actually lived in Pacific Palisades, where, he told me, he had worked for many years in the movie business, as a producer. Sean Westin was a small man in his late forties with luxurious, curly red hair and heavy, black-framed glasses. His grandfather had produced musicals at Warner Brothers in the 1930s, and his father had produced biblical epics in the 1950s, but even with his pedigree, Sean told me, he had just a small handful of credits to his name. Nevertheless, he hadn't let his professional frustrations turn him cynical or wolfish, as he had seen it go down for other movie business people pushed to the barren edges of that happy hunting ground. Sean remained essentially comfortable, good-natured; he carried the ineffable comforts of sunshine and money. It wasn't as if he were a stranger to worry. He worried about his health, about the fidelity of the young women in his life; he worried about the time it took for his calls to be returned; lately he had been worrying about global warming and the ongoing assault on civil liberties. But none of these disturbances could get the best of him; they could not subvert the essential peacefulness of his mind.

At this point in his life Sean was barely in the film business. He ran a company called Mr. Motto, which created and manufactured bumper stickers, with slogans that ranged from the banal, such as I LOVE MY AIRE-DALE, or SUPPORT THE TROOPS, to goofy, such as I BRAKE FOR JEWS, or ASHAMED TO BE IRISH, to the deranged, such as HONK IF YOU LIKE TO SHIT IN YOUR HAT.

That's one of mine! Sean cried out, gesturing excitedly at a white pickup truck that was just passing us. It's bumper sticker said KALASH-NIKOV ON BOARD. Really? I said, that's pretty intense. Oh come on, it's all in good fun, he said. People want to communicate. I nodded, wanting to be agreeable. There was something tender and guileless in Sean. You hated to bring anything negative into the conversation; you didn't want to burst his bubble.

He glanced at me appraisingly, as if deciding whether or not I could understand what was coming next. I've got an intuition about this whole thing, he said. You know, in the movie business, we like to think we've got all these scientific methods that will tell us if a movie is going to make money, but it's all voodoo; that's why so many people get wiped out. The Japanese come in with all their business plans and flow charts and scientific audience tracking research, and next thing you know, half of them are running back to Tokyo in a barrel. The movie business is instinct; it's basically a little buzz you get.

So what do your instincts tell you?

We got ourselves a motley crew, I'll tell you that. We've got three guys working for IR. They won't say so, but this is a company perk, a little thank-you from on high because these guys did great business, they are major earners.

What's IR?

Oh, International Resources. Spot traders. Mostly oil and gold, but if it comes out of the ground, they buy and sell it. Coal, uranium, gas, even diamonds. They can buy and sell futures on that stuff ten times a minute, bang bang. I don't even know how they keep track of the shit going down. These guys are the grabbiest, pushiest take-no-prisoners bastards ever walked the face of the earth. They make stockbrokers seem like yoga teachers. Talk to one of them, they really do believe that the dinosaurs died and their bones turned to oil just so some Metal Man a million years later can buy a BMW and a bottle of Cristal. Only thing worse than a Metal Man is an arms dealer. Ever spend much time hanging out with arms dealers? I shook my head no. I didn't even know any dentists; where the fuck was I supposed to meet an arms dealer? Which I did not say. Man, you do not want to do that, Sean said. You really want to steer clear of arms dealers.

Who else?

Do you know who Michael Piedmont is? I nodded yes, and Sean lowered his voice. He was sniffing around the movie business a couple of years ago; this was before the indictments and the plea bargains. He was looking to be a big-shot producer. Believe me, there were a lot of people more than willing to take a meeting with him. But he couldn't adapt to how we do business. Word was, all he really wanted to do was meet Sharon Stone or Hilary Swank. I should go over there and let him know his cover's blown. I sort of wonder why he's even here. I guess he's doing this the way I am.

Why are you doing it?

Me? Just for the fun of it, really. No particular reason. Maybe I'm a little bored. I like to travel, and to be honest I don't have anyone to travel with at the current time. My wife's Iranian, and she just opened a carpet store, very high end, one- to two-hundred-thousand-dollar rugs, antique, silk, all of them hand-knitted by teeny tiny hands, and the shop takes all her time. The kids from my first marriage are grown, and the boy Maya and I had together is so in love with his nanny, I can't get near him. So what the hell, right? I can afford it, it's here, so why not? If I don't like it, I won't do it again. If I really hate it, I'll just leave. There's no big deal. Being around beautiful women makes me feel great. I just feel so alive. And, to tell you the truth, I like hookers. They're really a lot of fun; they're very realistic, very little bullshit. They're more like men, in terms of being direct. This idea that they're all crying themselves to sleep, it's just not true. And people talk about how dangerous it is for the girls; that's bullshit, too. I mean, dangerous compared to what? To being a cop or a fireman? To working in a coal mine or a steel mill? More dangerous than building a bridge or washing windows in a high-rise? More dangerous than working in a nuclear power plant or driving a truck? I once developed a project about industrial accidents—more people lose their lives like that than in war, did you know that? Hooking's an easy job. What's the big deal? You're lying around in bed, some poor putz comes in, you snap a rubber on him, boop boop boop, he's over and done, and the money's on the dresser top. So every once in a while, a hooker's found dead. Not that that's not a terrible thing. And, by the way, I've never known this to happen, and I've known hookers since I was fifteen years old. It happens more on TV than in life, but it happens. What I'm saying is it happens to everyone who works. People get killed on movie sets, too. You ever hear of Vic Morrow? How's that for a waste of life? He was doing a goddamned *remake*. But when a hooker dies, people like to seize upon it because we live in a puritanical society. What about you?

Me?

Yeah, what brought you here. Is this your first time?

Yes, it is. My uncle gave it to me as a cheer-up present. That's a hell of an uncle. Westin sounded skeptical, so I had to add My girlfriend was, shall we say, less than faithful to me. Westin nodded sympathetically, and then, speaking in little more than a murmur, he said It must be fun, being a woman. You know? Having so many people wanting to fuck you. I thought women found that dehumanizing, I said. Westin laughed at the idea. I'll take it; I'll take it any day of the week. To have people obsessing about you, willing to do anything or pay a shitload of money to touch you. How bad can that be?

Just then, I felt a hand suddenly land on my shoulder, horror movie style. I looked up and saw Castle looming over me, also horror movie. Everything all right here, gentlemen?

We nodded eagerly.

You mind switching seats with me for a sec? Castle asked Westin, and Westin waited a moment, expecting Castle to offer some reason for the request, while I was filled with hopeless hope that Westin wouldn't move. Castle maintained his commanding silence until Westin relinquished his seat—though not without a sarcastic little *voilà* in its direction, as if the entire matter were rather silly.

Lincoln oomphed down next to me, patted my knee a couple of times. Do you have a dog? he asked. Me? I said. No, I don't. Wish I did, but I don't. I love dogs, he said. When I was a kid, all I wanted in life was a dog. There was this FBI agent, very interested in my father, he had a dog. Captain. A little black and white dog, maybe part Cocker, had those ears. He walked the dog around the playground where I hung out. One day he lets the dog off the leash, and Captain runs up to me, jumps up, licks me all over my face, like we've known each other all our lives. Pretty soon this FBI agent lets me walk his dog. Then he says he's going out of town, can I come over and feed Captain, gives me the fucking keys to his house. Extraordinary. Before I knew it, I was more a part of this FBI agent's family than I was of my own. He never laid a finger on me, but he seduced me, and pretty soon I'm telling him everything he wants to know about the old man. It would have been enough to put him in prison, if he'd stayed around, but . . . Castle splayed his fingers out, to connote taking flight. Unfortunately, that left me with a mother who hated me for fucking up her marriage and an older brother who used me as a punching bag.

That's amazing, I said. Sad story.

Yeah, very sad. I think that's why I got into the travel business. Figured somewhere along the way I'm going to run into the old man, though he may be dead and buried in Moscow for all I know. He'd be about eighty-eight by now.

A lot of people live longer than that, I said.

Well, you never know, Castle said. I keep my eyes peeled, like Ahab looking for the big fish, except I don't want revenge, obviously. He clapped his hands together, signaling a change of subject. Anyhow, Avery, there was something in your paperwork that puzzled me. Some irregularities. His tone was good-natured, yet I was on guard. Castle gave the appearance of friendliness. The large space between his two front teeth, the melancholy cast of his bloodshot green eyes, his powerful, darkly furred forearms, all contributed to an aura of tolerance and forgiveness—I assumed he had seen enough of life's blurred edges, sudden reversals, and broken promises to give him a philosophical nonchalance. How upset could he be that I had fudged a few items on the forms I'd filled out? How much of a stickler for truth and accuracy could a man be while fronting an international pimping firm?

Irregularities? Are you sure?

Castle patted my knee again, and this time left his hand there. You didn't mention your occupation or any employment.

I'm sort of between things. Is it a problem?

I was figuring maybe private income.

I wish.

Yeah, sure. Though I've seen it exact a terrible toll.

We were silent for a moment. Then Castle said, I did an Internet search on you. How come you didn't tell me you're a writer by trade?

Maybe it's someone else, with the same name.

Like a condor folding its wings, Castle laid his arms across his chest. He tucked his chin down and looked at me in such a way that implied Oh please, come on, don't embarrass either of us.

All right, I said, you got me. And before Castle could ask why I would try to obscure the fact of my profession, I added I really didn't want to put that on my application. I didn't want you to think that this was some sort of writing assignment.

Castle let that hang in the air a few moments and then asked, Is it?

Oh my God, no. I shook my head, laughed. Are you kidding me? Absolutely not. Writing is about the last thing on my mind right now.

I saw you writing in a notebook, on the plane.

Force of habit. Listen, do you want to know why my uncle Ezra gave me this trip?

He said you were having girlfriend troubles.

That stunned me for a moment. Ezra had spoken to Castle about what Deirdre had done to me? One of the most upsetting and degrading aspects of having been cheated on is wondering how many other people know about it, and how it colors their thoughts about you. I understood why some people—men, particularly—keep it a secret if they've lost their job or received a bad diagnosis from the doctor. They don't want to be that person. They don't want to be culled from the herd, left behind, or eaten.

To say the least, I managed to say. Then I decided to go further: I always sort of suspected her.

Castle raised his ghostly eyebrows and then went back to work on my knee, this time slipping in a couple hard squeezes between the pats. You don't need to make excuses for her. She can burn in hell. Demons can spread her legs and pour hot lead into her pussy. I blanched at the violence of this. It was all I could do to stop from turning away. I'm into men's liberation, Castle said, as if this explained it all. So. Let me ask you a question, Avery. You ever really give it to someone in an article and then there's all this blowback? You ever really piss anyone off?

You mean like letters to the editor? I asked.

Well, I was thinking more like someone wiring your car so it blows up when you switch on the ignition.

Iceland slipped serenely past the windows. A barn. Extravagant clouds like steam surrounding a half-dormant volcano. Castle stretched out in his seat. Unfenced pastures with small horses and swaybacked red cows. Castle's voice was mild, amused. When I was a kid—and this was way, way before your time—there was this columnist named Victor Riesel. He was what my parents used to call a real sonofabitch. He had a column in the old *New York Mirror*, but it ran all over the country, syndicated. About 1955 or '56, Riesel writes a column about how some dinky little union with connections to the Lucchese crime family is shaking down contractors. The story runs, and that night Riesel goes to Lindy's up on Broadway and someone comes in and throws sulfuric acid at him, right in his face. They rush him to St. Clare's Hospital—I always remember that part because that's where my brother was born. But the doctors can't save his eyesight. No one did any time for it, either. The guy who threw the acid was this young kid named Abraham Telvi, and when he realized he'd just blinded someone with a national following he started bellyaching, wanted more money, and he ended up with two bullets in the head in Little Italy. The guy who really engineered the attack was the guy they called Johnny Dio, but they never got anything to stick on Dio until the early '70s—he was serving time for some crazy kosher meat scam when he died in Danbury Prison hospital, in 1979.

Kosher meat scam? But Castle waved off the question. Outside, great steaming fissures in the rocky world, gray geysers shooting up forty or fifty feet and then dissipating into mist. Reykjavik was in the near distance, it looked clean, utilitarian, and slightly past its prime, like an Olympic village built twenty years ago. A long thick braid of white clouds curled a half inch above the horizon.

We're almost there, Castle announced, and I'll tell you what: you're going to absolutely love Icelandic women. They're not the brightest people on Earth, but they're very, very friendly, and oh my, are they ever sexual. He sighed dreamily. Word of warning? Don't let them drink too much. Some of them really go overboard.

My stomach turned over. It seemed best for my overall peace of mind and certainly better for the book I wanted to write if I could get through this trip without having sex with a paid escort. But I also sensed a certain distance between my resolve and my current state of mind. Crossing an ocean, being suddenly far away from anyone who knew me, created anonymity, and with no one to watch, no one to know, who could say what I would end up doing?

9

AN HOUR LATER, I was with Sigrid. You know what would be nicest for me? I said to her. I had allowed myself to be seated in a therapeutically designed chair, and now my knees were up as high as my chin. I would have to struggle if I wanted to stand. Sigrid sat across from me. She had a spacious, friendly face, polite, reserved, with little tugs of resignation at the corners of her mouth. Her dark brown hair framed her pale oval face. There was something transparent in her, plain, but a plainness that was alluring, the plainness of something unmarked, undiscovered, a stoical, pioneer plainness. She looked like a woman stuck in a ho-hum job, in a car rental kiosk or a bank. She was dressed in a dark skirt and a white blouse, as if she had stopped to have sex with me on her way to work.

No, what would be nicest? Was she mocking me? Her voice was foggy, thick. I wasn't quite sure how I had ended up with her. As soon as the minivan had arrived at the hotel, the men had been shepherded into a conference room on the ground floor of the Royal Reykjavik, a room with a blue and white carpet and dark purple draperies, recessed lighting. A buffet breakfast had been put out for us, and we ate nervously. The women were already there, waiting. At first, I couldn't tell one from the other; they were all simply beautiful. A basket full of kittens, just as Castle had promised, but most of the men were unexpectedly reticent, diffident. The Metal Men, Webb, and Cobb all gravitated toward a sturdy-looking blonde with bright lips and fingernails, long curling eyelashes, dressed in a silver jumpsuit; she looked as if on the days she wasn't working as a prostitute she was a superhero. The others seemed to be milling about, as if waiting to be chosen. I had expected it to be like the Oklahoma land grab, yee-haw, hats waving, spurs digging into horseflesh, the native population running for their lives. Instead, the guys circled the buffet table, slowly filling their plates with scrambled eggs and bacon, little triangles of cheese with caraway seeds, tomatoes grilled to black.

Eventually, the Icelandic women made their way to the buffet, and each one attached herself to one of the men. Was it at all based on our questionnaires? Sigrid had just come up to me at the buffet and said Hello, and then took my plate, as if everything was settled. She was in front of the breadbasket, and she asked me with a simple movement of her eyes if I wanted some bread. I shook my head No. If she was trying to act somehow maternal, that really wasn't the right foot to start out on. She saw the look of concern on my face. Don't worry, she said, after, if we want to remain together that's good, but those who don't can choose again. Again? I wanted to say, but didn't. Considering the underlying depravity of the whole situation, I felt stiff and shy. We went to a table, pretended to eat, and then Sigrid asked me if I'd rather come to her apartment than stay at the hotel—It's so plastic here, she said—and I leaped at the chance. How much better for my reportorial purposes to go to where she lived, and how much better for my peace of mind to be away from the others, for a while.

We drove back to her apartment in her car. Sigrid and I barely spoke. She seemed absorbed in the music playing from her car stereo, some sort of sexy international hybrid, Brazilian, French, maybe West African. I had never been able to figure out where people developed a taste for that sort of music, or where they found it. It all seemed like the sound track from a movie I had missed or a party I hadn't been invited to. We stopped at a traffic light; she shifted the car into neutral, leaned over, and kissed me on the mouth. You're a shy one, aren't you, she said.

You took me by surprise, I said.

There was something in that remark that pleased her, or so it seemed. I had no real hold on what was going on, exactly. In fact, I had never been in such an ambiguous, confusing situation in my life. Because at the root of our being together was a transaction that would mean sooner or later we were going to be in bed together, every gesture she made, her rhythmically tapping her fingers on the steering wheel to the coffeehouse samba, her small shudder of fright when a couple of guys on mopeds buzzed past us, her considerateness in cracking the window before lighting up her cigarette, her kissing me, of course, and her little ersatz insight into my so-called shyness had to be weighed against the strong possibility that everything she said and did was a lie, or, to put it less stridently, a show. Her name was probably not Sigrid, and though I told her I was Avery, that could just as well could have been made up, too. All that was true was the transaction that had come before; the true identity beneath our masks was that I was a man who had somehow come into enough money to allow me to be on this side of her funky little car and she was a woman whose life had come to this.

I was in an unreality more total and opaque than any I had ever experienced under the spell of any tequila or drug, more insanely inevitable than a dream, I was way the hell over the rainbow. Yet the more I thought this—and I was quite literally repeating to myself *This is just so unreal*—the less the concept of *unreality* meant to me, and what took its place was the suddenly seductive notion that there could be no unreality because there was no cardinal, ruling reality, and what the world (space, time) actually consisted of was countless competing realities, some of them parallel, most intermingled, and what I had all this time been calling the Real World was simply a series of routinized actions and perceptions, nothing more persuasive than the sum total of my rickety life. This improvisation of cordiality and attraction being acted out between Sigrid and myself was as valid as any of the transactions large and small that comprised my daily life heretofore, no less genuine and valid and frank than the *Hi, how are you?* I exchanged with the Egyptian who manned the newspaper kiosk near my apartment, or the little beckoning finger I raised at the corner diner when I wanted the waiter to bring me a refill of coffee. There were the lies you told to trick someone out of that which they would not give you under other circumstances, and then there was this, the lies you told with the understanding that they would not be actually believed, the lies you *agreed to tell*, and the lies you agreed to hear. You did not believe these lies, and you did not expect the lies you told to be believed. All that decency demanded was staying in character.

What I was not prepared for was the pleasure I felt in this strange, luxurious darkness . . .

We pulled into the little circular drive in front of her red corrugated apartment house with its green roof and white trimmed windows, surrounded by tall green shrubbery and presided over by an extremely tall but empty flagpole. Out we go, she said. An orange cat patrolled the parking area, and it approached Sigrid, its tail flicking. Come on, she said to me, taking my hand, up we go.

In her apartment, I must admit I felt a degree of paranoia. *Where am I?* I wondered. A wave of exhaustion went through me, disorienting, belittling. It seemed as if only an hour or two ago I was in my broken home, and now, somehow, I was *here.* My mind reeled at the strangeness of this. Okay, I'm in an apartment in Reykjavik, a two-minute ride from the hotel. Her mango-colored Scana had smelled of vitamins and cigarette smoke. I had happened to glance in the backseat and noticed the upholstery bore the marks of a child seat that had once been there, chalky indentations in the black vinyl; the vanished seat left an impression of itself like a picture that had been taken down from its customary spot on the wall. Was there a child somewhere? Or was it merely someone else's car, or a car Sigrid bought used?

I cleared my throat, looked at her wide, mild face. What would be nicest for me is if we just talked—for a while. I couldn't believe I had added those last three words. Was I trying to assure her that eventually there would be more than talk? Had I just taken people-pleasing to the next dimension? After a lifetime of sucking up to a series of fathers, was I now going to use those skills on a woman whose job description began and ended with making me comfortable? I wanted to ask her how old she was, but I held off. Why offer her an invitation to lie? Women in this business always say they're younger than they really are, unless, of course, they were underage, in which case they may tack on a year or two.

Okay, no problem, she said. She narrowed her eyes, a slightly jokey imitation of a woman grappling with her own passion. I like to talk. She crossed her long legs, gestured expansively. What do you want to talk about? From the outside came the sound of a bus changing gears—a pneumatic wheeze followed by a roar. I glanced at my watch. It was nine in the morning. People were on their way to work. I felt a tug of longing for the simple things of life; like many men without regular employment, I sometimes believed that a strict schedule and a set routine might be the answer to life's difficulties. Behind Sigrid's chair, against the white wall, was a six-shelf bookcase, made of lightly stained wood, and filled with books, most of them in English. I squinted, tried to read the spines. L. Frank Baum, Maxine Hong Kingston, Jonathan Franzen. What a great country! I see you like to read. She glanced over her shoulder. Oh those, well, not so much now. I have some trouble with my eyes, and when I read it's not so good. Trouble with her eyes? Wasn't that a symptom of syphilis? I wondered if I ought to tell her that I was a writer—but how stupid would that be. Still, books, that would be an opening.

Do you have a favorite? I asked. Book? A favorite book? No. She shook her head, and I wondered how I could have asked such a ridiculous question. I rubbed my shoulder, as if to soothe a bruise. What time was it in New York? Four in the morning? Five? Deirdre was padding on her way to the bathroom for a sleepy predawn pee. For such a youngster, she had the urination habits of a woman three times her age.

There's something inherently awkward in this, isn't there? I stated this as casually as possible. I had learned from journalism that a certain degree of candor loosened tongues. It never ceased to amaze me. Even people in public life were lonely, longed to be listened to, *heard*. If you were able to create a mood of safety and frankness, there was no telling what you might hear.

Yes, awkward, Sigrid said, but how do you mean? I shrugged . What was she asking me? Were we having a language problem? I don't know, I said, and moved my hands back and forth as if trading one heavy stone for another. This, you know, this. It's all the same, she said. Life is nothing. We live, we die, we do, we don't do. Someone might be dreaming us. A big hairy giant sleeping in a cave, this could be his dream. I suppose so, I said. I fought back an urge to cheer her up. I guess life is a mystery, I said. She agreed, but then added A murder mystery. Wow, I said, you really have that Nordic pessimism thing, don't you?

You don't like me? She asked this with a remarkable lack of emotion. Well, no, it's not that. You're very beautiful. Thank you. For a moment I was afraid. Of me? I touched my chest, indicating harmlessness. Yes, if the Americans don't like you, then they send the bombs over and everything—she threw her hands up in the air, made a surprisingly convincing explosion sound. And then they go up and down the streets in their Humvees with machine guns. She made the sound of rounds firing. I had never met a woman who could make those sounds. Don't worry, I said, I come in peace. Your president is an insanity on the world. I myself was no friend of the president, but I did not want to join in with Sigrid on these matters. I felt as an American I would have to absorb the world's displeasure with my country. It was part of the deal; you got plenty to eat and plenty of fuel, and in return you had to suck up a certain disdain worldwide. Also, I didn't want strangers to think that the sort of man who staked himself out against the current president was also the sort of man who went on sex tours. I felt the opposition ought to occupy a higher moral ground, and my telling some Icelandic hooker that I was a liberal wasn't really fair to other liberals, 99 percent of whom were working hard on their monogamous relationships. Let's not talk about politics, Sigrid. Do you mind?

What zodiac sign are you? she asked. Well, Sigrid, I said, I'm a Leo, but I'm thinking of having it changed. She didn't react, not so much as a smile. What sort of hooker wouldn't even laugh at your jokes? Was this where her anti-Americanism had led her? Had it completely wrecked her sense of humor? Or was laughter something she kept in reserve, in the spirit of not kissing you with her mouth open, or not letting you touch her left breast, the breast presumably reserved for her true love.

I noticed something in the corner of the adjoining room, the gleaming reddish back of a cello, propped up in a corner with its strings to the wall. It looked startlingly and ethereally beautiful standing there. I wanted to touch it, this emissary from a better world, this instrument of articulation that allowed us to hear the sad keening sound of the unpolluted universe. Sigrid could see I was looking at it. It's not mine;

it's my brother's. He plays in the Icelandic Symphony, but not so much anymore. He is spending most of his time working for the musicians' union.

I nodded. So tell me, I'm very curious about my tour leader. Mr. Castle? Yes, what do you make of him? She looked a little uncertain, and I rephrased the question. Is he a pretty nice guy? *Oh shit, how lame,* if only I could take that back. Interview questions are like tennis serves; you bop a couple into the net, and you lose the point. But Sigrid answered. She had to; it was part of the job. Mr. Castle is the boss but he doesn't act the boss, I like that. Well, that's good, I said. I'm glad to hear he's treating you right. She seemed not to understand or maybe wasn't listening. She picked a small piece of flesh off her lower lip and then placed it on her tongue.

Would you like to have a coffee? She rose from her chair, loomed over me. No, no, I'm fine. Water? Okay, that would be great. I had to rock back and forth a couple of times in order to get up, and then I followed Sigrid into her kitchen. It was small, modular, spotless. We were on the third floor of her building. The window over the sink looked out onto a parking area, enough for about 100 cars, most of them gone. An old man in a blue jumpsuit was cleaning the cement, hosing it down with water so hot that half of him was obscured by a cloud of steam. Here heat and hot water are all free, Sigrid explained to me. (Maybe she had once been a tour guide. Her English was certainly up to the task. But a day of dragging idiot tourists around, and what do you have to show for it? A sore throat, a splitting headache, and a hundred bucks?) In winter, Sigrid said, we use hot water instead of shovels to clean the snow away. She opened the refrigerator. There were a couple of withered apples, a bowl of something covered by a crumpled dome of aluminum foil, a can of Fanta, and a bottle of water. So I see the bottled water craze has come to Iceland, I said. I would have thought the water here would be very drinkable. She pulled the bottle out, opened a cabinet, and took out a glass. It had a red stripe around the middle. Our home water is clean but . . . She made a childish face of displeasure, pursing her lips, and wrinkling her nose. In my duress, I found the gesture unbearably poignant and alluring. What? I asked. It tastes bad? Yes, maybe like someone has put an egg in it.

There were four red chairs around the blue enamel kitchen table. Sigrid seemed to understand that, for now, at least, I felt more secure talking to her in the kitchen; she gestured for me to sit, and then she opened the can of Fanta and sat across from me. She took a small sip, and shivered with pleasure. Skål, I said, lifting my water bottle to her in what I assumed was a universal Scandinavian salute. You're a nice guy, she said. Perhaps you would like to wash off. My instinct was to quickly say No, but, in fact, I felt disheveled and stale from the flight, and the thought of a shower was wildly appealing to me. Maybe later, I said, at which she shrugged. The water tasted transparent and cold, as if it had just come off a glacier. I wiped my mouth with the back of my hand. My face felt coarse. It made me think of the other men, back at the Royal Reykjavik, naked by now, banging away like conquering heroes, trying to plant some deep romantic kiss on some woman's mouth while she thrashed her head back and forth, trying not to offend or irritate, but nevertheless hoping to keep a modicum of personal privacy and dignity for herself. Hoping.

The light here is so strange and beautiful, I said. In Iceland. I gestured, waving vaguely in the air over my head. The sun, I guess, it comes from a different angle. She took another drink of orange soda. I noted that she had a bit of a sweet tooth. What did that mean? Younger than she looks? Recovering alcoholic? Junkie? This time the sip was not so restrained, and a moment later she burped, rather loudly and without the slightest self-consciousness. I was trying not to think of this human being in purely sexual terms, but that belch seemed to suggest she would be an uninhibited lover, a maker of deep animal noises. This was a lot more difficult than I had imagined. Being exhausted didn't make it any easier, that was for sure. Lust was like a fever, more likely to overtake you when your defenses were down, when reason, self-control, and all the other departments of superego were closed for siesta.

Do you have any other brothers or sisters? I asked her. Yes, two more, both older. A brother, an engineer. He works at the geothermal plant. She rubbed her fingers against her collarbone. And a sister, a doctor, but she doesn't live here exactly now. She is with Médecins sans Frontières. Doctors Without Borders? Yes. Wow, that's wonderful, that's really fantastic. Sigrid shrugged. There's plenty of sick people right here in Reykjavik. But, I insisted, Doctors Without Borders, those people are really great, they take incredible risks and they do so much good. I was about to add that I donate a hundred dollars to them every year, but it was enough that I had already said *wonderful, fantastic,* and *incredible* in the space of three seconds, I didn't have to go to any further lengths to convince this woman that I was a goofball.

Well, as you can see, Sigrid was saying, I am not the one in my family who has made a big success. How about you? Brothers and sisters? No, none, I'm an only child. But I *do* have four fathers. Sigrid nodded incuriously. She might not have quite understood what I had just said. A seagull landed on the sill outside the kitchen window, peered in for a moment, tilting its head left and then right, and took off again. Yep, I said, four of them. Sigrid leaned forward, placed her hands on the table, and folded them, like a country person settling down for a good long talk. Are you married? I hesitated a moment before answering. After all, I could be anyone I wanted to be. It wasn't quite the elasticity of identity of being in an Internet chat room, where your gender, age, and appearance could be matters of pure fantasy—and, yes, I had indulged myself in that sort of tomfoolery during early visits to cyberspace—but being here in Sigrid's kitchen—if that was really her name, and if this was even her apartment—offered me an opportunity to, if not reinvent myself, then, at least, to make a few judicious revisions. Why not married? Or I could be a widower. Why not a brief marriage to an actress who was stabbed to death by an obsessed fan? Why not a couple of great kids? Yes: Brendan and Collette. Brendan skateboards and is dyslexic; Collette is only eight but is building a harpsichord. Yet I lacked the energy for invention, at least right now. Maybe I could be that person with the next woman, in the next country. For now, all I could do was shake my head No, and when she asked And no children? I shook my head again, but this time with my eyes lowered, as if I were ashamed.

Nobody wants to have children now, Sigrid said, in her husky melancholy voice. I think the world ends with us. She pinged her fingernail against her soda can. Some of the sea birds, they break their own eggs because nature informs them that next year there will be less food. The scientists have studied this. The mother birds abort the unborn ones because of the scarcity is coming. She shook her head, impatient with her own English. You understand? she asked. Yes, yes, I think I read something about that—which was untrue; I had never read about that, not a paragraph, not a word, not a letter—and then I added A year ago. Sigrid stood up, so suddenly that I tensed. For a moment I thought she was coming after me, was going to take me by the throat and throttle me for pretending I had read something about birds destroying their own eggs. But she was merely making another visit to the refrigerator. Time for my vitamins, she announced. I didn't turn in my seat to watch, but listened to the refrigerator door open, the sound of plastic moving over the metal bars of refrigerator shelving, the squeak and rasp of a cap unscrewed from a bottle . . . What certainty did I have that at any moment two or three Viking thugs weren't going to come charging in and beat the living hell out of me?

Fear! Everything in the Fleming presentation had been reassuring, designed to conceal the one dark red unspeakable fact that all of us were engaged in a criminal enterprise, all of us were violating if not the laws of Iceland—who the hell knew *what* was permitted by law on this hunk of loamy lava?—then some other set of laws, the ones that governed how people are meant to treat each other. Sigrid reached over me and picked up the water bottle, swigged from it to wash down her vitamins, and then, when she put the bottle back onto the table, she remained behind my chair, and a moment later she lay her hands gently on my shoulders, rubbed them a couple of times, and then began to massage my shoulder, neck, and back. Pleasure trickled through me, slowly. You're nervous, by which I took her to mean tense. I rotated my shoulders, moved my head back and forth to stretch out the muscles in my neck. I guess so, a little. The gull was back in the window; this time its visit was even more fleeting. Sigrid's grip on me was strong, commanding, impersonal. But why did it even *have to be* personal? What did I want? You turn on the radio; it plays music; you like the music. What difference does it make that the disc jockey in some radio station has no idea who you are or even if you are listening? And of course whoever made the music doesn't know you, you have never crossed his mind, except perhaps as a possible customer, and that's not you, that's just the money, but who cares? The important thing is you hear it; its having nothing to do with you is beside the point. All right, up you go. She cupped her hands under my arms and pulled up on me. A nice warm shower is what you need.

It seemed frankly churlish to refuse. Wasn't her life difficult and complicated enough without having to put up with my irregularities? What was I supposed to tell her? That I had come on this trip as an observer? That I was not the sort of man who would have sex with someone he didn't love and who didn't love him? *Come on!* I could adopt the persona of the shrinking violet, a sort of ambivalent touch-me-not who signed up for worldwide debauchery but could not exactly bring myself to act on the opportunities being offered me. Who would that guy be? Anyhow, I was already standing, already allowing myself to be led like a blind man out of the kitchen, into the little T-junction at the center of her apartment—kitchen behind, living area ahead, bedroom left, bath right. Yeah, that's a good idea, I said. And then I had a temporary solution to my dilemma. You're not going to get in there with me, are you? My God, that sounded much, much more lame than I was prepared for. And this is what I was saying *without* a persona; this was really me. I had no idea I was that lame. It was like catching an unexpected glimpse of yourself in a mirror and seeing, really seeing, for the first time what's happened to your ass. Just for you alone, Sigrid said, with a little laugh in her voice. I woke at first light and bathed and drove to the hotel. It struck me like poetry. What an extraordinarily beautiful thing to say: *I woke at first light and bathed and drove to the hotel.* Wouldn't it be wild if I somehow fell in love with her, and she with me, and I spent my life in Iceland? And why not? English was widely, if stiffly, spoken; the weather wasn't as brutal as the country's name implied; my occupation was certainly portable, and, in an environment without many celebrities or trendsetters, I might be able to produce pieces that actually had some value.

Sigrid's bathroom was small, warm, and damp, and had a faint sulphuric smell, not altogether unpleasant—the odor was not so much rotten as rugged. Mica, quartz, fossils, cold hard mud. Feeling prim almost to the edge of panic, I looked for a way to lock the door, but there was none. What kind of country had bathroom doors that did not lock? There was no tub, just a stall shower, flimsy, with a shower curtain decorated with daisies. A little tangle of hair blackened with gooey shampoo was caught in the drain at the bottom of the stall. The showerhead was rusty from the mineral-rich water that flowed through it. The hot-water faucet had a red dot on it, the cold a blue. I turned them both halfway and quickly peeled out of my clothes. There was a rough, sky blue cotton towel resting on a Sesame Street footstool; I assumed the towel was for me and the stool must have belonged to whomever the missing car seat was for. Yet she had said she had no children, her friends had no children. Back home, childless couples bought toys, games, treating themselves as if they were their own children. But car seats? I didn't know; I would never know. That was the thing with a hooker—everything but the body was a lie, and then the body turned out to be the biggest lie of all.

The stinging hot shower was hard and sulfurous. Memories of Norman Blake came streaming out the showerhead. If I could choose one thing in my life to have not happened to me, if I had veto power over only one thing it would probably be my mother's third marriage and the introduction of that disappointed bully, that vengeful and resentful, hard, hairy, and indomitable man, who, on top of all the pettiness and capacity for sudden cruelties, had a hellish kind of breath, like a pile of manure set on fire. Even now, years later, I could not eat a boiled egg or egg salad without enduring a grim reminder of my mother's third husband, with a cock like a sock in its sleeping state, a cock like a Nazi salute when it was getting ready to rumble—this terrible, unwanted knowledge was mine thanks to Blake's ceaseless self-display, his lunatic lack of personal modesty. In the shower, I reached for a block of dark brown soap. I could hear music coming from another apartment, an American black voice singing *Good morning little schoolgirl*. Who was that singer? Muddy Waters? Buddy Guy? Suddenly the music cut off. Whoever had been listening to it must have realized he'd had it on too loud. The soap barely made any suds . . . *suds* . . . very strange word, something childish, even primitive about it. The bar of soap leaped like a toad out of my hand and hit the floor. As I bent for it, I imagined momentarily being assaulted from behind, my head crashing into the noisy metal wall, and when I was upright again I thought of Sigrid in the next room. What must it be like for her to have a complete stranger showering in her apartment—if this was her apartment—and to know that, if I so chose, I could enter her body? What ineluctable sequence of abuses and addictions had led her to this moment? My heart filled with pure, blind pity. Was she out there wringing her hands, pacing, hoping that I would somehow have a heart attack and die? Or was she letting her mind go blank, just hitting some internal DELETE button over and over until nothing was left?

The water truly did reek of egg. I sniffed my soaking forearm. Not *too* bad. I finished quickly, toweled off, stood there naked for a moment holding my clothes. It passed through my mind that it might be prudent to masturbate. No, that would not do. I did not fly across the Atlantic Ocean for a quick toss-off in a hooker's bathroom.

I got back into my stale clothes and walked into the living area, and, as I had feared, Sigrid was not there. In here, her voice called out from the bedroom, and now I really had no choice but to go in there, but I did so with my resolve ratcheted up to its highest level and in full possession of my moral senses. Even if she were waiting for me in a naked pose of scientifically calibrated irresistibility, even if experts in the male response had worked out various postures that years of art history and extensive questionnaires had revealed to be universally alluring, I would venture no closer to her than the edge of the bed, though even as I stated this to myself while moving ever closer to the sound of her beckoning voice I knew there was no way I could give myself anything better than an even shot at fulfilling what suddenly seemed an impossibly high standard of behavior.

Sigrid, we have to talk, I began, even before I reached her bedroom. Step by small hesitant step I drew closer. I composed what I would say next, and as I tried to put the words together I struggled to pay attention to myself. My inner voice, however, was muffled; a howl of fear and another of desire drowned the poor thing out. Yet, deaf as I was to myself, I continued to articulate. I don't mean we have to talk like there's something I have to tell you; I don't mean it like that. She might *not* be completely naked—sex in these situations might be permissible but *not* obligatory. Surely I cannot be the first man who wanted a bit of chitchat before rutting. Of course, she might be in some condition worse than nudity: she might be in a leather halter; she might be swinging from a harness; she might, for all I knew, have sprouted immense wings and be hovering over the bed like a harpy.

Sigrid was merely sitting on the edge of the bed and she smiled at me the moment I walked into the room. She was a nice person. The walls were bare, painted a dark pumpkin color. There was a round blue rug on the floor. The bed was heavy, mahogany, old-fashioned in its dark, ponderous way. This had to be someone else's bed, once upon a time. This was a hand-me-down. She probably took it from her parents' house, a weird little legacy . . . Feel better? Sigrid asked. Not only did her smile seem genuine, but her voice was intimate, concerned. She really did want me to feel relaxed. Much better, thanks. That shower was a good idea. Good! You want to lie down on my bed. She patted the mattress. I'll give you a . . . She squeezed the air with both hands, indicating massage. Okay, I said. I was stunned by my answer, by the quickness with which it came. You put all your clothes on, she said, looking me up and down. Yeah, I did. I was a little chilly. *My God, why would a man lie to a hooker? Under what circumstances would I absolutely and without fail tell the plain unvarnished truth?* Well, now you may take them off. *If I don't do as she says, she's going to think I'm a cop.* My essay began to compose itself. *Sigrid, well-read and stately, had to make a quick decision about me. Her most basic question was was I a cop?* Was was? That can't be right. But how else can it be said? Sigrid snapped her fingers, as if to awaken me from a trance. I blinked myself back to the world we shared, and she patted the bed again, this time more insistently. It seemed wisest to keep things light, and so I pressed my hands together as if I were preparing to swan-dive and then I flung myself onto Sigrid's mattress. The headboard pounded against the wall. Careful, it's new paint. She stood up, checked the wall, licked her thumb, and rubbed it over the mark. I remained facedown, with a toreador's relationship to my thoughts.

It's good, Sigrid said, and then joined me on the bed. She was on her knees, leaning over my back as she had at the kitchen table. She pressed the whole of her weight down on me and then released, did this a few times, bouncing me up and down. There was no more pleasure in this than there was in having a coat-check girl help you on with your coat. You'd really have to be scrounging for physical contact if you could make do with this, or to take it, as people will, as the beginning of something, an intimation of some further intimacy. Once, ten billion light-years ago, Gene Jankowsky had told me *I gotta tell you, man, I was so lonely and need-*

ing, you know, the human touch, I almost got a haircut. Up and down, up and down, Sigrid said in her husky voice, and then, just as I was about to lift my weary head and turn toward her, just as I was about to say Thanks, but that's enough, I really would just rather get my bearings here, Sigrid changed the rules of engagement by suddenly and very, very forcefully grabbing my ass, a hand on either cheek, squeezing away with a kind of eroticized rage. It's time for the moment of truth, Avery No-name, she said. Well, the moment of truth, I could not quite bring myself to say, is that I am definitely not having sex with you. I did, however, manage to squirm out from under her weight; she was a lot denser than she looked, as if her bones were steel and her blood especially thick, in order to get her through the Arctic winters. I rolled onto my back and looked up at her with what I hoped was an expression of forbidding skepticism, no easy pose to strike, even under ideal circumstances. Come on, Sigrid, whatever happened to *The customer is always right?* She didn't appear to be familiar with the phrase or the concept. The customer isn't always white, she murmured. What I'm trying to tell you here, Sigrid, is that . . . My God, I could not say it. I wagged my finger back and forth gesturing No no no, hoping that that would suffice, and even if it didn't, it gave me the little bit of extra courage I needed to finally state my case. I'm here to talk to you, not to have sex. Okay? No sex. I want to get to know you; I just want to talk. She rolled away from me, jammed her hand beneath the waistband of her skirt, and scratched her behind. Cleared her throat, paused, her eyes went flat and lusterless as she surveyed her own internal well-being, and then she cleared her throat again.

What do you want to talk about? What is a nice girl like me doing in bed with a man she does not know? Well, no, I said, I wasn't going to ask that. Even though that was the question, the exact question, though, perhaps, more felicitously phrased. The one question you were never supposed to ask a prostitute was the only really important question you could ask. I like money, Sigrid said. I like to have money, I very much want the things money can buy. And I don't like working a regular job. With this, I can have my own hours. You understand, I am one of those people who do not belong. In Iceland, we have a saying, *Too smart to be a soldier, and too dumb to be a general.* My father said that is the definition of me.

Here's what I'm curious about. I was seated on the edge of her bed now; I smoothed the wrinkles out of my trousers. Oh! More questions? Haven't I told you enough? You're the kind who wants more than just the body. You want the soul, too? This is why I don't work in an office or for some boss. My thoughts are my own. Of course they are, I almost whispered it, trying to soothe her. I really wasn't trying to *pry*. I wondered if she knew that word, but I couldn't think of another one to take its place. She shoved my shoulder playfully. You can always have a blow job. She pushed her lips out in an exaggerated pucker. She was scrutinizing my face for a reaction, and I hoped I was managing to appear distant and bemused, though I was also aware that a part of me was thinking *I guess I'll go for it*. Her fingers walked along the bedspread, leaped up onto my thigh, and then marched in place. I thought, *I am not going to smack her hand off me. If she unzips me, goes down on me, then so be it*. But now Sigrid's long ivory fingers were walking in reverse, scuttling down the promontory of my thigh, while she tilted her head to the left and to the right. *Welcome to S&M*, I thought. *She may as well be in black leather*. First I put it in my mouth and then I hold your balls. Is that so? I managed to say. Then I give the balls a squeezing. Oh, really? Is that what you'd do? I meant to say it in a teasing way, as if I were one of those people who looked upon desire, sex, and orgasm with a certain amount of world weariness.

There was an urgent knocking at Sigrid's door, angry and entitled. I leaped from the bed, my heart spitting ice. So it was a setup, after all, I thought. However, Sigrid herself looked more than a little frightened, so if it was a setup she didn't seem to be in on it. She also looked strangely helpless, as if the largest part of her instinctively submitted to fate. She just didn't have any fight in her. She clasped her hands together and looked imploringly at me, as if it were up to me to do something. Sigrid? a voice called from beyond the door. It's Mr. Castle. His voice entered the apartment like smoke. Avery? I just heard from your uncle. He left a message. He needs to talk to you immediately.

10

I DON'T THINK I had ever even said the word *minivan* before, and now there I was, sitting in the back of one, for the second time that day. The driver was a young Icelander, a boy about twenty, in jeans, a gray turtleneck sweater, and eyeglasses with turquoise plastic frames that might be worn by a librarian in a distant galaxy. His brown hair was a mass of careless swirls, but his expression was funereal, and when I pulled the minivan door open and stepped into the minivan's warm, leathery-smelling interior, I had the feeling that something terrible had happened. I glanced over my shoulder. Sigrid was three stories up, looking down at me from her kitchen window. She gave me a sad farewell wave, as if we knew each other. And then I saw Castle and Gabrielle, both of them waiting for me inside the minivan. Has something terrible happened? I asked them, closing the door behind me. They were sitting in the third row; I sat in the second.

It didn't sound that bad, Castle said. But I told him I'd give you the message. The kind of person I am, if I don't do it right away, it doesn't get done. Gabrielle was writing figures in a notebook, frowning. She looked at me through the tops of her eyes. I tell him, Lincoln, it can wait. She made a breathy, dismissive noise. Then, turning toward her husband, she said You are going to end up in a clinic, with tubes running in and out of you, and a heart machine. Castle smiled indulgently. I am going to outlive you, my dear. I am going to outlive everyone. Gabrielle's eyebrows shot up, her eyes opened wider. You want me to tell you what you are going to do? You are going to lose fifteen kilos, okay? To me, you are a beautiful man, but you cannot carry this extra weight around because it is killing you.

Gabrielle's worry over Castle keeling over made me think that something had happened to Ezra and they were choosing not to tell me yet. I sat quietly, with my hands folded in my lap, and watched Reykjavik roll past my window. We passed a small park. A couple were holding hands, looking at a small kidney-shaped lake, as if they were waiting for ducks to feed, but there were no ducks. A massive gray church steeple loomed in the distance, carving out an inverted *V* against the steel gray sky. I was sorely in need of sleep, and in my exhausted state I had no defense against anxiety. What would I ever do without Ezra? He's all right, isn't he? I asked Castle. Ezra? Castle said. His eyes were shut, and he was leaning his head against Gabrielle's shoulder, while she continued with her sums. Oh, don't worry about Ezra, he said. He'll bury us all. *Liar!* I thought.

We pulled in front of the hotel. Castle had told me to check my e-mail for a message from Ezra, and I walked quickly through the lobby, to the business center, a little glassed-off section near the elevators, where there were three computers for guests' use. (On my way across the lobby, I noticed Tony Dinato, sitting in a club chair, writing post-cards.) No one was using any of the computers, but even so I had to go through a lengthy and, in my state, practically intolerable sign-in procedure with the hotel employee whose job it was to log guests on and off the Internet.

I had been hoping to go through the tour without making any contact with the outside world. I thought it would be easier that way. I was never much for e-mail anyhow; days often passed without my receiving anything in my online mailbox except for advertisements for pain relief, penis enhancement, cheap mortgages, and computer virus protection. Today, however, there were several messages, from my agent, my new editor, Deirdre, and the real estate agency, too. But I went first to Ezra's.

Kiddo! Heard from your mother. Never more beautiful, I'll give her that. She came all this way without even calling you first, as best I can gather. Pretty nutso, if you ask me. With this type of person you're dealing with extreme unreliability. I told her, Naomi, you've got the body of a young girl; that doesn't mean you've got to have the mind that goes with it. I don't know what she's going to do next. In the meanwhile, I hope you are splendid. I guess it won't come as much of a surprise, but I love the hell out of you.

I sent an immediate reply.

Dear Uncle Ezra,
   I don't know what she's up to. She told me she hated my piece in Esquire and she said she was going to give me hell for it. Where is she now? The most important thing is for her NOT to know what I am—ha ha—doing.
   P.S. Your friend Castle might be the devil. As far as I can see, he doesn't cast a reflection!! Which makes this like The Twilight Zone, with free sex!
Love, Avery

My hands were shaking, and now that I was close to my (as yet unseen) hotel room, the lure of sleep was powerful, but I could not leave without seeing what Deirdre had written to me. It might have been that knock on the head I suffered on Fifty-sixth Street, but I still somehow believed Deirdre could make everything that had happened between us in the past month disappear.

Hi, Avery—are you there yet? If you are, I'll bet you'll be checking your e-mail. You love e-mail and you always need to know if someone out there is thinking of you. (LOL) Anyhow, I wanted to make sure you had something to read—

How dare she assume that I, not twenty-four hours into the trip, would be nervously tapping into the Internet to see if anyone was looking for me. Deirdre's view of me was always a little too bemused for my taste. I found her tone so offensive, my most powerful impulse was to delete to message and then, before I could reconsider, it was done in a keystroke.

There was an e-mail from Resnick and Driscoll, the real estate company Isabelle Rosenberg worked at, and when I clicked it open the note was from her. I was awfully glad to hear from her, though I had to admit to myself that my sense of anticipation upon finding word from her did not match the rush of feeling I experienced when I saw that Deirdre had written, a burst of longing that, even as it passed and disappeared, still left behind a detritus of lust and fury, all the debris of love without the love itself, like a comet will leave traces of the galactic garbage that comprises its fiery tail.

Hi, Avery—Just to let you know that I've asked everyone in the office to stop showing the Perry Street apartment. A colleague wanted to show it to a prequalified buyer, and I said in front of the whole office You can't! That's Avery's apartment! You should have seen the looks on their faces. They don't seem to get it. When we Israeli-Colombian girls see what we want, it's best to get out of our way! Anyhow, I hope you're having a nice trip. You never exactly told to me where you're off to, but I hope you travel safely and have fun. Make sure and call me as soon as you get back so we can get this apartment settled. I can already see you sitting in that beautiful front room, with all that original molding and northern light.
Isabelle.

I clicked on Reply so I could send a message back to Isabelle, though normally I would have spent some time contemplating what to say.

Dear Isabelle,
What a treat to hear from you. Yes, by all means reserve the petite manse of Perry for me—

I was vaguely aware that that petite manse business was a little forced and just maybe a little crazy, too . . .

By the time I'm back, the money will be in place. Then—

I paused for a moment; my fingers hovered over the keys, but they were still moving, as if anxious to get on with their work. I lowered them back into place.

I can have my new apartment, which will be a perfect place to celebrate your handsome commission. I'm thinking salad of hearts of palm and avocado, Chablis, a loaf of Italian bread from Zitos. (Yr not on one of those low-carb diets, are you? You BETTER not be. Don't change a hair for me, not if you care for me, Stay little valentine stay . . .)

I paused again, stared curiously at the screen, as if this message were being composed collaboratively by me and the hotel's computer. And then suddenly something quite gross and lustful seized my mind and I wrote it down just to see it.

How about this? You come over, we drink the champagne, we get a little light-headed, and then you give me a look with your dark eyes and I start kissing you all over, your face, your ears, your neck, and even the palm of you hand, and then you grab my hair and give me just that little bit of encouragement I need, and the next thing I know, I've got my tongue deep in the human honey of your pussy, which I guess from your eyebrows is sublimely hairy, and you are coming so hard your thighs beat against the side of my head, ding dong ding dong.

I sat back in the chair. I was breathing through my mouth and if anyone had been there to see me, I would have looked deranged. I was aroused by my own erotica, like Genet titillating himself in his cell by writing *Our Lady of the Flowers*, only mine was lousy. My fingers continued to wave in midair. *Okay okay, delete*, I said to myself. But instead I clicked SEND, and a heartbeat or two later the little spasm of insanity was on its way to Isabelle.

No, I shouted, grabbing the top of my head with both hands. But how to stop it? There was only one solution: I must disconnect the computer. I fell to my knees and groped chaotically beneath the desk for the plug, but by the time I found it I realized it was too late, if it had ever been possible. I remained under the desk for a few extra moments—it was weirdly relaxing there—and stared at the bristling weave of the carpet. At last, I crawled out again and sat heavily in the chair. In a box at the top of the screen, written in green letters: YOUR MESSAGE HAS BEEN SENT. I sat there trying to imagine just how such a thing could happen—how I could have been so careless, so gross, and how, as well, a few ill-advised lines of smut written in a trance in Iceland could make their way to a computer terminal on Seventh Avenue South, how I had most likely blown my chances for that apartment, and how my finger, one of the least heralded, least respected, least important parts of my body, could commit an act that would plunge the entirety of me into a cauldron of undiluted humiliation.

I FINALLY MADE IT to my room, took another sulfurized shower, got into the bed—I had yet to unpack. I fell asleep fast, like a dog being euthanized. First of all, a dreadful dream about my mother. I'm sitting with her in her Costa Rican apartment. She's as tan as a wallet, wearing a red one-piece bathing suit, with white sunblock smeared on her nose and lips, like she's going to go out surfing. She offers me a drink, in a silly girlish voice, like You want a drinky-winky? And I am somehow offended, and I say No thank you, Naomi. And she takes offense at THIS, that I called her by her name. I'm your mother, you think you could call me Mom? No thank you, Naomi, I say. She's getting angry, and I start saying Naomi Naomi over and over. I am goading her on but feeling horribly frightened at the same time. *She's going to hand my head to me*, I'm thinking, and I start stealing these furtive little glances over my shoulder, just to check on the door, so I can get out of there if I have to. But then, there IS no door. I mean, where there once was a door is a solid brick wall, and someone's knocking from behind it. I wait for my mother to say something, but she gives no acknowledgment that anyone is knocking. She is rubbing her fingers together; they are making this insectlike clicking sound. Click. Click. And from behind the door, bang, bang. Finally, I say Who's there? Shhh, my mother says, and I only say it louder: Who's there??

It's me, a voice said, Sigrid, and by now I was half awake, but still pretty much in the dream, too. Hello? I said. Hello, she said back. And it really was her, not in the dream but in the hotel. I scrambled out of bed, just in my boxers, and I somehow made it to the door without falling on my face. Sigrid? I said, still not sure what was happening. Open up please, I've come to see how you are.

And somehow the sound of her voice dropped like a stone in my dark heavy blood and created a little wave of love. At the time—and I *know* that three-word preamble is often utilized by scoundrels—but, at the time, I somehow believed that Sigrid had come to my room because she actually cared about me, that against all odds and defying all logic there had somehow developed between us a small but real connection. I'm not 100 percent certain I was awake; part of me might still have been in dreamland with my mother and that brick wall. But the next thing I knew, I was fumbling for the lock, opening the door, and when I saw her—dressed in black, with stockings, high heels, as if she was on her way to work, which she was—I reached for her, touched her shoulder, and instead of saying How did you know which room I'm in? or How did you get past the desk? I said Come in, come in, and once she was inside my room I gathered her in an embrace not really any different from one I would give to someone I loved, someone I knew.

As I held her, she moved closer. Tenderness, tenderness, the fragile consolations of tenderness. And it was tender, even though it wasn't real. Elevator music isn't really music, either, but it can trigger memories of music; it can create music in your mind. Out of nowhere seemingly I remembered something I read at least ten years ago written by Karl Barth: Women in their whole existence are an appeal to the kindness of men. Yes, well, how do I say this? The moment she touched me in this provocative way, the resolve I had to get through this trip without becoming Part of the Problem was practically gone.

Sigrid smiled shyly, stepped back. So? she says. Everything is okay? I took her by the wrist and steered her toward the bed. *Am I really going to do this?* I asked myself, but it was like someone had just pitched me off a roof and I'm asking myself *Am I really falling? Am I really getting closer and closer to the ground? Is this really the last moment of my life?*

And so: the bed. It still held the visual echo of my brief sleep, a big fetal dent at the edge of the mattress. I aimed my fall so I filled it again and pulled Sigrid in after me. She laughed merrily, slid next to me with surpassing grace—the way she responded to my tug, the willingness to be pulled into the bed, her responses were exactly as I have always fantasized but have never really experienced. In every other instance in which I have dived or rolled onto a bed and attempted to pull a woman in with me, I have always sensed some little hitch of hesitation, coming either from her desire not to be dominated or from some concern about personal safety, no matter how carefully I have wrapped the whole thing in playfulness. It's always been What are you doing? Or Avery, you're twisting my arm. When I think of all the things I wish were different in my life, I can't help but wish my experiences with women had been a little more joyous, by which I mean a little less fraught. I cannot wholly blame this plodding *seriousness* on the women I have slept with, but, still, I think it would have been possible for someone possessing a measure of erotic anarchy to shake me up and bring a little light to what has on balance been a slightly melodramatic, even morbid, experience. But now, I was with a professional, and holding onto Sigrid and feeling the effortlessness with which she followed me onto the bed was one of the least fraught, most graceful moments of my life, and it struck me that what was in store—or at least *could be in store*—might be a revelation, the way dancing with a great dancer can suddenly reveal you to yourself and from then on you are never again wholly without grace.

I rolled onto my back and casually gathered Sigrid to me. It crossed my mind that her pretty white blouse and black skirt were liable to get wrinkled, but nothing in Sigrid's manner suggested that anything so mundane was on her mind.

And so the grand presumption began.

Because if I knew anything in this world, anything at all, I knew that the contents of Sigrid's mind were not available to me. The inner-Sigrid may have been screaming in rage, My blouse! He is ruining my new blouse! This fucking American baboon, I'd like to scratch his eyes out! Or maybe she was more of the melancholy type, and her mourning for her blouse was more resigned: Oh, there goes another pretty satin blouse. I don't know why I even bother. Everything I touch turns to shit. Or maybe Sigrid was one of those women for whom being with a man, any sort of man, was a reliable source of pleasure, like a veterinarian who works with dogs, dog after dog, sick dogs, shy dogs, snarling, nervous dogs that must be muzzled even to have their ears checked, gassy dog leaking the stench of festering meat, whatever the day brings, all that is certain is there's a dog on the table, there are dogs in the waiting room, and there are more dogs on the way. The doctor may love dogs, but would she treat them without charging a cent? Maybe so, in some earlier period of her life. But not now, now she has become a professional. Spending the day with some thirty dogs, sticking her finger up thirty canine rectums, drawing canine blood, all free of charge? Not possible. Nevertheless, it is no accident that this is how she spends her workday. She loves dogs. And Sigrid loves—or at least *loved*—men, and what better way to make a living than sticking her fingers in us, taking our blood, sending us trotting home with our noses wet and our tails wagging?

She slipped her rough-skinned hand beneath my T-shirt, snuggled closer to me—it was all so affectionate. Or reminiscent of affection. We were in a play about affection. We were in a play about sex. We were in a play called *Irresistible*, I was playing the role of the man exhausted after a long journey—and I was perfect for the part!—and Sigrid had the role of the girlfriend, or the girl, who had a few ants in her pants, and was glad to see me and who wanted to comfort me, help me relax. Of course, I use the word *me* advisedly. It was me, but it was me playing the part of me, and it was me also playing the part of not-me. Similarly, Sigrid was involved in at least as many roles as I was. The psychoanalysts, looking at an ordinary couple, used to ask How many people are in this bed? Well, here we had at least six, maybe eight, maybe ten. Maybe none.

The astonishing thing was you could choose, choose what you knew, choose what you felt, and believed. You entered a state of double and triple thinking. Being in bed with a whore is like being press secretary for a president. You believe his story even when you know it's not true, and you also believe in his right to lie.

I rang down the iron curtain between what I knew and what I wanted to know. One moment, she was clearly and totally a hooker who had come to my room because the whole thing has been prebooked and paid for. An ambitious hooker, or a conscientious hooker, who thought she needed to pick up where we were when Castle came to collect me. But then I felt the weight of her leg as she cozily (or calculatedly) draped it over me, making a seemingly accidental half contact with my genitals, and I also detected a kernel of something sweet in her breath, the last olfactory echo of a sucking candy, or perhaps some breakfast marmalade, and the information that was once so luridly mine—the information that she was a prostitute, a *whore*—was suddenly unavailable to me, was superseded by the flesh and blood of her, and the flesh and blood of me, and some larger universal force of which we were both a part.

I am going to help you relax, she said to me, and she shifted her hips so the contact between us was more emphatic. Before long, my clothes were off and her hand was working me over, and her tough little tongue was banging into my ear with all the oomph and anger of a shoulder trying to break down a door. I couldn't tell if what I was experiencing was Sigrid's sexual gestalt, or if this was just how she kept her autonomy around johns. Maybe she felt some specific irritation with me. I felt unusually hard and at the same time vaguely numb, and then suddenly I was in her mouth and within a minute I ejaculated, wondering, as soon as it was over, *If an orgasm can be bought and sold, then does that make it no more intimate than peeing into a plastic cup?* and, second, *Can I still tell myself I am maintaining my journalistic remove from the tour?*

I decided I could.

I covered my eyes with my forearm and was overtaken by an avalanche of . . . what? Happiness? Far cry. Regret? Not really. Relief? Just trace elements. Ennui? Perhaps, or in other words: Yes. An annihilating boredom with myself, my body, the world. I felt a pubic tug, a little gnat's whine of pain, and I lifted myself up on my elbows, looked down where Sigrid had been at work. She was peeling off my condom. I didn't even know I had one on. Some dazzling whore-craft to roll it on me without my knowing. She gave my cock a little pitty-pat-pat and then she made a wait-right-here gesture and rolled out of bed, smoothing down her skirt, her blouse—these things suddenly mattered to her again. She disappeared into the bathroom, and I waited for her in bed, in my T-shirt but otherwise naked. Who dressed like this? Someone in the movies . . . Oh right: Porky Pig. A few moments later, Sigrid reappeared. She had a warm wet washcloth, and she swabbed the dreck. I scrambled under the covers. How did it turn out that she had kept her clothes on? She asked me if I wanted her to stay or go. I shrugged, turned away. Some terrible mood was coming on, rushing in like darkness. She took this to mean Go, and she started to leave, following the ancient wisdom that one of the things men pay prostitutes for is to get out without a fuss when it's over. But before she was halfway across the room, I said Oh you may as well stay. I had no idea that's what I wanted, but there you have it.

11

AN HOUR LATER, I was awakened by the sound of a single piece of paper sliding beneath the door to my room. I am not a deep sleeper, but I don't know if I have ever before been jolted out of sleep by such crumbs from the sonic table. I scrambled up, my heart pounding, and then I stumbled hastily across the room to read the message, expecting the ill-defined worst. What a relief to see that all it was an announcement of a day trip to the Blue Lagoon. I stood there, holding the sheet of paper, my heart bobbing like a little rowboat lashed to the dock during a storm. Sigrid, too, had fallen asleep. She was a thumb sucker, the first undeniably true thing about her, and as she sat up, she dried her thumb on the bedspread.

Feeling I must experience whatever the tour had to offer, I readied myself to go downstairs. When I told Sigrid I was going to go to the Blue Lagoon, she assured me it was not only beautiful but beneficial to one's health. I asked her if she wanted to come along—I couldn't help myself; I felt close to her and somehow obligated. She said she was happy to make the trip, but it was pretty obvious she wanted to be free to go back to her old life, and down in the lobby she gave me a quick dry kiss and walked away from me, wriggling away with increasing speed, like a trout that has been unhooked and released back into the cool rushing water.

Those of us who were going to the little side trip convened in the Royal's main bar. It was called the Mojita and it was meant to look as if it were some stylishly seedy old place resurrected from old Havana, during the reign of Batista and Meyer Lansky, when whoring, Christianity, and free enterprise were the Cuban style. I was the first to arrive and I sat at the bar. The bartender was a young blond guy with the tattoo of an iguana crawling out of his shirt collar. I ordered a coffee, a club soda, and a glass of red wine—I didn't know what the hell I wanted.

A few moments later, I heard the click of heels, turned on my stool, and saw Gabrielle. She was dressed in khaki pants and a safari jacket, with a silk scarf poofed up around her neck. Where is Sigrid gone? she said, as she slid onto the stool next to mine. Gabrielle was freshly perfumed, though it seemed she had tried on one kind, decided against it, and covered it up with another. Oh, she went home, I guess. What? Gabrielle's voice was sharp with concern, as if I had just told her Sigrid had been rushed to the hospital. She began rummaging through her shoulder bag—out came cosmetics, a calculator, a small biography of Frank Lloyd Wright, and, at last, her cell phone. She flicked it open as if it were a switchblade. Are you going to call her? I asked, to which Gabrielle nodded curtly. Oh, don't, I said. It was my idea. I asked her to leave. Gabrielle stopped. You sent her away? For what problem? There was no problem. I don't need her for sightseeing. Gabrielle held her cell phone, kept it at the ready. There was no problem? She raised her eyebrows inquisitively, frowned. No, I said, she was great. Gabrielle clicked her phone shut, dropped it back into her bag. In French, she ordered a glass of red wine. Then, to me, she said Sigrid is a beautiful young woman. I smiled, nodded. But I think you should have done what Lincoln suggested. You remember? Back in New York? She glanced over her shoulder, making certain we were alone. Didn't Lincoln talk to you about upgrading? she asked. Didn't he offer you the Platinum Membership? With Platinum you get our best girls. Believe me, I said, reaching for the club soda, then the coffee, and finally settling on a sip of wine, Sigrid is all the woman I can handle. The bartender brought Gabrielle's wine. She picked it up, cocked her head at me by way of a toast, and then said All we want is for you to be happy, Avery. It's not rocket surgery.

We sat in silence for a few moments. Then she began pitching me on the upgrade again. One of the men, she said, was not so happy with the girl he chose. It was all to his specification, he saw her, it was Hello, how are you, nice to meet you, come up to my room. But these things are very mysterious. There was no magic. And so he wanted to change. And as a Platinum member he could do this, no problem. I just can't, I said. Anyhow, all the women are great. Of course they are, she said, and patted my arm. But I'm sure Romulus was glad he signed up for Platinum, because as soon as he told us that he wanted a change, we sent up a new girl.

Really? I said. I was surprised that Gabrielle would be so indiscreet, but I did know how to do my job, at that point. What did he want? She answered me without hesitation. Someone more maternal. Older, with the full body. A full body? You mean pregnant? She laughed, patted my arm again. Both she and Castle liked a lot of physical contact. It wasn't enough for them to just talk to you; they had to have access to your skin, as well. Not that full, she said. But, yes, the mother type. To me, it comes as a relief, not to have everyone wanting someone the most crazy young. Do you have motherly types available? I asked. We do our best, she said, with a shrug meant to imply modesty. Why? Do you want someone like that? I shook my head, more emphatically than necessary.

Soon, the others came straggling in, and we boarded a tour bus large enough for seventy passengers, though we were fewer than twenty. A few of the men had taken a pass on the little side trip, opting to use the time for bed rest or more sex. The Metal Men, however, were there, talking animatedly with each other and more or less ignoring the women they had chosen, as was Jordan, who was drifting in and out of sleep, his head tilted semi-lifelessly on the shoulder of his companion, a slouching, gum-chewing girl with bright green hair and an odd spattering of birthmarks on her face. She held his empty sleeve and idly stroked the cuff, like a little girl caressing a stuffed animal while she drifts off to sleep.

I sat next to Romulus. He wore expensive-looking slacks and a sweater that was so soft it could have been edible. When the bus started making its laborious U-turn around the hotel's parking lot, I asked him Everything going well? He made a disgusted face and said Not really.

An old maroon Jeep swung around us. The driver, an athletic, self-sufficient-looking woman in her twenties, had her long bare arm hanging out the window. Romulus craned his neck to get a better look at her and then pointed his video camera at her and did his best to record her as she drove away. Gotcha, gotcha, he said under his breath. When she was well out of sight, he turned back toward me and said I don't care about paying a little extra here or there. But I don't like being hustled. I asked him how he was being hustled, and he rearranged himself on the seat, arched his back, rubbed the small of it, wincing a little. Our friend up there, he said, indicating Castle with his eyes, who was seated with Gabrielle at the front of the bus. Castle seemed to sense he was being discussed. He turned in his seat and looked directly at us, bit his lower lip, pointed, and then turned around again, putting his arm around his wife. Did you see that? Romulus asked. He might have very good hearing, I said. He's got very good something, Romulus said.

We were silent for a half mile or so, schoolboys on a class trip who have just been shushed by the teacher. Finally, motivated by curiosity and a need to do my job, I asked Romulus Did he hit you up for more money? Romulus nodded. He knows what you want, he said in a low voice. And the more you want it, the more he'll screw you.

He turned in his seat to face me more directly. He had a broad, stubborn face, the face of a man who has endured, the placidity of someone not terribly invested in what you might think of him. Look, he said, I've been a businessman since I was ten years old, and I know how to make my profit without sucking the air out of someone's lungs. You do it one transaction at a time, and every transaction is important. Every transaction involves the totality of who you are as a business. My father taught public high school in Bethlehem, Pennsylvania. He made shit money and he was a bit of a snob—but he taught me and my brother to act honorably. This guy? He jutted his chin in Castle's direction. He's churning my account.

So you didn't like the woman they had for you? I asked. She was all right. She certainly had all the necessary equipment. She could have been a model, I guess. Nothing wrong with that, I said. No, there's nothing wrong with that. But . . . Romulus breathed out a long sigh. I'm on vacation, right? So I kind of like to go with the flow, and right now, right now I'm in the mood for someone more my own age, and with a little meat on her bones. You know how they say *A boy's best friend is his mother?* Anyhow, he sent someone new—but not what I wanted. He sent me someone older, but still she couldn't have been more than thirty. I wanted someone my mother's age, not my mother's age now, but her age when I was like twelve.

I laughed, assuming he was kidding, but as soon as the nervous bark was out of me I realized Romulus was as serious as an Oedipus complex. I tried to cancel out my laugh with a few coughs, and then I asked So did Castle have one for you, someone the right age?

He said it would be a little tricky, plus he wants an extra five thousand if he can arrange it. He made a world-weary face, like a guy standing on his front porch who sees that once again the goddamned paperboy has thrown the *Times* into the boxwood hedge. Not that I care, but put this right on the questionnaire, and I would have expected it. One of my lawyers went with Fleming last year; he tells them right up-front that he likes flat-chested brunettes, and that's all he saw. So I figured these people know what they're doing.

It struck me that a lot of things that John Q. Public wanted to do with his dick were forever baffling to me. I'd never been able to get into the spirit, say, of any sexual congress that involved special outfits. Naughty nurse's whites, chambermaid's apron, executioner's hood, cowboy boots, even stiletto heels and garter belts—it all seems awfully goofy to me. It's not that I can't imagine my way into the excitement of these erotic accessories, and if I were to find myself in bed with some-one who needed a bit of rubber, leather, or silk, I suppose I could have accommodated her, get into the spirit of the enterprise. Ditto for hand-cuffs, nipple clips, whatever. But my penis and I, we are a simple people. All we really ever wanted was to go through the mating rituals, without the actual reproductive consequences, and to be adored.

Romulus tepeed his fingers, then tapped them together. The thing is, he said, once a woman's been a mother, she knows how to treat a man; she knows how to give of herself, deeply. He leaned out into the aisle, peered down at Castle, shook his head. I built a very successful company out of nothing. No capital, no backers, just me and my will to succeed.

I asked him what sort of company, though as soon as the question was out I regretted it. I wanted him to talk about sex, not about his business success.

I own CutMax, he said, as if anyone would be familiar with that. We've been selling knives door to door for nearly two decades, and you want to know how many returns we've had in all that time? Under five thousand.

I nodded sagely, not adverse to giving the impression that I knew something about selling door to door and was perhaps something of a connoisseur of the well-crafted knife, as well, but I was really trying to devise a way to get our conversation back to the kind of woman he wanted to pay for.

I don't design them, he said, I don't manufacture them, and I don't retail them. We send the specs out, the knives and our other products get made in China or Santo Domingo, and we pick them up in Philadelphia. Direct sales, door to door. I myself did it, back in Pennsylvania. I sold Christmas cards, magazine subscriptions. When my father was on summer vacations, he sold Kirby vacuum cleaners. Also door to door. America was built on door to door. Was this what I always wanted to do? Hell no. What was my dream? Just to make a good living, nothing fancy. When I was a kid, I used to beat my brains out, trying to come up with some kind of invention. And I almost did. I almost invented Velcro. Same way that Swiss lucky bastard came up with it, too. Walking through the fields, looking down at my cuffs, and seeing all these burrs hanging off my pants. The difference between him and me was he had a lot of family money backing him up. I had a father who could barely pay his own bills and a mother—let me tell you about my mother. I once gave her a little yellow glass necklace I got at Walgreen's, gave it to her on her birthday, and she burst into tears and told me it was the nicest present anyone had ever given her, that piece-of-shit necklace I paid three dollars and twenty-five cents for. She was a hell of a lady, a very special person.

From selling knives door to door, I said, to having all these beautiful women. Not too shabby.

But, despite my little tug on the conversational reins, Romulus wanted to make sure I didn't somehow think it was he himself who was peddling these knives door to door, and as Iceland rolled barrenly by he gave me a history of his company, how it had gone from a hundred-thousand-dollar-a-year company to the fifth largest seller of kitchen wares in the country. Then, abandoning brevity, sparing me, it seemed, no salient detail, he explained how his company's training program worked, how he had figured it out so that the company profited whenever it "hired" new salespeople, all of whom were required to invest nearly a thousand dollars, to cover two weekends of workshops and a sample case of CutMax's best-selling knives. Those who prevailed in the program soon made enough money to justify the initial outlay, the vast majority of hires sold enough knives to relatives and close friends to more or less break even, and the duds went their merry way, though Romulus claimed to believe that even those who failed at knife sales learned enough in their training period to increase their chances of success in some subsequent endeavor.

Meanwhile, we were closing in on the Blue Lagoon.

So how did you hear about Fleming? I asked Romulus, but here the direct approach stiffened him. How did *you?* he shot back, and so I told him about my uncle's connection, which seemed to satisfy him. My West Coast sales manager, he said. He likes to go to Thailand; in fact I think he's planning to move there, at least on a part-time basis. He took me there once, insane holiday. He shrugged, flicked his fingers dismissively. Not really my taste. Half these Thai girls are like boys, and most of them are insane. They talk in singsong and do these fake little dances. He arched his back, reached behind himself, and massaged his left kidney.

Truth is, I should just go home, Romulus said. I've got a fantastic wife. How about you? Are you married? I shook my head NO. I was starting to feel some anxiety over my ability to remember everything he was saying. I struggled against the urge to reach into my back pocket for my notebook.

All right, then, Mr. Question Man, listen, you want to know why I'm here? A couple of weeks ago I'm sitting at home, my wife is asleep. It's maybe midnight, no later. To me, the night's still young. I was in meetings all day with some investment bankers who are telling me they've got someone who wants to buy my company. Not that I want to sell, but you have to take those meetings, you got to know what's out there. So I'm stimulated. I'm jazzed. And to be honest with you, I'm sort of lonely, too. I have a couple of drinks to take the edge off, and the next thing I know I'm in the bedroom. We've got this beautiful bedroom, overlooking a lagoon I built, absolutely gorgeous, we got about twenty Belgian swans in there, and I'm waking my wife up and telling her Hey I can't sleep, and she sits up but *doesn't even take off her fucking sleep mask* and she tells me there's Ambien in the medicine chest, and I tell her—I guess the drinks had something to do with this—that what I really need is a blowie. A blowie? she says, as if she'd never heard of such a thing. A blowie, you want a blowie? She's really trying to make me feel like a loser. I'm used to that. Mary used to be a tennis player, ranked and everything, so she's very competitive, she likes to put people in their place. So I tell her Yeah, a blowie, also doing business as blow job. Is that a crime? Does that make me some kind of freak? I've just spent a day with people who are talking about putting five hundred million dollars in my pocket. You can move mountains with that kind of money. You know what I'm saying? All I'm asking is for her to open her mouth and let me put my dick in. What is the big deal? But forget it. Those days are past between me and Mary. It's not about blame, it's about what it is, and what it is is pretty dead. So there I am, down in my study, drinking my single malt, listening to Steely Dan, and doing the one thing I promised myself I would never do: feeling sorry for myself. It just didn't seem right. I've worked so hard and taken so many chances and so many knocks, and now I'm in a position 99.9 percent of men would envy, and where am I? Up on my hind legs like some yappy little dog, waving my paws in the air and begging my wife for a little pat on the head. Do you see what I'm saying? With all that beauty around me, the grounds, the swans, the art, the live-ins, all the toys I ever wanted, and I'm sprouting a woody and don't have anywhere to put it except here. He showed me his hand, and looked at it himself, with some disgust, as if it were an impostor he has just exposed. It's against nature is what it is. Any other species, the male gets to a certain point of power, he can have all the sex he wants. But I was getting more action when I had six people working for me and the main office was my Honda. To me, that makes absolutely zero sense.

We arrived at the Blue Lagoon. The parking lot, granite gray and moist, was essentially empty, save for a couple of tour buses, a rusty blue Volvo station wagon, and three mud-spattered motorcycles. As we got out of the bus, the chalky Icelandic sky was torn asunder by the screaming roar of a squadron of B–1 bombers, in V-formation, wings swept back, noses jutting forward like pterodactyls craning for a drink over a glacial pool. It was as if death itself was winging over us, a dark miracle of technology. I felt a cold sickness at the core of me, helpless and small, and all I could think of was the payload in those long bellies, and the hell that was going to rain down on whoever our enemies were right now. The Metal Men, however, were catapulted into a kind of instant exuberance at the sight of the B–1s. They clapped their hands and then turned them into fists and thrust them into the pale Arctic air. Hap took out his Sony and pointed it in the air, recording the planes in their flight.

Our pilot used to fly one of those, Castle said to me. He startled me; I thought he was already inside the domelike entrance to the lagoon, arranging our tickets. Castle followed the path of the B–1s with his finger. Those puppies can really move, he said. His voice was full of admiration, crosshatched with sarcasm. It was the voice of a man who had made peace with his appetite for destruction. They weigh almost two hundred thousand pounds, and that's empty. They go about a thousand miles per hour. Something that size? Filled with explosives? Rockwell builds them, with four huge GE turbofan engines. And they've got such fantastic electronics, it makes our plane look like something the Red Baron should be flying. They've got everything from repeater decoy systems to wind-corrected bomb and missile dispensers; they've got situational awareness, automatic terrain-following high-speed penetration, jamming capabilities, and superprecise weapons delivery. He continued to point, though now the sky was empty. *Where are they going?* I wondered to myself.

You know what I love? The names they give them, Castle said, showing me his big gapped smile. *Ol' Puss, Seven Wishes, Global Power, Reluctant Dragon.* I often wonder what my old man would say now that the U.S. rules the sky, the earth, the seas. He's probably spinning in his cockamamie Moscow grave.

Inside the dome that served as the lagoon's entranceway and staging area, we were given bathing suits, towels, and a key to a locker. The men's changing room was dank, poorly lit, with a wet smell in the air just short of mildew. The Fleming men were surprisingly modest as they shed their clothes and wiggled into their swimsuits—gray, vaguely diaperish things that might have been worn in strong-man competitions fifty years ago. We met the women again on a narrow wooden deck built at the edge of the lagoon, where a few other tourists sat at round patio tables, drinking mineral water or beer, and slathering themselves with a thick salty paste, a by-product of the deeply saline waters, meant to accelerate the lagoon's magical properties. Surrounding the milky turquoise lagoon were mineral-rich outcroppings of rock; truly we were in a lunar spa. Vaguely gaseous steam rose from underwater spouts here and there, and a few of the visitors—all men, none of them ours—trudged toward the smoke with zombielike slowness, their bodies caked with white paste.

The clouds, driven by a low moaning wind, raced overhead, blocking out the sun one moment, making way for it the next. The cool rays strobed against the chalky blue water. The waters, always warm, were said to be healing, as if the stuff could actually permeate our skin, mix with our blood, flush out our poisoned, withered organs, go around and around our circulatory system like a squadron of fairies, bestowing new life on the pancreas, the liver, the kidneys, the bones. The women we had come here with were meant to be healing, too, I thought, all these specially chosen creatures Castle had gathered up for us, based on the supposition that regular women—the tap water of the gene pool—were not fine enough for our heightened sexual sensibilities, nor sufficient to cure homeliness, or loneliness, or flickering libido.

This water comes from over a mile deep, Castle said to me. He had a Dixie cup filled with the white paste, which he handed to me. His chest was corrugated with waves of silver and gray hair and his stomach was hard and round, with a long deep scar on the left side and a fuzzy chocolate mole on the right. His legs looked spindly, fragile, hardly able to support him. What is this stuff? I asked. It looks deadly.

He clapped me on the shoulder. You're sort of a worrier, aren't you.

The young wiry woman who was with Jordan was holding his hand and leading him into the phosphorescent glow of the lagoon, while the other women huddled together on one side of the deck, whispering to each other, touching each other on the wrist, the shoulder, like schoolgirls, but without the mirth, without even much energy, exuding, if anything, a certain low-key collective nervousness, which I credited to their general discomfort at being in our company, let alone our intimate company. Jordan and his companion walked through the lagoon until they were waist-high in the weird blue water. It would have been nice if the water could have healed him. A cool breeze was blowing. I hugged myself to get warm. Jordan's girl seemed eastern European, Romanian maybe, or Spanish; she might even have been a Gypsy. She had long, finely articulated arms and wore a dozen or so thin silver bracelets on each wrist; her emerald hair was gathered in back by a maroon scrunchy. Despite her thinness, she moved with a stolid determination, swaying from side to side, as if she learned to walk in a bog.

A few men, not with our group, stood together in the middle of the lagoon. One of them, tan, with a ponytail, and a body that seemed to have gone to fat only recently, had a tattoo of the Virgin of Guadalupe on his back, the long curling dark hairs of which grew through the Virgin's extended hands, her lips, and her eyes. He was watching the girl with Jordan, and his jaw was working back and forth. He was clearly furious about something. One of his friends put a steadying hand on him, and he shook it off impatiently. His friends stepped back a little and nodded sympathetically. One was a heavyset guy with a shaved head who looked like the world's most enormous baby, with a nose like a knuckle and dark little eyes the size of watermelon seeds; then there was a young guy with a long face, who wore an Egyptian ankh and a heavy turquoise and silver bracelet; and the third was a middle-aged man with a Brutus haircut, implacable blue eyes, and a starburst of milky white scars on his shoulder. The four of them walked away from us, going deeper into the water, joining the other men who were trudging as if in a trance toward the spout of smoke coming off the back end of the lagoon.

You'll be a million times warmer in the water than out here, Castle called out. He hopped off the deck and was ankle-high in the thermal drool. He bent down—his chest suddenly fleshy, loose—and scooped up handfuls of water, threw it on himself, his belly, his neck, his underarms.

The lot of us were standing, shivering and uncertain, at the edge of the lagoon, while Castle beckoned us in. I hopped into the water. It felt like liquid silk, soothing yet disquieting. The sun's skittering light reminded me of a lamp behind an immense fan, how the rotating blades continually cut into the rays. The water was completely opaque; I looked down and it seemed as if my legs ended just below the knee. The bottom was cool, with a sleek mineral slide to it, ground-up quartz and shale, milled and remilled of all impurities, a kind of wet talc, soft but unyielding. It didn't have the elemental slurp and ooze of a river bottom nor the evolutionary clutter of an ocean's floor.

Castle, meanwhile, was gesturing ever more energetically, urging his crew into the lagoon. The Metal Men had already ventured in, and Romulus, looking worried, out of his element, like a man whose pride rested squarely on his feeling in control, was dangling one foot in, looking back over his shoulder at the women, whose conference had taken on more and more animation.

I was looking directly at the four other men, for no other reason than they happened to be at the compass point toward which I was heading. The huge angry baby of a man had his hand on the back of the darkest of the quartet, grazing the edge of the hair-pierced Virgin. The man with the scarred shoulders was nodding emphatically. And it was exactly then, with a fateful mental *ping*, that I realized these four guys were hatching a plan, and that the plan was going to involve violence, and that we globe-trotting johns were going to be the object of that violence. These men, I sensed, were either the fathers, uncles, brothers, or lovers of some of Castle's escorts, and they were here to avenge the honor of the women or of their family.

I think we're about to have some trouble, I said to Castle.

Castle splashed some water on me and then feinted left and right, like a boxer daring me to retaliate. I raised my voice, hoping the four men wouldn't hear, though by now they had stopped the Dawn of the Dead slog toward the fountain of steam. They had turned around to openly stare directly at us. There's some guys here, I said. Big angry fucking mean-looking guys. That woman with Jordan? I think one of them is her father or uncle or something.

Despite my alarm, seemingly nothing could stop Castle from jamming the heel of his hand onto the water's surface and launching a gallon or two of it in my direction. I dodged most of it, though a bit of healing water hit my forehead. I don't think you understand, I said. These guys . . .

Yeah, yeah, these guys, Castle said. I've been watching them. I don't think in Iceland we're going to have any trouble. Other places we've gone, we've had little incidents here and there. What kind of incidents? I asked. Well, you know, jealous boyfriends, troublemakers, usually young guys who maybe resent a little that some older Americans come in and scoop up all the most fabulous women. We had that trouble in Prague, once. But Reykjavik has always been smooth sailing. Those guys really look as if they're up to something, I said. Castle shrugged. What am I supposed to do? This is a public place.

Romulus, the Metal Men, Sean Westin, and Jordan were in the water. Most of the women, I noticed, had disappeared. The one who was with Sean, a cheerful-looking girl with frosted pink nails and her hair in ringlets, ran back to where they had been standing, retrieved a towel that had been dropped onto the deck, and quickly made her way toward the changing rooms. There were an awful lot of canaries dropping dead in the coal mine.

By now the four men had disappeared. The spot in which they were standing was taken by an elderly couple, who moved with their arms extended as if trying to keep their balance on a tightrope. They had slathered so much magic mineral salt onto their faces, shoulders, and arms, they looked as if they were prepared for some aboriginal rite of passage.

Jordan, I noticed, had disappeared, too, but then, just as I noted that, he burst through the surface of the water, gasping for breath, his arm flailing. A moment later, the man with the Madonna tattoo rose up as well, grabbing Jordan around the throat and pulling him under the water again. I tried to shout out, but someone gripped my ankles and a gasp later I was upended. The supposedly healing waters were choking me now, rushing up my nose, into my mouth, and all the while I was also being punched in the side of the head, the face. I blindly tried to grab hold of whoever was doing this to me, but my swings were panicked, aimless, as were my kicks. My face was pressed against the lagoon's flaxen floor, and now I was swallowing sand, too. A foot was placed at the back of my neck, at which point this most remarkable fact began to impress itself upon me: someone was trying to end my life.

In some inchoate way, I was never more firmly on my own side than I was at that moment, never more convinced of my right to live, to thrive, to vanquish my enemies. I tried to stand up—in fact, I think I did make it to my feet for a moment—but I was tackled again, and this time he, whoever he was, sat on my back and pressed my head down with his hands. I wondered furiously why no one was coming to my rescue, but something akin to an inner voice had begun to command me, a calm, authoritative voice that instructed me not to waste precious time wishing for intervention when clearly none was forthcoming. *Best to twist away if you can, he'll lose his balance*, the voice suggested. It was urgent but calm, this voice; if I had been a different sort of man, I might have mistaken it for the voice of God. I managed to twist away and my attacker floated off of me, but not before pummeling me with his heels and clawing at me, as well—he caught the inside of my ear, which promptly began to bleed, sending a latticework of red threads into the milky blue water. Then the idiot bastard sat on me again. This time he'd figured it out a little better; he was more centered. It felt as if the weight of a grand piano had been placed on me. I felt flattened out, and now it seemed that I wouldn't be able to get him off of me, which awakened in my dying heart not a sense of panic, or even any particular urgency, but a great sonorous sadness. Poor Avery. Drowned in Iceland, of all places. Somehow, even riding the downward trajectory of this sur-rendering self-pity, I found the strength to corkscrew my upper body and grabbed onto the hard hairy leg of the murderous man on top of me. I don't understand how women can tolerate having a man on top of them; it's really unpleasant. I sank my teeth into the hairy softness of his thigh, biting down with all my savage strength. I heard his muffled and distant howl through the water, and I continued to bite and even grind my teeth back and forth to maximize the pain I was causing.

A moment later, his weight was off of me, but I didn't ease up on my bite. I was on my knees now, still chewing away at my attacker, who was pounding on my back and screaming, grabbing my hair, trying to work his fingers into my eyes. I tasted his blood spurting into my mouth, salty and oily, abhorrent. Even as he attempted to gouge out my eyes my attacker was trying to get away from me, and I opened my jaws, let him go, just as one of the Metal Men grabbed me under the arms and pulled me up.

A little greasy circle of blood was around me, round as a lifesaver.

Castle was helping Sean, who was hyperventilating and bleeding from the nose.

What passed for security in this place, a stocky girl with Heidi pigtails, a teenage boy with acne on his back, and the grizzled old veteran of many long dark winters who sold us our admission tickets, had finally arrived, but when the man with the Madonna tattoo and his band of vigilantes scrambled out of the water, and onto the deck, the lagoon's employees made no attempt to apprehend them, and when they hurried off, through the warming house, past the changing rooms, down the long windowless corridor leading to the entranceway and the parking lot, no one made an attempt to slow them down, no one followed after.

In my little group, there was chaos, everyone speaking at once. And how not? We had been attacked! By madmen! Someone took our measure and wanted to do us a great deal of harm, not only to terrorize but to annihilate us. Jordan's injuries, Romulus's long lonely nights, Sean's essential good nature, my nights on the sofa, my having refrained from actual intercourse with anyone in Iceland—all of it meaningless to them. These men had come here with the sole purpose of inflicting pain on us, making us suffer, perhaps even taking our lives. And not only that; they had gone to the trouble of driving out to this otherwise deserted lagoon, paid their admission, gotten their little tickets, had their tickets torn, walked into the changing room and put on their trunks, and then waited in the so-called healing waters for who knows how long for us to appear. How they must hate us! All that trouble, all that inconvenience, not to mention the risk. The vehemence and single-mindedness of their hatred whipped us, its collective object, into a frenzy; we were all speaking at once, overgesturing, turning this way, that way, pointing here, there, no there, there, no there, *there for Chrissakes*, not really making that much of whatever cuts and bruises we had incurred, anesthetized as we were by the adrenaline rush.

As for me, the taste of blood was still in my mouth. I waded back into the lagoon, cupped a handful of the healing waters, and shamelessly squished it around my mouth and spat it out. And as the pinkish stream splashed into the lagoon, I felt not only the bright shining exhilaration of having survived but an almost equal happiness that at least a few pages of my book had just, for all intents and purposes, written themselves. This was better than finding fifteen Airedale pups sleeping in a urine-soaked cardboard box in a puppy mill in Concord calling itself Longacre Meadows; this was better than that moment in the Florida retirement community when I happened to be having lunch with the president of the owners' association and his wife walked into the kitchen wearing a bright turquoise terrycloth robe and tearfully informed him that their drug-addicted nephew, who had been staying with them over the past few days, had disappeared with all of her jewelry.

Castle was not saying much. He was stroking his chin and gazing out at the ring of lunar peaks surrounding the lagoon. He looked haggard, unlucky, like a gambler staring at the roulette table after all his chips have been raked off. He was calculating his losses.

12

YOU WOULD HAVE THOUGHT getting out of Iceland as soon as possible was an easy decision, even if it did suggest we were capitulating to the men who had terrorized us at the Blue Lagoon. But for the men who hadn't been with us, who had skipped the side trip, probably because they were having too much fun with the women they had chosen, the idea of heading on to our next stop without fully exhausting the time that had been allotted for Reykjavik was completely unacceptable. Even when Castle and Gabrielle assured the group that Oslo would be every bit as pleasurable as Reykjavik, a few of the guys continued to grumble, though, really, it was mainly Webb Doleack. Well that's fucking ridiculous, he said to the group, which Castle had convened in one of the Royal's conference rooms. If you'd been there, Sean Westin said, and seen those animals. But Doleack was not one to be reasoned with. If I'd been there, I guarantee you none of that shit would have gone down. He shook his head, clearly meaning that those of us who had weathered the attack had not been able to sufficiently defend ourselves, which amounted to not only a failure of nerve and will but a kind of national disgrace.

What about finding those monkeys and teaching them a lesson? Doleack asked the group. It didn't strike me as much of an idea; I was chewing gum to get the taste of blood out of my mouth. But Linwood, who hadn't really been hurt but whose pride was injured—only he knew for sure what cataclysms of fear he felt back in the blue water—went along with Webb's plan. We could contract it out, he said. There must be all kinds of people who we could give a few hundred bucks to, and they'd gladly take care of the whole thing.

Okay, then, gentlemen, Castle said, ignoring both Doleack and Linwood, we will meet in the main lobby at eight o'clock this evening, and we shall be in Oslo in time for iced vodka, smoked salmon, and . . . other delicacies.

Gabrielle raised her hand. May I say something please? Of course you can, my dear. Castle made a low sweeping bow. The important thing, she said, is we are all okay and now we go on our way. I want to tell you gentlemen how great you all are being. As she spoke, Castle stroked his chin and nodded his head in agreement. You are the most fantastic group ever, without doubt. With this incident, it's been a challenge—but also an adventure. At this, Castle nodded even more vigorously, though there was something frozen in his smile, and Sean, who was standing next to me, singsonged out of the side of his mouth, Someone feels a lawsuit coming on. And so, Gabrielle continued, we enjoy these last two hours and a half here, and then off we go quickly to Norway for the best time yet. And as a very special promotion, Lincoln has arranged—she glanced at Castle and he put up four fingers—four brand-new companions for any of you who would like to meet someone new before we leave to Oslo. Isn't that great? To which one of the Metal Men shouted back That's great, Gabby, but we're still going to sue your ass. There was general laughter, and Gabrielle—Gabby? when did *that* happen?—gave him the thumbs-up.

Do you call her Gabby, too? I asked Sean, to which he shrugged, nodded. Jesus, I said, it's like with Jordan, everyone's calling him Jordy. And that's a problem? Sean asked.

Gabrielle had her hands up in the air. Her confidence about addressing the group was increasing, and she was one of those people for whom an increase in confidence meant speaking more loudly and gesturing broadly. Would you like to see your new companions? she called out. Are you all ready to take a look at the new recruits Lincoln and I have brought in for you? The response to her urgings was a little flat, though agreeable. A few Yeahs and a scatter of applause. Len Cobb, standing behind me, clapped his hard hands together. They made a loud, hollow sound, like a basketball bouncing in an empty gymnasium.

I was standing next to a compact man with a small sunburned nose and close-cropped colorless hair. He looked like a farm implements salesman or, what he in fact was, a pilot whose career hadn't quite gelled, probably because of personal difficulties—alcoholism, contentiousness. Bring them in already, for Chrissakes, he said softly. Don't make such a big production out of it. He wore a blue jacket with white piping and a little pair of silver wings pinned over the breast pocket. He was freshly shaved, and the tang of his aftershave lotion mixed with the smell of beer on his breath. I'm Beau Clark, he said, I'm your pilot, and that little sonofabitch over there—he pointed to another smallish man, standing next to Piedmont—is my brother Francis, who's flying with me, though if you were to ask him he'd say I was flying with him. Oh, I see, I said, extending my hand. Well, thanks for the ride. You're very welcome. Pretty good plane they've got us on? I asked, as if I might have a special interest in and knowledge of aviation. Oh, the plane's great, he said, with a bit of teasing in his voice. I like to bust Linc's balls, but you want to know the truth? I nodded. Truth is, flying Fleming is always a good experience. The clientele. *What about the clientele?* I wondered. But that's all he said: the clientele, as if the men who came on these tours were legendarily great guys. And from a flying viewpoint, he said, not only do you get well-maintained equipment, but it's basically a series of short hops with plenty of down time in between. Sounds great, I said, though I noticed he didn't say new equipment, but well-maintained, which suggested fairly old machines, lovingly tinkered over and kept aloft.

Oh, it's great, all right, he said, make no mistake about that. My brother and I will always be grateful to Mr. Castle. He took a chance on us when no one else in the industry would. Beau then watched with obvious pleasure as the color fled from my face, and then he laughed and gave me a playful bop on the shoulder. You should have seen your face, he said, and then, calling out to his brother, he said Hey, Francis, how you doing over there? Francis gave him a little salute, and then

Beau pointed up at the ceiling, which I took to mean they had to begin making preparations—but for what? The upcoming flight to Norway or a bit of debauchery? Francis tapped the face of his watch, nodded, and moments later the two brothers walked out of the ballroom together.

Soon after Beau and Francis were gone, the door opened again and the four previously unviewed Icelandic women came in. I felt some terrible mixture of despair and quickening interest. They marched in single file, like four waitresses coming in for the dinner shift. The first in line, who could not have been more than twenty years old, with some childish plumpness still in her heart-shaped face, waved at the men with a kind of hyper vigor, like someone in a rowboat signaling for help. A few of the men waved back at her. It was all a bit of a joke. She stretched her mouth into a large, comic smile, which looked half a parody of happiness and half a grimace of fear. As to the other women—the first in a busily patterned pantsuit, with a sensible haircut and the soft sorrowful gaze of a hospice volunteer; the second gaunt in a dark blue dress, worn with fishnet stockings and square-toed shoes; and the third, with powerful calves and heavy thighs, in an absurdly short denim skirt— they each had the air of someone who knows her time is being badly used, but who is required to go through the motions nevertheless.

Dr. Gordon had his hand on Jordan's arm and was pushing him to the edge of our group. Jordan's resistance was undercut by his fealty to his father's commands. Come on, Dad, he was saying. I'm okay with how it is now. Don't be absurd, Dr. Gordon said, his voice shimmering with scorn. She was in on it, and you know it. He shook his son's arm. Now, look, that young one there, you see her? You better make a move before someone else snaps her up. Dad, Jordan pleaded. But Dr. Gordon gave him a shove, and Jordan stumbled toward the women.

Okay, gentlemen, two more hours, Castle called out, and then we meet right here, bags packed. An irritating edge of bossiness had crept into his voice, and I thought to myself *He's used to failing.* The men began dispersing, and suddenly I was the only still point in a sea of activity. I wasn't quite sure what was happening. Were the women already upstairs? How did the other men know who was to go where, and when? Where had I been when all these arrangements were being made? I drifted toward the exit, hoping that Sigrid would and would not be waiting for me in my room. The couple hours of sleep I had managed to get since landing in Iceland, rather than refreshing me, had only created a dark backdrop against which the glittering multifaceted diamond of my exhaustion could be displayed. Regardless, I thought it might not be the worst luck in the world if I were to find Sigrid, bathed and perfumed, propped up with a book in my bed, with the covers drawn chastely up to her breasts . . .

But Castle called out to me before I was out of the conference room and when I turned toward the sound he waved me over with proprietary urgency. All I could manage by way of resistance was a sigh and a frown, but beyond that, delay seemed an exercise in sheer pointlessness. This trip was not quite so gratis as Uncle Ezra had implied, but then again nothing in this sad and beautiful world comes to us free of charge, free of complications or obligations; even the milk we drink from our mother's breast comes with a bill that we are eventually meant to pay.

That was a hell of a thing you did back there, Castle said, draping his arm over my shoulder. The biting? I said, showing my teeth, trying to make light of it. Look, the most important thing here, Avery, is that whatever happened back at the lagoon—and I can promise, by the way, that I'm never bringing another group to that place, that place is nuts—the whole thing stays there, we lick our wounds, we learn our lesson, and we move on. I need you to be my eyes and ears on this one, kiddo. Okay? I don't want the guys getting involved in vigilantism. And we sure as hell can't have them throwing their money at some local goons to take care of things. You understand? *Of course I understand,* I thought. *I speak English. What's not to understand?* I was slightly sickened by my own ill temper; I was poisoning myself.

A woman in a beige dress and an apron came in with a vacuum cleaner. She might have been Indian or Pakistani. She cast a brief apologetic look in our direction and then started the machine, which, in the empty conference room, seemed as loud as a jet engine. Castle was forced to practically shout. The thing about these guys is that they think they can buy justice, or payback, or whatever they want to call it. They think they can buy anything.

I knew I was tempting fate and could possibly get myself thrown off the tour, but I could not help but ask, So tell me, are there things you think money *can't* buy? Castle waved me off. Oh please, that's a childish question. There are so many things money cannot buy, I don't want to waste my time or yours enumerating them. Castle brushed coppery wrist hair away from the face of his watch and checked the time. Okay, see you back here in one hour and fifty-two minutes. Are you packed? I shook my head no. The cleaning woman vacuumed a coin up, and it rattled around in the hose; she stared at the canister, as if wondering if she should open it up and retrieve the coin, but then she sighed unhappily and continued moving the head of the vacuum cleaner over the dark blue carpet, back and forth, steadily, as if she were rolling paint. Then you should pack. You'll see, once we're in Norway you're going to be really, really happy. Trust me, I know. I've got an instinct for these things, Avery.

I just have a few things to put in order, I said. It won't take ten minutes. Great. Then you have time to enjoy yourself right here. Castle put up a finger, tapped it thoughtfully against his chin. Sigrid, right? Yes, Sigrid. May I ask you how she is? I noticed she didn't come with you to the Blue Lagoon. She's fine; she's great. No complaints. Then you find her satisfactory? I wondered why Castle was essentially asking the same question. She's great, I said, careful to keep my tone noncommittal; she's an interesting person. I'll be honest with you, Avery. I came very close to discontinuing Sigrid, though I personally find her to be a very nice person, she takes terrific care of herself, and she's the kind of girl you can have an actual conversation with. Why were you going to fire her? Castle smiled and pointed at me, with that annihilating joviality you find in salesmen. That's something I'm not going to talk about, he said. But did you get a look at Magdalena? There's nothing about her not to like. She's with Lenny, and they're having a ball. And the Metal Men? Oh man, the Metal Men are over the moon. One of them, I won't say which one, told me that this has been hands down the greatest experience of his life. Here's a guy, good looking, young, absolutely loaded, with all the opportunities any man could want, but he's never been with such a beautiful, talented girl before, someone whose only focus is to make him extremely happy. You think that when some animal is having sex he's thinking *Oh, I hope she doesn't think this or I hope she doesn't want that?* No, they're just doing it, my friend, they are in the moment, like

Zen masters. Isn't it funny that when a woman wants to criticize a man, she'll say He's a dog. You know what I say to that? I say I only wish, but thank you anyhow, I appreciate the compliment.

And Tony? Castle said, smiling, shaking his head, as if now we were going to discuss some lovable eccentric, about whom we both had had occasions to worry in the past, but who now was giving every sign of being out of the woods. Tony is winning that lottery over and over; that, my friend, I can promise you. People ask me where the satisfactions come from in this line of work. You want to know where? The Tonys of this world. Look, I'm not saying anything about him that he wouldn't—and hasn't—said about himself, but his life until now hasn't exactly been a grand buffet of pleasures. I'll tell you something, if Tony needs to engage the services of an escort, I am really glad he came to me and didn't take his chances on the so-called open market, because there he would most likely be cheated, disrespected, and overall eaten alive. Guys like Tony, they come into a bit of money and figure Well, it's now or never, I want to have this experience; just like people want to go to the Louvre or see Angel Falls, they want to experience some of the wonderful things, things that may have been denied them over the course of a difficult life. They want to taste the sweetness of life. But if the Tonys try to do it on their own, most of the time they spend just cooling their heels in some overpriced hotel suite, or ending up with some hard-as-nails street hooker and having a depressing experience. Where's the justice in that? What did Tony ever do to deserve to be treated like that?

The listening aspect of my job was proving, for the moment at least, to be more than I could manage. I felt trapped with Castle, which made me long to be in my own room, the thought of which created a surge of ancillary longing for Sigrid, which may have been Castle's aim all along.

At last, I extricated myself from Castle's moist verbal embrace. In the lobby, waiting for the elevator, I felt none of my previous self-consciousness about the hotel staff, and what they might be thinking about me: did they think I was one lucky bastard or the scum of the earth or some marginal man who had to pay thousands of dollars for what most people enjoyed as freely as they enjoyed the sunlight or the sight of children happily playing in the park? All of these nervous thoughts about the desk clerks and the bellhops, the restaurant staff and the bartenders and the cleaners and the waiters and the cooks and the handymen were subsumed by my anxiety that at any moment Castle would come hurrying out of the conference room with yet one more thing to say. I watched the numbers count down on the lighted display above the elevator doors, and when the doors slid open I darted in and stood off to the side, with my back against the wall, hoping to make myself invisible should Castle come into the lobby before the doors slid shut.

The elevator stopped at the next floor. The doors opened to a young woman with short reddish blond hair and broad shoulders. I recognized her from the breakfast buffet and, as far as I could remember, she had gone off with Michael Piedmont, which may have been exactly what she had wanted, if she had been tipped off about how supernaturally rich he was, though there was, of course, a chance that she had viewed him with horror and alarm, seeing only a man in his early forties who had committed an act of self-vandalism so extreme that it was difficult for him to walk, whose body was desecrated by a kind of long-term feeding frenzy to the point that anyone having relations with him was facing the prospect that even the most gingerly pursued sex act could lead to a heart attack or stroke, after which she might find herself trapped beneath the landslide of him, gasping for air.

She pushed the button for the third floor, even though it was already lighted. She moved as far from me as the elevator car would allow. It was as if even proximity to a man was something she chose to avoid when she was off the clock. We arrived at the third floor. I waited for her to get out, and then I followed behind her at what I hoped would be perceived as a respectful distance. She stopped at Room 340 and knocked lightly. It's me! Her voice was girlishly airy, not entirely real. Piedmont wasn't about to come racing to the door to let her in and so she was still standing in the corridor when I walked by, and I may have passed a little too close to her. Fuck off! she said. Creep. I could think of nothing to say, no way of striking back, no way of ameliorating the insult. I cast my eyes down and hurried toward my room; my face was burning. I heard the door opening behind me, heard Piedmont's wheeze, and then the woman said Oh God, what's been going on in here? Look at this place!

I unlocked my room door with the electronic key, but someone—it had to be Sigrid!—had fastened the security chain, stopping the door after six inches. Hello, I called, and Sigrid's voice answered Avery, is that you? Icelandic women knew little about safety. You don't say Avery, is that you, you don't give away the name; a bad person at the door could so easily say Yes, it's me. But then I wondered *Maybe it is, maybe it is a bad person at the door.*

Just then, the door across the hall opened. Len Cobb was standing there, immense and totemic, covered only by a bath towel wrapped around his waist. Other than the couple of corkscrews of hair in the hollow of his chest, his skin was smooth and seemed to radiate an inner glow. His knees, however, were a mass of scars, wormy pink welts. Hey, come in here for a sec, would you? Cobb waved me in, while checking up and down the corridor for anyone else who might be around. His eyes were reddened, as if he had been drinking or weeping. I was just, um . . . I pointed to my door, which was being unlatched and opened by Sigrid, whose dark hair was slicked back and who looked kind and cozy in one of the terry cloth bathrobes supplied by the hotel. Just for one sec, okay? Cobb said. I need some help.

He wanted my help in opening his minibar. I angled around the bed, stepped over a pair of pants that had been dropped onto the floor, as well as a sports bra, and a pair of women's underpants about the size of a false mustache, and then I crouched in front of the mini-bar, which was in the cabinet beneath the TV. A nearly naked round-faced woman with curly blond hair sat on the edge of the bed with a small towel on her lap. She hadn't bothered taking off one of the sleep masks that had been in the complimentary toiletry bags Stephanie had given each of us on the plane. Who have you brought in here? Cobb's girl wanted to know. Is he going to video us? It's just a friend; he's going to get this damned minibar open. That's right, I said, in what I hoped was a reassuring tone. The pliable little key to the minibar was in the slot, and it had been twisted practically into an *S* shape. I think I turned it the wrong way, Cobb said, in a worried voice, as if he had just run over a cat. He massaged his forehead with his long fingers. Oh man, he said to me, softly, did you ever miss someone so much it's like you're going crazy?

The woman on the bed lifted her sleep mask. Her blue eyes were cool and inexpressive. You're with Sigrid, yeah? I nodded yes. *They don't miss a trick.* I finally got the key out of the hole and did my best to bend it back into some approximation of its former shape. I don't think this is going to work, but we can give it a try, I said to Cobb. I'm so hungry, the woman said, rubbing her tummy. The little joke dislodged her towel, but she didn't seem to mind, or notice. Her heavy thighs were pressed tightly together; her pubic hair grew out in long arcing swirls. I slowly worked the key back into the hole. What could be in that cold box that would be worth all this trouble? Cobb picked up the towel and tossed it back onto his companion's lap. For God's sake, he said. I slowly wiggled the key back and forth until the lock tripped and the door opened. Inside was an assortment of soft drinks, Scandinavian beers, chocolate bars, nuts, sugar wafers, breath mints, and dollhouse bottles of liquor. Voilà, I said, standing up. The girl tucked her hair behind her ears, sat straighter, a look of concentration on her face; she took eating rather seriously. I will like a bag of M&M with peanuts inside. She stuck out her hand, but I knew it wouldn't be politic for me to give candy to Cobb's girl.

At that moment, Sigrid walked in. Why are you in here? she wanted to know. She was in platform shoes, a bright turquoise sweater, white jeans, and her hair was plaited into pigtails. Alarming swaths of bright pink scalp. Cobb turned his camera on her and began recording her. I am waiting for you in your room, Sigrid said, looking away from the camera. Hello, Sigrid, the girl on the bed said, and Sigrid said Hello, Magdalena, and then Magdalena got off the bed and the women kissed each other on either cheek. Magdalena, not noticeably concerned that she was the only one in the room naked, squatted down in front of the minibar and took not only the M&Ms but a bottle of Perrier and a Twix bar.

I should be with you, Cobb said to Sigrid. How tall are you anyhow? She said I don't know, in the way you measure. Do you know the metric system? Fuck no, he said. Good old American feet and inches. She stood next to him. She took the camera out of his hand and tossed it on the bed. The top of her head came up to the groove between Cobb's chin and his lower lip. His dark eyes widened. You're tall, he said. She pointed down at her shoes, not wanting to be given credit for the inches they added. He took her by the shoulders, turned her around, and looked at her from behind. Sigrid was looking directly at me now, and her expression was slightly offended, but in a good-natured way, as if Cobb was a joke we were sharing and she were saying Can you believe this guy? Magdalena sat on the bed and emptied the bag of M&Ms into her hand.

How about we trade? Cobb said to me. It seemed a barbaric idea, and, frankly, I would have much rather spent this last time in Iceland with Sigrid, if only because I sort of knew her, and now, with a degree of comfort, or at least familiarity, I was starting to piece together a series of questions I could ask her. Yeah, we should trade, Cobb said, his voice becoming more animated, let me hang out with . . . He pointed at Sigrid, and she supplied her name. You can come back next time, she said, and you can tell Mr. Castle you are requesting me. There's not going to be a next time, Len said. Why don't we work this out right now? How about this? he said to Sigrid. Avery can scrimmage with Magdalena and I stay with you. Why don't you ask Avery? Sigrid said. Me? I cried out, pointing to myself. I'm not the boss of anyone. But can we just trade people as if they were slaves? Hey, Cobb said, taking offense, I was traded six times. Does that make me a slave?

Magdalena finished the last of the M&Ms and said For extra money, we can all do it together. No way I'm doing a four-way, Cobb said. Magdalena was unfazed by his refusal. Just two thousands of dollars, she said. No, Magdalena, Cobb said, no, you and I, no more. One thousand, Magdalena said, lifting one finger and then moving it back and forth like a metronome. Cash. She rocked back on the bed and then sprang to her feet. She skipped across the room, collecting her clothes, humming to herself.

Just then, Tony knocked on the half-open door to Cobb's room and let himself in without waiting for an answer. He wore only a pair of yellow terry cloth shorts and a pair of flip-flops. He was breathing shallowly, and his delicate fingers moved in the air in front of him. Oh Len, I'm sorry, but there is something happening in Webb's room. I hear the most terrible sounds coming through the wall, and when I knocked on the door, Webb said Go away and when I said Is everything okay? he said Get the eff away or I will effing kill you.

Eff? Magdalena looked to me for an explanation. What means eff? It means the letter *f*, as in *fuck*, but Tony doesn't want to say *fuck*, I said. He'll pay to do it, but he won't say it. Hey, you know what? Tony moved closer, and pointed his finger at me. You don't know what I'm about. If you did, you'd be very surprised. For a moment, it seemed as if I was about to have my second physical altercation of the day. This was by far the most violence I had known since that stretch of childhood under the rule of my third father. If only I had exercised that newfound capacity for physical confrontation back then, everything in my life might have turned out differently. I realize this might be one of those fatal errors built into standard-issue masculine mental equipment, but still I could not help but think if I had even once knocked Norman Blake back on his ass—oh, what a world that would have been!

Now, however, my back ached from the violent twisting at the Blue Lagoon, and—though this may have been my imagination—I still had the taste of blood in my mouth. Despite the theory that my life could have turned out better if I had been more willing to mix things up physically, at this point I would rather have rolled over than thrown a punch. Look, man, I'm sorry. Can we just drop it? Tony nodded, lifting his chin, pressing his lips together, with a manly implied smile. What about it, guys? Cobb said. Can I get a little privacy here?

But his privacy was only further violated by the entrance of Jordan, who came hurrying in, along with his new companion. He was able to get the youngest girl after all. She wore a hotel bathrobe and her eyes pulsated with fright; Jordan was in his blue Oxford cloth shirt and his Brooks Brothers boxers. His left leg, like his face and neck, was covered in burns that rose off of him like mountains on a topographical map. Webb's gone crazy, he said. He's got his girl by the back of the neck, and he's running her up and down the hall. I think he's going to smash her head into the wall. Sigrid gestured impatiently while she said something in Icelandic to Jordan's girl—I guessed it was something along the lines of You saw this and you let it happen?—and then she said to me, We better see what is happening here. He's with Enir, she's my cousin. And my friend, added Magdalena.

Please stay here, I said. This guy's pretty tightly wound. Magdalena finally had her clothes on, which was a relief. I could not bear her nakedness anymore. It was simply too sad, the whole thing was, these women, the tour, the world.

Tony followed me into the hotel corridor. It was empty and strangely silent. Maybe on the other side, Tony said. There was something priestly in his personal scent: incense, candle wax, angry little secrets. We could walk around. I nodded and then asked Do you want to stop in your room and get some pants? Tony looked down at his terry cloth shorts, shrugged. I got these at Saks Fifth Avenue, in New York, and I chose them for their versatility. You can sleep in them, but you can also go out in public. You really can't, I wanted to say.

By now Jordan and Len were out in the corridor. Maybe he brought her back to his room, Jordan said. We should call Castle, Len said. If Webb's flipped his shit, it's up to Castle. Right? It's his baby; he's got to rock it. But even as Cobb spoke, we could see Doleack coming around the far corner near the service elevators, strolling in a relaxed way with Enir, who was nodding agreeably while Doleack held forth on some subject, counting off conversational points on his fingers.

At first Webb didn't notice the four of us standing outside Len's room, but when he did his expression changed from a kind of snarl to one of ostentatious forbearance, as if he was going to give us a moment to explain ourselves and then attack us with everything he had. He took Enir's arm and quickened his pace, until he was standing before us, at which point a smile crossed his face like a scratch mark across glass, and he said I presume you gentlemen are looking for me. His eyes went from face to face, ending at Jordan, where they fixed and hardened. He had not allowed himself to be drawn into the collective pity and protectiveness the others felt toward the injured boy, that much could be said for him. He treated everyone equally.

You know what I never heard about, he said to Jordan, putting his hand on his shoulder. What the hell happened to you. The U.S. Army happened to me, Jordan said, glancing at Doleack's hand, but doing nothing to dislodge it. I was trying not to look at Enir. There was a quality in her face that touched some chord of pity in me, and I was reminding myself that pity was one of those things we were no longer meant to feel, pity had somehow undergone a transformation from what decent people were meant to feel when others suffered into a form of condescension, and a rather convenient transformation, at that, for those who were not suffering or not exactly decent.

So you were a soldier, Doleack was saying. Mind if I ask you what a nice . . . Doleack paused, made something of a show of looking Jordan up and down. Oh, let's say upper-middle-class boy like you was doing in the military? Just trying to do the right thing, Jordan said. Then as now, then as now. Really? That's very admirable. Judging from your father, I'd guess it doesn't exactly run in the family, military service. Dad served, Jordan said. We all do our part. He just had better luck than me. So what happened to you? Doleack asked—his tone practically demanded an answer. But Jordan just shook his head. Bad luck, he said. Pure and simple. Doleack nodded. The answer seemed to satisfy him.

So? he said. What are you guys doing out in the hall? Some kind of powwow? We all traded glances. I think you know, Jordan finally said. No, I don't. Bring me up to speed. We were wondering if you were having some kind of trouble, I said. Trouble? Webb looked at Enir, whose eyes were lowered. What kind of trouble? Well, I said, if you're not having trouble, then it doesn't really matter. We don't need to spend time talking about nothing. No, I'm interested, Doleack persisted. What kind of trouble did you think I was having?

You had your girl by the back of the neck, Jordan said, and you were running her around. Really? Was I? Is that what you saw? Doleack moved his face close to Jordan's. But Jordan did not back away, nor did his voice betray the slightest fear. Fuck you, Webb, he said. You can't scare me. I'm a suicide bomber. You think I care what happens to me? Then Len Cobb did that thing men do for each other when they are trying to save a guy from being beaten: he put his arms around Jordan and held him fast, as if Jordan, even missing an arm, was a wild man who must be somehow prevented from doing Doleack grievous harm. Jordan struggled against Cobb's grip, but Len was too strong. I felt something ought to be done about Doleack, but I didn't want to try and pin his arms down. Instead, I inserted myself between Jordan and Doleack and thrust out my arms, as if I were directing traffic and the two men were trucks on a collision course.

Doleack looked at me appraisingly. His eyes were like antifreeze. He seemed to have something in mind, a response to my efforts at peace-making, a few choice words to send my way, or perhaps something a little more forceful, but before Doleack made his move something caught my eye, a glimpse, an image as sudden and piercing as a dart. I lowered my arms, put one hand on top of my head, and stumbled backward a step, another. I was so manifestly stunned, so visibly poleaxed, so violently and vertiginously thrust into a world that made even less sense than the one I had been inhabiting since stepping inside the Fleming waiting room back in Westchester, that all of them, Doleack, Jordan, Cobb, Tony, Sigrid, Enir, and Magdalena, were aware that something strange had just happened, though none of them would have guessed that I had just seen, turning the corner and heading toward the east wing of the hotel, my one and only mother, followed by a wild-haired bellboy wheeling her sky blue valise.

13

IT TOOK MORE than riding the minivan to the airport, more than being whisked through immigration, more than reboarding the Fleming jet, more, even, than watching the tarmac speed past the oval window while the pilot taxied onto the runway for me to feel safe in the knowledge that I had, indeed, eluded my mother and was, at least for the time being, safe from her. I wasn't sure what I was so afraid of—it was more of an instinct, really—but it took being fully airborne for me to even begin recovering from the shock of seeing Naomi in the hallway of the Royal, and even as the plane, which seemed like a thing gone wild, climbing at an unusually fast speed, with something frantic in its acceleration, even as the plane was airborne, I could not help but worry that she had somehow managed to find her way on board and was sitting a few rows behind me.

Never in my life had I wanted so desperately to avoid someone. Surely there were men alive who upon being surprised by their mother, no matter how decontextualized she might be, no matter how long it had been since last they had last seen each other, and no matter how long a list of grievances against her they carried with them at all times, would feel, as their primary emotion, something in the general category of joy, men who would not press themselves as close to the wall as possible and hardly dare to take a breath, men who would not place their finger on their lips and widen their eyes with panic, in the hopes that those around them would also fall silent, but, of course, men like these were not on the first leg of a sex tour when the unexpected meeting took place.

That was half of my problem as the plane strained and shook its way toward our cruising altitude, its wings dipping left and right, the turbines revved to a high whistle. The other half was that Webb Doleack was sitting near me. Boarding had been a hurried affair, and Webb might have taken that seat without anything in mind more complicated than efficiency, but it did not strain the boundaries of probability for me to imagine that Webb wanted to finish what had begun ninety minutes ago in the hallway, and so, for the first several minutes of the flight, part of my mind groped for possible reasons why my mother had appeared in Iceland, while the other part prepared for some kind of assault from Doleack, though the more I thought about this possibility the more confident I became that I could hold my own against whatever Doleack might try. After all, we were both in a seated position, and, astonishingly enough, I was beginning to see something in myself of which I had had, heretofore, no inkling: a ferocious animal nature, an ability to defend myself with something rather more potent than avoidance, sarcasm, or dark thoughts.

That the woman I had glimpsed at the Royal was not my mother but merely someone who looked like Naomi was a hope I couldn't completely abandon. I had made no more than two seconds of visual contact, and even those hadn't been under optimal conditions—not only was she, whoever she was, at least a hundred feet away, but she was turning the corner and was partially obscured by the bellboy, while I was in the middle of a thicket of people, one of them unraveling. Any defense lawyer can tell you there's nothing quite so unreliable as an eyewitness; the image the eye captures is printed on stock permeated with prejudice, fear, fantasy. What we see is not reality but light beamed into our brains, which is then interpreted in accordance with what we already know of the world. That woman in a fringed jacket, suntanned or dark skinned, with wiry, graying hair, could have been any American tourist of a certain age; she might have been Israeli; she might not even have been a female. In a world of billions, you'd have to say the odds were that who I had seen back in Reykjavik was not my mother.

But if it was—then what? With Webb Doleack near me, fussing with the seat, tilting it far back, bringing it up again, toeing off his shoes, violently rubbing his eyes while letting out a low ruminative rumble, I tried to force myself to think in an orderly fashion, something I hadn't been really able to do since Iceland, if not before. Actually, it was before Iceland when logic abandoned me. I was hardly being rational in the departures lounge when I started thinking Castle cast no reflection. I was hardly being rational when I was screaming at Deirdre on the phone with that poor driver five feet away from me. When *was* the last time I had thought clearly? Peeking at Deirdre's diary, the aborted rendezvous with Chelsea, even sneaking out of the emergency room before I could be properly looked after . . . All right, that was then and this was now. Now, I needed to be logical and I needed to be sensible. Someone—Uncle Ezra, Andrew Post, *someone*—must have given my mother enough information to piece together my itinerary, and if that were so, it would not strain credulity to think I hadn't seen the last of her. In fact it strained it rather less than believing that I had seen her in the first place. All right then. I needed to act. Because if Naomi were to catch up to me, the grudge she carried over my article in *Esquire* would seem a mere pittance of animosity next to the revulsion she would surely feel upon seeing me on a sex tour. (I could not possibly be alone in this. None of these guys, no matter what they might say, would want their mothers to know what they were doing.) But the avalanche of embarrassment would be next to nothing compared to the trouble her presence would cause me. She might very well get me bounced off the tour. Surely Castle would choose to protect the rest of the tour members, *the paying clients,* from the psychological saltpeter of having someone's *mom* on their trail. Life was too hard and too short for that kind of thing, and even though the $135,000 each of them had paid was not a fortune for the likes of Piedmont, Cobb, or Linwood, and really a trifle compared to the quarter of a million dollars a middle-aged CEO, about whom I had recently read in one of the tabloids, had dropped in five hours in a strip club, getting nothing more for his money than three bottles of bogus champagne, a dozen lap dances, and a spoonful of semen in his shorts. Nevertheless, Castle might, in light of the investment the others had made, feel duty-bound to cut me loose. And if that were to happen, my book would never get written, my contract would not be fulfilled, and the apartment on Perry Street would not be bought, the thought of which derailed that particular line of deliberation, and sent me careening into the memory of the demented e-mail I'd sent Isabelle, in which I offered to put my tongue inside her.

It wasn't as if I had never thought such a thing; in fact it wasn't as if I hadn't thought similar things about a great many women, wondered about their bodies, made educated guesses about the lay of the land, how they would smell, how they would taste, would they be wild or mild, focused or loosey-goosey, but all speculations were harmless. Admittedly, they were mine, and they were, I suppose, to some extent, *me*, but I had always remained blameless, because they were merely *in my mind*. Maybe some women could see evidence of these thoughts in my eyes, or detect it in the little slur of my voice, and maybe there were women who just assumed I, along with most other men, was thinking these things, or was, at least, capable of thinking these things. But, nevertheless, I had never said anything like that before, at least not so it could be heard by another person. The shame of it, the wreckage. I felt myself sinking into despair, and I tried to buoy myself up by imagining I could still repair the situation, undo the harm, if I appeared at Isabelle's office with a sufficiently large check. At least a sufficiently large check offered some hope. Getting bounced off the tour, coming home with two pages of notes, and resuming my life on the sofa on West Fifty-fourth Street would ensure that Isabelle would never forgive me.

I needed to get as much on paper as I possibly could, while I was still on the tour. And this new sense of urgency immediately directed itself toward Doleack, if for no other reason than I was seated an arm's length from him. First, however, I would have to decrease the level of animosity between us, which turned out to be easier than I imagined. Doleack might have had a foul temper, but he was as quick to calm down as he was to explode, and when I leaned toward him and said I'm sorry about that craziness back at the hotel, he shrugged and said I wasn't hurting Enir, or running her around, or doing anything like that. He spoke in a mild, bemused voice, as if we were discussing a misunderstanding that had taken place months in the past. Well, I said, the whole thing about this trip is that what we do is our own business, which I immediately regretted because it seemed to imply that I didn't really believe Doleack's story. Did you see that beat-up blue BMW following behind the bus taking us to the airport? Doleack asked. That was Enir, she followed me out there, for a final good-bye. I nodded, hoping to conceal every trace of my skepticism—it was too much like hearing about hookers who are so transported by the john's sexual prowess that they refuse to take the money.

I decided to talk a little about myself, hoping a few moments of confessional candor would elicit a similar response from Doleack. I was living with a younger girl, and she told me she met someone and she was having sex with him. I never saw it coming. I think she was fucking him for a couple of weeks without my having the slightest idea. Doleack nodded, not with any particular sympathy, but with a kind of forensic comprehension. Women are very good secret keepers, he said. Their sex organs are internal. I never thought of that, I said, with entirely too much enthusiasm. I reached into my jacket pocket, pressed my thumb on the RECORD button of my tape recorder.

I was pretty torn up, I said, hoping to stress my own vulnerability— though it did occur to me that Doleack might be repelled by the thump of excessive breast-beating. Doleack almost certainly subscribed to the masculine credo of not letting what women do or don't do count for too much in the general scheme of things, though even in hypermasculine subcultures such as maximum security prisons a sizable percentage of men react powerfully to the infidelity of a wife or a girlfriend. So for me, I continued, this is really about trying to blot out that bad experience with a lot of good experiences. And then, for good measure, I added My sausage has been in the deep freeze for a while. There's pills for that, Doleack said, tilting his chair far back, lifting his hips and smoothing out the front of his trousers. He looked as if he were getting ready to disengage.

So how about you? I asked, rushing things. Doleack, with a furtive glance over his shoulder, a quick check up and down the aisle, reached into his zipper jacket and pulled out an ampoule, snapped it easily in half, and swallowed its clear contents. *Just what he fucking needs, more*

testosterone. Doleack swallowed, made a face, and then chased the testosterone with a couple of Tic-Tacs. I had to press for some answers before
the juice kicked in.

What made you decide to fly Fleming? I asked Webb. What do you
mean? Doleack asked. I don't know what you're driving at. What's to
decide? You're offered a chance to have sex with some truly spectacular
individuals, who's going to say no to that? Do you know anyone who
could have that and say no? I knew from experience this was going
in the wrong direction; Doleack was asking *me* questions. Well, Webb,
there's a lot of men in America. I think it's safe to say most of them
aren't on this plane. Something had to put you in the mood to do this.
You want to know my life story, is that it? Webb asked. The whole sad
story? That would be great, I said, and then, before he could object, I
asked him if he had ever been married.

I was married to Marie Lois Simmons Doleack. She was a flight attendant on the Delta shuttle I used to take between Washington and
New York, a trip I made with some regularity in the old DOD days. She
was a big girl, not fat, not an ounce of fat on her, but tall, with broad
shoulders, and wide hips, and strong legs. She took excellent care of
herself, diet, grooming, manners, she was the whole package. She was
from a military family, raised up in Alaska, she was very methodical in
everything she did: first you did this, then you did that, then the next
thing, all by the book. *By the book*, it was one of the things she said. You
had faith it was in the book for a reason, people had figured it out,
they'd tried it and it worked. Me, I always sort of suspected if it was in
the book it was already out of date. Everyone figures with my Defense
background I was a military man, but no, that wasn't for me, that wasn't
how I chose to serve my country. My area of expertise was business,
handling multiple bids. People in the press love to scream about how
we overpay for everything, armor, toilet seats, hammers, but that's bull-
crap. We always got the best price.

I'd be seeing her once, twice a week for six months and never got
more than a nod and a polite smile, but then one day, this was back
when Delta used to run a hydrofoil on the East River between La Guar-
dia and East Thirty-third Street—what would take you an hour at least
in a car you could do in fifteen minutes on the hydrofoil. Marie was

standing near the rail, and I tapped her on one of her big old shoulders and said Hey you better be careful none of that water sprays on you, or we'll have to put you in a taxi and take you straight to New York University Hospital and get you a cholera shot, and she said Really, you'd do that for me? That was how it started. By the time the hydrofoil docked on the East Side, we had already arranged to have dinner that night. Doleack went silent for a moment. He was one of those men who frown when they feel grief, or even tenderness, as if there is someone soft inside of him who is trying suddenly to be heard and who must be stared down, and silenced. We ate at a restaurant, I don't think it's even there anymore, near Gramercy Park, called La Colombe d'Or. I had no idea where to take her; I called my sister, she's an expert on restaurants, and she said Oh take her there, and order the cassoulet, but Marie wouldn't touch the cassoulet. She ordered a spinach salad, with dressing on the side, and she said to me I'm going to keep my figure until I find the right man, and then I'm going to marry him, have a couple of kids, and get as fat as a hog. Doleack cleared his throat, a rough, angry sound, like someone peevishly dragging a chair across a bare floor.

Did you have children? I asked. I pitched my tone between solicitousness and persistence. It was something you learned to do, like moving the dial on the coffee grinder so you could get the consistency you wanted—fine, extra fine, espresso. Nope, Doleack said. Negative on that. We spent two years trying. Every time Marie got her period she'd cry, but I'd say Marie, what the fuck do I care? Let's raise Jack Russells—we were both crazy about those little ballsy dogs. Let's buy a farm somewhere and get some horses and saddle them up and ride the hell out of them, and then jump into a nice pond naked as the day we were born. I meant it, too.

She stopped flying. She thought maybe all that compression was the problem, and you know sometimes women's cycles get screwed up if they're up in the air too much. Marie went through all the possibilities. By the book, of course. And step number three, or maybe it was four or five, anyhow she made an appointment to get the plumbing checked, and that's when they discovered she had a cancerous cervix. Next stop, Sloan-Kettering in New York. We had one more dinner at Colombe d'Or, and once again she did not order the cassoulet, but she had a taste of mine. She said how good it was, so rich and smoky, but I could tell it wasn't really her thing, especially going into the hospital the next morning and surgery the day after that. Doleack reached into his pocket, and I wondered if he was going to snap off another ampoule, but he just kept it there.

She never got out of that place. When they opened her up, everything was a million times worse than what they had originally thought. She died like she lived, total efficiency. First one thing went and then the next. It was like closing a summer house room by room. She lost her sight, boom, her ability to walk, finished, everything in order, one after the other, very methodical, like putting sheets over furniture, turning down all the thermostats. Her kidneys shut off, and finally her lungs started to fill, and that was it. She was thirty-one years old, we didn't have a living will, or any of that sort of thing, we thought we would live forever, but there she was propped up in the hospital bed filling out the forms, putting her initials in the boxes—all four of her initials, I could never figure out how she squeezed them in. You know the last thing she said to me? She could hardly talk, it was all mumbles and morphine, but she whispered right in my ear I'm going to miss you.

Oh God, I said, this life has so much suffering. I had meant it to be consoling, but Doleack's eyes flashed with annoyance. I'm sorry, Doleack said, I don't happen to think you can compare losing Marie with any ordinary fucking little everyday tragedy. He took a deep breath. But in order for you to understand that, I guess you'd have to know something about how things were between Marie and me, and you don't, do you? You don't have the first idea about what we had. And I am not going to go into a lot of X-rated detail here, I will leave that to your imagination, but I will tell you that it is absolutely one hundred percent impossible for two people to be more compatible, more in tune with each other physically, than we were. With Marie, every light in my body went on. Every nerve was saying Okay, Webb, this is what we've been waiting for. And believe me, it wasn't like she was some expert. Sometimes she'd just spaz out, and I had to hold her hips and tell her Whoa, you're going crazy here, just find a rhythm and keep it. What made her so great to me had nothing to do with so-called skills. It was something much more mysterious, mysterious and basic; it was just her body, the specific gravity of it, the texture. Her pubic hair was long but very soft, extremely silky; you could rest your cheek against it and want to fall dead asleep, I've never touched anything like it, it was like corn silk. She was very wet when it was time, but never too wet; there was always this little bit of . . . I don't know what to call it, there was always some substance, like a little pinch of arrowroot in the gravy to give it more body. She was what she was and maybe she was just one of a kind, but I would really like to find someone, another woman who can make me feel like I've found perfection. Because you know what? Do you know what you have when you don't have perfection? He put up his hand, telling me not to bother answering. You have something less; you are making do. Is that the worst thing in the world? Answer: No, not really. But once you've had perfection, it feels pretty shabby to have anything else. Doleack pulled his plastic cube of breath mints out of his pocket, tapped one into his mouth. He offered one to me, which I accepted because when someone offers you a Tic-Tac they are telling you that you need one. So, Doleack asked, does that pretty much answer your question?

I knew enough not to say yes. You always wanted more; you always moved the finish line back when you were interviewing, no matter how surreptitiously. You never wanted the subject to feel there was nothing more than needed to be explained, justified, amplified, apologized for. I suppose so, I said. You go around, sleeping with women, hoping to feel what you felt with Marie. Doleack nodded but raised his eyebrows. Well, nothing quite so pathetic as that. I do manage to enjoy myself. I may be on a quest, but I make sure the journey is pleasant. After all, it's still sex. I love getting my dick sucked and I love fucking. And then, without another word, without a yawn, or even a shift to the left or the right, without putting his head farther back, without stretching out his legs, without a change in his breathing, Doleack fell into a sudden deep sleep; it was as if he were an appliance and someone had just kicked the plug out of the wall.

I gazed for a moment at his sleeping, defenseless face. Of course I was saddened by Webb's story. How could I not be, especially since I could not help but see in it certain similarities to my own? We were both chasing phantoms. But Deirdre was still alive, and really mainly separated from me because of my own pride, and longing for her did not belong in the same category as Webb's longing for Marie. How could I compare the tragedy of his losing Marie to death to my losing Deirdre because I really wasn't capable of sustaining the relationship? Yet even to conjure Deirdre in this self-abnegating way brought her to sudden life within me, and I said her name, softly, so as not to awaken Doleack.

I inched my little tape recorder out of my pocket, peeked down at it, and—cue: music, close-up of eyes bulging in horror—I saw that I had somehow failed to press the RECORD button. I had just pressed PLAY and the blank tape was blithely revolving.

I had blown it. I started madly running my hand through my hair, and then stopped, looked around to see if anyone was paying attention to me. Tony's hands were folded, and his eyes were shut; his lips moved in what seemed a pious mutter. Len Cobb was listening to his iPod and eating a ham sandwich and drinking a comically small can of beer. Stephanie was strapped into her seat and appeared to be dozing. But she sensed I was looking at her and she opened her eyes suddenly, to return my gaze. I gave her a small wave, meant to suggest my own harmlessness, but she interpreted the gesture to mean I needed her for something, and though the plane was still tearing through the gloomy gauze of nocturnal northern clouds and seemed a long way from leveling off, Stephanie unclasped her seat belt and, using Tony's and then Len's seat back for balance, she made her way toward me.

I quickly got up, to stop her before she walked all the way to my seat. I don't need anything, I was just waving. Are you sure? she asked. I'm already up, I could get you—a drink? Some fruit maybe? No, nothing, I'm fine. I touched her elbow, meaning only to say she should go back to her seat and relax, but she stiffened at my touch. *She must think we're all monsters.* Mind if I chat with you for a minute? I asked. Sure, if you'd like to. I'm going to make myself a cup of tea. You're welcome to join me. I followed her into the galley. It was about ten feet by four feet, lit by three overhead lights. It wasn't exactly shipshape. Salt or sugar grit was on the counter. Four badly stained napkins were balled into a corner; it seemed as if they'd been used to mop up a spill and then shoved aside. A whiskey tumbler with a *V* chipped out of its rim stood next to a similarly disabled wineglass. I don't know what I was expecting. Something better. I see you were having a nice little chitchat with our friend, she said, opening a metal drawer and pulling out a tea bag from a rat's nest of tea bags. I wondered if the pilots were similarly lax in their housekeeping. I wasn't greatly concerned with cleanliness or tidiness in general, but I did think that those involved in aeronautics ought to be particularly neat, focused on crossing every *t* and dotting each *i*, just as you would not want to look up from the examining table and notice your doctor had soup in his mustache.

Well, since you asked me a question about how I like working this route, do you mind if ask you a question, too? Not at all, I said, be my guest. She pressed the flat of her hand lightly against her collarbone, to signify sincerity or harmlessness. Do you think the guys spend much time wondering what all these women think of them? Hmm, I said, that's a good question. Well, don't *you* ever worry about that?

Yes, I see what you're driving at, I said. But aren't the women in a business and we're the customers? I think salespeople tend to like their customers, if they're successful. So you think they like you? Stephanie asked, her smile as thin as fishing line. Maybe, I said. They might prefer us if we were a fabulously good-looking collection of perfect gentlemen, but on what planet was that likely to happen? Prostitutes are like psychiatrists, ambulance drivers, tutors, and personal trainers; they've got to be used to human wreckage. We're all selling something that's precious to us: our backs, our skills, our time. Think about it. You sell your time, your own precious, finite portion of your allotted stay on Earth, and you say here's an hour of it, give me ten bucks, or a thousand, whatever. The women have something men want, and they are selling it, and maybe not being that crazy about the men is part of the job. But let's face it—eight hours of work for a month's worth of income, it balances out, don't you think?

Right now I'm not thinking of them, Stephanie said. She had filled a teacup with water and then stuck it in the microwave. What I wonder about is what it feels like to be *you*. She lowered her voice, so it was just loud enough to be heard over the hoarse hum of the engines. I've had experiences with men who thought that maybe they were a little too good for me. It's like having your soul scoured out with a Brillo pad.

You feel like a complete stranger to yourself, except for the raw pain. The microwave's timer rang, and Stephanie took out her cup of tea.

I don't see how a man could think he was too good for you, Stephanie, I said. I'd think any man would feel pretty lucky—She stopped me with a quick shake of the head, a frown. Don't flatter me. If working on these routes has taught me any one thing, it's where I fit in on the beauty scale. It's been a real education, I'll tell you that. I hear some of the men rating the women on a ten-point scale, young, thin women, with the perfect waist-hip ratio, which you've got to understand is still the most important thing to men. And do you know what they give these women? Once in a while a nine or a ten, but mostly eights, sevens, I've heard sixes. So you can imagine what they'd give me, like a minus twelve. She sensed I was about to object, and she raised a silencing finger. You can't tell me my own experiences. There is nothing quite like it, being with a man who doesn't think you're pretty. Being with someone who is thinking to himself *Damn, I could do better than this.* So I've got a theory, and I'm trying to live by it, but it's hard. What's your theory? She took a sip of her tea. She gave no indication of pleasure or disappointment; she experienced the tea the way she would experience reading the words *she sipped her tea.* My theory is that everyone needs to know exactly how attractive they are, where they fit in on the universal beauty continuum, and they should try to refrain from contact with people who are either much more or much less attractive than they are. Find your level and stay there. This holds true for friendships, too, by the way. In fact, if a woman wants to know where she fits in on the beauty scale and she can't quite get the truth out of her mirror, she should ruthlessly appraise her five closest women friends and just put herself somewhere in the middle. That'll get you pretty close to the truth.

Go to any beach, any bar, any high school cafeteria, you see the gorgeous ones with the gorgeous ones, the fat ones with the fat ones, the frightened little homely ones with glasses and their shoulders hunched up, they stick together. My girlfriend calls it beauty apartheid. But for men, forget it, it's a different game, they don't have to stay in their beauty ghetto; they can get a free pass out if they're brilliant, or funny, and they can always buy their way out. That's what this whole trip's about, isn't it? Buying women who wouldn't want to be with you for free? In other words, you completely hate us, I said. Stephanie shook her head. We're just rats in a maze, Avery. We can't really help how we behave. And the truth is—I like men. I love them, really. I like to argue with them, and I like having a man on my arm the way some guys like walking around with pit terriers on a leash. I like their energy, their directness, and you know the stakes always seem raised when the men are around. They want so much and so they're willing to put it all out there. I like that. Are you sure I can't get you something to drink?

But before I could answer, Jordan, standing at the front of the plane, was calling out for everyone's attention. Though it was warm in the cabin, he wore a zippered jacket, a silk paisley scarf with long black tassels. He held a cocktail glass with something bright amber in it, and he hoisted it up, like a cavalryman at the head of the table proposing a toast. His eyes were hectic. He swayed back and forth to counteract the movements of the plane. I want to propose a toast to my father, he called out, his voice thick and slurred. His empty sleeve, which he had tucked into his pants pocket, had come loose and waved about on its own. In the harsh light of the plane, his burns seemed particularly livid; you could almost feel the searing pain that had preceded them. Come on, you fucking guys, he called out. Everyone raise your glass. You fucking guys, fucking fucking . . . He fell silent, blinking rapidly. He seemed to be rapidly descending into debauchery, simply too frail to withstand the past twenty-four hours. Dr. Gordon, as well, seemed worse for wear. His blue blazer was rumpled, and his cottony white hair was disheveled. I have to tell you, Jordan was saying, I wasn't sure I even wanted to come on this trip. It was my father's idea. It all just seemed sort of random to me. All I wanted was to be home, crawl into a hole and never come out. But—Dad, I'm always going to listen to you, from now on. So Dad, come on, man, you've got to stop beating yourself up. What happened, happened. You couldn't have stopped me if you wanted to. Not your fault, not your fucking fault. Jordan adjusted the height at which he held his glass, so that now it extended straight out at the other passengers. He smiled wildly, like an escaped convict reveling in his hours of freedom before the inevitable recapture. Thank you, Dad; thank you,

Mr. Castle; thank you, Gabby; thanks to everyone at Fleming Tours, and thanks to all you guys, you've all been really great. He drank whatever was in his glass in a long swallow, shivered theatrically, and then stumbled back to his seat.

Have you decided to go for the upgrade? Stephanie said to me.

14

LATE-NIGHT LANDING at Gardemoen Airport. The moon shone behind the bright broken clouds, transforming them into smashed-up pottery. On the ground, a Royal Jordanian jetliner that had been scheduled for takeoff was still on Norwegian territory, delayed by security concerns. It had been cordoned off by the *politi*, who stood in formation, with their hands behind their backs, stiff and still as toy soldiers, while air marshals and intelligence officers questioned the plane's passengers. Because of the fracas concerning the Royal Jordanian 757, the Fleming jet was directed to a far runway and we had to deplane via a portable stairway and walk across the chilly damp tarmac to a side entrance of the main terminal, with the wind whipping at the hems of our jackets and the backs of our necks.

Except for the wind, the night was nearly silent. Even the jets on the tarmac, the planes circling above, the lone takeoff: silent.

Michael Piedmont was walking in front of me, the heels of his shoes clicking away, and for a few moments I lost myself in contemplation of his bulky body. It was darkly compelling to think about all that had been consumed to fill and stretch Piedmont to such an extent, the second helpings, the third, fourth, and fifth helpings, the blueberry pie eaten with a spoon while standing up in the kitchen, the bowls of popcorn scarfed down while lounging on the sofa, the scoops of ice cream bigger than cantaloupe, the chops the size of hot-water bottles, the gravy-stained shirt fronts, the olive oil–spotted ties, the crash diets, the catastrophic bowel movements, the dire warnings from one doctor and then the next, the resolutions made, the despairing capitulation to his own ravenousness. Just as Dr. Jekyll turned himself into a monster through his own curiosity, Piedmont had made himself horrible through appetite, but for him there was no going back, now he was Hyde without the Jekyll, Hyde forever, Hyde ad infinitum.

Piedmont wondered who was walking directly behind him—perhaps he felt my eyes upon him—and because it was not easy for him to look over his shoulder, he stopped walking altogether and turned around to face me.

His face lit up with a pleased smile, as if he and I were old friends and what a nice surprise it was to bump into me in Norway, of all places. There was something genuine and compelling in that smile, a kind of human warmth I had perceived in many successful people. Even corporate thieves like Scrushy or Lay, men accused of ruining thousands of lives, bankrupting municipalities, triggering suicides, were apparently quite likable when you were with them. After they were brought to justice, some of the jurors remarked that they had never in their lives met men so genuinely warm and amiable. It might have been an act, a lie, but it was a lie that shared a border with truth. The rich and successful men I had interviewed in the course of hacking out a living had one surprising thing in common: they seemed to genuinely *like* other people. Even men who were known as ruthless had a kind of animal comfort around other human beings. In fact, the successful people I had met were not only friendly but *seductive*. You wanted to be on their team; you wanted to go where they were going. The snarlers, the screamers, the pouters, the injustice collectors, the curators of their own little museum of slights and snubs—in my experience, these were the men who had never made it, or who were slipping; these were the failures, like my father number three, vicious, vindictive Norman Blake, who hated you because he was quite certain that all you and he really held in common was a low opinion of him.

Piedmont fell into step next to me, and held on to my forearm for balance and support. What a terrible plane, he said. Next time we'll take one of mine. I've got a brand-new Gulfstream just gathering dust. You do? Piedmont snorted out a laugh and shook my arm. Come on, friend, he said, you know I do, and you know who I am. I saw it in your eyes back in New York. There was no point in denying it, though I was disappointed to learn that my initial recognition of Piedmont had been noticed—I wondered if my studying the men, my note-taking, and my occasional dictations into my recorder were not half so discreet as I had imagined. And by the way, Piedmont continued, Lincoln told me you're some kind of a writer and you're probably here taking notes and plan to write this whole thing up. That's really not true, I said, with such great conviction I almost believed it. I think it's hilarious that people even write books anymore, Piedmont said. Since my return—I assume you know about my time in jail—I do lectures, seminars, audiotapes, video, and I'm going to do a book, too. But how many people are going to download a book? Too much work. I've got a cousin who's a big-time New York writer. Maybe you know her. Chandra Colt? I shook my head no. Well, she's a terrific girl, bright, motivated, and she's written six books. Mainly fiction books. Anyhow, she sat down and did the math and figured out that over the course of twelve years of writing, if she added up everything she earned, she was making under fifty cents an hour. I said Chandra, if you're willing to work for that, then I suggest you get a job in one of the Nike plants down in Indonesia or somewhere. The weather's better, the cost of living is a lot less, and with your brains you could be in a management position within a couple of years.

I mean, what is a book? Piedmont asked, stopping a few dozen feet before the terminal door. If you put it in relation to where information technology is in general? It's antique, to say the least. It has its roots in a world that doesn't even exist; it's like an ear trumpet or cure by leeches. I wrote a piece about that, I said. It's coming back, cure by leeches. No, it's not, Piedmont said. Maybe a couple idiot doctors here or there are bleeding people, and they get their face on TV, and someone like you writes an article about them because it's different, but trust me it's not coming back. We've progressed and old things get left behind.

How about what we're doing? I said. The world's oldest profession hasn't been outmoded. Piedmont looked at me quizzically. This is all about progress, too. If the women back home were a bit more on the old-fashioned side, a lot of us would be happy running after them. But women today are in a transitional phase, somewhere between what they once were and what they will be, and it makes them difficult to deal with. They're touchy like teenagers, but I always say if you're going to act like a teenager then for crying out loud *look like one.*

We cleared immigration in moments. The immigration officer barely glanced at me, didn't even ask to see my passport, just waved me through. When we got into the main terminal, several liveried drivers were holding small hand-lettered signs saying FLEMING TOORS.

Want to share a car? Piedmont asked. You're a good conversationalist. I nodded yes, understanding that what Piedmont meant was I like the look in your eyes when you listen to me. Castle was standing with the chauffeurs, assigning people to the various cars, but Piedmont ignored him and summoned one of the drivers—a sour-looking middle-aged man who should have been driving a hearse. Piedmont's weight might have announced to the world that he was helpless in some ways, but he was used to people doing what he asked, and his assumption of authority and primacy communicated itself to the driver, who made a curt little bow in our direction and then said in English that we should wait for him near the exit door while he fetched the car. Fetch? I said to Piedmont, as soon as the man was gone. But Piedmont wasn't interested in words.

We waited for the car beneath the overhang. It was dark blue late in the evening, and there wasn't much traffic. A fine mist fell past the streetlights. I looked out at the twinkling red lights of a distant radio tower and thought to myself *Ah, Norway.* But beyond that my mind might as well have been buried alive.

WE CONVENED in the lobby of the Hotel Christofer, a decent enough place, though perhaps a few years past its prime. The dark mahogany lobby was a little *too* dark, and the carpeting was on its way to becoming threadbare. The night manager was a solid-looking woman in a lavender pantsuit and high heels. A bellman, tall and sepulchral, approached me and asked, in that overly pronounced English-as-a-second-language way, if I would care to have a little bit of help perhaps with my luggage. He had the smell of medicine on his breath.

I had had four hours sleep in the past three days.

Before long, the men on the tour were in the lobby, even our pilots. Stephanie was on hand, too, holding a clipboard and talking with the night manager about room assignments, while she clicked her ballpoint pen rapidly. Castle came in, leaning heavily on Gabrielle. It seemed he had twisted his ankle or hurt his knee. He was alternately wincing with pain and smiling bravely. Gabrielle steered him to the front desk. He leaned back on it and mopped the perspiration off his face. Gentlemen, a word please, he called out. When we were finally quiet enough for him to be heard, he announced Because of the lateness of the hour, we've taken the liberty of ordering room service for each of you. When you go to your rooms, your meal will be waiting for you. We trust it will be to your liking. Our choices were made based on your own stated dietary preferences. But tomorrow, Gabrielle broke in, you will be offered a full buffet with many, many choices.

Stephanie gave me the electronic key to Room 420. Here you go, she said, with chilling impersonality. Is this a good room? I asked, not that I expected an answer, but I just couldn't let her move on as if there had never been a moment's friendship between us. They're all good rooms, Stephanie said. You did upgrade to Platinum, didn't you? I shook my head no, and she shrugged and then quickly turned away, lest I attempt to further engage her.

I took the elevator up to the fourth floor with Jordan and Dr. Gordon. Jordan's high spirits in Iceland were still coursing through him. Yet whatever satisfactions Dr. Gordon had derived from giving his son a chance to exercise the privileges of his class and gender had by now been dissipated by the inevitable tedium of travel, though something may have occurred back in Reykjavik to depress him, some failure of personal hydraulics or some sad absence of desire. Dr. Gordon looked old and ragged, and his eyes, usually communicators of irony and disdain, were full of melancholy. The skin on his face hung loosely. His shoulders were slumped and he massaged the heel of his right hand, as if he had just signed a thousand checks. How you doing there, Jordan? I said. I'm sad about leaving Iceland, he said. I know my girl turned out to be sort of a loser, but the new one they found me after was fantastic, and, actually, I liked the first one, too, until the thing at the Blue Lagoon, which I'm not sure was even her fault. I've never been so happy to leave somewhere in my entire life, Dr. Gordon said. It's a perfectly ridiculous country with all the charm of a Wal-Mart. Come on, Dad, Jordan said. Let's enjoy this. I am enjoying it, Dr. Gordon said, in a voice so glum I laughed aloud, at which point they both looked at me, and I was forced to say Sorry, I was thinking of something.

On the fourth floor, I walked toward my room, without saying good-bye. As I made my way down the stolid, stately corridor—green carpeting, cream walls, old oil paintings in gilded frames depicting adventures at sea—I heard Jordan saying, No, stop it, you can't come in. I want to talk to her, Dr. Gordon said in his peeved, insistent way, but Jordan, fresh off the erotic high of Reykjavik and ready for whatever Oslo had in store, held his ground. It's fine, Dad, he said. There's nothing to worry about. That's nonsense! Dr. Gordon cried. Dad, Dad, come on. Jordan's voice was soothing. This is what we wanted—remember? This is what we hoped for, except it's even better.

I remained in front of Room 420, listening, stalling. On the other side of that door, I assumed, was a Norwegian girl who had already been paid to keep me company. I took a deep, steadying breath, engaged the card in the slot, it clicked, and I waited for the little emerald light to come on, and then I opened the door. Honey, I'm home!

A man, an Olav, an Alf—who knows what his name was?—was in my room, wearing nothing but a blue silk tank top and doing push-ups next to the bed, poised on his fingertips and his splayed, stiffened toes. He looked up at me and smiled. His dark hair was wet with perspiration, as was his square, heavy-jawed face. His stout member hung loosely, swinging back and forth. Oops, I said, and closed the door, and stood out in the hall holding on to the door handle, my heart racing, and my mind questioning itself—had I really just seen that? I put my ear to the door, but all I could hear was the rhythm of my own blood.

I went down to the lobby to find Castle, and, as luck would have it, I found him right away, sitting with Gabrielle in the rustic little lounge off to the side of the main desk. They had a huge photo album between them—one of those dopey little numbers with a padded cover and the word *Memories* written in wedding invitation script. Avery! Castle said, as if I were a pleasant surprise. Sit down and join us. He slammed the book shut, placed it on his lap. There's a man in my room, I said. A man? Gabrielle said. Yes, a man, in my room. Doing push-ups. And please don't talk to me about Platinum upgrades. Castle and Gabrielle exchanged looks, trying to decide if I were insane, or if this was actually something that needed their attention. What room did you go to? Castle wanted to know, and when I told him, Gabrielle checked that against her room assignment sheet and she made a brief Gallic nod in Castle's direction, and he said Let's go up and see what's going on, okay? Nina was meant to be in your room, not a man.

Castle and I rode the elevator together. Are you sure it was a man? he asked me as we rose. I said I doubt it was a woman with short hair, broad shoulders, and a reddish penis. Well, Castle said, either way it's unacceptable. A lot seems to go wrong on this tour, I said. Castle's faint eyebrows shot up, his cheeks puffed out. Tell me about it—and this is one of the more uneventful trips. The thing about this business, you're dealing with a lot of variables, and the thing about variables is that they vary. You just never know. Your buddy Sean? He's on his way back to the airport—he's going back to LA. Really? What happened? Castle shrugged. He said it was a business thing. That's why I tell you guys, try to stay off your cells and your e-mail, but does anyone listen? Castle shook his head and answered his own question. No one listens. He's going back to LA in the middle of the night? I said. I wouldn't think there'd be any flights. Castle smiled, patted my shoulder. You're very detail oriented, aren't you. You should have been a woman.

I looked up at the security mirror perched on the upper-left-hand corner of the elevator car. I could see ghostly, ravaged me—added to the general filth of traveling, my hair was thick with the mineral deposits of Sigrid's shower and time spent underwater at the Blue Lagoon. Castle had already moved toward the back of the car, somehow out of range of the mirror's fisheye. Stand next to me for a second, I wanted to say.

We walked in silence to my room. Castle extended his open hand, and I gave him my key card. Click. The door opened. The curtains were open to the featureless dark blue night. The TV set was on, without the sound: a BBC reporter stood in front of a pile of smoking rubble. A wicker basket with a pyramid of oranges was on the sleek cherrywood dresser. The bed was expansive, untouched. The phone's message light was throbbing like a firefly.

Nina? Castle's voice filled the empty room. He stepped in, waved me along. We stood side by side. Nina? Are you here? The bathroom door opened and Nina emerged. She had wrapped a white towel around her waist; otherwise she was bare, having recently stepped out of the shower. She looked startlingly like Deirdre, the same skin tone, a kind of dense whiteness like the inside of an apple. Her breasts were frank, utilitarian, no more erotic than her freckled collarbone, her powerful cleft chin, possibly because she didn't bother to cover them. Like Deirdre, she had long, wavy rust-colored hair, but Deirdre's eyes were brown and Nina's were so icy and blue they almost seemed white. Sorry, she said, in a slightly begrudging way, as if we were the ones who ought to apologize. She grabbed a travel bag from the foot of the bed and disappeared back into the bathroom. Two minutes please, she called out through the closed door.

Well, it looks like you're all set, Castle said, handing the key card back to me and turning to leave. Wait a second. I put a hand on his arm to stop him. There was a guy in this room, right there, on the floor, doing push-ups. What can I tell you, Avery? He gestured, taking in the room. There's two men here, me and you. And then there's Nina, who I should tell you I would only normally give to a Platinum member, but seeing as you're Ezra's boy. Look, Lincoln, there was a guy here. I know what I saw. Castle breathed out a long, weary sigh. Are you trying to tell me that you *want* a guy, because if that's it, there's nothing I can do, that's a different tour. I don't want a guy. Are you sure? Because it sounds like maybe you do. Luckily, Nina emerged from the bathroom, and Castle said All right then, I'll leave you two little lovebirds alone.

As soon as the door clicked closed, Nina catapulted herself at me, as if (a) she knew me, (b) she was fantastically glad to see me, and (c) she was smaller than me. I strongly suspected that this enthusiastic greeting was part of her professional repertoire, as much a tool of the trade as the Singapore Grip or theatrical cries of pleasure, but mainly I was concerned with not landing on the floor. She hit me like a sandbag, with her arms around my neck and her knees gripping my sides, but she was expert enough to steer my fall toward the bed, which I hit with a thud of relief, only to be turned rather forcefully onto my back, at which point she began kissing my face with a fervency that bordered on the comic—in fact, it would have been hilarious if it hadn't been a bit frightening. Oh baby baby baby, she said, her voice husky and insistent. I turned my face this way and that, as if she might try to cut off my air supply. She put her hand between my legs. Still kissing me—or, really, making kissing motions and sounds on various parts of my face and head—she undid my fly, maneuvered her hand into my underwear. As unnerving as all this was, I nevertheless was as erect as a sailor on deck for inspection.

Nina suddenly stopped aggressing me with her pugnacious smooches, and we were still for a moment, simply two creatures in a nice Norwegian hotel, both of whom had recently been checked and cleared for sexually transmitted diseases. One of us was going to walk away with a few thousand dollars in her purse, and one of us wanted the temporary solace of touching a woman, and nothing more was in question but who would do what next. I raised myself up on my left elbow, cupped Nina's cheek with my right hand, and kissed her on her busy lips. You're very beautiful, I said, to which she answered Thank you very much, kind man. A few moments later we were out of our clothes. She had removed all of her pubic hair, which I found somewhat upsetting and far less erotic than it's meant to be, but, after all, it's not the end of the world. Deirdre once asked me if I wanted her to shave herself bare; she even said we could shave her together, it might be fun, she'd always wanted to try it; but I objected, somewhat vehemently. That reddish, wiry thatch was very alluring to me, and, in general, the sight of pubic hair was one of my limbic system's visual clues; it meant something special was going to happen. As to Nina—her pubic hair was her business. Literally. It was a little chilly in the room and we kicked our way under the covers. She petted me expertly. It was as if she had five hands. Her little fuchsia cosmetics bag was open. I saw condoms, lubricant, a tiny little vibrator. By the way, I said. Just to let you know? If there is a knock on the door, I am not going to answer it.

15

HOW CAN I EXPRESS what happened in those first few hours with Nina? Deirdre, Isabelle, Chelsea, if that was even her name, and then Sigrid, if that was *her* name, had each added to the deep seething storehouse of desire stewing at the center of me. By the time I was next to Nina, I could do nothing to control or even pace myself. I wanted her as if I had been seeking her. She patted me on the cheek—it wasn't a particularly sexual gesture; in fact, it may have been slightly contemptuous—and I caught her hand, turned it over, and pressed my lips to her palm. It was a reflex of the heart, just like your foot making a little whoopee kick when your knee is tapped by the doctor's rubber hammer. The hard wiring, the deep instinct of a man's drive toward a woman, was the most real thing about me now, more real than the book I was going to write, certainly more real than any moral qualms I might have. Nina knew it for what it was, and for what it wasn't, and she wasn't bothered in the least. She wasn't worrying *Oh no, this poor guy is in love with me,* she wasn't thinking *So this one wants to pretend it's some big romance,* she wasn't even thinking *Oh he's getting carried away, maybe I can milk him for an extra grand,* or maybe she was, maybe she was. I did this; she did that; I did another thing. Strike up the band! Once again, it was time to dance! Did she feel like dancing? Highly improbable. Did the great hoofers of yore feel like windmilling their arms and tap tap tapping their patent leather shoes five times a day when it was their turn to come out on stage? Once it was showtime, once the music began and the curtain parted, only the most discerning members of the audience would be able to sense that anything less than 100 percent was being given. Because Nina was such an accomplished dancer, because she was a professional, even I—Ginger to her Fred—attained a grace rare to my experience, and, unlike Astaire's partners, I even imagined I was in the lead.

When I turned her over, I placed my thumbs against the tattooed filigree work on her coccyx, pressing hard as if to splinter a violin. She looked back at me, her eyes flashing behind a veil of hair. Her deep womanly tides rose up from her—no matter what, we are human. There is no other meaning, nor shall there ever be; there is nothing but that.

The bed wheezed; the headboard beat like a fist against the wall.

Where was I?

I want to make a band, Nina said to me, as we rested in bed, waiting for room service. I sing and I write songs. She beat out a complex rhythm with her hands on her belly. And drums, too. I tried to encourage her to sing me one of her songs, but she said she couldn't, not without accompaniment. Who are your songs like? I asked her. I wasn't trying to suggest that her music was imitative or derivative, but that's how she seemed to take it. They are my own. I don't care to copy another band. She had a slight British accent; she may have taken a semester or two in London. I know, that's not what I mean, I said. I'm just trying to get a sense of what they're like, your songs. I mean, are they rock, are they punk, reggae? Reggae? Nina said, her voice rising. She seemed to find this wildly amusing. Like some nigger from Trinidad?

Reggae comes from Jamaica, I said, suddenly tight-lipped, suddenly moral, suddenly hoisted up into a position to pass judgment. I know that, she said, giving me a playful shove. Like a nigger from Trinidad—Don't say that, I said. I can't stand that kind of talk. It's a line from one of our songs, she said, smiling. Our band is called—in English you would say The Forbidden Zone. We take everything that is forbidden and put it in our songs. We want to come to U.S., where many things are forbidden. Where you cannot say this or that, and even certain kinds of sex are against the law. Many people in the U.S. are in jail for anal sex. They may go to jail and *have* anal sex, I said, but they're not in prison because they *had* it. She shook her head, as if deciding not to disabuse me of illusions about America. There's a lot of laws on the books that no one bothers to enforce, I said, somehow duty bound to clear up negative misconceptions about my country. I really wasn't prepared to deal with the anti-Americanism of the hookers I was encountering.

We will play in small clubs and rock out the house, Nina said, arching her back, stretching her arms out behind her. Her nipples were turned out, one looking right, the other looking left, like security guards protecting her heart. We shout forth all that is verboten, not just *nigger* but *cunt* and *ass*, too, and *Jeffrey Dahmer*, and *fuck you, Wal-Mart*. She laughed, amused by her own naughtiness. Yes, that will be pretty bracing, I said, rolling over, draping my leg over her midsection. No kings or queens, no one better than anyone else, that's what we sing, Nina said. Tear down all smokestacks and stop fucking up the world. You want to fuck up the world, then fuck up your own world, not mine or my children. You have children? I asked. Maybe one day, Nina answered, truthfully or not. I realized I was scratching my head, I didn't know why, exactly, but my scalp was more responsive right now than any other part of my body.

Nina sat up suddenly in bed, turned herself around, and crawled slowly toward the middle of the bed, stationing herself between my legs. She grabbed my dick, which was hibernating. She blew on it, a couple little aimed puffs, like a photographer blowing lint off the camera's lens. Do you know in China last year they put under arrest more than half a million people for prostitution? "Chinese Whore" is one of our songs. I shan't be singing, but they give me time for the most crazy drum solo. I didn't know they had prostitution in China, I said. I took a sharp involuntary sip of breath as she put me inside her mouth. I thought about asking her to stop, but it just wasn't a realistic option. Eventually my dick rose, like a tired old host gamely hauling himself up out of his armchair to greet a guest who has come too late for the party. Come on, Nina said, you must get ready to get set and go. It's all for you, baby. Anywhere you want it. I nodded agreeably, scratching my head. I did not want to make my scalp the focus of my sex life forever, but right now there was nothing better. Of course they jolly well better have prostitution, she said, taking my penis out of her mouth but continuing its stimulation with her hand.

Her palm was cool as marble. Now China has a free market, she said, and men are moving here and there. So they get rather lonely and need comfort. She put me back in her mouth and sucked very, very hard, like in a cowboy movie when someone is trying to extract the poison of a rattlesnake bite. Whoa, I said, touching the top of her head. She crawled back up the bed, thrusting her shoulders forward and then back, like a dancer imitating a lion crossing the veldt.

This is the last time I shall ever do this, she said. After you, no more, we will have brought this to a conclusion. She cupped her hands over her breasts and massaged them. I wasn't sure if she meant this to be erotic. I was, in fact, losing track of what was and what wasn't erotic, just as I had somehow lost the distinction between what was naughty and what was despicable. Uh-oh, she said, pointing to the pillow. I had leaked a little blood, the incessant scratching must have opened up the cut I got on Fifty-sixth Street—or was it Fifty-fifth? I had lost track of that, too. I was lost, so lost, I wondered if I would ever find my way back again. What happens to you? Nina asked. It's nothing, I said. I hurt myself back in New York. There was a knock at the door; a woman's high, timid voice said Room service please.

Nina grabbed the bloodstained pillow, whipped it off the mattress, and stowed it beneath the bed. They'll be quite peeved if they find this, she said. The management here is very calculating. To them success is a column of numbers. She wrapped a towel around her waist and opened the door. Nina towered over the graceful, petite woman who brought our food. The woman wore a beige hotel uniform, and her hair was covered by a sheer turquoise hijab. If she noticed Nina's naked breasts or that I was lying in bed covered by a pale top sheet that was somewhat the worse for our last hour's exertions, she gave no evidence. She rolled the cart in and kept her dark eyes fixed on the gray drapes and the thin sedate slice of the Norwegian night in between. There were two plates and a bowl on the cart, each covered by a pewter dome. I couldn't remember what we had ordered. When things come so easily, it's hard to keep track of them.

Nina began speaking to the woman in Norwegian, and the woman answered, though at no time did she make eye contact. Nina took the bill off the cart and put it in front of me. She had already taken a blue glass bottle of water out of the ice bucket, and she drank directly from it. I signed, without paying attention to the prices. I hope you're giving her a whopping tip, Nina said. These women are all frightfully poor. Take some dollars out of my pants pocket then, I said. My pants were on the floor. With pleasure, Nina said, and while she went through my pockets she continued to speak to the room service waitress, who was surely just trying to answer Nina's questions as succinctly as possible and get out of our room.

Her brother is working in a biochemistry laboratory in one of our most important universities, in Tromsø, Nina said. He is supervising the systematic importation of plants from his native home. These plants have proven medicinal value, which we enterprising Norwegians are learning how to synthesize. I nodded as she spoke, though I was having a difficult time understanding what she was saying—not the words, but the purpose of them. What did we order? I asked. Nina lifted one of the covers. Tomatoes with herbs, she said. She lifted another. Soup. She touched her finger on it and then brought it to her mouth. Beef. I don't remember anything we ordered, I said. You don't need to, Nina said. It's right here. Who needs memory if you have money? She lifted the next cover. Roasted beef sandwich and chips. We ordered well, I said. I just wish I remembered more. Nina put a french fry in her mouth and spoke while chewing. You American men are always so afraid you are losing your mind. I wonder why that is. Is a mental health epidemic in the U.S.?

After we finished eating, we showered. Nina washed her privates with disconcerting vigor, and then she insisted on treating mine with the same thoroughness. She held the bar of soap up into the spray of the shower and then tried to put it in me, which I resisted, instinctively. She smiled at my maidenly demurral, took the soap, and drew an X over my chest with it, and then hit me at the X's crossroads. It wasn't painful but it was spooky—maybe some kind of Arctic voodoo was being performed. Do you want me to tell you the secret to happiness? Nina asked, as she cupped her hands beneath the shower spray. Every morning when I wake up, I say Okay, Nina, today you shall kill yourself, and what would be the best method to achieve this? That's your secret to happiness? I asked. Yes, and you must do it seriously, no larking around. From your first waking moments the idea of ending your life must be more real than any other thought. You can even decide how it must be done. Shall you slit your wrists or take an overdose? You must think of it realistically. That could be dangerous, I said. I reached around her, turned off the shower. It was immediately cold without the water running over us. Of course it is dangerous, Nina said. But listen to what must happen next. You have one exact minute to come up with a reason why today is not the day to end it all. She smiled widely. I always find a reason, and it makes me happy for the whole day. Maybe the reason is something stupid and small, like oh today my boots come back from the shop, where the nice chap has fixed them, or maybe today is my Aunt Goola's birthday and I promised I would call her. Oh, oh, don't go, baby, she said, grabbing my penis, which was shrinking in the sudden cold. Where's my poor baby going? I slid the glass door open and stepped out of the tub, grabbing a large towel and wrapping it around my waist.

Let me, Nina said, taking the towel off of me and drying me from top to bottom. When she was finished with my front she pushed my hip bone to turn me around, and when she was finished drying my back she slapped me on the ass and said There we go. Thank you very much, I said, taking the towel back and wrapping myself up again. *This is what you get as a child*, I thought, *but you're too innocent to really enjoy it and then you get it now and you're not innocent enough to enjoy it.* She took my hand and led me back into the sleeping area, where the bed awaited us, covers and top sheet on the floor, and all but one solitary pillow thrown overboard. I felt doubtful that I could perform sexually again, and I had to remind myself that she was being paid to keep me happy and not the other way around.

What do you say we go downstairs to the bar and have a drink? I suggested. We have the minibar, said Nina. Oh, I don't want to do the minibar thing, I said. They charge triple prices for the minibar. *Uh-oh*, I thought, *now she'll think I'm a low roller*. But Nina ruffled my hair and said Now we must be friends for you to say that.

THE LOBBY BAR was already closed for the night, but we were able to be served in the pub next door. It was made to look something like a hunting lodge, with moth-eaten stag heads and crossed swords on the walls. We were greeted by a tall, elderly man in a worn black suit, who seemed to want to seat us before we changed our minds and fled. The only other customers left in the place were six smashed Norwegian men, who were red faced from booze and disputatiousness, and a trim Japanese man in a pinstriped suit who sat in their midst with his hands folded, a look of pained discomfort on his face, a half glass of beer in front of him. The man next to him, a beefy guy in a black jacket and white tie, leaned over to say something into his ear. Whatever it was, the Japanese man shook his head vehemently, as if his reputation or even his personal safety depended on it.

A young waiter in a red cutaway jacket and a bow tie brought a plate of olives to our table, hoping to further cement our relationship to the pub. Dressed, Nina looked much less like Deirdre. She was wearing a blue silk dress with a faint paisley pattern on it. Deirdre never wore blue. I've got red hair and white skin, she had said, if I wear blue, that's it, I'm a flag.

What shall we have? Nina asked. She pushed the olive dish a little closer to me. Say what you will about the lack of feeling between a man and his paid companion, there was something in that gesture that filled me with sudden warmth, as if I had just gulped down a cup of tea. I didn't know Nina and she didn't know me, but I knew how she smelled, the slightly sour floral scent of her skin, the distant whiff of chicken stock simmering in the little waxed wrinkles of her armpits, the hot minty taste of her mouth, and the bumpy cool oatmeal texture of the inside of her, and she had heard my helpless whinny, that involuntary song of surrender I make when I come, which probably told Nina a lot more about me—animal me, faintly girly me, wounded me, bury my heart at wounded me—than most of the people with whom I supposedly had decent relationships could be said to know.

I leave it to you, I said. Whatever you like. She tilted back in her chair and signaled the waiter, who came over with small late-night menus. She ordered before he could put them down, and he nodded but did not immediately turn around. He lingered for an extra few moments, looking first at her and then at me, and in all likelihood pieced the story together. A little match flame of shame sparked up within me but was quickly extinguished by a gust of simply not caring what anyone thought. It was the most exquisite freedom. It may have been what Fleming was really offering.

Do you mind if I ask you a question or two? I said to Nina. If I can go first, she said. Am I making you tremendously happy? she asked. Is everything to your liking? You're great at sex, if that's what you mean, I said. Really and truly great. Thank you, Avery. I jolly well appreciate it. And I'm sorry I tried to put that piece of soap up your bum. I laughed nervously and told her it was okay, no big deal. Mr. Castle is going to ask you for an evaluation of my services, and then he will tell my Norwegian boss, who is a shit. Last month I was given a rather shabby evaluation, so now I'm a bit nervous. Well, there's nothing to worry about. I'll definitely give you five stars.

The waiter brought a bottle of vodka, icy and opaque, two small glasses, and a plate of cut-up herring, each glistening piece skewered by a toothpick, each toothpick topped by a green ruffle. Nina waited for him to leave and then filled her glass and mine. She drained hers in one gulp, filled it again. I think Mr. Castle operates on a ten-point scale, so if you say give Nina a five that will mean I'm a cooked goose. This chap in April, it was a complete disaster. I thought my boss was going to give me the heave-ho, but maybe filling my place was not so easy. Most of the girls who do this work here in Oslo are Africans and Asians. None of the Ukrainian girls come here, I don't know why, and the Norwegian girls who do the job are maybe a little bit ugly or with problems. She poked her finger against the inside of her arm, tapping the vein. Still, I know he's keeping an eye on me and would like to replace me, so that is why I mention the evaluation.

So tell me about your boss, I said, as casually as possible. It's a man? Nina made a philosophical gesture. It depends what you call a man, she said. Maybe he's a man, he could be, but maybe more a snake notwithstanding. So tell me something about him. I smiled, as if the two of us were in on something, running our own little scam on the outskirts of the larger enterprise, as if we were close, as if there were things she could tell me that she might not ordinarily tell anybody else. How did you meet this guy? Oh with Nils, you don't meet him, he meets you. He's full of moods and angers and has the most crazy crooked face. To demonstrate, Nina hooded her eyes and twisted her mouth. Then she glanced over her shoulder, to make certain we weren't being over-heard. I was working one night at Benetton, and he came in and . . . She waved her fingers as if dispelling smoke. That's the end of the story, for now. She picked an olive off the plate and placed it in my mouth. I had no recourse but to chew it, though it was sour and loathsome. Nina refilled her glass and then topped mine off, too, though it was already almost full. She was looking at me with more intensity than she had when we were having sex. If you like we can make a private arrange-ment, she said. I will tell you everything you want, and you will pay me extra money. It's a you win–I win situation. You get what you want, and with the extra money I can buy a National Steel guitar for my boyfriend, because when we were in Bergen a fortnight ago our van was robbed.

Her boyfriend. I could almost see him, a lanky, loose-limbed man-boy with shaggy hair and a fringe jacket, a black gaucho hat, walking the street with two guitars strapped over his chest. I don't really have extra money, I said, as if that made me a little bit less of a jackass than she might be assuming. I was told everything was included, so I brought very little. Maybe, Nina said, what to you is a little is to me a lot. Anyhow, no problem. I can take your big strong hand, and we can go to an ATM, which is ten meters from the hotel. All I want two thousand U.S. dol-lars, and then I will tell you all how I decided to become a part of the adult travel industry. I'm not sure I have two thousand dollars in my account at home, I said. I'm not like the other men on this tour. And then I added, financially speaking, that is.

I heard the door to the restaurant open; then I heard the famil-iar clomp of Michael Piedmont making his way. He had an exhausted, sick expression, and he was blinking rapidly, as if having trouble staying awake. Next to him was a rather plain woman in a fuzzy white sweater and white skirt. Her eyes were bright blue, her lipstick bright red, her hair was bright yellow, and the beret she wore at a jaunty angle was bright green—all the colors of her seemed to come from a Lego set. Piedmont's shirt collar was bent backward, and the rim of it was sub-merged in his shirt back; the woman with him busied herself with turn-ing his collar up and then patting down the points, as if to coax it into staying put.

He came directly to my table. The chair was too small for him; he perched upon it like a candy apple on a stick. The woman stood off to one side, until he motioned for her to sit.

Nina? she said to Nina, uncertainly—making sure, I guessed, that it was the name in use for this particular job. Nina said something to her in Norwegian, and the women exchanged brief kisses.

Piedmont didn't bother with introductions. Rebekah and I are going out to an after-hours club to hear jazz, he said to me. That sounds like fun, I said. You have to have the whole package, Piedmont said. Dinner, dancing, going out. It makes it more fun. You should come with us. I'm pretty tired, I said. The last time I slept was in New York. Piedmont looked at me sympathetically, as if I'd just told him I had cancer. Oslo has a thriving jazz scene, he said. They love jazz. And you know what? I love jazz, too. My first computer company was called Giant Steps, which I named after one of Coltrane's albums, on Atlantic. Ahmet Ertegün called me personally, I had nothing at the time, I was just a baby, and I thought he was going to threaten to sue me or something, I was really shaking in my boots, but he was calling to wish me luck. Wasn't that nice of him? That was very nice of him, I said. The Turk, Piedmont said, nodding. I have a Piedmont computer back home, I said. I know, you already told me. What do you want? A rebate? You're asking the wrong person if that's what you want. They kept my name because it has buyer recognition, but I have nothing to do with the company anymore. When I had my little playdate with the law, they took the whole thing away from me. He rotated himself in his chair to call for the waiter, who was already on his way over with the food Nina had ordered.

I watched as the waiter put a plate of sliced beef in a dill sauce in front of Nina, and the same thing in front of me. Piedmont arched his brows and pressed his lips together as he regarded our food. Sorry about that, I said to Piedmont. About what? About mentioning my company? Hey, I'm doing fine. I make an obscene amount of money giving talks, seminars; people are throwing money at me all the time. Pretty soon I'll start another company; that's the beauty, that's the thing nobody gets. Once you're on the merry-go-round you can just stay there. Look, I was never that computer oriented in the first place. It's not like I was writing software. I manufactured the things; it could have been toasters. You understand? I had real smart people working for me, a cool product, and I knew how to get it built at a good price.

One of the Metal Men wandered in; it was Olmo, his boiled face and deep-set eyes a mask of defiance. He moved his shoulders as if he were hearing a great song, but he didn't really look very happy. He had changed into a blazer and slacks, a white shirt and red tie. The woman he was with would have looked like a hooker if she had been standing on line at the Motor Vehicle Bureau. She wore a shawl, a short leather skirt with silver doodads in it, like an old Wells Fargo pouch, fishnet stockings, and clunky high-heeled boots. She was heavily made up, and she seemed mean and vulnerable, like one of the transsexual hookers who patrol downtown Manhattan at night, who look as if they could stab you and then go on a crying jag. Olmo stopped when he saw us, furtively, like a man stepping out on his wife who sees his brother-in-law. Mr. Olmo, the Great Mr. Olmo, Piedmont called out in a merry voice, as if there were something intrinsically humorous about Olmo.

Olmo and his escort drew up chairs, but the table was too small for them to fit around it. Olmo sat more or less behind Nina, and his date was behind me. Piedmont was no longer resisting the pieces of herring, nor was he abstaining from the olives. We're going out to listen to some really great jazz, he said to Olmo, and you're welcome to join us. Okay, Olmo quickly said, but without enthusiasm. I glanced over my shoulder to see if his date even knew what was being said, but as soon as I turned I was brought up short by her implacable eyes, so much like stop signs they might as well have been octagonal.

A moment later, Len Cobb walked into the restaurant. Piedmont boomed out a greeting and waved him over to my table. Cobb was dressed in a dark blue Italian suit, a white shirt, light brown loafers so soft looking they seemed made of nectar. He had a fresh-looking bump on the side of his forehead, about half the size of an egg. He walked slowly, but his legs were long and he was at the table in a moment. He was clearly out of sorts. He seemed even unhappier than he had been with Magdalena back in Iceland; with his chin jutting out and his lips pursed, he was making something of a show out of remaining calm, while communicating how upset he was. If Piedmont noticed this, he chose to move right past it. Where's your friend? Piedmont asked. You gotta go get her; we're all going out to hear some jazz. He said the word *jazz* in some vaguely Louis Armstrong voice.

Who told you I like jazz? Cobb said. I just assumed you do, because you're black, Piedmont said. Don't all African American people like jazz? Ooh, that's cold, said Olmo. Despite himself, Cobb smiled, shook his head. This is not what I expected, he said. Not at all. Did you get a bad one? Olmo asked. Because you can switch. You can have mine, actually. Cobb shook his head. I don't know. Maybe it's me. This kind of money? I thought I'd be seeing something I never saw before. Like what? Olmo said. Like a girl with two pussies and ten breasts?

What is he saying? Nina asked me. I'm not sure, I whispered. He's not happy with the girl? she asked me. She pronounced it *gull.* Then, without waiting for an answer, she cried out at him, Who is your girl? But Cobb didn't answer. He was extending his lower lip and stroking his chin, like a general trying to figure out how it had all gone so wrong. Who is your girl? Nina repeated, even more loudly.

Maybe you were expecting too much, Piedmont said. They're just human beings; it's not going to be that different. It is what it is. It's a lot of money is what it is, Cobb said. I never thought I'd be paying for pussy, especially not this much. Don't think about the money, Piedmont said. You can never think about the money. We live in a prison, and the bars are made of dollars and cents. Cobb nodded reasonably, the way you do when someone recites a Zen koan or some other pithy piece of spiritual advice, and no matter how faulty it may sound you don't want to be rude because, in the end, you're touched the person would want to enlighten you, and, also, you're embarrassed for them, spouting off little sayings. I went to the exercise room, Len was saying, but it's closed until morning. I just need to ride a stationary bike or get on the treadmill, I need to move. If I don't get a certain amount of exercise, I start to lose it.

Who is your girl? Nina said, yet again. I wanted to tell her to stop asking that, to, in effect, shut up, and it was interesting to realize that I was not only too polite to say that but actually a bit afraid.

Marit, Cobb finally said. She'll be right down. Marit's great, Nina said. She's the most beautiful of all the girls. You don't know how lucky you are. Cobb responded with a baleful stare and then busied himself with removing a speck of lint from his lapel. Maybe if you're not happy with Marit, Nina said, you can't be happy at all. Get out of my face, Len said. You don't know the first thing about me. Marit's great, Nina said, her voice continuing its rise—soon, it seemed, she'd be shouting. There are too many men in Oslo who want to fuck her. That's her problem, Len said. No, Mister, that is your problem. You understand me? Your problem. Len reached into the olive plate and plucked out the single wrinkled, dented black olive Piedmont had left behind and threw it at Nina, hitting her in the forehead.

Oh no, I thought. *Now I have to be gallant, now I have to come to her defense?* Come on, Len, I said, none of that. You could have hit her in the eye. Control your woman then, he said. Hey, I said, I can't control anybody and anything, and I don't want to. Nina, in the meanwhile, had retrieved the olive, which had bounced off of her head and landed on the floor, and she threw it wildly at Len, missing him by several feet.

These are the moments we will always remember, Piedmont said. Food fights at the Christofer. He slapped his hands on his stomach, smiling happily. When I was in the gulag there'd be a food fight every Saturday night, it was like a tradition. We had guys in there, some of them pretty quote unquote successful out in the world, doctors, lawyers, hedge fund managers, spot commodity traders. And I'll tell you something, a lot of the men in there are going to look back at their time inside as some of the happiest months of their lives. There was always something going on. Greatest food fight of my life was in La Paz, Olmo said, with these awesome fucking guys from Dodge Phelps. We'd just fucking killed the copper market. Nothing in life is worth it if you don't have fun doing it.

What are they talking about? Nina asked me, in an annoyed—and, frankly, annoying—manner. Our relationship, such as it was, was already on the rocks. Michael is an important businessman in America, I said to Nina, in a low murmur, hoping she would get the idea that these little sidebar comments needed to be kept at a discreet level, and he got in trouble over his company's stock and had to go to jail for six months. Prison? Nina said. That man was in prison? She did murmur every word, except, of course, prison, which she fairly barked out. That's right, Piedmont said to her. A lot of fine people have gone to jail, some of them prisoners of conscience, some of them framed. Ralph Waldo Emerson visited Henry Thoreau when he was in prison, and he said Henry, what are you doing in prison?—to which Thoreau famously answered, Waldo, what are you doing *out* of prison?

This may have wowed them in Aspen, but Nina didn't seem impressed. She looked at me, her eyes alive with sparks of delight. Her finger lunged at me like a little dog at the end of a leash. You see? Mr. Castle promises us all the men have passed many tests, all are clean, honest, and good. Back and forth the finger went; I almost wanted to lean forward to offer her the relief of finally poking me in the chest. Believe me, I said, there's nothing to worry about. He's a very important man back home. He's streamlined the lives of many people.

Why, thank you, Avery. Piedmont pressed his hands together, bowed, saluting the divine within me. Don't think I don't appreciate it. What does *streamline* mean? Nina asked me. It means what I should have done to my own fat self, Piedmont said. Slimmer, sleeker, faster. He put his hands on his knees and, from a seated position, thrust his chest forward, like a Sumo wrestler about to engage. Any of the ladies who end up with me, he said to Nina, are lucky ladies. Isn't that right, Becky? Rebekah was plucking at the fuzz on her white sweater and might not have recognized the name Becky as having anything to do with her name. I am respectful, I am generous, and I have such a tiny little penis you hardly even know it's there.

What is he saying to me? Nina demanded of me. I don't know, I said. Don't ask me; talk to him; he speaks the same language I speak. You don't need to filter these things through me. She furrowed her brow at the word *filter*, increasing my impatience. Talk to him, I said, not me. The ancients, Piedmont was saying, tilting his head in an erudite manner, believed that having a big cock was a sign of imbecility. Priapus, who was always pictured with a shlong halfway down to his knees, was an idiot. All the A-list gentlemen had modest, even *delicate* genitalia—I like to think of myself as following in that noble tradition. With all these extra pounds, what used to look like a toe now is more like a nipple. He laughed and patted Rebekah on the top of the head. But you've got no complaints, right? Her smile was quick, startled. She leaned over and whispered into his ear. Well, that's very neighborly of you, he said. And then, to the rest of us, he announced, No complaints, she's very happy with my dainty ding-dong. As the great artists always say, Less is more. Isn't that so? he said to Rebekah. It is like fucking a giant bear, she said to the rest of us. Piedmont thrust his arms into the air, as if he had just scored a goal at the World Cup. Are you interested in monster cocks? Olmo asked no one in particular, and no one paid it any attention.

Cobb's woman, Marit, appeared—brunette, sleekly built, with long fingers and a sideways way of looking at people, as if only the corners of her eyes worked—and the lot of us left the Christofer. We walked in pairs, out into the moist, mild Oslo night, through the quiet downtown, where all of the shops and most of the restaurants were closed. In the distance, I could see a harp set upon a platform which was attached to pulleys being lifted up the side of a narrow, cast-iron building. Since Piedmont, with Rebekah at his side, was leading the way, we walked very slowly, and if there had been anyone out in the streets to observe us we would have made an odd sight, moving with a physical solemnity that was almost funereal. Though maybe we would have been made out to be pretty much what we were: four johns and four hookers, out for a nightcap.

Was I the only one who was entertaining the possibility that we were now being led into an ambush? Do you have any idea where we're going? I asked Nina. People in Norway love old music, she said, but just try to give them something brand-new, that's the day you learn what these people really are. Jazz! She pretended to spit in the street. What does jazz have to do with anything? Jazz is for some old man sitting around in his expensive flat in a silk robe. She extended her pinky, symbolizing, I guessed, everything fey, piss elegant, and done for. I myself harbored no such resentments against jazz, but I didn't care to engage in some debate about musical forms with Nina, whose own becalmed career in the music business was clearly on her mind and was, in fact, the principal reason she was in my company in the first place, for surely if things had been going well with the Forbidden Zone, if they were touring, recording, or even enjoying the prosperity of hope, she wouldn't be walking through Oslo with me. (Of course, if my career had been prospering, I would probably not be here. So there.)

Piedmont had to stop twice to catch his breath, Marit dropped her cell phone and it broke into pieces, but eventually we made it to the jazz club, which was recessed from the street a hundred or so feet, in a courtyard full of life-size statues of jazz musicians. The musicians portrayed looked vaguely like Dizzy Gillespie, Charlie Parker, Gerry Mulligan. The courtyard had an ersatz old-timey feel to it, with shiny black cobblestones, each one smooth and uniform, and the only light cast by a half-size streetlamp, against which leaned one of those generic jazz statues, this one of a vaguely Miles Davis-ish trumpeter with rippling muscles, a wife-beater T-shirt. In short, this place looked about as hip as a jazz club in Disney World.

If there was any criminal premeditation in leading us here, Nina seemed not to be in on it. She was looking around at the statues and shaking her head with obvious displeasure. This is what you'd rather do than have much more fucking, she said in that tone of voice you use to remind a child he has made a choice and is going to have to live with the consequences of that choice.

The club called itself Birdland. We entered through a glass-and-metal door, like the entrance to a supermarket. We were in a small vestibule, at the top of a steep spiral of metal stairs leading to the music—a fierce, chaotic drum solo was in progress. The vestibule was lit by a string of red Christmas lights. The eight of us were crowded together; Rebekah said Now go downstairs, in a commanding voice she probably wouldn't have used in her own language. We followed her down the narrow, corkscrew stairway, getting closer and closer to the drum solo, which grew louder and more oppressive with every step we took. *Descents into hell might sound something like this*, I thought.

The downstairs of Birdland was small and dark, a smell of extinguished candles in the air. A long bar was on one end of the room, bathed in indigo light, with no one behind it making drinks, and the reflection of three quarters of a tenor saxophone floating in the smoky mirror. There were twenty, maybe thirty small round tables in the club, most of them empty. On the bandstand, the drummer—a manic-looking blond guy in an oversize turtleneck sweater—had finally stopped his solo and was back to keeping time while the saxophonist, a black man in his fifties, with carefully cut salt-and-pepper hair, played his solo, alternating lightning tours of chromatic scales with plaintive bluesy three-note riffs.

The manager came over, greeting Rebekah first with a kiss to either cheek, and then welcoming the rest of us. He was a man in his forties, with scimitar sideburns and a long, inquisitive nose. His name was Arne, and he treated us as if he'd been expecting us. He was particularly attentive toward Cobb, grasping his elbow as he shook his hand, and repeating a couple of times what a pleasure it was to meet him. Arne might have recognized Cobb from his NBA days, but I had the feeling he was confusing Cobb with someone else. So this is the Oslo jazz scene, Piedmont was saying, with evident pleasure. I looked around, taking the place in. The other customers were an indecipherable crew—a couple of old-salt types, in knit caps and long curving churchwarden pipes, a young Asian couple who held hands and stared raptly at the musicians, a table of four guys who looked as if they were up to no good—drunk, keeping time by slapping their open hands against the table, and frequently looking in our direction.

Are those friends of yours over there? I asked Nina. Who are you meaning? she said, crossly. I tried to think of where things had taken a wrong turn for us; was it when I basically refused to walk with her to that nearby ATM to withdraw extra money? Over there, I said, those four guys checking us out. She looked at them, making not the slightest concession to discretion. I don't know them, she said. They keep looking this way, I said. And why not? Nina said.

Piedmont was having four bottles of Mumm's brought to us. A bartender had somehow materialized and was now a graceful black silhouette in front of the neon blue lighting. Also materializing was a stocky young woman, satirically dressed in a crinoline party dress and combat boots.

I caught Cobb's attention and pointed to my forehead, to a spot corresponding to his swollen bruise. What happened? I silently asked. He clicked his fingernails against the tabletop and looked at me silently, with no intention of answering. Then he slowly turned away—and this might have been a trick of the light, or it could have been simply because my brain was deprived of proper rest and was starting to fade, or it could also have been that my brain wasn't so much starved for sleep but had ingested the wrong stimuli and was now infected like a hard drive corrupted by a virus, but whatever the reason, or the unreason, whatever flames of irrationality were licking at me, when Cobb refused to answer my question and turned away as if I were not worth bothering with, I could see, *actually see,* the broad-shouldered waitress walking toward us with a tray and eight glasses, right through Cobb's head.

The bottles were uncorked, the glasses were filled, and Piedmont, whose party this seemed to be, made a toast. To freedom, my friends, to our lovely hosts, and to fellowship. Nina was drinking her champagne before Piedmont was halfway through the toast; the rest of us said Here here or Skål, and we clicked glasses, click click click.

The quartet's piano player was a woman. Her back had been to us, and all I had noticed of her, as she punched out shimmering little chords of accompaniment, was her wavy red hair and the way it bounced up and down on her black tuxedo jacket as she moved to the rhythm. She played a solo, skittering and discursive, you'd have to be totally committed to listening to it in order to hear it at all, and when she was finished there was a smattering of polite applause. She looked over her shoulder to acknowledge the audience's good manners, and it was almost as if Deirdre was there. I knew I was really looking at a Norwegian jazz pianist, I knew that woman at the black Baldwin upright, in her tux jacket and tight faded jeans, her enormous dollhouse chandelier earrings, I knew she was not Deirdre, yet the resemblance was shocking. The coloring, of course, and the feminine swagger, that nonchalant, otherworldly confidence that is yours when you have always been loved, when your parents are bright and humane, when your ears have a kind of dewy sheen from all the encouraging words they have heard. I never really had to leave her. I could have fixed the situation. It wasn't hopeless; it wasn't lost.

Suddenly, a wave of longing for Deirdre came crashing to the shore of the little island that was myself, and then everything was unbearable: the way I was living my life, the way I had always lived my life, the things I had failed to do, the things I had done, and what I was doing right now, the reason I was here. I was left with nothing but devastation, a sudden opening into a loneliness and sadness so great that it threatened to pull me in. If I were to be pulled in, into that darkness, that terrible darkness, I feared I might be lost forever. Which is to say that the tears that suddenly sprang to my eyes might have been tears of sadness, but they might also have been tears of terror. Terror might have stuck its staff into me like a dowser's willow crook, and hit the underground stream where the tears had been all along. The piano player was into a slow, bluesy version of "Over the Rainbow."

Nina rubbed my back in rapid little circles. Someone refilled my glass. Leave him alone, Piedmont was saying. At one point, unable to support my head any longer, and wanting the privacy of at least not being able to see the others, I pitched forward and brought my forehead to rest on my forearm, almost tipping the table over. I heard the champagne bottle sliding; I think Cobb caught it because I heard Olmo say Good hands, Len. I heard Nina saying Hello? Are you going somewhere? Presumably she was speaking to me. I heard Len telling someone he was planning to go for a five-mile run as soon as possible, and I heard one of the women say something in Norwegian to one of the other women to which she replied with a admonishing No. Olmo was telling the story of Hap's unsuccessful proposal of marriage, just as he had back in Westchester, but this time adding that Hap was a legendary womanizer who had slept with probably a thousand women and wasn't it funny that the one woman he proposed to—and who was almost certainly going to pass—had oversized calves. From there, Olmo was saying that the three of them were thinking of getting out of the business and starting their own hedge fund. The men didn't seem to care about this, and the women might not have known what he was talking about. I didn't know what a hedge fund was, either, not in any detail; I didn't know what distinguished it from a mutual fund, or why the word *hedge* was in it. Was it a hedge against inflation, a hedge against the overall direction of the market? My mind circled around and around this question. The voices of the others were distant, muffled, like the scream of that bastard whose cry of pain I'd heard underwater at the Blue Lagoon.

My own exhaustion was circling me like a boxer eager to end the fight; I closed my eyes for a moment, and, boom, I was gone. A few moments later I came drifting back. I opened my eyes. I was in the backseat of a car. A pale yellowish tuft of stuffing poked out of a slit in the

upholstery, next to where my head lolled. Nina was on my left, someone else on my right; the driver had a steel gray crew cut, protruding
ears, a white silk scarf wrapped around his neck. My eyes burned, my
eyelids were as heavy as my legs, and the next thing I knew I was waking
up in a bed, on top of a down comforter, darkened beneath my chin
by saliva. I had been dreaming of the sky over Fifty-fourth Street; I had
been looking at it when the waiter from my corner coffee shop came
out to smoke a cigarette, his see-through pocket full of lottery tickets. I
rolled onto my back. Where was I? A bare lightbulb was directly above
me, screwed into a socket in the ceiling, which was surrounded by expanding ripples of wedding cake plaster. I turned away from the light's
glare, noticed a window, partially open, uncurtained, a flat, hard darkness beyond.

I felt compelled to get out of this strange bed, but some need for
safety kept me still, because, having no idea where I was, I didn't know
what I would do once I was upright, or where I would be, or what I
would find. I heard music from the next room, the throb of it at once
nostalgic and disorienting—it was a letter from home, but who was
sending it, how had it gotten here? All that separated me from the
music was a wooden door, painted eggshell blue. I got to a standing
position—the compact, overheated room did a kind of visual hiccup
as the blood momentarily drained from my head—and, thinking that
the worst that could happen to me had probably, without my entirely
knowing it, already happened, I smoothed down my shirt, and opened
the door to whatever was awaiting me on the other side.

Here were my thoughts, in the order in which I had them. *Big room. Not
so warm. Len Cobb is beating up Nina. Olmo and Piedmont have been drugged,
and now they are on a black sofa with their heads thrown back, their mouths
open. Isn't that the drummer? God, water pipes are so lame. Hookahs, hookers,
that's weird. Nina seems to be getting away from Cobb. There's an iPod, there's a
speaker tower. Marijuana. Smells good, feels bad. What clutter. Distant ring of cell
phone—Eine kleine Nachtmusik. I must help Nina. Oh my God, Nina.*

At which point I lurched forward, shouting out her name. I don't
think anyone in the room had at that point realized I was a factor. One
of the Norwegian girls said The dead are now coming awake, and Nina,
who was on the floor, propped up on her elbows, looked my way, with a

weird little Oops of a smile, at which instant I realized that Len wasn't doing anything wrong, not really, certainly not in any actionable way. His dark trousers had been replaced by dark naked legs and he was merely fucking Nina, and hot on the heels of this deeply embarrass-ing—even shaming—clarification was the further clarification that my other two traveling buddies were not the recipients of some knockout drug but were doing their best to enjoy side-by-side blow jobs, admin-istered by Marit. Wasn't Nina meant to be for me? I could have walked into a booby trap, stepped on a land mine, so sudden and intense was the explosion of searing, irrational jealousy. There are men, and I am not one of them, for whom jealousy is a springboard into acts of vio-lence, and there are others, take for example *me*, for whom jealousy is a springboard into an overwhelming sense of shame. Shame and wretch-edness and smallness and insignificance and exclusion.

Len was energetically jabbing his finger in the air. At first I thought he was pointing at me, in a threatening way, but then I saw he was point-ing at Rebekah, who was already out of her white sweater and was now wriggling out of her matching skirt, folding it neatly and placing it on a wooden chair, painted, like Rebekah herself, in a primary color, in this case blue. She was wearing lacy red underwear. Her breasts were heavy, rather maternal. She held one with her left hand while her right hand pulled her underpants to one side, revealing a pink exfoliated crotch. Her eyes were looking in my general direction, though not ex-actly at me. Then she turned around, shook her ass at me. It was clear I was meant to be aroused by this, and I was, to some extent—my penis was not exactly ready for action, but it stirred. I waved her over, think-ing it would be better for everyone if we went back to the bedroom. I couldn't stand watching Nina and Len fucking. And Olmo and Pied-mont sitting shoulder to shoulder like two men on a roller coaster—that wasn't much easier to take.

Where are you going? Piedmont demanded of Rebekah. To your friend, she answered. No, no way, let's all stay together. Piedmont tilted his head back so he could see me as if I were in the viewfinder of an old black-box camera, and said Don't take her away; it's one for all and all for one. Now Marit was fellating only Olmo; the woman who had come into the restaurant with Olmo was working on Piedmont. I got a look at her because she took a break, sat back on her heels, like a woman on a riverbank exhausted after hours of scrubbing clothes. She had hiked up her shirt to expose her sheer copper-colored brassiere. Her belly was divided into three distinct folds, each one the width of a celery stalk. Despite the tough mask of pancake makeup and mascara she wore over what had once upon a time been her face, she looked as if she were struggling. She caught her breath, swallowed, bowed her head. Later, when I had sex with her, I learned her name was Maud, I mean the name she used. This was the first, and probably will be the only, time I participated in an orgy. More than that I cannot say.

Except I can say this, too: you can't *always* care about what you do, and how you behave. You can't *always* care about right and wrong, even if you have God on your side, which I did not, even if you have God, or some idea of God, in your hip pocket, even if you carry a flask of his blood in your jacket, it doesn't matter—there are times when you just don't care anymore. You just do the bad thing, because you are frightened, or curious, or bored, or angry, because something or someone tells you to, or because you are consumed with desire, maybe not consumed, not starving, maybe just somewhat hungry, just wanting a few more sips from the great chalice of earthly pleasures, just enough to top you off. It happens. To all of us. The most you can hope for is that you don't sin too often, and that you don't break a major commandment. In other words, steal but don't kill. You could get by with breaking all the commandments except the one that warns you thou shall not kill; even though it got shuttled down to number six (sic!), it's still the commandment that matters most. Go ahead, if you must, and worship false idols, fantasize about a new Mercedes or the woman next door, and if you hit your thumb with a hammer and happen to take the Lord's name in vain I think the Lord can deal with it, I really do.

All right. I *can* say something else about the orgy. It was great, mad fun. It was as close as I've ever gotten to being an uncivilized man. Maybe the Metal Men experienced similar highs blasting mountains, grabbing whatever they wanted. Maybe Dr. Gordon felt something akin to this after splitting a patient's sternum and holding his heart. Maybe Tony felt thrust far beyond the earth's persistent gravitational pull when he scratched off the winning numbers. But, despite the irregularities of my early life, I had always closely adhered to what was expected of me. I got my assignments in on time, I paid my rent, left an 18 percent tip when I dined out, looked—with one notable exception—both ways before crossing the street. Now, however, in the drummer's front room, with Olmo singing Who likes monster cocks? and Marit continually repeating the rather obvious yet somehow remarkable observation Now, boys, we are really doing it up, I was feeling for the first time the pleasure that can be derived from blithely violating the boundaries that had long ago been so carefully pointed out to me while I was walking around the parameters of my life like a good dog on a leash. The occasional confrontations with the unappealing bodily facts of the many animals writhing around were more than made up for in the forbidden, mindless, pleasure of sex for sex's sake.

16

WE WALKED BACK to the Christofer around eleven in the morning, two by two, the original couples restored, reeking and depraved. I could barely put one foot in front of the other. Everything felt so askew, I would not have been surprised to find I had put my pants on backward. All that propelled me were visions of my bed and fantasies of occupying it by myself, tossing and turning in a cool ecstasy of privacy and autonomy. I thought about that bed awaiting me with the fervency of a shipwrecked sailor floating in the middle of the ocean, clutching to one piece of jetsam, keeping despair at bay with a dream of dry land. Even at the height of morning commerce, Oslo maintained its dreamlike hush. A truck went by as quietly as a golf cart. Two workers carrying cases of wine into a restaurant moved themselves and their cargo with such grace you could have thought they were stealing the wine rather than delivering it. Piedmont was in front of me, the back of his shirt dark with sweat. Rebekah kept a guiding, encouraging hand on his elbow as he clomped along. Behind me, Marit had asked Len about the boy with the scars and only one arm, and Len launched into a discourse about Jordan, in which Jordan emerged not only as a war hero but as a man in whose person resided all the great virtues: loyalty, compassion, honesty, and courage. I don't know what kind of trash you're used to, Len said, but he's a good man, a very, very good man. He makes me afraid, Marit said.

I heard a sharp intake of breath. What are you shivering about? Len asked her. I was thinking of him, Marit said. Then don't think about him. And don't go shivering either. You understand me? Don't do that. That's very rude.

When we arrived at the hotel I made my hasty good-byes and returned to my room, but it was occupied by two housekeepers. They may have been mother and daughter. The older one was standing with her hands on her wide hips, surveying the damage, her face an olive oval ensconced in a floral scarf. The younger one, bareheaded, in jeans and a lilac blouse, was beginning to gather up the bed linens, grasping them with swift, harsh gestures, as if they were delinquents who might try and break free. They didn't react to my walking in; they seemed neither startled nor aware. Sorry, sorry, I said. But even my voice couldn't move their eyes toward me. How much time do you need? I asked. We are cleaning room now, the older one said. Twenty minutes? I offered. More, she said. I took a last longing look at the bed—even without sheets and pillows it looked inviting—and then made my way back down to the lobby.

Stephanie and Gabrielle were standing in front of the elevator as I got out. They had just gotten back from the Munch museum, and they were laughing at one of the souvenir postcards they'd picked up at the gift shop. Stephanie greeted me warmly, but Gabrielle looked concerned. She appeared prosperous, cultured, and busy in her pleated skirt, soft wool sweater, and white blouse with a big floppy bow at the top of it. Where is Nina? Gabrielle said. Her tone seemed to suggest I had done something terrible to Nina, and I shook my head. But everything is fine? she asked. No problems? I really didn't want to evaluate Nina's services just then; it seemed particularly awkward to be doing so in front of Stephanie. Gabrielle, however, was determined that I answer; I finally said No problems at all, but even that wasn't enough and the inquiries continued until I said She's great, she's a beautiful woman, I'll be seeing her later on. Gabrielle smiled; like most people, she was receptive to information that made her life easier. Lincoln was sure you would like her energy, she said. Yes, I said, her energy. Are you ready? Gabrielle asked Stephanie, stepping into the elevator. Are you going to have a coffee or something? Stephanie asked me. Yes, I am, I said, and then, remembering my manners, I asked her to join me.

We went to the restaurant where last night's strenuous festivities had begun. The room seemed not to have fully recovered from a long night. The slightly skunky smell of beer was in the air, and a large table had been pushed into a corner and piled high with white linen table-cloths and red napkins waiting to be laundered. The waiters working seemed to have just rolled out of bed, and they moved nervously, with the overly solicitous manner of unfaithful husbands hoping to hide what they had been up to the night before. Our waiter asked for our room numbers, and I detected a slight hesitation from Stephanie, which made me wonder if she felt uneasy about my knowing which room she was in.

Across the room, Tony and Dr. Gordon shared a table, along with a sharp-faced young woman who patted her close-cropped hair as though comforting herself while she spoke on her cell phone. Tony, whose back was to us, was gesturing emphatically, and Dr. Gordon, who looked even grayer and more fatigued than he had when I saw him last night in the elevator, was nodding weakly, a look of dismay in his large wet eyes.

I think someone better keep tabs on Dr. Gordon, I said to Stephanie. He looks like he's going to end up in the emergency room. I'd like to put Tony Dinato in the emergency room, Stephanie said. He's gone completely off his rocker. He has? Stephanie looked at me with surprise. You mean he hasn't come after you with his Bible stuff? I shook my head no. Well, he will. I'm surprised he hasn't gotten around to you yet. Maybe he thinks I'm a lost cause, I offered. He's tried to convert two of the girls so far, Stephanie said. He's proselytizing hookers? I can't even get these women to laugh at my jokes, I said. Stephanie nodded. I think winning all that money and then this, it's been too much for him. I think he's snapped. Maybe when we get to Latvia he'll have better luck. A lot of the Latvian girls are very religious.

The waiter came with coffee, croissants, little fluted tubs of pale white butter, a basket of miniature jam jars. His hands were shaking; he had nicked himself shaving, right below the nose. You're going to love Latvia, by the way, Stephanie said. The girls there are some of the most attractive of all the countries we're going to; I've actually heard some guys say they're the most beautiful women in the world, tall and fair, and even the older ones are very fit. Yet very religious, I said, distancing myself from the pleasures awaiting me. Don't worry about that; there's nothing you can imagine and for sure nothing you could physically accomplish that these girls can't handle. They're all so glad not to be living under communism any longer. And they believe in Fate, which means that for them whatever is happening is meant to happen. It makes them very accommodating.

The thought of the Latvians and their believing in Fate and, especially, their being very accommodating—we all knew what accommodating meant—had a slightly sickening effect on me, as would a detailed description of the next meal when you haven't begun digesting the last one. In fact, the idea of getting back on another minibus that would take me to the airport and then onto a plane that would take me to another airport, where another minibus would await me, made me as weary and anxious as the thought of meeting yet another woman who would be somewhat nice to me as a way of paying the rent or buying her boyfriend a new guitar.

In Riga, Stephanie said, you're probably going to meet Anastasia. She might be a little young for you, but she's great. A little dark-haired beauty. A lot of the guys have gone for Marianna, but I think she's generic. Too blond—or maybe you don't think it's possible to be too blond. She looked up toward the ceiling, to organize her thoughts. You like dark-haired women, don't you? I find myself caring less about what anybody looks like, I said, but I might as well have said nothing. Then there's Lubov. What I like about her—I know this is silly—is how she holds her head, like she's ducking under a doorway that's too low for her. She's supercute and full of attitude. All the other girls look up to her; she's sort of a leader. Maybe Yulia, if you like big. She's a folk singer, not only Latvian songs but songs from all over the world. She has fantastic hair, too, dark red. I like red hair, I said. Stephanie shook her head. You should stick with Lubov, she said. Or Yana, very intelligent, loves books. The only thing is she's too tall for you. I think Len when I think Yana. And I'll bet Romona ends up with Jordy. She'll want to take care of him. Stephanie laughed, shook her head. It's the greatest show on Earth, she said.

The names sound Russian, I said. The Russian girls were very popular, Stephanie said, back in the day, but we've stopped going there since the war. Because our governments are not really getting along right now, some of the girls were getting a little sarcastic. It was very disappointing to Mr. Castle. He especially liked taking the guys to Russia. I think his father was part Russian. More like pro-Russian, I said. And when Stephanie looked at me uncomprehendingly, I said His father was a Communist. He was? That's wild, that's about the cutest thing I ever heard. Anyhow, we dropped Russia and we put Latvia on the itinerary and you know what? The guys had a better time in Riga than they ever had in Moscow or St. Pete. One guy said—Stephanie looked over her shoulder to ensure privacy and then silently mouthed the name of a well-known, recently retired congressman—that Vilnius is like a small town filled with beautiful sex-crazed models. Except, let's face it, I said, they're not sex crazed. They're doing it for money. Stephanie shrugged. Those two things aren't mutually exclusive. I love flying—but I also love getting paid. So I combine the two. Especially the Latvian girls, they don't like the local men. The men are like twenty years behind the women when it comes to being modern. The Latvian girls say that the Fleming guys treat them with a lot more respect than the guys they meet in their regular lives. Which is great, I said. Just when our country needs us the most, we're putting the ass back in ambassador.

Stephanie lowered her eyes and began giving her coffee far more attention than it required—you don't really have to stare at the surface of your coffee while sugar dissolves.

I heard a rapping at the window, and when I turned toward the sound I saw Cobb, who was on the sidewalk outside, dressed in black satin shorts and a T-shirt, jogging in place. He gave me a wave and took off on his run.

He's self-medicating through exercise, I said to Stephanie, and then I reached for the little pile of postcards she had next to her coffee cup. Do you mind? I asked. The topmost postcard was the inevitable reproduction of *The Scream*, but the next was a less familiar Munch, a painting of a lithe young girl, her lower half tentatively covered by a blue robe with white lining, her hands knitted together behind her head. She is offering her tender breasts while five sets of feverish red and green hands monstrously grope their way toward her. The next card showed a man painted against a violent background of flame and smoke. He was naked to the pubic bone, with a red slash across his throat and ominous green paint at the back of his shoulder. His gaze was steady, wry, and somewhat contemptuous, as if by looking at him we were invading his hellish privacy, for which he was going to forgive us because he was doomed and we were not worth being angry with.

He sort of looks like Castle, I said, sliding the card across the table. She did not so much as look at the card as bat her eyelashes in its direction. No, really, I said. He bears an uncanny resemblance. It's called *Selvportrett I helvete*, Stephanie said. *Self-Portrait in Hell*. Here's another one. She reached over for the postcards, found it. This is called *Self-Portrait with Red Background*. See, he gave himself a nice green suit to wear, and even a little vest. I like the way he has his hand in his pocket, like a businessman. Very satisfied with himself.

I looked at the postcard. Munch's face was scorched by red light. The painted red background surged like a sea of fire. Do you ever think that maybe we're in hell? I asked Stephanie. And that Lincoln Castle is . . . you know, an extremely bad person, so bad he's not even a person anymore? Stephanie looked disappointed, as if she had expected more of me, something better. I realized I could draw a map of my whole life with every point along the way another woman I had disappointed. But it was too late to change that now—not in Oslo, not on a sex tour. No one really expects you to get your life on firmer footing while you're on a sex tour. It seems, I said, that he doesn't cast a reflection in a window or a mirror. What mirror, Avery? Any mirror. Things that reflect, in general. She broke off a piece of croissant. I wouldn't worry about it, she said. But that wasn't nearly enough to put things to rest. I said I felt there was something strange about him, from the very beginning. And then Stephanie said What's the beginning? You understand? Can you ever really say where anything begins?

I shook my head. I didn't know what to say to that. If we can't find our way back to where something began, what hope do we have of ever understanding why we are where we are? Are you all right? Stephanie asked me. Just tired, I said. Long night? she asked, with a box-cutter smile. It took me by surprise. Such disappointment, such antipathy—I was surprised she felt anything so intense. Did she have some sort of feeling for me, or was she just showing bitterness about the whole enterprise? Many long nights, I said. Two months on the sofa, a flight across the Atlantic Ocean, then an insane night in Iceland, then the attack, then . . . I gestured, implying I would spare Stephanie the gory details. But she was having none of it. Then what? she asked. More insanity? Yes, much more. Aw, poor you. She took a prim sip of coffee, crossed her legs. Her disdain for my mental health, probably meant to have some chastising effect, a way of putting me in my place by reminding me I was a john with a john's predictable miseries, only made me feel more sympathetic toward myself. In fact, I was just about to launch into my familiar twelve-bar blues called Four Fathers when my attention was seized by the sound of the door to the restaurant squeaking open, and when I turned toward the sound there she was, weighing in at 115 pounds, wearing the striped black pants and the green satin blouse, Naomi Cohen Kaplan Kearney Blake Jankowsky.

Avery? Stephanie said, with some alarm. My mother's here, I murmured. I'm looking right at her.

Naomi saw me, too. Confoundingly, she was with Romulus Linwood, the goddamned steak knife king, who had already confessed to me that he was looking for someone a little older, a little more maternal. Mom stopped her progress into the Christofer's restaurant so abruptly that she stumbled for a moment. But then she turned and began walking away. It seemed, at least for the moment, that she was no readier to see me than I was to see her. I was momentarily paralyzed by uncertainty. Should I run after her or hide? My legs trembled uncontrollably.

You do not allow your mother to walk away in such a situation, no matter how dense and detailed your case against her may be. You do not allow your mother to be in the company of some guy on an around-the-world sex tour. If your mother has traveled from Costa Rica to Norway to slap you across the mouth because of a (perhaps ill-considered) article in *Esquire*, then just take it like a man, for God's sake. Be a good Latvian and accept your Fate. Hey, Mom, I shouted out, as I set out for the door connecting the restaurant to the hotel lobby.

I got there just in time to see the elevator doors sliding shut. Romulus and my mother, I assumed, were in the elevator, rising up to whatever floor he had been booked onto. The numbers above the elevator door remained dark; all that was illuminated was the arrow indicating that the car was rising.

I went to the front desk clerk and asked him to ring Castle's room. I didn't care how irregular it might be, or what he might think of me. All I wanted was for him to tell me which room Romulus was checked into. I was directed to the house phone, while the desk clerk—a frugal-looking man with neat gray hair and a bureaucratic mustache—put me through to Castle's room. I stood there listening to the low guttural ring, like the death rattle of all communication. The house phone was on a marble-topped table, which it shared with a couple of pots of African violets, a yellow bowl with a blue stripe filled with red and white peppermint candies, and a wicker basket filled with small, imploding apples. I couldn't see an apple without thinking of Kearney, Father Number 2, who ate five of them a day and smoked apple-scented pipe tobacco. Though he smoked, drove recklessly, and went through several cans of Old Milwaukee beer every night, Kearney maintained a nervous relationship with his own health. He weighed himself morning and evening; he respected the federal dietary guidelines as if they were constitutional amendments, including the green and yellow vegetables and the six glasses of water daily, which he didn't even bother to drink cold. Apples were always in abundance in what was then the Kearney household. They were on the table near the front door, in a large bowl next to where keys and loose change were deposited. When I was six or seven I helped myself to fifty cents, having no idea that for all the casualness with which Kearney emptied his pockets into the bowl at the end of the day, he nonetheless kept an uncannily exact count of what was in there, and those two quarters hadn't been in my pocket for more than fifteen minutes before I was dragged back into the front hallway and raged at as if I were on my way to a life as a career criminal. Kearney's soft, handsome Irish face was suddenly as hard as a horseshoe. He grabbed my arm and tattooed it with a thumb-shaped bruise, and reminded me that my father, whose flickering existence in my memory was on full life support, wholly dependent upon information supplied by Kearney and my mother, was dead and in the ground because he couldn't keep his hands off of other people's property, and did I want the same thing to happen to me? Even as a hairless little blob I recognized the injustice and the sheer *tackiness* of what he was saying, but when I opened my mouth to protest I saw my mother, standing a few feet behind her second husband, her eyes dim behind a mist of fear, her finger, with its wrinkled knuckle and long scarlet nail, placed imploringly on her lips.

A dull marimba ring announced the arrival of an elevator. For a moment, I thought it was my mother emerging, but it was Gabrielle, who stepped out of the brightly lit car, wearing a smart black suit. A pair of glasses hung from a long matronly chain and came to rest on her bosom. She wore a short dark skirt and a white satin blouse. She carried a small biography of Thomas Edison; she was probably on her way to lunch. I called out to her, and she turned slowly toward me like a shopkeeper who must somehow produce a labored smile even though you have come into the store ten seconds before closing time. I need to get hold of Romulus, I said, rushing to her side. Oh yes? She put a step's worth of distance between us. May I ask why? There didn't seem time to come up with some bogus excuse, so I simply said He just left with my mother.

Gabrielle had eyes like a nurse—promising understanding, even compassion, but always at a distance, always with a reminder she had important business elsewhere. Remember? I said. He was into older, more motherly types? He said this. He said it to me, and he said he told you, too. You were trying to find him someone else in Iceland. Don't you remember? He asked for someone else? Yes, of course I remember, he wanted a change, but there were many changes after, you know, after the Blue Lagoon. Fuck the Blue Lagoon, I said, improvidently. This has nothing to do with that. He wanted a change before any of that happened. He said he wanted to be with someone more motherly. Gabrielle shook her head, slowly at first, and then more emphatically. The act of shaking her head created its own momentum, a physics of denial, the way a lie will pick up velocity once you have started it rolling. Look, I said to her, Romulus walked into the restaurant with my mother. They saw me, they disappeared, and now I would like to see my mother.

Your mother is *here?* a voice behind me said. I turned toward it with the same hopeless fear I turned toward the Town Car when I heard it materializing on the edge of consciousness. It was that old devil Castle, wearing one of his festive silk shirts. He looked at me with his head cocked to one side. Apparently, I said. Apparently? What are you talking about? Either she is or she isn't. My mother is here in the hotel. Like there was a man in your room? Castle said. No, not like that. Other people saw her, too. Maybe you better tell me what's happening here, Castle said. I mean everything. I don't know what's happening, I said. I rarely see my mother. She lives in Costa Rica. Costa Rica? Castle said. Is she in the business? What business? I asked. You know, he said, with a wave. Our business. I wasn't aware you and I *had* a business, I said. Adult services are legal in Costa Rica, Gabrielle said, though she was still shaking her head no. I paused for a long time, giving them both a chance to fully consider what they were implying about my mother. Then I said, enunciating every word, My mother is not involved in prostitution.

Then what in the hell is she doing here? Castle said. Can you please tell me that? I have just never heard of something like this. Have you ever heard of something like this? he asked Gabrielle. No, she said. Her head stopped shaking back and forth, though her glasses continued to swing from their chain. Castle returned his inquisitive gaze to me, with even more intensity, as if Gabrielle's never having heard of someone's mother showing up on a sex tour was the final proof of its irregularity. I don't know why she's here. All I know is she is, she's here, she's with Romulus, and I need to speak to her. Well, Castle said, don't expect me to tell you Romulus is in Room 625. I opened my mouth to further argue my cause but then realized what he'd said. I didn't want to further compromise him with my thanks; I nodded brusquely and walked quickly to the elevators, jabbed my thumb against the call button a number of times, and just happened to glance toward the restaurant at the moment Stephanie was coming out, perhaps in search of me. I waved her back in and flashed my fingers a number of times, hoping to indicate that I would be back in fifteen or twenty minutes, but Stephanie didn't seem to know what I was trying to tell her and gave me a puzzled look. I was forced to call out to her, I'm going to get my mother. Instead of going back into the restaurant, however, Stephanie walked over to Castle and Gabrielle, both of whom looked glad to see her. By now, I was in the elevator, and the doors smoothly shut out the sight of the three of them exchanging continental kisses. *Of course, of course,* I thought, *they're a team.*

I pressed the button for the sixth floor, but the slow-moving elevator stopped on two, and Webb got on. Avery! he cried out, clapping me on both shoulders. You're the only guy in this whole outfit who doesn't give me a pain in the ass. He looked rested and relaxed, though his eyes held a glint of Webbian menace. He was in the company of a frightened-looking woman in her early twenties, her dark hair cut like an English schoolboy's, her milky green eyes showing enough anxiety to get her detained at any major airport. She wore a blue leather skirt and an orange T-shirt lettered in blue and saying SOMMERJOBB. She seemed aware that it was her misfortune to have ended up with Webb, and, indeed, as the doors closed and the elevator resumed its laborious ascent, she stepped a foot or two away from him. She carried an ice bucket, heaped with cubes and crowned by a pair of silver tongs, in which was reflected the elevator's illuminated ceiling.

Webb was full of hijinks, showing a playful, teasing side that carried glaring hints of sadism. He hadn't yet grabbed his Norwegian companion by the back of the neck and run her up and down the corridors; instead, he commandeered the ice tongs and began dropping ice cubes down the back of her shirt. She hunched her small round shoulders and twisted her torso, creating space between her T-shirt and her skin, and allowing the ice cubes to fall to the floor, with minimal contact with her skin. But, wary as she was of him, she did not want to passively endure his childishness. She grabbed a handful of ice herself. Oh no, you don't, Webb said. His voice was sharp, loud, full of concern, as if by retaliating and putting ice down *his* shirt she would be placing him in serious jeopardy. Even smiling and pursuing Webb with her handful of ice, the girl looked seriously unnerved. She had the gummy smile chimps dressed in formal wear show to the camera, when their lips are stretched back by the fish hooks of terror. She jiggled the ice cubes in her hand, and then, with the whoop of a girl who has always tried to hold her own with her rambunctious brothers, she lunged toward Webb and shoved the ice cubes down the front of his shirt. You're going to stop my heart, you crazy bitch, he shouted out. She seemed to take some encouragement from this and began taking ice cubes one at a time out of the bucket and tossing them at Webb, who energetically dodged them. He picked out an ice cube himself, grabbed her behind the neck—his specialty, it seemed—and forced it into her mouth, and then he held her mouth shut so she couldn't spit it out. She was saying something in Norwegian, muffled and full of high notes, and she was doing her best to pull his hands away from her mouth and jaw. But Webb was hardwired to resist whenever force was used against him. The girl struggled to remove his hand—she scratched him, tried to bite him, shook her head back and forth—but all her efforts only made him grip her tighter. I thought he might end up killing her.

Let her alone, Webb, I said, but my voice lacked resonance, it was flat and without authority; it was a voice I knew well, a voice I didn't like to hear: the voice of my childhood. I cleared my throat, repeated my warning, which, the second time through, sounded as if it had a little something behind it, if not the power of enforcement then at least a bit of humanity. We're just having fun, he said, tossing a quick glance my way. Come on, Webb, I said, trying to strike a tone that implied both reasonableness and determination, and a couple of hand gestures that suggested that here we were once again, going over ground we had already covered, and now it was time for him to behave and act like the generally good fellow I knew him to be. Hey, I don't tell you how to treat your fucking whore, so don't tell me. We were already nearly at the fifth floor. Somehow knowing we only had another couple of moments emboldened me. I moved closer to him, drew my shoulders back, stuck my chin out, clenched my teeth. Just leave her alone, Webb. The woman was trying to free herself by turning her head left and then right, and her eyes were showing a great deal of white, like a horse in a burning barn. I didn't have a plan of action; I had never known what to do when words failed. But suddenly it seemed like a good idea to cause Webb a bit of pain, enough to make him let go of the girl, and I elbowed him in the ribs with all my might.

His reaction was far beyond the cries of impending calamity he emitted when his escort dared to threaten him with an ice cube. He *shrieked*, high and shrill as a smoke alarm. Life is moments, isn't that what people say? Well, it's billions and billions of moments, so there has to be a lot of editing if you are going to tell anyone anything, and in my editing I like to linger here, with Webb shrieking, with Webb grabbing his side and holding it, as if I might have split him open and his organs were in danger of falling to the ground like trinkets out of a piñata. The girl's mouth was finally uncovered and she spat out like a rotten tooth what was left of the ice cube. It hit the faux-marble floor of the elevator car and bounced hectically here and there before settling in a corner. The girl tenderly touched her own chin, the sides of her mouth, and she said You're crazy, which I assumed she was saying to Webb, though there is, I suppose, an outside chance she meant me. Like many men who have had scant or no real experience with physical force, I was filled with illusions about it, and I was reveling in my quick strike at Webb. This was even better than the Blue Lagoon, where my violence might have been somewhat more extreme but, also, wholly reactive and rooted in self-defense. Taking a nip out of someone's thigh when they are trying to drown you doesn't exactly make you a warrior.

But now, in the elevator, my moment of unalloyed triumph was over; once Webb had ascertained that he hadn't been hurt, his eyes locked in on me with a predatory calm that verged on delight. I ought to have known full well that he was going to come after me, but I was, nevertheless, unprepared. Webb lowered his head like a bull, and then he ran his shoulder into my chest. I either fell or flew backward. My head hit the back wall, where a framed poster advertising the Christofer's restaurant hung, a slightly faded, out-of-date-looking photograph showing a whole salmon on a silver platter and a bottle of champagne. I heard the glass of it shatter beneath the force of my skull. The elevator stopped; the doors opened. This is my floor, I said, in a surprisingly composed voice. Webb was sweating profusely. His rather small hands, squeezed into fists, circled around and around, like someone gathering up a skein of yarn. I was particularly focused on his gold and garnet ring that sat upon the fourth finger of his right hand, as large as an acorn. What better reason was there to wear such a thing than to now and then ram it into the bridge of someone's nose? Well, it's been real, I said, moving past him. I heard the elevator doors shut behind me, and I stood there for a moment, trying to remember which room Lincoln said Romulus and my mother were in.

At that point, I had no idea that my collision with the back of the elevator had reopened the gash on the side of my head, nor did I realize that my scalp was bleeding. I rapped on the door to Room 625, waited.

You're covered in blood, Romulus said to me, as soon as he opened the door. Once he said it, I felt it. Somehow my skin's registry of the greasy warmth of my own blood hadn't yet been transmitted to my full consciousness, though, in fact, a little puddle of blood had pooled in my ear, and there was blood on my neck, my collar, and halfway down the front of my shirt. Romulus had opened his door enough to allow me to see a pie slice of his room, enough to put to rest the hope that the woman I had been seeing since Iceland as my mother was in fact some other middle-aged woman, a tan, well-taken-care-of woman in simple, expensive clothes who, because of my own inflamed sense of guilt over the *Esquire* piece, or because I was simply conjuring the worst thing that could befall me on this trip, merely (and intriguingly) *appeared* to be my mother. But none of that was the case: the woman seated in a chrome and leather chair near a tall mahogany dresser was without question Naomi Cohen Kaplan Kearney Blake Jankowsky. Now, all I needed to figure out was why she was in the knife king's room.

What are you doing here? I asked her.

Oh my God, Avery, I knew it, I knew it, you're covered in blood, she said, rising from her chair. Her face was puffy, pale here, red there. She had been crying. She made her careful steps toward me—she always walked as if she were sneaking off somewhere, as if the creak of a floorboard would give her away. Romulus gave up on the idea of denying me entrance. He further opened the door and stood to one side, making room for my mother, who continued her cautious pace toward me. Contrary to what I would have predicted, I was glad almost to the point of mania to be seeing her, even here, even now. Naomi, I said, reaching out for her, Mom.

MY MOTHER was staying on the Christofer's top floor. She hadn't expected to be in Oslo, and the hotel had been fully booked, except for the vast, pricey Explorer Suite, which, out of kindness, the management let her have for less than the going rate, so once again, I thought, her haphazardness and helplessness had worked in her behalf, and someone, a man, in this case a middle aged Norwegian with deeply recessed eyes and a shock treatment haircut, had intervened on her behalf—though to complete the old pattern she would have to marry him and I would have to change my last name to Reichelt. After taking our leave of Romulus, we rode the elevator, not exactly in silence but making talk so small that it was worse than finding ourselves with nothing to say. On the eighth floor, the elevator stopped and opened to Dr. Gordon, who seemed awfully surprised to see me. Are you going down? he asked. Not at the moment, I said, and then the three of us stood in silence, like people in a book of photographs waiting for someone to turn the page. When the doors finally slid shut, my mother said Who the hell was *he*? Dr. Gordon, I said, he's from Evanston. That old guy's on this trip with the rest of you men? He's here because of Jordy, I said. Yeah? Who the hell is Jordy? Jordy is Jordan, his son. The trip's really for Jordy. Oh my God, Avery, that has got to be the sickest thing I've ever heard. I made a low, bitter laughing sound. Stick around, I said.

Up in the suite, I followed my mother into the sitting room. She stood by the window. Despite all the time in the sun, her dark hair was even darker and more lustrous than it had been when she was young. She was quite tan, and her skin practically sparkled with the moisturizer she used to counteract the effects of all that sun. Dark and rich, she looked like food. She had parted the curtains and gripped the right panel with one hand. She was intent, motionless, with all the concentration of a spy looking out for a signal of some kind: a blinking light, a white van circling the block, a man in a bowler walking a Cocker spaniel. I could live here, Naomi finally said, letting go of the curtain and turning again to face me. Except for the weather, she added. That I could do without. Romulus told me winter lasts half the year. Well, it's not really an issue, is it, I said. You're in Costa Rica. She waved dismissively, which, I thought, strongly suggested that things weren't going well down in Nosara.

What were you doing in Romulus's room? I asked her. She shook her head, as if the question was rife with complications, though I couldn't understand how *anything* could be going on between her and Romulus, much less anything complicated. I was just hanging around this hotel all day waiting for you, she said. I was very grateful for the company, believe me. Rom's a sweet guy, and he really needed someone to talk to, and I was more than happy to oblige. What was I supposed to do while I was waiting? Eat? She patted her stomach. Anyhow, the winters here aren't as bad as the ones we had in Chicago. The part I couldn't take is the darkness. Mom, I said, trying to haul her back to the matters at hand. I'm the kind of person, she said, who is light sensitive. If I don't get a few hours of light, I mean real light, sunlight, then I can go into a full-blown depression. In that way, Costa Rica has been a miracle for me. All these years I lived with SAD without knowing what it was. She narrowed her eyes, as was her way when she probed for information. Do you know what SAD is? she asked. It was actually something I *did* know—I had even written about it for an in-flight magazine, a piece about light boxes that counteract the winter's long gloom—but at the moment I couldn't recall what the letters stood for. Situational . . . I began. No, she was quick to say. Seasonal. Seasonal Affective Disorder. And before you snipe at it, let me tell you, Avery, it's real. It's as real as erectile dysfunction or an enlarged prostate, or any of the other things they throw billions of dollars at because men suffer from it.

So, I said, Mom. I brought my hands together, squeezed them. What's going on? Why are you here? But the winters here? she said. They're not supposed to be too bad. Nothing like what we—I never said it wasn't real, Mom. All I'm asking is why you're here. What were you doing in Iceland and now . . . I fell silent; for a moment I didn't know where we were.

Norway, she said. She had no more hesitation jogging my memory than she had doubting my veracity, or in assuming I knew rather little about the world. She really couldn't muster much more respect for my autonomy than she had back in the days when she changed my name as if it were a shirt. It may be difficult to grant full dignity to someone whom you've toilet-trained; it might be a long day's journey into empathy to ever fully respect someone after dealing with their diapers.

So this is about the *Esquire* story? I said.

No, it's not, but, yes, I have not forgotten your little story in that magazine. All right, then let's talk about it, I said. I have to tell you, Mom, I didn't think it would upset you. Really? she asked. Because I'm so insensitive? No, not because you're so insensitive. What has insensitivity got to do with it? Then what? Why didn't you think it would upset me? Because I'm not educated? Because I didn't finish college? I had two years, and then I had the misfortune to fall in love. I was foolish. I thought falling in love solved everything. I was an idiot. I was a foolish fucking idiot. Okay? Is that what you wanted to hear? Her voice wobbled momentarily and her eyes reddened, and I felt a searing stab of remorse. I had only wanted to protect myself from her, not to hurt her.

I didn't think it would upset you because there's nothing in it that you don't already know. I tried to make my voice soothing. But she waved it away as if my words were a swarm of gnats. And now the whole world knows it, too, she said. You held me up as an object of ridicule, and you slimed me with your patriarchal bullshit. As she said the word *bullshit*, she looked at me, as if for the first time. Her eyes engaged mine with a sudden frankness, and she even smiled.

Look at you, she said, shaking her head. Look at *you,* I countered. How much do you weigh right now, Avery? I don't know, I said. How much do *you* weigh? I weigh a hundred nineteen pounds, which is exactly what I weighed when I met your father. Which father? Stop it, you know which father. Your real father. They're all quite real, Mom. Your biological father. Is that better? I nodded, and Naomi went back to the subject of her weight. It's five pounds more than my weight when I was with Andrew. It's about the same as it was with Norman, and it's actually less than it was with Gene. Gene and I loved to eat. He taught me how to make goulash and stuffed cabbage, and all kinds of other Hungarian delicacies. What are you laughing at? I'm not laughing. I'm smiling. All right, then what are you smiling at? I'm smiling because you even remember your weight in terms of the men in your life. You're like those kids who give shape to the past by remembering the names of their teachers. Those guys weren't my teachers, I'll tell you that much. That's not what I'm saying, Mom. I'm saying that you can't even think of yourself just as yourself; it's always connected to which marriage you were on. Women are about connections, she said, with a simple shrug, as if that's all there was to say about it. Women are about connections, I said, because they come out of a history in which being connected to a man was their only hope for survival. In which they weren't able to make their own money or run their own lives. But it doesn't have to be that way any longer. My mother looked at me quizzically. Let me get this straight, she said, you're on a sex tour *and* you're giving me lectures about feminism?

She sat at a round mahogany table and gestured me into the chair opposite to her, which put the windows at my back. We sat in silence for a few moments while she took off her rings and placed them in a row. Mom, I said, why don't you just tell me what you're doing here.

As soon as you called me from that emergency room, I started making arrangements to come and see you. You sounded so terrible, and so strange. You were slurring; I could hardly understand you. It was the most terrifying thing. You're all I have left in the world. I couldn't just let you slip away; I had to see you. And then when I got to New York and found you gone? She shook her head, remembering her own ordeal. How did you know where to find me? I asked.

A mother does what a mother must do, she said. All my life, I've been too passive. That part of your article I had to agree with. I guess I was always looking for someone to rescue me. But no more of that, not for me. Now when I set my mind to do something, I don't let anyone stand in my way. As she spoke, she took off her necklace. Between your uncle and your agent I found out enough, and then I got in touch with some very nice woman at Fleming Tours, and when I told her it was an emergency she gave me your itinerary. Well, she'll be losing her job, I said. I can promise you that. Aren't you glad to see me? she asked. Well, I don't know, Mom, it's pretty strange. You're here. I can hardly believe it, but here you are. That's not much of a welcome, Avery. All right, Mom, welcome, I'm thrilled that you're here. Who on an around-the-world sex tour wouldn't want his mother along for the ride? She had stacked her rings one on top of the other, and now she toppled the tower and they rolled around the table. I hate sarcasm, she said. It's oppressive. You know what it's like—clouds that block out the sun, but useless clouds, clouds that don't ever rain. Big dark empty clouds. She looked at me through the tops of her eyes and then began organizing her jewelry again. Why didn't you just wait for me in New York? I asked.

Listen, Avery, I didn't come all this way to argue with you. I wasn't going to pay New York prices for two weeks in a hotel, just to wait. Do I think what you're doing is terribly, terribly wrong? Of course I do. You're a grown man; you can make your own decisions. But I'm a grown-up, too. And my decision was when my son calls and says he's been run over by a car, I am going to be there for him. She let the necklace slither out of her hand, winding it into a curl on the tabletop. I wasn't run over, I said. I was hit. I never should have called. She shook her head. You don't give an inch, do you, she said.

The phone made its high electronic purr, and the red message light trembled. My memories of my mother and the telephone were a series of images of her hurrying to answer whenever it rang, as if she was always expecting a call that could change everything. She would make her nervous little steps toward the ringing, her mouth slightly open, her hand extended, and she would snatch it off its cradle and say Hello in a practically breathless voice. She was similarly avid about the mail. She often peeked out of our front window, looking for the postman, and when the mail fell through the slot in our front door she scooped it up immediately, rifling through whatever had come as if she were waiting for an exit visa. Though this time she didn't answer the phone, the question remained: what *had* she been expecting, what *was* she waiting for, all those years? And this long-unanswered question led to a more somber inquiry, not about her but about me: why in all the years granted me had I failed to fathom the source of my own mother's unhappiness? What had driven her from marriage to marriage? What did she want, from what was she running? What did she think about when she was alone? What most did she wish for? What most did she fear?

Did you have a good flight? I asked her. I was feeling a pressure between and behind my eyes, a desire to cover them, close them. I got out of the stiff, functional hotel chair and made my way toward the sofa, with its satin stripes, grape and vanilla. Naomi's eyes widened. You don't seem well, she said, and she heard the edge in her voice as much as I did so she repeated the observation, but softer the second time. I'm fine, I said. A bit tired. I'll bet you are, my mother said. As she said this she pointed at me, and then at the side of her own head, and then at me once more.

I was bleeding again. The human head, in addition to its other freight, is awash in blood.

I excused myself and retreated to her bathroom. The stark, dazzling cleanliness of Norwegian things! The shallow white parallelogram of a sink gleamed; the tile floor looked as if it had never been stepped on. Open-heart surgery has been performed in rooms less clean than this one. The mirror was spotless; I hated to disturb it with my unshaved, unkempt, bleeding upper half. I turned on the bright silver faucet. The water was icy, and I brought a couple of handfuls to my face. What a pleasure. I felt Deirdre's hands on my waist and I backed into her, causing her to tighten her grip on me, such are the simple pleasures, the little mercies life can offer. Where would we be without these things, without contact, without caresses, without the knowledge that someone wants to touch you? I hated to do it, but I needed one of those towels. I needed to dry my face, and I needed to press the towel against the side of my head to soak up that persistent trickle of goo. I pulled the pristine towel off its equally pristine crystal rod. I looked around the bathroom and saw that I was alone. I knew all along Deirdre was not there, that I had imagined it, I wasn't *that* far gone, but thinking that, saying to myself *Of course it was my imagination,* was not nearly so convincing as the feel of her hands on my hips. The chic little black telephone fixed on the marble wall rang, and this time Naomi picked up. I heard her say Hello, with her familiar little interrogative warble.

I wandered back into the suite, tying the towel around my head so I wouldn't have to hold it any longer. Tying a towel around your head is difficult for beginners. It kept flopping down in front of my eyes. I'm sorry, it's just not possible, my mother was saying to whoever had called her. Who could it be, if not Romulus? Well, thank you, that's very nice of you, she said, softly. I finally got the towel wrapped right, and I walked to the window, wondering if my mother's suite on a higher floor might give me a better look at Oslo. First, the sky, bluebird blue, with the long narrow clouds gliding along like albino alligators. I looked down at Seventh Avenue, an artery jammed with the plaque of traffic, mainly yellow taxicabs except for one nonambulatory ambulance, stopped in the middle, its warning lights spinning out a frenzy of red shudders. I snapped my fingers. Of course! I finally remembered how I'd gotten to the emergency room after my mishap back in New York. Someone had called an ambulance. Finding that missing piece filled me with confidence and sweet relief. I turned from the window and said Mom? But she put up a finger to quiet me because she was still talking to Romulus, who, I gathered, was having a problem taking No for an answer, since he had been primed to believe he would have at least ten days of life in which no woman would deny him anything, though surely neither Castle nor Gabrielle would have dared to suggest, even in the heat of, say, encouraging Romulus to spring for the Platinum, that he would have access to another tour member's mother. Okay, okay, my mother was saying, now you're just exaggerating. Exaggerating what? I said, reaching for the phone, ready to take it out of her hands and start shouting threats at Linwood, who I imagined was making some overtly sexual remarks, but my mother turned her back to me and tossed her shoulder in my direction, as if to shoo me away. I'll call you later, she said. No you won't, I said, loud enough for Linwood to hear. Yes, she said, I remember. Room 625. But Rom, I suggest you participate in the program that's been arranged for you. And with that she hung up the phone and stood with her back turned toward me, shaking her head.

This is really too much, Mom, I said. What am I supposed to do? she said, still not facing me. Well you're certainly *not* supposed to be forming relationships with men on the tour. She nodded her head, took a deep breath. Who is he anyhow? I don't know anything about him, she said. He says he's rich, but he doesn't seem rich. He's a door-to-door knife salesman, Mom. And what difference does it make? Why are you here? The towel I had so carefully tied around my head was slipping, covering my eyes, and I was forced to unwrap it. An inkblot of blood had seeped into the center of it. You poor thing, she said. I knew I did the right thing, coming here. We've got to get you to a doctor. I don't need a doctor, Mom. I'm okay, I'm fine. I just need a little rest, if anything.

The curtains were parted and I leaned over, tugged on them to close the gap. My mother folded her hands, placed them on the table, and she said When you got married straight out of college I was very upset. Did you know that? No, I said, I didn't. Well, I was. You seemed so young and so uncertain. She, of course, was madly in love with you. Why of course? I asked. Oh, stop. What are you, fishing for compliments? You were quite a catch. So charming and so handsome. That's insane, I said. You're insane, she countered, with considerable force. You know, Avery, one day you're going to have children, and you'll understand how painful it is to see them making mistakes, especially if they make the same mistakes you yourself made, that's what hurts the most. It's what a friend of mine down in Nosara calls the old double whammy. You feel bad because your child is in trouble, and you feel bad on top of that because it's trouble that maybe he inherited from you.

I tried to take this in, I really did. I nodded, swallowed, gave it time. But, finally, I could not stop myself from saying You actually think your friend in Costa Rica coined the phrase *double whammy*? What in the hell is wrong with you? my mother shouted.

It might have been the architecture of the room, or perhaps it was the silence that followed her outburst, but my mother's voice seemed to echo. I don't know if you ever outgrow the deep, instinctual fear of being shouted at by your mother. My heart curled up in my chest, like a caterpillar that's been poked with a stick. I was not used to my mother shouting at me—she left the heavy lifting of child rearing to the fathers, while she herself tried to keep me in line with quick, urgent glances, pursed lips, and an occasional tug at my arm when she would walk me into the next room to counsel patience. You're just making things worse, she'd say to me. You're digging a hole for yourself. What's the point of arguing? He's tired. He's had a bad day. You know how he gets. Sometimes the little boy needs to act like the grown-up. Don't make me ashamed. He's been so generous. Just go upstairs and be quiet; I'll take care of it.

Listen to me, she said. I really want to put things right between us. I thought so as soon as I heard you were hurt. You did? I said. Yes, of course, but now, here, seeing what you're doing, it seems more important that ever. This thing, Avery, this thing between us, this thing that goes around and around in your head, it's gone on long enough; it's time to put it right. Put what right, Mom? I really don't know what you mean. I mean you and me, that's what I mean, that's what I want to put right. The whole mess of it. Starting with your father, your real father, who stood over your cradle and wrung his hands and gritted his teeth so he wouldn't cry, that's how happy he was, that's how crazy about you he was, that's how much he loved you. Oh Mom, don't. I don't think I can take this. Not now. Well, you're going to have to, because I came a long way to talk to you, and who knows when we're going to have another chance. Your father, your father was the love of my life, and being

able to give him something so precious, giving him that, a baby, his son,
it was the most wonderful thing I was ever able to do. That's not very
modern, I realize that. But I loved that man. You think we didn't know
anything about birth control? We had it all—better than there is now,
if you ask me. But I said Plant your seed in me, we'll keep it in there,
protect it, we'll let it grow and grow and then one day a child will come;
I don't care if I'm too young, I don't care if it hurts. I was just a kid, and
I was scared to death. My mother had filled me with such horror stories
of childbirth, I was sure I was going to be torn into shreds.

The telephone rang. My mother gave no indication of even hearing
it. Andrew Kearney was a different story, Naomi was saying. What we
had in common was we both loved your father. And that wasn't enough.
I never should have married anyone when I was so unhappy. I was still
madly in love with Ted. I married hastily and it ended. Is that a crime? I
wanted to be loved, and I wanted to love someone. Do you think I don't
know I made a mistake? I go over these things, over and over them.
They say that having time to think is a luxury; well then bad memories
is the luxury tax.

I guess it was the name-changing thing that ended up bothering me
the most, I said, hardly feeling it, but saying it anyhow out of loyalty to
myself because I had felt it for so long, it was a feeling that had amassed
enough seniority to have the right to be expressed, even if its time had
passed. I know, Avery, I know. But we were in a complicated situation.
First of all, you hardly remembered your real father. And given the
circumstances of his death, I thought it would be best if I could start
you on a fresh path and not have you carry around a name filled with
so much sadness. I didn't want all the kids in school to ask a lot of questions about your name, like Who is your father? Where is he? How did
he die? And the other thing was, your father stole money from Andrew,
and having that name in the house could have been a problem. But
didn't you just say that you and Kearney loved my father, and that was
the main thing you had in common? It's never that simple, Avery. You
know that. Everything has layers; every little string has a hundred knots.
Come on, you're a writer, you should know this.

Ringing. At first, I thought it was the telephone; then I realized it
was the door. Is this going to be Romulus Linwood? I asked my mother.

She frowned. Get over it, Avery. Given the nature of your little journey, I don't think you can begrudge me striking up a conversation with
someone I meet in a hotel lobby. The doorbell rang again. Avery? a
voice called out. It's me, it's Nina. Are you in there? Can you open the
door?

I got up to let her in, but my mother reached for me with great
urgency. No, Avery, please. I know who's at the door, one of the prostitutes, right? This has got to stop, Avery, I mean it. You can't do this.
It's a little late for that, I said. If you let her in I'm leaving, she said. I'm
going to get up and go right down to Romulus's room, and I'm not
kidding.

I hear you in there, Avery! Nina called through the door. Please open
for me, I have massive information. Hold on for a second, I shouted
back at her. Then, to my mother, Come on, this is insane. I can't just
leave her out in the hall. I'm going to let her in and see what she wants.
I could tell by my mother's expression she was uncertain what to do
next, and so I pressed my point. Please, Mom, it'll be fine. Oh, you're
full of charm, aren't you? That was the one thing Gene worried about.
Gene? Well, you know, he was such a basic, honest person, he didn't
trust charm. And he saw how you would try and charm people, work
them this way and that, spin things so you'd get your way. He thought
there was something just a little bit sneaky in you.

Gene said that? About me? I felt what little strength I had desert
me. It was like staggering around, trying to keep your balance after
being hit by a wave, only to be hit by another. Nina rang the doorbell
again, and then again. We all know what you did to help Heidi, Nina
said though the door. In the elevator with the ice. That was good, Avery.
Oh, don't take it so hard, my mother was saying. There are things he
did for you, you don't even know about them. He couldn't have loved
you more. It was one of the main reasons I married him. Because I
knew Gene Jankowsky loved you. It was the main thing we most had in
common, did you know that? The main thing. He was all about art and
a sort of hippie nature-worship thing—which, by the way, I understand
a lot more now than I did then—and our sex life was a disaster. Especially after Norman. Blake? I cried out. I hate even hearing his name!
I know he was moody, my mother said. Why do you think I put up with

it? Not that it was right, not that I don't wish I would have thrown him out on his ear the first moment I noticed he was being so hard on you, not that I haven't cried myself to sleep many a night thinking about the things I let that bastard get away with. But nature had been very generous with Norman. Oh please, Mom, this is really making me ill. She smiled, placed her hand over her heart. Oh my, she said. You're like a child. Don't you want your mother to have been happy at least once in her life? You were happy with Blake? Well, that's what I'm saying, yes, I was, in that way. If only he hadn't been so goddamned grumpy. Grumpy? Mom, he was a sadist. She shook her head. You love to argue about words, don't you.

The doorbell rang again, and this time the knocking that followed was louder, made by a heavier hand. Avery, open up. We're getting out of here. It was Lincoln Castle. Meet in the lobby in ten minutes. I looked at my mother. I have to see what's going on, I said. She waved, conceding the point, and I opened the door. Castle and Nina hurried in, as if to gain their perch inside the room before I changed my mind.

What's going on? I asked Castle. Webb got carried away, he said, and we're getting out of Dodge. If we don't, we're going to get bogged down in a real mess. He got carried away? I asked. How far did he go? Don't worry, Castle said. We're not taking him with us. He can clean up his own mess. Nina was at my side now. She linked her arm through mine, leaned her head against my shoulder. Well, look at that, Castle said. That's what I like to see; that's what makes it all worth it. Do you mind? He reached in his pocket, pulled out a digital camera, and before I could object or turn away he pressed the button and the little window in the camera's corner, no larger than a postage stamp, exploded in blinding white light.

Are you all right? Naomi asked. She held a flute of white wine; she was tilted far back in her leather seat. We were in the Fleming jet, banking over the choppy gray Baltic, coming in toward Riga. Our pilot, Beau Clark, or maybe it was his brother Francis, was chatting up Piedmont near the back of the plane, laughing at everything Michael said. Clark may have misjudged how close we were to the Riga airport because suddenly he was walking very quickly—almost running—toward the cockpit. That's a disquieting sight, isn't it, I said to my mother. Seeing your pilot running. Yes, well, she said, if you're in a certain kind of mood everything seems like it's a sign that something bad is going to happen. I looked around. Stephanie was sitting with Len, who seemed to have plunged into still deeper despair. Tony was wrapped in a blanket; all that was visible of him was his face, his open mouth; he was sleeping, but he looked dead. Linwood was talking to one of the Metal Men and making something of a show of being absorbed in conversation, exclaiming Why that's fascinating, and I've always wondered about that, in the same spirit, it seemed to me, that I, in sixth grade, tried to prove to Polly Greenwood that I was over her by laughing uproariously whenever she passed by, usually enlisting whoever was at hand to flesh out the ruse, but, if need be, prepared to go it alone.

The Riga airport was a long glass box, nearly empty. There's something I want to tell you, my mother was saying. It's good news, at least I think it is. It's good news if you make proper use of it, anyhow. We were walking through Pasu Kontrole and then through Deklare jamo nav. It was as if we weren't even there. Latvian security officers, wearing green jackets with red patches, paid us no mind. I could use some good news, I said. Okay, my mother said, when we get to the hotel. Riga was sedate; the buildings thrust out their chests like unbowed soldiers in a defeated army. They dripped decoration: painted plaster princesses and sword-wielding centurions were perched over doorways, embedded in pastel walls, wedding-cake swirls, cornices, columns, chalices. Nothing was simple here. You looked at it and you gasped for breath. What peaks of whimsy were these people attempting to scale? Though it was daylight, every car in the city drove with its headlights on, as if traffic was one immense funeral procession. We checked into the Hotel Guttenberg, on a little side street, across from a tile-encrusted Greek Orthodox church. The reception area was small, stifling; there was a little bar off to one side and a line of tall, ladder-back chairs against the wall. All the men were crowded in; we could smell one another. Maybe our parents will hook up, Jordan said to me, as we all waited for Gabrielle and Stephanie to expedite the paperwork and get us into our rooms. You never know, I said. The clerk behind the desk was a toweringly tall middle-aged man with long gray hair and a cautious, uncertain face. He wore a dark blue jacket, green shirt, a black tie. Call your director, Gabrielle was saying to the clerk. Let him know we have come a day early, and he will tell you to give us our rooms.

There was no extra room for my mother. You guys are going to have to bunk in together, at least for tonight, Stephanie told me. We shared the elevator with Tony Dinato, who looked as if he hadn't entirely woken up from his nap on the plane. Have you noticed that I'm angry with you? Tony asked me. Why in the world would you be angry with me? Because you didn't tell me that your father was the artist who made the Jankowsky Cross. He reached into his shirt and pulled out the cross. Will you look at that? my mother exclaimed. What a small world. Tony put the cross back in his shirt, gave it a comforting pat. I heard you were going through some religious conversion experience, I said. That is true, Tony said. Is there, I asked, some sort of contradiction? Between the conversion and what we're doing? Yes, there is. But there must have been a reason why I chose to come on this trip, and I'm going to see it through.

Our room was at the end of a long corridor, and then a sharp turn to the left, and down a couple of stairs. We opened the heavy wooden door and stepped into a suite of sorts, a blend of a small hunting lodge and an attic. Rough-hewn posts, exposed beams, not a right angle to be found. Twin beds with brown and gold spreads, and one of those Eastern bloc television sets that manage to look simultaneously futuristic and antique. French windows covered by lace curtains opened up to the quiet lane below. I'm so hungry, my mother said, I noticed some nice cafés on our way over here. What did you want to tell me when we were in the airport? I asked. She looked puzzled. You said you had some good news, I prompted. She patted me on the arm and smiled; my curiosity was pleasing to her. I'll tell you over lunch, she said.

Out on the cool, quiet, pastel street she said We have to be careful. I don't want to end up at the same restaurant all the men are going to. We're not having anything more to do with them. Is that so? I said. Yes, it is, she said. You're a nice man, too nice for this kind of meshugas. You've gotten sort of Jewish down there in Costa Rica, haven't you?— and the next I remember, we were standing side by side in the Jewish Museum of Riga, a sad, threadbare place, with nothing much on display: old newspapers under glass, photocopied pages from old newspapers, flimsy little booklets set out on a folded-up Ping-Pong table like take-out menus from a Chinese restaurant. We were the only visitors in the place. What are we doing here? I asked my mother, but she was transfixed in front of a little glass cube, inside of which were two silver spoons, keepsakes from the circumcisions of two Latvian children named Solomon and Isaac Etelson. This is who we are, she said in a whisper. She moved a few steps and gazed at the next display cabinet, which showed a handful of walnuts, painted gold. I followed her. Another held nothing but an old wooden top, striped red and blue. Next was a picture of Theodor Herzl, with his fierce black beard meant to lend gravitas to a face that would have appeared juvenile without it. He had expectant, dark eyes, and he stood with his arms folded over his chest, like a man patiently hearing you out before he launches into his passionate rebuttal.

Before the Nazis, my mother said, eighty thousand Latvian Jews, after the Nazis less than two hundred. Think about that. And when I failed to appear sufficiently horrified by this statistic—though I don't know what, short of suicide, would have given evidence that I had fully absorbed its significance—she looked at me as if I didn't have feelings and said You're part Latvian, you know that, don't you? On which side? I asked. On *my* side. She thumped her hand against her chest, and her voice rang out in the room, with its high ceiling and bare wooden floors. Startled by her own vehemence, my mother looked around. An elderly woman with a mist of pale orange hair was seated in a folding chair near the pamphlets, her hands resting in her lap, her jaw set. Oops, my mother said, maybe we better get out of here.

We walked down a flight of scuffed, uncared-for marble stairs that led to the street. Our footsteps echoed. I gripped the banister, afraid I might pitch forward. The world floated insubstantially before me, no more convincing than the Shroud of Turin. I never felt all that Jewish, I said to my mother. She frowned sympathetically. But do you believe in anything? I don't know, I said. I guess I just would like to go back to New York. Maybe see Deirdre. Glad to hear it, but that's not believing, she said. That's just more wanting. I nodded; she was right, of course she was. I was silent for a moment. I listened to my heart—not for it to speak, and to somehow impart its vast, vascular knowledge, because that's simply nonsense, that's a dream; I listened to it just to hear it thump, doing its thankless grunt work. I'm an animal, I said to my mother. I believe in my body. I believe in my hair and my hands and my eyes and my belly. I believe in my desire. We stood in front of the old gray building, with its tall ponderous doors, the indecipherable plaques screwed onto the facade. All the men on your trip believe in their desire, she said. I think the whole point of God is to give us something else, something just as compelling as our desires and our appetites. People think God is there because people are so afraid to die, but that's only half of what it's about. We also need something big and powerful and all-seeing and all-knowing, just to free us from being slaves to our own bodies.

We took a taxi, a little gray Mercedes, back toward the center of town, past old wooden houses, broad and gray, with ancient clapboard siding and bleached shutters hanging crookedly. They looked derelict and damp, like places where Bill Sykes would hide from the police. At that moment I knew Isabelle was no longer holding on to that apartment on Perry Street for me. The funds had failed to transfer. A new buyer had appeared who trumped my offer, and Isabelle and the owners had found a way to negate my offer and my earnest money and were now moving on without me. How had I ever so misconstrued her friendliness for anything more than a way to do business? Oh yes, and there was that other thing: the e-mail about her vagina.

I covered my eyes with my hand. I felt the loss of that apartment as a kind of extinguishing of hope. Are you all right? my mother asked. I shook my head no. I was doing this whole thing for money, and the money was going for this apartment I found. But I'm never going to be able to write the book. The pitch I made for it was complete fantasy, and I'm never going to be able to fulfill my contract. And on top of that I said something really crazy to the real estate agent and even if I had the money she wouldn't want to do business with me.

All right, my mother said, first of all, your money situation isn't what you think it is. What are you talking about? I asked her, but she waved off the question. And secondly, what could you have said to a real estate agent that would make her so angry? It doesn't matter, I said. Of course it matters, my mother said. It's important to remember everything matters and it all makes a difference. Our lives are so short, and everything that happens in our life span is really important; there is nothing wasted, there's nothing that doesn't count. You can't say I'm going to do this, but it doesn't really count. It all counts, and everything is connected to everything else. I'll put it in your terms, Avery. Think of everything that has ever been said and everything that has ever been written, every book, every poem, every conversation, every scrap of paper, every encyclopedia, in English, in Chinese, in French and Spanish and Italian and Russian and Korean and Arabic, in Swahili, in Farsi, and then think of your life. What are you next to all that? You're like one half of a letter in one word; that's your life, that is you front to back, up and down, over and out. But that doesn't make what we say and do less important. It makes it *more* important.

My mother had a *Riga This Week* booklet she'd picked up at the hotel, and she was looking at the restaurant ads in it. Look at this, she said, turning the pages in the booklet and showing them to me. Ad after ad promoting strip clubs, gentlemen's bars, and escort services, along with hotels, tour buses, and beauty shops. Everything's for sale, I said. You can say that again, she said.

Why do you say I don't have to worry so much about money? I asked her, and when she said I'll tell you once I get a little food into me I felt such exasperation I closed my eyes and the next thing I knew we were sitting in a restaurant called Peterburga. The walls were mint green with gold leaf trim, ornate sconces, a somber mahogany floor, upholstered chairs, heavy curtains, a collection of old samovars in a locked display case. My mother looked very happy over her bowl of dark red soup with sprigs of dill floating in it. Oh, I'll have to hand it to them, Naomi said, this is the best borscht I ever had. We were the only customers; it was late for lunch, but the owners clearly needed the money and weren't going to close if there were a couple of tourists to be fed. We sat at the window, facing the street. The waitress came to refill our water glasses. She wore a festive green vest with braiding, and flowing pants. She had long platinum hair with bangs, an angular face, glossy pink lipstick the color of a little girl's toy hot rod. Is good? she asked in a weary voice. Serving us hadn't been her idea; she would have rather gone home. This is the best borscht I ever had, my mother said. She dipped her heavy spoon in, held it out toward the waitress. It's the fresh dill, isn't it? The waitress smiled uncertainly and then said I shall bring other food. I want to go home, I said to my mother, and she started to touch my hand but then stopped. I know you do, she said. Do you want me to go with you? I was a little taken aback by the question. Do you want to stay here? I asked. She shrugged. I wouldn't mind getting to know that adorable knife salesman a little better. She saw the look of what I suppose was horror on my face, and she laughed. I'm kidding, she said. Of course I'll go back with you. If there are no planes, we'll take a balloon. And here's part of what I wanted to tell you. You can forget about all those financial pressures and writing your cockamamie book. The Jankowsky Cross is more successful than ever. Much, much more. Is this for real? I asked. It's as real as it gets, my mother said. People are scared, people are lost, mothers are sending crosses to their kids in the army—I don't know what the hell's going on, but I heard from this man named Bud Burdette who is head of Calvary Products, and he told me that sales of the Cross are up over six hundred percent in the past year. So what were you getting? Something like twenty thousand dollars a year? I nodded yes. Well, the next check will be for at least a hundred twenty thousand dollars. How do you like that, Avery? That's a lot of money just for being somebody's stepson, and you don't have to chase after a bunch of prostitutes to get it, either. She narrowed her eyes. Or was needing the money just an excuse to do what you wanted to do anyhow? Maybe I should go home, I said.

It was a warm spring day. A group of office workers in dark slacks and leather jackets walked past the window, puffing on cigarettes, a smear of lilac smoke drifting in their wake. Then a tall, broad-shouldered young woman with henna in her hair, talking excitedly into her turquoise cell phone. A man was approaching us on a Vespa. He had a large shaved head, a Roman nose, an angry face; he wore a leather jacket, a red-and-yellow scarf around his neck. (Where had I seen that scarf before? On the edge of understanding, I saw a flickering image on the Town Car bearing down on me on Fifty-sixth Street.) The Vespa sped past. A gasoline can was in the carryall on the back of it.

And then, as if being marched to the Bastille, the Fleming men and their Latvian escorts filed past on the sidewalk. If they had stopped and looked through the window, we'd have been face-to-face. I had an impulse to hide, but where could I go? The waitress came with our meals, fried lamb with sour cabbage for my mother, poached perch with trout caviar for me. Do you see what I see? I said to my mother.

Jordan led the way, his empty sleeve flapping like a wind sock at an airport. He was with a rather pessimistic-looking woman with a Joan of Arc haircut, who walked with her hands clasped and her head down. Dr. Gordon was behind, walking with Gabrielle, who kept a steadying hand on his elbow. Then came Tony and his girl, Len with his, and then, one after the other, the Metal Men, with three fair-haired, tall, rather formally dressed women, none of them touching, just simply marching along. Piedmont and Romulus were next. These men, in whose company I had been so false, and so often irritated—it astonished me to feel my heart go out to them. Piedmont was walking on his own, no cane, no walker, and doing a very credible job of it. He carried a little paper bag of nuts in one hand and a family-size bottle of ginger ale in the other. Romulus was tapping his watch and then bringing it up to his ear. Behind them were the companions they had chosen for the rest of the day: an athletic young woman with teased hair and stonewashed jeans, with something of the rural lesbian about her; and a dreamy-looking woman with an oval face and sloping eyes, a wide mouth, long fingers, a slender and studious-looking woman in her early twenties, who, under other circumstances, would have reminded me that life is full of beauty, and would have awakened in me a quick flash of urgency, a ripple of desire, but right now was just another layer of darkness.

My interest must have somehow caught her attention because she turned and looked directly at me. Shit, I said, not moving my lips, this could be awkward. She wore a bright red-and-yellow-striped silk scarf, knotted casually around her neck. Just relax, my mother said, not moving *her* lips. You're just another man. And she was right; the woman might not have been looking at me; she might have just been checking her own reflection in the window. Next was Lincoln. I turned slowly away from him in my chair, but I glanced at him over my shoulder. He was walking alone, his face drained of all joviality, his hands behind his back, his eyes on the ground. I held my breath, against him suddenly looking up and seeing me. The waitress was seated at a table near the back, typing on her computer. The click of the keys was like chopsticks against the side of a bowl.

We ate our food. I was so worried, my mother said. I thought I'd find you had slipped into a coma. I cried for the whole flight from San Jose to New York. And then when you found out what I was doing, I said, maybe you wished I was in a coma. Will you stop? she said. Don't your grudges have a statute of limitations? Remember why I'm here. She raised her eyebrows. I'm here because I love you and if I hurt you then I want to make up for that, and I want you to live your life, every single day of your life, secure in at least that one thing, that your mother loves you, and always has. Thank you, Mom. I took her hand. I love you, too. She put her hand on top of mine, stopped me from letting go. Will you promise me never to disrespect women? she said.

We were outside now. Someone had closed the curtains to the restaurant, dark gray curtains with silver threads in them. The sky was pale violet, cloudless. A jet, distant and translucent, raced by, followed, a moment later, by its roar. There goes our plane, I said. Don't worry about planes, my mother said. If you want to get home, there's always a way. We passed an old woman sweeping the street. She wore a gray smock with an orange safety vest; her broom looked as if it had been made in the fifteenth century.

Oh! Look at this! Naomi pointed to a little café on a corner, one of those three-steps-down places. A plain red sign over the door announced its name—KAFEJNICA—and under that sign was a smaller sign that said ELVIS. Let's go in for a coffee or something, Naomi said. I still love Elvis. Then she added Do you think it's the same Elvis, our Elvis? Of course, I said. There's only one Elvis, even Elvis Costello would agree with that. We sat at a Formica table in the dark bar. The table was orange; the chairs were brown and white. Posters of Elvis's sad, terrible movies were on the wall: *Harem Scarum; Girls, Girls, Girls*; as well as framed publicity photos, mostly Late Elvis, when he was living and singing as if he just wanted to get it over with. One of his gospel songs was coming through the speakers. His voice was deep, earnest, with that renegade edge of teasing. *I believe that someplace in the great somewhere, a candle glows.*

A young woman wearing jeans cut off at the knee, sheer black hose, and dark orange high heels brought our coffees, with a shot glass full of sugar and another shot glass of milk. Elvis fell apart when his mother died, my mother said. He was never the same after that. That's when all the self-destructive behavior took over, after Gladys died. Is that why you love him? I asked. Do you enjoy being a wise-ass? she asked me. Because I hope not, it's very limiting. I'm sorry, I said, the thing is I don't feel very well. She frowned sympathetically. I'm not here because I love Elvis. I'm here because I love you. And I have to tell you, I don't like the looks of that thing on the side of your head. It doesn't matter, I said. I'm fine. Really? Do you really feel all right? she said, hopefully. Well, that's an interesting question, I said. It's hard to assess because the mind trying to make a judgment about its own function is the same mind that is being evaluated. There you go with words, she said. Well, it's not just words. I'm really trying to figure it out. I walked out between two parked cars. Oh, Avery. Don't even remind me. What a terrible thing. I always told you to look both ways. It might have begun before that, though, in the little supermarket when Deirdre told me about Osip. Who's Osip? my mother asked. Or maybe it was when I started calling myself Osip, or when I made an appointment with the woman who called herself Chelsea. Maybe I should never have walked out of Roosevelt Hospital. There are so many possibilities. All I know is this: I am lost, I am so lost, and I don't know if I can find my way back.

I looked into my coffee cup. We should get back to the hotel, I said. You probably need to rest. I know I do, anyhow. My mother finished her coffee and, seeing I hadn't touched mine, she drank half of that, as well.

Outside, a blackened piece of lace floated by, carried by the wind.

There's nothing like European coffee, my mother said. I feel like jumping out of my skin, in a good way. We were on a cobblestone street, walking past little art galleries, wine shops, a strip club, a gambling casino. In front of us was our hotel, with its pink facade, the top-floor windows bright with sun, the lower floors dark. A minivan was parked in front, and four hotel employees were ferrying luggage on board.

I guess there's a woman waiting in there for you, my mother said. Will you promise me you won't take advantage of the situation? Remember, Avery, just because you can do something is no reason to do it. Don't forget, the universe knows when you do something wrong.

The little white blanket of time we are given isn't large enough to pull over our heads; there is no darkness possible, no hiding place; we are always in the light. But what if that isn't true? I said. What if it really doesn't matter, one thing happens, another thing happens, you screw someone, you don't screw someone, you just keep moving, and none of it adds up, there's no final tally. You have to act as if it matters, Avery, or else you go mad. Okay, but what if I've already gone mad? Then you just have to find your way back, honey, that's all you can do.

We walked into the hotel, and Lincoln Castle was standing at the desk, wearing a pair of reading glasses, frowning, and running the index finger of his right hand over a long printout, while holding in his left a credit card. He heard us come in. I could see from his expression that he was sorry to see me, but he quickly covered his initial reaction with an all-purpose smile. Avery, he said, I was wondering if I'd see you again.

It seemed a strange thing to say, until I put it together with that printout, and I realized he was in the process of checking out of the hotel. Where are you going, Lincoln? I asked.

We've had a bit of a mix-up here, he said. He was about to say more, but then he fell silent. He breathed a long sigh; his eyes went from me, to my mother, and back to me. Look here, Avery, let me be up-front about this. This is the end of the line for you. What is that supposed to mean? I asked. It means we've had a major change of plans. We're leaving.

We're leaving?

No, Avery, that's the thing. Not you, not your mother. He made a polite, though possibly ironic, bow in my mother's direction. The rest of us.

Why? I asked. What happened?

What happened is that the Riga police picked up some lunatic with a full can of gasoline who was going to set fire to this hotel. That's what happened. Oh my God, I said. I was also going to say I think I saw him, heading in this direction on his Vespa. But I knew that would only make matters worse for me. What's that got to do with me? I asked.

I don't know, buddy. Maybe nothing. But we've got a consensus here, and the consensus says you just don't fit on this trip. I'm running a business here, okay? I've got to take care of my people. If it makes you feel any better, both my wife and Stephanie were on your side. And Steph's hard to please, so you've got something to be proud of there. But the rest of the guys? Castle shook his head sadly. Then he handed his credit card over to the desk clerk.

Kicked off a sex tour? Was I really going to be the first man in the history of sex tourism to be bounced off the trip? I made a couple of wild narrative calculations, trying to imagine how this would not only go into my book but might actually improve it. After all, being kicked off a sex tour was even more extraordinary than going on one. But the narrative thrusts were circular, essentially frantic.

May I ask why I'm being kicked off the tour? I asked Castle. Well, first of all, he said, you never even paid for your spot, so let's get real, okay? You can't lose what you never had. That's just bullshit, Lincoln. Just tell me.

The clerk slid the credit card receipt across the desk for Castle. He was one of those men who sign with a flourish. Then he turned back toward me, folded his short arms over his barrel chest. Okay, first of all, you completely freaked out Diana. Who's Diana? I asked. I don't know anyone named Diana. In Iceland? he prompted. I was with Sigrid in Iceland. Castle made a sour look, as if I were being pedantic. Sigrid is Diana, Diana is Sigrid, he said, with exaggerated patience. Then the whole thing at the Blue Lagoon. How does that become my fault? I cried. It's just circumstances, Avery. Let's not play the blame game. Plus I got a complaint from the hotel in Reykjavik, that you were pulling the plugs out of the computers. You want to hear more? I nodded yes. Romulus says you've been busting his chops. Tony says you've been making fun of his religion. Tony's wearing my father's cross! I shouted. Castle put up his hands. I'm not here to argue, he said. I'm just telling you. You're sitting with Sean, you seem like you've made a nice connection, and then the next thing we know he's on his way home. I don't know anything about that, I said. But go on, I added, this is good, I should hear all this. And even with Webb. You're blaming me for Doleack? I asked. How do you get that? Avery, please, there is no blame. No one believes less in blame than me. But then I learn that right before Webb goes nuts you completely humiliate him in front of his girl, right there in the elevator. And then, there's the other thing, the thing you'd probably me rather not talk about. Not in the presence of your lovely mother.

I put my arm around my mother and said Naomi and I don't have secrets from each other.

All right, Castle said, have it your way. The little orgy in Oslo? Does that ring a bell?

I sensed my mother had turned her head and was looking at me, but I kept my eyes on Castle. Yes? I said, doing my best to sound unconcerned.

Well, apparently you were a little scary. Shall we say a little above and beyond the call of duty? I have no idea what you're talking about, I said. Well, confidentiality requires that I say no more, so we'll just leave it at that. I did nothing at that so-called orgy that everyone else wasn't doing, I said. That's not what I heard, said Castle. And then we have the little matter of today. Today? What are the charges about today? No charges, Avery. You have to stop thinking that way. There's no bad and good or up and down or right and wrong; we're just here talking. But it did seem a little odd that once we got here everyone else hooked up with a beautiful woman and you were nowhere to be found. I was with my mother! I cried. She was hungry and she wanted to go to a museum. Well, said Castle, be that as it may, just at the time when you have so mysteriously disappeared, some lunatic decides to protect the virtue of all these innocent Latvian virgins by setting fire to our hotel.

Lincoln folded his copy of the credit card receipt and placed it in his breast pocket. Take care of yourself, Avery. I'm sorry things didn't work out a little better, but at least you got a taste of what we're about. And I truly do hope you enjoyed yourself, at least as much as you are able to. And Naomi, it's been a real pleasure meeting you. Have a safe and pleasant journey.

We were too stunned to prevent him from leaving. The door swung open, capturing in its glass the budding boughs of a nearby cherry tree, and then it closed again and Castle was gone. Well, my mother said, did you? Did you enjoy yourself, at least as much as you were able to? I nodded. She made a small, mirthless laugh. Well at least you can be honest about it, she said. Now what am I supposed to do? I said. I have a contract to write a book about a tour I've just been kicked off of. That moment of confidence, in which I'd thought I could use this reversal of fortune as a narrative twist, had passed, and in its wake I felt doomed. I think you'd better get back to New York, while you still can, Naomi said. I think you have this much time. She described a half inch with her thumb and forefinger.

We went up to our room. I dozed in a chair while my mother closed up our suitcases—we hadn't really unpacked. Come on, she said, shaking my shoulder. We have to hurry. I'm a dead man, I said, shaking my head.

Taxi! I rocked back and forth, with my hands on my knees. My mother, hoping only to calm me down, began talking about Deirdre. You know, those few hours I was in New York? When I was trying to find out where you were, I went to your apartment and I found Deirdre there, right in the lobby, picking up her mail. She was so happy to see me. Such a beautiful girl, and so gracious. But I don't kid myself, Avery. She was nice to me because I'm your mother and she misses you and loves you and wishes more than anything that you were with her. It was perfectly obvious. She was sleeping with a Columbia student, I muttered. Well, the very nice thing about being a pot is you don't have to call the kettle black. Where are we going? I asked. Up to the sky, she said cheerfully. She tapped her purse; I guessed there were tickets inside of it. Do we have reservations? I asked. Just leave that to me, she said. The grass on either side of the road was a bright milky green. There were billboards advertising beer, corn chips, soap. They all showed young women, blond and cheerful, almost manic; they were like a natural resource offered to the rest of the world. The country was having a close-out sale on blondes.

Did Deirdre really say she wanted me back? My mother shrugged. Not in so many words, but I got that sense from her. And that stuff about the Jankowsky Cross? Is it really selling that well? I don't have exact numbers, but, yes, I think we can expect a real increase. But you don't know for sure, right? There's nothing wrong with being optimistic, she said.

There was blood on my passport, but the control officer didn't seem to care. Off came my shoes. My socks were black, thin, worn. I emptied

244 / Scott Spencer

my pockets. Coins. A pen. A set of keys to the apartment on Fifty-fourth Street.

The sun had broken through the clouds. The runway threshold markings glistened like crushed diamonds in the light, and the control tower cast its long shadow across the field, like the numeral 1 painted onto the tarmac.

Welcome aboard.

Up we go, my mother said, when we were finally aloft. Shredded clouds raced by. My hands were shaking. Turbulence? Nerves? Then, suddenly, the clouds were beneath us, stately and white, rolling one after the other, out toward a distant point, like gravestones. Okay, here we go, my mother said, tilting me back, covering me with a dark blue blanket, patting my shoulder. And then she brushed her open hand over my eyes so the wrinkled pink of her palm touched my eyelashes, and my eyes were closed, and I went into the sweetest softest most soothing darkness I had ever known, and she said Okay, baby, that's it, just relax, and before you know it you'll be home.

Acknowledgments

THANK YOU to the Bogliasco Foundation and to the John S. Guggenheim Foundation for their generous support during the research and writing of this novel. Jo Ann Beard, Lynn Nesbit, Dan Halpern, and Millicent Bennett all gave me valuable advice about the manuscript. Thank you as well to Lorrie Moore, who used the title "Willing" for a wonderful short story years ago and who graciously gave me permission to use it for this novel. While I was in the process of writing this book, four people died, all of whom have been integral to my life's joy and without whom my life has become less comprehensible. Their names, in the order of passing: Butch Conn, Charles Spencer, George Budabin, Carolyn Hougan.

Quoth the raven, "Nevermore."

About the author

About the book

Insights,
Interviews
& More...

Read on

Meet Scott Spencer
From Brawling Dishwasher to Distracted Novelist

Marion Ettlinger

SCOTT SPENCER is the author of nine novels, including *Endless Love*, which has sold more than two million copies. His other novels include *The Rich Man's Table*, *Men in Black*, *Waking the Dead*, and *A Ship Made of Paper*.

What has been your most unusual job?

I'm going to give a multiple answer to this. Once, I had a job washing dishes in a hospital, a short-lived position that remains vividly in memory mainly because the guy washing dishes next to me—we were both in our early twenties—squirted hot water on me and the hostilities ended in a fistfight, the last one I've ever had. That same year I had a job delivering mattresses, which remains a kind of negative gold standard of occupational misery, and ever since then I have gotten through difficult situations by saying, "Well, at least I'm not delivering mattresses." Later, a published writer, with two books out and a third on the way, I still needed a day job, and I was hired by a consulting firm to evaluate Title I remedial reading programs in public schools in some of New York's most impoverished neighborhoods—Brownsville, the South Bronx. A couple of years after that I was subpoenaed by a grand jury and compelled to give evidence against my boss, who was billing the city for two or three times the hourly wage he was paying me. I wanted to tell the court that, even so, I was being overpaid since I really had no credentials, but I had the sense to realize this would only make things worse for my old employer—he sat there in the front row and looked at me with sad, accusing eyes. But what choice did I have? Did he really think that the eleven dollars an hour he had been paying me would buy perjury?

You have written for **Rolling Stone, Harper's, The New Yorker,** *and many other magazines. What has been your most rewarding experience as a journalist?*

A friend of mine working as a private investigator for the United Steelworkers Union put me on to a story about the infamous Marc Rich, who turned out to have the controlling interest in an aluminum factory in West Virginia, and *Rolling Stone* sent me on an assignment that went from Ravenswood, West Virginia, to Zug, Switzerland, where I went with about ten USW members, most of whom were out of the country for the first time in their lives and who were there to confront the aptly named Rich in his off-shore lair. Some of the most enjoyable journalism I've done has involved talking to musicians whose work I admire—Sonny Rollins, Al Green, Ornette Coleman, Gillian Welch, and Levon Helm. I listen to a lot of music, and I often press whatever it is I'm crazy about onto my partner, my children, my friends.

What, if any, music do you listen to while writing?

I don't listen to music at all when I'm writing. In writing, the word is everything, and in music the word is just another face in the crowd.

A Barnes and Noble profile of you notes that "the film version of **Endless Love,** *directed by Franco Zeffirelli, was (as* **TV Guide** *put it) 'a notorious disaster,' but it marked the film debut of three* ▶

Meet Scott Spencer *(continued)*

future stars: Tom Cruise, James Spader, and Jami Gertz." How do you feel about that?

Ah, the movies. *Endless Love* was a debacle for all involved. At the time of its release, many critics called it one of the worst adaptations of a novel of all time. It *did* introduce a few young actors, but I think it was a disaster for Franco Zeffirelli, and I know it was a setback for Judith Rascoe, a first-rate screenwriter whose reputation is otherwise unsullied. Selling that novel to the movies may have been a bit of bad judgment on my part—but how was I to know? I'd never made any money before, and I went out and bought a car, and then a house. The car is in a landfill somewhere, but the house still stands and I'm living in it. Many years later, I wrote a novel about a novelist and called it *Men in Black*; the same year it appeared, the movie about space aliens called *Men in Black* was released, utterly eclipsing my novel and giving many people the mistaken impression that once again I had sold a book to the movies. But this time I had nothing in my pocket to offset the rude remarks! There is, I suppose, a fundamental conflict between the written word and movies, but many, if not most, novelists remain fascinated by movies, and we often wonder what our stories and our characters would be like if some genius director and some gifted actors got their hands on them. It goes beyond wanting some two-hour full-color advertisement for our book. We love the movies, their size, their energy. Yet how often does it really work out? How many times—if ever—can we say, when we have read and loved a novel, that the movie adapted from it was better or even as good as the book?

Five years separate A Ship Made of Paper *from your follow-up novel,* Willing. *Is that customary for you? How much of this time was spent working on the new book?*

I am not a fast writer. I make mistakes; I digress; I change my mind. And I'm not the hardest person

> ❝ *Endless Love* was a debacle for all involved. At the time of its release, many critics called it one of the worst adaptations of a novel of all time. ❞

to distract. Here are some of the things that—
or who—distract me when I am "supposed"
to be writing: Jo Ann, my girlfriend; phone
conversations with my friends; my mother and
my children; Shep, my dog; Nell, my other dog;
Rocket, my other other dog; Campbell, my duck;
the Internet; and tennis.

What is on your desk right now?

As given to distraction, digression, and second and
third thoughts as I am, my desk is even less orderly
than my mind. Here is what's on it right at this
very moment: a laptop; a stack of bills; a bottle
of water; a cup of coffee; an ashtray, just in case;
a picture of my son and his girlfriend; a picture
of my girlfriend; a picture of my daughter and her
dogs; a picture of my parents taken before I was
born, with my father in his Army uniform and my
mother looking exceptionally beautiful; a black
pen; a blue pen; a green pen; a book of postcards
based on the cover art of paperback noir novels;
a pack of gum; four stones I brought back from
my grandfather's village in Latvia; my notebook;
a little glass bowl filled with different sizes of
paperclips, though I doubt I have used even one
paperclip in the past five years; and a shopping list,
which I see now my girlfriend has placed on my
desk in the hope that I will soon go to the store,
and which I will add items to and sneak onto *her*
writing desk. Eventually, I suppose, one of us will
make the run to the Stop and Shop. ∽

> ❝ My desk
> is even less
> orderly than
> my mind. ❞

After *Willing*

MY LOT IN LITERARY LIFE has been to write about people who behave badly, and my central characters struggle with the mystery of their own motives from page one straight through to the end of the novel. In my first novel, a sci-fi comedy, the narrator was a frustrated research scientist whose loneliness and vanity led him into the employ of a secret organization that conducted illegal experiments on human subjects. In my second book, the protagonist was a bit of a social-climber who accidentally hit his stepbrother in the head with a fireplace poker, ending his life. And in my third, the narrator, a well-meaning and well-spoken stalker, sets fire to his girlfriend's house as a way of getting her to pay attention to him.

A writer's imagination is a kind of darkroom where the images of the eye or the mind's eye are transformed into language. This darkroom is as closed and mysterious as the darkrooms of the early photographers, and the chemicals in which the writer bathes his images are the stuff of his own life, his character, his culture, his history, his ambition, his soul. Unless you stock your darkroom with premixed chemicals, what comes out of it will bear a distinctive mark, and that's why the most individualistic and idiosyncratic writers are those whose works tend to bear the greatest similarity one to the other.

With *Willing*, I thought I was taking a departure from my other novels and, in some ways, I was—I have never written about so many characters at once, nor have my characters ventured abroad before. But in the most fundamental way, I was attempting in *Willing* what I seem always to attempt—the creation of complicated, not always wholesome characters who could lead me in to a deeper understanding of the darker edges of the human psyche, and could tell me something about desire, selfishness, generosity, love, and hate. Writing about people who behave badly is to risk the wrath of critics and readers; in *Willing*, however, I was putting a couple of extra shells in the gun aimed at my own head.

If you are going to write a comedy about grossly overprivileged men jetting around the

> 66 Writing about people who behave badly is to risk the wrath of critics and readers; in *Willing*, however, I was putting a couple of extra shells in the gun aimed at my own head. 99

globe in pursuit of sex with prostitutes, you have to be completely unacquainted with the laws of Cause and Effect not to at least *suspect* that you might be in for a rough time. I was, in fact, prepared for the worst. I summoned spectral feminist critics who would excoriate me for my failure to grasp the tragic and criminal nature of prostitution. (It's painful and time-consuming to fret about how you are going to be misread and misunderstood, but it's still easier than writing.) I wondered if sex workers themselves might somehow take me to task for my portrayal of them. I wondered if citizens of the countries visited by my characters would find glaring errors in my descriptions of their homelands. I even found time to wonder if people reading this novel would wonder if I myself had traveled the world in pursuit of rentable flesh.

When you publish a novel that deals with a sex tour you prepare yourself for questions about what you did to research your book. As understandable as these questions may have been, they failed to recognize that the reality of a novel resides within the novelist. There were, nevertheless, quite a few morally acceptable ways of gathering factual and psychological information about the international sex trade. First and foremost was the novelist's ability to extrapolate. It may sound strange, but a part of what I came to understand about what happens between hookers and johns I learned from taking lessons with a tennis pro—how you can feel so inferior to someone whom you are paying, how the ludicrous praise for the prowess of your forehand creates its own special world of illusion, an alternative universe of italicized cognition in which bald-faced flattery is recognized as such, but is also believed, and in which you live in a Let's Pretend world, but you, in fact, do all the pretending.

And beyond the writerly knack for extrapolation, there were other avenues toward understanding what might take place on an international sex tour: conversations with hookers and johns; reading historical, sociological, and political books about the sex trade; studying the various Internet sites devoted to sex tourism; and, of course, hours, weeks, months, and, finally, years of contemplation. ▶

> 66 There were, nevertheless, quite a few morally acceptable ways of gathering factual and psychological information about the international sex trade. 99

After *Willing* (continued)

Somewhere in the third year of this long contemplation, I began to despair over my choice of subject and setting. I write nearly every day. This meant that about twenty-eight days a month I spent hours thinking and writing about prostitutes and the men who employ them, and it was beginning to wear me down. How did I ever get into this? I often wondered, and said as much to those who I felt might feel sufficiently sorry for me. At one point, I was overcome with a kind of horror over what I was writing about and I stopped working on *Willing* altogether, and began writing another book. In one ecstatic fortnight I wrote thirty pages of a new novel (a novel I have returned to now), but the story I was trying to tell in *Willing* and the themes I was trying to work through continued to gnaw at me and I really had no choice but to return to it.

When I finally did finish writing it, I was happier and more relieved than I ever had been upon completing a novel. I usually experience a kind of postpartum poignancy as I put the final touches on a story, but at the end of *Willing* I felt as if I had finally found a way out of a world that was to some small extent driving me mad. Yet, at the same time, when I stepped back I realized that the final draft of *Willing* was startlingly close to the book I had originally imagined—closer, in fact, than I had gotten to the originally imagined end product in any of my other books.

And with that realization came a terrific onrush of protectiveness. This book had done what I had asked it to and now it was time for it to go out into the world and there was nothing I could do to shield it from whatever rough treatment it might encounter. One thing I was sure of: I had written a book that offered any number of temptations to be badly read. For example, there is throughout *Willing* a number of references to *The Wizard of Oz*, beginning with a blow to the head that initiates Avery Jankowsky's trip to the surreal world of sex tourism, and continuing throughout the book, with references

> " At the end of *Willing* I felt as if I had finally found a way out of a world that was to some small extent driving me mad. "

to L. Frank Baum himself, tin men, and people going over the rainbow, and culminating, in the final page, with Avery aloft.

The second thing I wanted my book to be was my response to living in a country at war, a strange war in which the well-off did not fight and interest rates and gay marriage were as much on the country's mind as war. I wanted *Willing* to be read as a book about Americans abroad, about human instinct subverted by money, about survival, illusion, and our sinking reputation around the world.

And on top of all this, I wanted readers to experience the book not only as humorous, but funny, and I was worried about that, too. If I am known for anything as a writer it's for telling love stories, preferably about obsessive, brokenhearted men. In *Willing*, few of my so-called strengths were brought into play—no obsessive love, no blind obedience to the heart's most urgent commands, and when it came to the sex that took place between my characters, I was steadfast in my refusal to go into much detail about that aspect of the action. I have always believed that by describing the sex act I can reveal something interesting, tender, and unguarded about my characters, but in the case of men having sex with prostitutes I thought that the actual sex would be the least revealing and true thing I could concentrate on, and so, for the most part, I skipped it. I thought it would be like reporting point by point on a set of tennis played by the teaching pro and the huffing and puffing student.

Which brings me to the novel's eventual reception. A number of critics and readers expressed disappointment verging on outrage that there was so little sexual activity in a novel about a sex tour. I accepted this criticism, though I was skeptical, too. Often, reviewers, afraid of seeming straightlaced or less than hip, will criticize a novel for not being transgressive enough, when in fact nothing could make them happier or more comfortable than to read ever so slightly updated versions of the same book they ▶

> **If I am known for anything as a writer it's for telling love stories, preferably about obsessive, brokenhearted men.**

have been reading their entire lives. Some read the novel as darkly funny, but others, less attuned, perhaps, to my sense of humor, seemed to suggest that my novel belittled prostitution by failing to take note of the damage it can do, or the pleasures it can bring.

My worry that women would find the subject of the novel so distasteful that they would end up disliking it on political grounds turned out to be basically groundless, though there was some suggestion of prurience on my part by a couple of female bloggers. And the worry that my novel would be faulted for its lack of verisimilitude turned out to be groundless as well: in one stunning turn of events, I learned that sometimes we go into the unexplored regions of our own imagination and end up colliding with outer realities in the most unexpected ways.

Within a couple weeks of *Willing*'s initial publication, the governor of my home state of New York, Eliot Spitzer, a former attorney general who rose to power largely on the strength of his rectitude and moral clarity, admitted to a long involvement with a call-girl ring that was charging him around five thousand dollars per visit. One book reviewer said that with Spitzer's fall from grace (he immediately resigned) I had somehow won "the literary lottery." Though I am still waiting for my Literary Lottery check, the Spitzer affair was nevertheless astonishing to me. My father, Charles Spencer, who is sadly mentioned in *Willing*'s afterword, was born Spitzer, and if he had not changed his name I would be Spitzer, too. So here was my almost-namesake falling from grace for pursuing the same sad pleasures as my imaginary characters.

Compounding the strange mix of fiction with current events, one of the alleged principals of the call-girl ring Spitzer favored turned out to be living about a half mile from me, in a fairly isolated spot in upstate New York. One afternoon, while I was doing a phone interview to help publicize my novel, I heard that rare thing outside

❝ One book reviewer said that with [Governor Eliot] Spitzer's fall from grace (he immediately resigned) I had somehow won 'the literary lottery.' **❞**

my window—the urgent noise of traffic. Cradling the phone beneath my chin, I parted the curtains and saw several black sedans speeding past my house; presumably, they were on their way to place her under arrest. ⁓

An Excerpt from Scott Spencer's *Endless Love*

One of the most celebrated novels of its time,
Endless Love *remains perhaps the most powerful
novel ever written about young love. Riveting,
compulsively readable, and ferociously sexual,*
Endless Love *tells the story of David Axelrod
and his overwhelming love for Jade Butterfield.*

*David and Jade's lives are consumed with
each other; their rapport, their desire, their sexuality
take them further than they understand. And when
Jade's father suddenly banishes David from the
house, David fantasizes the forgiveness his rescue
of the family will bring and sets a "perfectly safe"
fire to their house. What unfolds is a nightmare, a
dark world in which David's love is a crime and a
disease, a world of anonymous phone calls, crazy
letters, and new fears—and the inevitable and
punishing pursuit of the one thing that remains
most real to him: his endless love for Jade and her
family.* Endless Love *is available in trade paperback
from Harper Perennial.*

ENDLESS LOVE

A novel

SCOTT SPENCER

"The sensations aroused
are akin to the
legendary thrill of
riding a roller coaster.
The speed, the fear, the
anticipation sharpen
the pleasure of walking
quietly on solid
ground."
—*Washington Post*

"A moving story of first
love when it's so intense
you feel it might break.
It's everything a novel
should be."
—Bob Greene,
Chicago Tribune

WHEN I WAS SEVENTEEN and in full obedience
to my heart's most urgent commands, I stepped
far from the pathway of normal life and in a
moment's time ruined everything I loved—I loved
so deeply, and when the love was interrupted,
when the incorporeal body of love shrank back
in terror and my own body was locked away, it
was hard for others to believe that a life so new
could suffer so irrevocably. But now, years have
passed and the night of August 12, 1967, still
divides my life.

It was a hot, dense Chicago night. There were
no clouds, no stars, no moon. The lawns looked
black and the trees looked blacker; the headlights
of the cars made me think of those brave lights
the miners wear, up and down the choking shaft.
And on that thick and ordinary August night,
I set fire to a house inside of which were the
people I adored more than anyone else in the
world, and whose home I valued more than
the home of my parents.

Before I set fire to their house I was hidden

on their big wooden semicircular porch, peering into their window. I was in a state of grief. It was the agitated, snarling grief of a boy whose long rapturous story has not been understood. My feelings were raw and tender, and I watched the Butterfields through the weave of their curtains with tears of true and helpless longing in my eyes. I could see (and love) that perfect family while they went on and on with their evening without seeing me.

It was a Saturday night and they were together. Ann and her husband, Hugh, sat in front of the empty fireplace, on the bare pumpkin pine floor. (How I admired them for leaving their good wooden floors uncovered.) Ann and Hugh, sitting close, paged through an art book, turning the pages with extraordinary slowness and care. They seemed enraptured with each other that night. At times, their relationship seemed one of perennial courtship; hesitant, impassioned, never at rest. They seldom took each other for granted and I had never seen married people whose moments of closeness had such an aura of triumph and relief.

Keith Butterfield, my age, the oldest son, and whose passing curiosity in me had been my original admittance into the Butterfield household, also sat on the floor, not far from his parents, where he fussed with the innards of a stereo receiver he was building. Keith, too, seemed to be moving slower than normal, and I wondered if I was seeing them all through the gummy agony of a dream. Keith looked to be exactly what he was: the smartest boy in Hyde Park High School. Keith couldn't help learning things. He could go to a Russian movie and even as he concentrated on the subtitles he'd be picking up twenty or thirty Russian words. He couldn't touch a wristwatch without wanting to take it apart; he couldn't glance at a menu without memorizing it. Pale, with round eyeglasses and unruly hair, in blue jeans, black undershirt, and beatnik-y sandals, Keith laid his hands on the spread-out parts of the stereo, as if he wanted not to build it but to cure it. Then he picked up a small screwdriver and looked at the overhead light through the mango-colored plastic handle. He pursed his lips—sometimes ▶

An Excerpt from Scott Spencer's
Endless Love (continued)

Keith looked older than his parents—and then
he got up and went upstairs.

Sammy, the younger son, twelve years old, was
sprawled out on the couch, naked except for a pair
of khaki shorts. Blond, bronze, and blue-eyed, his
prettiness was almost comically conventional—
he looked like the kind of picture little girls
tuck into the corner of their mirror. Sammy was
somewhat outside the Butterfield mold. In a family
that cultivated its sense of idiosyncrasy and its
sense of personal uniqueness, Sammy's genius
already seemed to be taking the form of profound
regularity. Athlete, dancer, paperboy, bloodbrother,
and heart throb, Sammy was the least retiring, the
least internal Butterfield; we all really did believe,
even when he was twelve, that one day Sammy
would be President.

And then there was Jade. Curled into an
armchair, wearing a loose, old-fashioned blouse
and a pair of unflattering shorts that reached
almost to the knee. She looked chaste, sleepy, and
had the disenfranchised air of a sixteen-year-old
girl at home with her family on a Saturday night.
I scarcely dared look at her; I thought I might
simply hurtle myself through the window and
reclaim her as my own. It had been seventeen
days since I'd been banished from their home
and I tried not to wonder what changes had
taken place in my absence. Jade looked at the
wall; her face seemed waxy, blank; the nervous
knee jiggle was gone—cured by my banishment?—
and she sat unnervingly still. She had a clipboard
wedged between her narrow hip and the side of
the chair, and she held in her hand one of those fat
ballpoint pens that have three separate cartridges,
a black, a blue, and a red.

I still believe the statement that gives the
truest sense of my state of mind that night is
that I started the fire so the Butterfields would
have to leave their house and confront me. The
trouble with excuses, however, is that they become
inevitably difficult to believe after they've been
used a couple of times. It's like that word game
children discover: you repeat a word often enough

and it loses all meaning. Foot. Foot. A hundred times foot, until finally what is foot? But even though the truth of my motive has worn a little thin (and through its diaphanous middle I can detect other possible motives), I can still say that indeed the clearest thought I had when I lit the match was that starting a fire on the porch was somehow a better way of rousing the Butterfields from their exclusive evening than a shout from the sidewalk or a stone against the window—or any other desperate, potentially degrading signal I might make. I could picture them: sniffing the smoke sent off by the pile of old newspapers, trading glances, and then filing out to see what the trouble was.

This was my strategy: as soon as the papers catch fire, I hop off the porch and run down the block. When I'm at a safe distance, I stop to catch my breath and begin strolling back toward the Butterfields, hoping to time my arrival with their emergence from the house. I'm not sure what I planned to do then. Either jump right in and help put out the little fire, or stand transfixed, as if surprised to see them, and hope that Jade or Ann would see me, wave, invite me in. The point was not to allow them to go another day without seeing me.

I don't recall debating this plan of action. Nerved-out and lovesick, I simply proposed it and then a short time later was lighting a match. I waited for a moment (my legs shaking from their desire to vault off the porch and run like hell) to make certain the fire had really taken hold. The flame lifted the corners of that stack of papers pages by page, increasing the depth of its penetration but not the breadth. I could have put it out by stepping on it a couple of times and I came close to doing so, not out of foresight but panic. I remember thinking: This will never work. ∿

Have You Read?
More by Scott Spencer

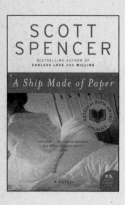

A SHIP MADE OF PAPER

No novelist alive knows the human heart better than Scott Spencer does. No one tells stories about human passion with greater urgency, insight, or sympathy. In *A Ship Made of Paper*, this artist of desire paints his most profound and compelling canvas yet.

Daniel Emerson lives with Kate Ellis and is like a father to her daughter, Ruby. But he cannot control his desire for Iris Davenport, the African American woman whose son is Ruby's best friend. During a freak October blizzard, Daniel is stranded at Iris's house and they begin a sexual liaison that eventually imperils all their relationships, Daniel's profession, their children's well-being, their own race-blindness, and their view of themselves as essentially good people.

A Ship Made of Paper captures all the drama, nuance, and helpless intensity of sexual and romantic yearning, and it bears witness to the age-old conflict between the order of the human community and the disorder of desire.

"This haunting, intelligent love story registers, with acute sensitivity to irony and politics, what is passionate, absurd, unsettled and unsettling in romance and race in America's middle class. This is Scott Spencer at his strongest."   —Lorrie Moore

"Spencer's latest novel should cement his reputation as the contemporary American master of the love story."   —*Publishers Weekly*

Don't miss the next book by your favorite author. Sign up now for AuthorTracker by visiting www.AuthorTracker.com.